THE LOTUS: BLACK SKIES (BOOK ONE)

CONNIE SUTTLE

Subtle demon
Connie Suttle author
subtledemon.com

Paperback ISBN-13: 978-1-6347809-4-0
eBook ISBN-13: 978-1-6347809-3-3
Hardback ISBN-13: 978-1-6347810-2-2

Published by: SubtleDemon Publishing, LLC
PO Box 1487, Mustang, OK 73064

Cover by Renee Barratt @ The Cover Counts.

To Walter, Joe, Larry, Dianne, Sarah, Mark, Denise and Brett.
Thank you.

ACKNOWLEDGMENTS

As always, this book is the result of collaboration. If it weren't for the support of my editor, my cover artist and my beta readers, it would be less than it is. All mistakes, as usual, are mine and no other's.

About the Author:
Connie Suttle lives in Oklahoma with her husband and a conglomerate of cats. They have finally banded together to make their demands, which has proven disconcerting to all humans involved.

You may find Connie in the following ways:
Facebook: Connie Suttle Author
Twitter: @subtledemon
Website and Blog: subtledemon.com

ALSO BY CONNIE SUTTLE

Blood Destiny:

Blood Wager

Blood Passage

Blood Sense

Blood Domination

Blood Royal

Blood Queen

Blood Rebellion

Blood War

Blood Redemption

Blood Reunion

Blood Recall

Blood Alliance

Legend of the Ir'Indicti:

Bumble

Shadowed

Target

Vendetta

Destroyer

High Demon:

Demon Lost

Demon Revealed

Demon's King

Demon's Quest

Demon's Revenge

Demon's Dream

God Wars:

Blood Double

Blood Trouble

Blood Revolution

Blood Love

Blood Finale

Saa Thalarr:

Hope and Vengeance

Wyvern and Company

Observe and Protect*

First Ordinance:

Finder

Keeper

BlackWing

SpellBreaker

WhiteWing

R-D:

Cloud Dust

Cloud Invasion

Cloud Rebel

Rose and Thorn

Black Rose Queen

Queen of Thorns and Roses

Future Wars:

Buffer Zone

Black Zone

Wraith Zone*

Lion and Raven:

Raven, Red

Exile, Ancient*

Dragon Witch:

The Dragon and Mrs. Muir

The Dragon Queen of Seoul*

The Lotus:

Black Skies

Storm Warning*

The Seer:

Betrayal*

* Forthcoming

A NOTE FROM THE AUTHOR

Events in this book take place on an alternate Earth—specifically CG-Earth 17, a Control Group world. While many things are the same as in your world, and your world's countries are more than similar to CG-Earth 17's, many things (customs, habits, prominent people, etc.) are also different.

And, as always, all mistakes belong to the author and nobody else.

Thank you for reading.

— Connie

CHAPTER 1

Dragon Lair

Hidden Mountain, North Korea

Lóng Lingyun

Wrapping the fingers of my brother, Lóng Hàoyŭ, around the glass of fifty-year-old Scotch, I urged him to drink.

He couldn't see—the White Flower had rendered him blind. And, as I suspected might happen, he was slowly going deaf, too.

This was the price he'd paid for harming the Lotus.

He'd done it because our parents told him to. How foolish they were to make such clumsy attempts on her life. Now, my brother was suffering, and, as was usually the case, our parents were the cause of it.

"What can we do?" Lóng Chenguang, Hàoyŭ's twin sister and the youngest by nearly an hour, pleaded. She was a talented witch in her own right, but she'd already tried everything she knew to prevent her brother's blindness.

Nothing had worked. The white jade flower had outsmarted both of us in this.

"Our parents will not be pleased if we fail in our assigned tasks," Hàoyǔ growled. While he could not become dragon as I could, he held the fire and spirit of the best of us.

"Then I say this," I began while my younger siblings listened attentively. "We let others accomplish our tasks. All it will take is a bit of urging to bring the human enemies of the Lotus to the forefront of this battle."

"You mean Kang Dong-hyung and his minions, the Go sisters?" Hàoyǔ asked. "They're in prison right now. How will they accomplish anything?"

"Our sister can get in and out of there with little effort, while fooling human recording devices, eh?" I said. "A few words of warning and a bit of information is all it will take. I believe Kang still has his fingers in many pies outside his prison walls, if you understand my meaning. Besides, I have looked into this carefully. Kang and the Go sisters still fear the one who might identify them in their most famous crime. That particular human is recently returned to South Korea."

"You mean those kidnappings and murders?" Hàoyǔ breathed while a slow smile crossed his features. "Chenguang, it will take little convincing to turn Kang's mind in that direction. Tell Kang that the reason that boy is still alive is due to the Lotus' interference."

"That's not true, brother," Chenguang insisted. "We all

know she was too young to do anything about any of that. Somehow, the boy survived, but like you say, it won't take much to convince Kang that he has two enemies and both of them should die."

"Meanwhile, I can assign a few of my dragon colleagues to help Kang," I said, sipping my own glass of scotch and reveling in the burn as it slid down my throat. "Plus, there may be other, ah, buttons to push to get Kang and his female spiders out of prison, to properly track their prey."

"You mean Undersecretary Chen?" Hàoyǔ demanded. "I warn you, it will take much convincing to get that old coward away from the safety of his office."

"Leave that to me," Chenguang reassured her twin. "He may be suffering the same malady as you, but he still has his own soldiers hidden among those belonging to the state. How effective might they be against the Lotus and this other —*human*?"

"I believe we've found our solution, my dear siblings," I laughed. "And our parents will be pleased by the outcome, will they not?"

Black Skies Headquarters

Seoul, South Korea

Sang Hae Jin

"Captain, the doctors say my wrist won't heal for another

eight months at least," Seo Min-ho set a file folder beside my gaming computer. "Team Owner Wu Chang says he already signed someone to a one-year contract to cover the time I'm out."

"Min-ho, this had better not be an attempt to remove you from the team," I slapped the folder with the flat of my hand.

Min-ho and I'd become very good friends once I'd been recruited to the Black Skies Gaming Team. His wrist injury happened at the end of the previous season and ended up costing us the world championship.

A German team had taken the championship from us at the last moment, leaving us in second place. Sure, we were South Korea's pride in the gaming industry, but second place still burned. I didn't blame Min-ho—the blame went to Chung Minjun, the team's backup player, who'd screwed up so badly it cost all of us.

As it was, he was still the backup, but his employment hung by a thread. I figured a replacement would be found—but only as a substitute, not a replacement for Min-ho.

"It's temporary—Team Owner kept saying that over and over," Min-ho reminded me after my anger became apparent. "He says the replacement player insisted on a single-year contract. It has something to do with a day job or, I don't know," Min-ho shrugged.

"It better be a year, and less than that if your wrist heals and I have anything to say about it. Is it somebody we know?"

We knew just about everybody who'd ever clicked a mouse in the gaming industry, and whether they were any good.

"Team Manager has the details. He said we'll get them during our next meeting."

"Then we won't get them, will we?"

Team Manager Chen Ling's responsibilities fell off his shoulders much like water off the proverbial duck's back. What he didn't do he forgot about, and that meant just about everything that didn't pertain to his fondness for (illegal in South Korea) gambling.

He was Team Owner's cousin, though, so there wasn't anything the team could do about it.

"Well, let's have our own meeting, then, and let the others know we'll have a replacement for the next year. When are they coming?" I thought to ask.

"Next Monday, or that's what Team Owner says."

"That gives us four days to make plans," I sat back in my chair and stretched.

"What plans?"

"To make sure they leave after the year's up," I grinned at Min-ho. "Nobody's gonna take my bro's place on the team," I added in English.

Min-ho's grin mirrored my own. "That's the Hae Jin we all know and love," he laughed.

The Hae Jin they all knew. If only they knew the *real* Hae Jin.

Four years ago, I returned to South Korea from the US after earning an MBA at Harvard. Two years ago, I got out of the South Korean military after serving my obligatory eighteen months for the country of my birth.

I thought about returning to the US after my military service ended, but my parents told me if I wanted to do what I pleased until I turned thirty, then I had to come home and do my military duty, then fritter away three years before learning to take over Sang Group, my dad's company.

I didn't go to the US specifically for college, though. In fact, I went when I was eleven. Anyone would be curious as to why an eleven-year-old might be sent to the States with only a married pair of servants to watch over me while I finished junior high and high school, and then while I graduated with an MS from Duke University before applying for the MBA program at Harvard.

I have a reason, although it isn't always a pleasant one to dredge up from memory. You see, when I was barely eleven and living in Seoul with my parents and younger brother, I was kidnapped.

Yeah, I'll remember those two bitches' faces as long as I live. They'd already collected the ransom from my parents when they decided to kill me.

What saved me?

The most implausible thing ever.

That night is burned on my brain—going in and out of consciousness while tied and gagged in a dusty attic somewhere in Busan, when the bitches went out to grab a bite.

They'd had me for three days and hadn't fed me anything except drugged food and a little water to go with it. Those three days were a blur of fear and misery—when I was awake enough to feel those emotions.

What brought me back to consciousness with a jolt were the small fingers worrying the knotted gag tied around my head.

Only the dimmest light made my eyes eventually adjust to the attic's near-darkness. I blinked to bring the face before mine into focus.

A small face.

Tiny fingers struggled with the gag's knot one of my captors had tied to keep me quiet. A small girl with a long braid falling over one shoulder put a finger to her lips to keep me from struggling against her efforts.

"I'm sorry," she whispered so softly I almost didn't hear. "I'll have to use the scissors."

I tried to swallow my nervousness, but my mouth was so dry I couldn't. "Stay still," she continued. "I don't want to hurt you."

I froze. She was going to cut the gag—the one that was tied so tight my lips and face had gone numb.

"Don't be afraid. Close your eyes and be still."

Those words—and that voice—float through my dreams still—especially the nightmares.

I dimly recall getting out of that attic—through a window so small I could barely squeeze past it—and then, my hand clutched tightly by the same fingers that had miraculously cut away the gag and the ropes around wrists and ankles, she led me along a high, narrow ledge while balancing herself with her free hand on the protruding bricks of a shadowy façade.

Only fleeting memories remain of the walk to a bus stop, a

bottle of water thrust into my hands, a train ride from Busan to Seoul and instructions to go with a specific cab driver selected by my small companion.

"What's your name?" I asked her, taking the wad of currency she'd shoved into my hands to pay the driver.

"No names. You can't say what you don't know."

"Huh?"

"Go with that cab driver. He looks like he might protect you—if your abductors are still around your house. You remember your address, don't you?"

"Yes, but," I started to argue.

"Go, now. I have to leave or we're both dead."

My legs unsteady, I strode toward the cab driver my rescuer pointed out. Briefly, I turned before I reached the car, only to find the girl was gone.

That night, the cab driver not only drove me home, he walked me to the front door. My parents at first thought my kidnappers had returned me as promised. Only after what seemed like hours did they come to understand that I'd escaped.

Less than a week later, with my kidnappers still at large and a dark cloud of fear hanging over the only home I'd ever known, my belongings were packed and the married servants were sent with me to the US, where my parents believed I'd be safe enough.

I'd tried to convince them about the girl, but those words fell on deaf ears. They were only concerned with me and my welfare. My last name was changed to Lee, which was my maternal grandfather's name, and I was sent out of the country lest the perpetrators try again.

I'd seen their faces, after all.

Over the years, I'd imagined finding that small girl, but had no name and fading memories. A private detective hadn't been helpful when I'd asked him to dig into the case once I returned to South Korea.

So I let it go, did my stint in the military, and then requested an interview for the only job I really wanted to do before taking the reins of Sang Group from my father—that of a professional gamer. I kept the name Lee for gaming purposes only; I planned to use my real last name once I took over the family business.

Ong Rae-Rae

"Remember what Doctor told you? That you needed to relax and take it easy or you'll die before you're forty?" Zhang Bao wasn't pulling any punches.

"Tae-hyun was being overly dramatic," I snapped at my friend, who also served as President and CEO of Ong Group's China-based factories and businesses.

"Tae-hyun wasn't kidding, Rae-Rae," he growled in English. "You came home from Taiwan unconscious and on a stretcher."

"After I decided to retool and retrain six factories in three months," I argued. "A mistake I will not repeat."

"I've already taken care of the relaxation part of this. Face it, you sneak off to do work when you're not supposed to. You have competent people working for you. All you should be doing right now is reading reports."

"Wait. You just said you took care of the relaxation part? What is that, exactly?"

"I signed you up for a year's contract with a friend of mine."

"Who does what, exactly?"

"He owns a professional gaming team."

"Huh?"

"The Black Skies team. Should have won the world championship a month ago, but due to the second-in-command's wrist injury, they lost the last game to the Germans."

"Of course they did. I need to know this because?"

"You'll be their second-in-command's gaming replacement—for a year. Also, it ties into a case Sea Eagle Investigations is working on—the hacking of corporations and government files in several countries. You said it yourself, remember? That those countries were hacked shortly after hosting a gaming tournament."

Sea Eagle Investigations was wholly owned and operated by Ong Group, but few people were aware of it. Zhang Bao was one of those people. I'd built that company from scratch, along with Osprey Technology and Robotics.

Both companies were at the top of their class in the products and services provided. Sea Eagle had recently been hired to look into the hacking of worldwide governments, so I was more than familiar with the case. That didn't mean I wanted to operate undercover in any way to solve it.

"I'm going to fire you," I told Zhang Bao.

"No, you're not."

"Yeah. As in yesterday."

"I have your signature stamp. Team Owner Wu Chang is a friend from Columbia University, and when I told him that you'd be near the top of the field if you chose to go pro, well, he was interested right away. The contract has been signed—don't worry, I've already gone over it and made any changes you'd make for yourself. You start next Monday. It'll be a perfect cover for a side investigation, don't you think?"

"Sure. Absolutely. Except that the entire country is going to think that Ong Rae-Rae is playing games and frittering away her time."

"I've signed you up with an alias. Nobody will know it's you unless you tell them."

"Because my face and hair won't give it away, huh?" I demanded in English.

"If I were you, I'd cut the hair and give it a few spritzes of purple or something, wear some blue-light-blocking glasses and fill the closet with trendy clothing."

"What's my alias?" I asked as nicely as I could while imagining the many, many ways that Zhang Bao might meet an untimely end. Or get fired.

By me.

"Manta. As in Manta Ray."

"Right. I want out of this contract immediately."

"Sorry. Can't. Also, Tae-hyun has given his blessing. He says getting you away from the office is the best thing for you right now."

"What about my swimming exercises?"

"There's a pool at a hotel not far from the team's headquarters. You can get a ride there every morning from one of those many bodyguards you employ. They'll be hanging around the team's base anyway, so you may as well make use of them."

"Sure. Right. Like I need something new to worry about."

"This. Is. Fun. Rae-Rae. You always have a good time when we play Ancient Wars together. Nobody can beat us; you know that."

We play against amateurs, Zhang Bao."

"You're fooling yourself if you think that. I know for a fact that we've gone against some of the elites, and they couldn't take us out. Mostly, it's because they can't take *you* out. Nobody can top your speed."

"Right," I drawled in English. Until then, our conversation had occurred mostly in Chinese.

"You have your own character to play if that's what you want," he went on. "Until now, nobody has even guessed who Madame Dragonfly is. I think it'll be a huge addition to Wu Chang's lineup. T-shirts ought to sell out overnight."

"Sure thing. You're delusional, you know that?"

"You're the boss."

"*Now* he remembers," I grumbled. "What about the hospital and school Ong Charities is currently building?"

"I already said you have good people in charge. Let them handle the hard stuff, all right? Go have fun. Beat up imaginary people and mythological creatures."

"I'm going to dock your pay and recall all your bonuses."

"Can't do that, nyah, nyah."

"Are you twelve?"

"No, but I am the youngest CEO in all of China."

"I can fix that."

"Rae-Rae, you don't mean that."

"I know. I'm still holding you responsible if anything goes wrong."

"Just let me know. I'll call Wu Chang and chew him out."

"Does he know I'm your boss?"

"He thinks you're a favored employee."

"I'm really thinking about firing you now."

"Ah, I have a meeting. Talk soon. Bye-bye."

Hae Jin

"Team Owner Wu Chang should pay you a bonus every time you end up in the newspaper, in the news or on the front cover of a magazine," Min-ho tapped my likeness on a magazine's glossy front. "Most eligible bachelor for two years running."

"I think my mother bribes them to do that."

"With this face?" He tapped it again before tossing the magazine in my direction. "How many girls throw themselves at you before and after tournaments?"

"I'm not discussing that, now or ever. Not interested in any of them."

"I know you're not gay."

"No, not interested in the boys who throw themselves at me, either."

"Asexual, then," Min-ho pretended to tap a diagnosis onto his phone.

"Shut up. I'm not that, either. Stop trying to fix what isn't broken."

"Are you sure it isn't broken?" Min-ho lifted an eyebrow as he stared at my crotch.

"Fuck off," I hurled the magazine back at him.

"Just checking," he laughed.

"You know we're contractually obligated to keep any ah, dates or liaisons quiet and out of the public eye," I said. "Although the twins flaunt that rule every chance they get."

"And I'm supposed to believe you have secret liaisons? Seriously?"

"Look who's talking. I've seen you go on a date maybe twice in the past year."

"That's twice more than you've gone."

"Shut up."

"Oh," Min-ho's phone buzzed in his hand. "Email from Team Owner."

"To all of us?"

"Yes. Check it out—it says, *Attention, Black Skies team members. A temporary team member will arrive on Monday. Please treat Manta Ray well. More information will come from Team Manager Chen.*

"Manta Ray? They're only going to use their gaming handle?" I rose to look at Min-ho's phone. "I've never heard that handle before."

"Probably something new they've chosen for the duration with Black Skies."

"Did you see this?" Park Shi-joon shuffled into the practice room holding up his phone.

"We saw. No idea who it is, and not likely to get anything from Team Manager either. We'll see him Monday," I shrugged. "All I care about is whether he's competent and mindful of his place."

"And by mindful, we mean respectful and willing to do whatever we tell him to," the twins walked in together.

"Slavery is outlawed in South Korea," Shi-joon verbally poked at Jeong Si-woo and Jeong Jun-woo. "Don't go overboard. You've made the unpopular list on social media already this year."

"Something else to think about—his social media. If he hasn't already set it up, it ought to be done soon," Min-ho observed. "Our fans want the scoop and they want it yesterday. Training and preseason gaming starts soon."

"Let's look to see if anything's been posted and we've been

left out of the loop," Jun-woo said, tapping on his phone to bring up the team's website.

"Won't be the first time that's happened," Shi-joon complained.

"Oh, here it says that a new temporary member will be announced Monday," Jun-woo reported. "I guess we'll all know at the same time."

"Has anybody started bugging us about it?" Min-ho asked.

"Only about five thousand fans," Jun-woo grinned and turned his phone around.

"Like I can see it from this distance," Min-ho retorted.

"Most of them are asking Hae Jin to respond," Jun-woo said, pulling the phone back and scrolling through the messages. "They also want to know the character the new player will specialize in."

"They'll specialize in whatever I tell them to specialize in," I said, scrolling through the messages myself. They ranged from the begging kind to the overly demanding kind, and I wasn't in the mood to answer any of them.

"Messages just doubled," Si-woo said.

"Great. By Monday, this will be out of control," I growled. "Min-ho, tell them we're not allowed to give out information until the official announcement is made. Text only with your left hand," I added. "Don't do anything to re-injure yourself. I want this imposter in and out of here as fast as possible."

"As you command, my Captain."

"Damn straight," I snapped in English. Whoever was

coming had already gotten on my bad side—just for existing in the first place.

Rae-Rae

"Cut it off, to right here," I made a chopping motion where my shoulder met my neck. "I'm about to hyperventilate," I added. My hair was my signature—long, thick, black, and hanging almost to my waist.

"But Chairman Ong," my hairdresser had actual tears in her eyes.

"Yeah, I feel the same. If I live long enough, surely it will grow back. What I need is enough hair to tie into a topknot. Oh, and once it's cut, dye the bottom three inches purple."

"I don't want to do this."

"I don't want to be recognized. Do this and I'll send your kids to college."

"I'll do it, but I don't have to like it."

"Same here."

"I know you'd send my kids to college anyway."

"True. I just need to be—in disguise for a little while."

"Chairman Ong, the glasses you asked for," Thiwat, my chief personal assistant, handed a designer case to me.

I stared at the purple-tinted lenses in the wire-rimmed aviators as the snipping began. I wanted to cry my eyes out and curse Zhang Bao at the same time. Instead, I sniffled once or twice, shut the case and closed my eyes, hoping that a year from Monday, all would be normal again.

Whatever normal for me might entail.

"WHAT ARE YOU DOING?"

"Packing. I hear you're partly responsible for my move to an uncomfortable bed in an all-male dormitory," I snapped at Tae-hyun.

"I didn't sign you up. I was consulted after the fact. I had no idea you'd be stuck in an all-male dormitory. Do you need a bodyguard?"

He was backhandedly offering the services of his husband, who was also my chief bodyguard.

"I will not be responsible for breaking you two up for an entire year," I complained. "Hu Lin will have to haul me to a hotel swimming pool and back, then keep watch while I exercise. That's enough for now. I hope nobody recognizes me. I cut my hair, dyed it purple, and ordered matching glasses."

"Rae-Rae, don't tease."

"I'm not. You should see this mess. When I pull it up, it looks like grape soda is exploding out of my head."

Tae-hyun cursed softly. "I didn't know this would happen. *Joesonghabnida*, Rae-Rae."

"Right. Look, I know you have your hands full with all your patients, while I just feel whiny. We'll talk later, okay?"

"What's your biggest worry? It can't be that you won't make the grade."

"That's the least of my worries. What part of all-male team leads you to believe I'll feel comfortable with any of this?"

"Yes, I doubt Zhang Bao took that into consideration when he signed you up."

"He tends to overlook things like that. I'm just one of the guys to him, I guess."

"He's bi, Rae-Rae. I'm sure he wasn't thinking about anyone giving you problems because—well, you're you."

"And I won't be me where I'm going. They won't know a single thing about me. While that's mostly for the best, it won't stop them if they want to get misogynistic."

"Surely you can wriggle out of the contract if that happens."

"I haven't even seen the contract. I have no idea what it says. He tells me he made modifications, and then didn't explain that, either."

"Hit them with one of your Peace Prizes. That ought to slow them down."

"I'm done talking with you. I have to go." I hung up without saying goodbye. That wasn't the way to treat my best friend since college, or the doctor who'd put my left foot back together after the accident four years earlier, but I wasn't in a good mood and it would surely deteriorate the longer I talked.

Yes, I was mad. No, I didn't know anybody I could take it out on.

Story. Of. My. Life.

Nobody asked me if I wanted this. They thought I needed it; therefore, I was going to report to my new job the following day.

I didn't even have an actual blood relative to complain to. Both my parents were dead. The one listed as my father on the birth certificate was also dead—killed by his mistress.

The only joy I ever got from Lee Ji-hoon was knowing we weren't related to begin with. All my other family members were also dead; whether by natural causes or murder it no longer mattered—dead is dead.

I'd grown up in a house filled with strangers, several of whom tried to kill me through the years in the hopes of getting their hands on the legacy left to me by my maternal grandparents.

That legacy included half-a-billion dollars, US, and twenty-five percent of the stock in Ong Group. All the attempts against me were orchestrated by one man—the man hired by my father-on-paper as CEO of Ong Group and whose name, which I curse often, is Kang Dong-hyung.

Kang Dong-hyung was currently serving a lifetime prison term for mass murder. I'd gathered the information against him at age eighteen and handed it to the NIS to verify. At age twenty, I stood in Ong Group's boardroom, wrestled the company away from Kang Dong-hyung and then watched him be arrested, along with six other board members who'd collaborated with him in his illegal and often murderous escapades.

Yes, I was decidedly wallowing in self-pity on that Sunday

afternoon. My father-on-paper, Lee Ji-hoon, didn't care about anything that happened at the company, as long as he could spend his days playing golf and drinking with his buddies, and spend his nights with one of his many mistresses.

Until his first and main mistress murdered him, that is.

"Stop thinking about that stuff," I warned myself. You see, I can't drink. I have a bad reaction to alcohol, similar to an allergic response. Just a taste of anything alcoholic would knock me out. I also have Graves' Disease, a form of severe hyperthyroidism. It was likely brought on by a childhood filled with neglect and attempted poisonings by the housekeeper and her sister—both hired by CEO Kang Dong-hyung.

The bitch housekeeper and her sister were also in prison for trying to stab me to death when I was nineteen. They'd done that after learning that I'd put the money and the company stock so far out of their reach they'd never get their hands on it.

It involved a good deal of computer hacking—not just of their emails, but those of CEO Kang's too. That's how I ended up with enough evidence to sentence him to life in prison.

As for bitch one and bitch two, well, they were sentenced to ten years each for attempted murder, after stabbing me. So far, they'd served eight of the ten, with two to go. What I knew that nobody else did, however, is that those two would go straight back to their lives of crime the minute they were released from jail.

It was up to me to find more evidence against them—enough to make sure they'd never breathe free air again.

"Pack your stuff, Rae-Rae," I shook myself out of the bad thoughts crowding my mind. "There's still plenty of time to find the right evidence to hang those two out to dry."

After I had two cases and a shoulder bag filled, I left the bags in the foyer of my penthouse apartment and headed for the kitchen. I wasn't hungry, but I needed to eat.

Doctor's orders.

Hae Jin

Team Manager Chen Ling grinned broadly as the team and I gathered in the dorm meeting room. Surprised that he'd made the effort to come, I barely glanced his direction before setting my coffee cup on a table and pulling out a chair.

Backup Chung Minjun had also made an appearance, when he hadn't bothered seeing the rest of us after the world championships.

As expected, even the twins ignored Minjun and chose seats as far from him as possible. The glower Minjun wore grew darker as Min-ho and Shi-joon also chose seats farther away.

"Fifty thousand messages," Min-ho chose the seat next to mine. His usual cup of bubble tea was set at his left elbow; he'd chosen to keep his right arm in a sling.

"Been trying to use it again, I see," I elbowed his left arm.

"Yeah. It's hard to remember, sometimes."

"I think a blanket statement ought to be enough on the website. If we try to answer all of the posts, we won't play again for two years."

"Makes sense." He sipped his drink.

"Ah, I'm glad to see you're all here," Team Owner Wu Chang breezed into the room. "Our new team member may be a little out of the ordinary, but I'm asking you now to make her feel welcome."

"Huh?" the twins spoke in unison as their heads jerked up.

"I can only give you her gaming handle. If she chooses to tell you about herself, that's her business. As of now, the contract states that she is to be known publicly as Manta Ray and nothing more. Manta, will you join us, please?" He motioned for someone to come forward.

Five heads jerked around, including mine. All I saw at first was the explosion of purple atop her head, the purple-tinted glasses she wore and how short and—yes—tiny, she looked.

"*Annyeonghaseyo*," she greeted us as she joined Team Owner at the front of the room. "I am Manta Ray. Please take care of me." She bowed to all of us.

Her greeting was met by dead silence that stretched out for several seconds. "Uh, hi," Shi-joon spoke in English, holding up a hand in a half wave.

"You speak English? That makes me so happy," she smiled at Shi-joon, who gulped. Her English was flawless. Shi-joon had just used up half of all the English he knew.

I squirmed in my seat, suddenly uncomfortable—until I realized what was happening. My body was speaking one language, my mind was speaking another. They disagreed greatly.

For the first time in what seemed forever, my body was hard.

Rock hard.

My mind, on the other hand, was shouting that this—apparent half-child with purple hair and glasses—was far from the ideal woman I'd envisioned. It was almost as if an alien had been dropped into our midst—one that *nobody* ought to be attracted to.

Damn.

Fuck.

Shit.

Alloftheabove.

CHAPTER 2

H*ae Jin*

"Have you played with any pro teams before?"

"Not to my knowledge."

Her answer—what did that even mean? You either had or hadn't. *Not to my knowledge* didn't make sense.

"What's that supposed to mean?" Si-woo demanded. "Have you played for a pro team before?"

"Not for. Definitely not for. As for playing with, do you mean with, physically, or against, in an actual game?"

"Either, I suppose," I waved off her answer.

"I've played against all kinds, from very talented to no talent, I guess," she shrugged. "Or so my gaming buddy says. He tells me we've gone against some of the best, but again, I have no real proof of that."

"Who's your gaming buddy?"

"I can't tell you that. He didn't give permission to out him in public, and while he felt duly obligated to sell me off into a year's servitude, my morals remain intact."

"Do you even speak Korean?" I scoffed.

"You have a little bit of a Boston accent," Manta held up a thumb and forefinger.

"MBA, Harvard," Min-ho supplied my background.

"That explains it, then. I assume you speak excellent English?"

"You assume correctly."

"Awesome." Awesome was drawled and drawn out, like what you'd hear in Atlanta, Georgia.

"He's more comfortable with English," Shi-joon supplied. "He says all kinds of things in English. I have no idea what he's talking about."

"Back to your experience. Which characters in Ancient Wars have you played?"

"Most of them—just to get used to what I may have to deal with."

"We'll begin practice tomorrow; I've held off starting until your arrival," I said. "I'll give you simple stuff at first, so we can see what your level is."

"That's not really necessary," she began.

"It is necessary. I'm the Team Captain and if I say that's what we'll do, then we'll do it."

"You're the boss."

"Yes. I am. In a few weeks, we'll broadcast several practice games, mostly playing online with selected teams. That includes our backup, Chung Minjun." I watched as her mouth tightened; I wondered if she'd studied the finals match for the championship and understood how badly Minjun had played.

"I'll be happy to take her on," Minjun volunteered.

"Sounds good," I narrowed my eyes at Manta Ray. "Let's see tomorrow what Miss Manta has when Minjun challenges her."

"Is there anything else?" she asked. I noticed her face had gone pale but didn't want to know what that was about.

"That's all for now, unless you have something to say."

"I have medication in the fridge," she said. "It has to be kept cold. I take it once a week for my hyperthyroidism. That's nothing to be concerned about—I'll take care of my needs myself," she added. "I provided a doctor's note to Team Owner, that says I need to eat something small or have a glass of milk every two hours, because of my condition."

"What happens if you don't get that?" Min-ho asked.

"I pass out and the paramedics show up," she said simply. "I get up at five every morning to swim. I've already set it up with the hotel down the street to swim laps every morning. I'll be back by six-thirty. If you want to change the schedule, please let me know in advance so I can act accordingly."

"The rest of us run together," I countered. I didn't add that before running at seven every day, I had Krav Maga lessons with a professional trainer.

"Also, due to a medical condition, I can't do that," she responded. "The documents are with Team Owner if you'd like more information."

"Now we know why girls aren't any good at gaming," Minjun sniffed.

"Your logic escapes me," Manta shook her head. "I need to unpack. See you tomorrow, pinhead."

Her last sentence was spoken in English, which meant Minjun failed to understand the insult.

"Say it in Korean, if you're going to say it," I snapped.

"All right. See you tomorrow, tiny brain," she told Minjun in Korean.

"That's enough. Never say anything like that again—to anyone on this team," I half shouted.

"You're the boss." She turned smartly and stalked out of the room.

"He insulted her first," Shi-joon reminded me quietly.

"That doesn't matter." I rose and shoved my chair violently under the table.

I knew Shi-joon was right—Minjun's insult was first and conceivably worse. He'd attacked her gender, when he didn't know the first thing about her yet.

I, on the other hand, had yelled at her for doing exactly what I'd told her to do. And, just like any other man on the planet, I tried to justify it to myself as I walked away.

Rae-Rae

I should have known better. I recognized Minjun's type

immediately. The closet misogynist who'd exact revenge at the first opportunity.

That's why, when I went downstairs on Tuesday morning to grab one of my injector pens and meet my bodyguard driver outside to go swim, I found my medication strewn across the floor of what passed for the team's kitchen.

"What happened?"

Hae Jin, who was doing his best to come in a close second in the misogyny category, stared at the now-warm pens before leveling an accusing look in my direction.

"Well, congratulations. That's around thirty thousand, US, in experimental medication that one of your teammates ruined," I said. "Unless you did it yourself."

"What?"

If I thought he was mad before, well, I couldn't have been more wrong. "Why the fuck would one of my teammates do this?"

"Because I wouldn't do it. Do you think the elves came by overnight just to prank me?" I demanded. "I could house, feed, clothe and educate twenty kids for six months with what's ruined on the floor right now."

"Clean up the mess," he growled and stalked away.

"Great. Second verse, same as the first," I said, gathering up useless medication and stuffing it into the non-recycle bin.

Ten minutes later, I climbed into the warm interior of Hu Lin's Cadillac Escalade. "I'll need more of the experimental medication," I told him, pulling the seatbelt around me to buckle in. "One of my teammates dumped the whole box on the floor during the night and now it's useless."

"I argued with Tae-hyun about this whole mess," Hu Lin confessed. "You don't need to be here—it'll be nothing but a headache for you. While you're swimming, I'll get Mr. Thiwat on the phone and ask for more medication."

"Just bring it one dose at a time, every Tuesday," I said. "So this won't happen again."

"Got it. Will you shower at the hotel after you swim?"

"I guess I'll shower at the hotel. I packed a towel and some clothes in my bag already," I toed the shoulder tote at my feet.

"How many enemies do you have already?"

"Two for sure, and I figure since one of them is the Team Captain, the others will follow suit. Meekness isn't my style, you know, so I'll be in trouble for the next year, guaranteed."

"Who's the other enemy?"

"The team alternate."

"The one who," Hu Lin didn't finish. He and I'd already had a conversation about that one—and what happened at the world championship barely a month before.

"Yeah. That one. I guess trying to call him out in front of the Captain was a mistake. This just means I'll have to go farther undercover to prove what happened—and what could happen again if they're not careful."

"It's too bad you can't get at least one of them on your side," Hu Lin steered the Escalade out of the parking lot, heading for the hotel. "How's the bed and your room?"

"Bed is barely functional. Room is okay—haven't seen any rodents or roaches yet."

"Make a list of anything you want brought in and I'll get it."

"I know. Thanks." I leaned back in my seat for the five-minute drive down the street. "I just—can't get used to this hair. I scared myself by looking in the mirror this morning. Things went downhill after that."

"Nobody will recognize you, so there's no worry on that quarter."

"Yeah. Tell me about it."

THE INDOOR, OLYMPIC-SIZE HOTEL POOL SMELLED OF chlorine and mist. Stuffing what little of my hair remained beneath my swim cap and adjusting my waterproof earbuds, I stretched in the bodysuit I wore for doing laps.

Hu Lin, occupying a chair near the door, checked his phone for messages while I dropped into the pool. I'd do thirty laps, starting with the butterfly stroke before going into a backstroke and freestyle before starting again.

When I'd first started swimming, I could barely do two laps, but then I was recovering from total exhaustion. Swimming, combined with the experimental drug I'd been given as part of a patient trial, was helping me keep my body mass at an almost acceptable level.

In fact, it had never been this good before, considering I'd nearly starved and suffered from malnutrition after being afraid to eat anything served to me as a child. The housekeeper's specialty was poison; that's how my mother died, slowly and agonizingly, after four years of eating tainted food.

Screw you, bitch Go Ha-eun, and your sister, too, I thought to myself as I climbed out of the pool half an hour later. The doctor had been paid to lie and say my mother's death was caused by something other than what it was, and my mother's murder had gone unremarked.

Father-on-paper had gone to see his main mistress the afternoon of my mother's funeral, as if nothing out of the ordinary had happened.

I, at four years old, had peeped through a doorway to see CEO Kang Dong-hyung hand an envelope of cash to the bitch housekeeper—a reward for getting the main Ong heir out of the way.

After my mother's death, there was only a four-year-old standing in the way of his gaining control of Ong Group and eventually murdering father-on-paper or pushing him out some other way.

Father-on-paper was so incompetent, it wouldn't have been difficult to do, either. "Chairman Sang called. I said you were in the water," Hu Lin held up my phone as I approached and grabbed my towel.

"Did he say what he needed?"

"He wants you to look over the budget."

"Is this what I get for owning thirty per cent of Sang Group?" I asked the rhetorical question.

"You do, and it's deserved," Hu Lin grinned at me. "That should teach you to help people out when they're about to get cheated out of a good invention."

"I tried to sell the stock back at the price I paid, and Chairman Sang refused every time," I groused.

"Because he knows it's in good hands," Hu Lin said. "I'll wait here while you shower—there's nobody else in there right now."

"Thanks."

"Thiwat is on the way with your medication. He'll keep the rest in the fridge in your office until I can pick it up and take it home with me. I haven't told Tae-hyun what happened yet. He'll be pissed."

"Yeah. Me, too."

HAE JIN

"So, what are you going to do? Minjun will want to play General Tang," Min-ho named one of the more powerful gaming characters in Ancient Wars.

"Tell her she has to play Court Magician Oh," I said, naming a lesser character.

"Why? There are others who are almost an equal match against Tang."

"If she has a temper, we need to see it now rather than waiting until we're in the middle of a match to find out she can't handle the pressure."

"While I agree with that strategy, now might not be the best time to test her on it. He's the one who ruined her medication and she probably knows it."

"All the more reason to test her now."

"You're the Captain."

"Yes, I am."

"She's here; somebody just dropped her off at the front," Shi-joon rushed into the gaming room.

"Tell her I want her down here in fifteen. It's time to see whether she's worth it or not."

"All right." Shi-joon walked out, shaking his head.

"Has she even had breakfast?" Min-ho thought to ask.

"Not my problem," I said. "That's on her."

"HE'S GOING TO PLAY GENERAL TANG?"

"That's right." I crossed arms over my chest and stared hard at Manta. To her credit, she didn't even blink.

"And I'm playing Court Magician Oh."

"Yes."

"Why did Minjun get to pick, and I didn't?"

"He has seniority."

"You're the boss."

"That's right."

Without another word, Manta took her seat at one of the gaming computers and put on her headset. I watched as she adjusted the seat to fit her height, which meant her feet weren't touching the floor.

Not my fault that she's short, I told myself.

On the opposite side of the round table, Minjun began to set up. On either side, the large, overhead screens lit up as Ancient Wars loaded. Minjun chose General Tang as his avatar; Manta chose Court Magician Oh. I chose to stand behind Manta; Min-ho moved to stand behind Minjun. Minjun's strength was in his ability to come out swinging. It was his downfall at times, too, especially if he went against someone who had more patience and a stronger strategy.

If this were a male challenger, you'd be offering advice, I castigated myself. *Min-ho is also holding back, because he doesn't have any advice to give on Manta*, I argued with myself.

I lifted my head and exchanged a glance and a shrug with Min-ho. It would play out as it played out, and there'd be nothing more to be done about it. At least we'd see a little of what Manta could do and why Team Owner decided to bring an untried female in over too many other seasoned players.

All of whom are male, I reminded myself.

Had I become something I hated, just because I'd tired of having girls throw themselves at me during every tournament?

Solving that riddle still wouldn't give me insight into Manta's strengths or weaknesses, I defended my actions.

"In five," Min-ho began the countdown.

"Three."

"Two."

"One."

"WELL, AT LEAST WE KNOW A LITTLE MORE. TWENTY-TWO seconds. Damn," Min-ho shook his head. "You didn't see the look on her face, either. It's like she was carved from ice."

Minjun had done what we'd expected, coming out immediately in battle mode. Most new players would have been taken by surprise.

Before General Tang could reach Court Magician Oh, Manta had already engaged and sent so many spells, daggers and magic bombs against Minjun's avatar that he couldn't even run for cover and regroup.

"I've never seen anyone move that fast," Min-ho shook his head again. "Do you think she studied Minjun's strategy?"

"Did she have time?"

"I don't know."

What I couldn't get out of my head was the moment Minjun's avatar died (without getting in a single blow against Manta's). Manta had stood, dropped her headphones onto the desk beside the keyboard, complained that the keyboard was too slow and needed to be replaced, and then walked out without looking at me, Min-ho or Minjun.

Then, I'd had the temerity to ask her where she was going.

"To get something to eat. It's been two hours," she flung out a hand as if delivering a slap in my direction.

I probably deserved it.

"TEAM PRACTICE AT TEN," MIN-HO DID WHAT I COULDN'T bring myself to do, and that was to tell Manta that we would be going into full practice days, beginning immediately.

"I'll be there," Manta finished off a small glass of milk and a croissant.

"Where are you going now?" I demanded as she walked out of the kitchen area.

"Brush my teeth." She disappeared in the direction of the stairs, which led to the second-floor dorm rooms.

"Dental hygiene is important," Min-ho remarked.

"Shut up."

FOR THE REST OF THE DAY, AND THEN FOR THE REST OF THE week, I assigned the weakest avatars to Manta. At times, I felt guilty for not letting her choose, but then I wouldn't have seen things I never expected to see.

We played three on three, using Minjun on one team and then the other, to fill in whatever slot I chose for him. With the avatars I assigned, Manta would play the hell out of the character, often revealing hidden talents the designer had given it that few, if any, had ever explored in their quest for the bigger and better.

Too, she'd use the weaker avatar to tease and taunt the opposing team's avatars, distracting them enough to give the advantage to her fellow team members. Enough so in most cases to give them the win, even when her avatar perished.

Whenever I'd give her an assignment, she'd bite her lower lip for a moment before saying, "You're the boss," and then make the best out of a seemingly hopeless situation.

A month went by like that, and then six weeks. That's when Team Owner gave the go-ahead to do an exhibition challenge with another Korean team, The Seahorses.

Fans would tune in for the online match, the game would be televised and ads would offer team T-shirts and other merchandise for the upcoming tournament season.

"What are you going to do?" Min-ho asked me two days before the exhibition match. "You really haven't done much to integrate her into the team as a whole; you're only using her to run interference while everybody else gets the real work done."

"I know." I raked fingers through my hair in frustration. I'd spent my time watching her carefully while she spun gold out of straw, as the old fairy tale goes. I hadn't given her any avatar to play that had tournament-level strength, yet. "What do you think?"

"Play Minjun, and then start correcting your mistakes."

I went still. *My mistakes.* Yes. I was making them. I had no idea how she really felt about what I was doing, either. She'd neither complained nor made any suggestions. Only the chewing of her lower lip showed any sign of emotion at all.

The exhibition match was on a Sunday evening, and the viewers signed up for the event had numbered in the tens of thousands, before hitting more than a hundred thousand, all across Asia.

"They'll want to meet Manta," I said absently.

"Then you should have thought about that before now."

"Do you still think I should play Minjun?"

"I do."

"Then you get to tell her."

"Wait, what?"

"You tell her."

"You have to come with me."

"Fine. Let's go."

"IF I'M NOT PLAYING, CAN I TAKE THE DAY OFF?"

"What?" Of all the things I imagined she might say, Manta was asking about taking the day off.

"You don't need me. Can I have the day off? I have things I can get done if I have the whole day for myself."

"What things?" I blurted without thinking.

"Stuff. Laundry. I haven't been able to cook anything for myself, so I want to do that, too."

I shouldn't have been surprised; over the course of a month-and-a-half we'd learned, slowly, that Manta couldn't eat spicy foods. Finally, Shi-joon had discovered that she'd had surgery for bleeding ulcers in the past.

Twice.

What had she done in her twenty-seven years that created bleeding ulcers?

"Fine," I found myself saying. "Take the day off. Don't stay here and support your teammates."

"Is that in our job description? If so, why haven't I been supported?" She studied me curiously.

"I think you should quit while you're behind," Min-ho remarked.

"You have something to say to me?" I barked at Manta.

"Only that you talk about teammates all the time, and then exclude me from being one of them. I'm only here for a year or less, so I understand you don't want to upset the balance. I can assure you both, however, that when the time comes, I *will* walk away from here and not look back. I have a day job to get back to, as strange as that may sound."

"What's your day job, then?" I snapped.

"I don't have to tell you that," she said. "Just be assured I do have one. Once I'm gone, you can go back to your band of brothers mindset and forget I was ever here."

Was I beginning to feel guilty?

Yes.

"Then take the whole weekend off. I don't care," I flung at her.

"Really? Thanks."

"Did you mean for that to happen?" Min-ho asked as Manta skipped up the stairs.

"You know I didn't," I muttered, feeling angry and ashamed. I'd cut her out of the exhibition game, when she deserved to be there more than Minjun did. The fact that she wasn't staying to watch the rest of us rankled, too.

"Why did I ever say yes?" I moaned, covering my face with both hands. "The fans will want to see Manta—she hasn't posted any pictures on the website, so they know next to nothing about her, still."

"Maybe we should post some. Too bad we don't have a functional kitchen. She apparently likes to cook."

"There isn't a lot you can do with a hot plate and a microwave," I let my hands fall.

"What would it take to get us a decent kitchen?"

"Probably more than Team Owner wants to spend."

"You're right. That's too bad. It might be nice to show the team in the kitchen, cooking something. We've never done that before."

"Then let's find a kitchen, somewhere. We can rent one, don't you think?"

"When?"

"Sometime after the exhibition matches?"

"All right."

Rae-Rae

I get the whole weekend, I texted Tae-hyun.

What are you going to do?

Sleep. Go over the second round of Chairman Sang's budget. Cook.

I'll buy the ingredients if you'll make lasagna.

I can do that. Have Hu Lin put everything in the fridge Friday. I'll make the sauce on Saturday so you can have lasagna on Sunday. I'll take a pan to the Sang's Sunday evening, so come pick up yours Sunday afternoon.

We'll be there. How about dinner out on Saturday night?

Sounds fine. You pick the place.

We will. See you then.

"Can you play basketball?" Min-ho arrived at my computer station Friday morning to ask.

"No. I can't run or jump," I told him. "I was in a car accident four years ago and my left foot was crushed. It's mostly made of bone fragments and titanium, now, and the doctor says if I mess it up again, I'll be crippled for the rest of my life. That's why I swim for exercise; water doesn't put that much stress on it."

"Why didn't you tell us this before?"

"You never asked before. You know, it's one of those reasons why girls aren't any good at gaming," I quoted Minjun's insult.

"Minjun should have been fined for that, and he wasn't."

"Minjun has other sins to pay for. In the grand scheme of things, that's just a minor fault. Are you taking the team to play basketball?"

"Tomorrow morning. When will you be going out for your weekend off?"

"Maybe around ten or so. You'll be gone by then, won't you?"

"Yes. We want to get an early start; the courts fill up fast on weekends. It's a way to blow off steam, especially before an exhibition match."

"Well, have fun. I'm going to dinner with friends, and then I'll cook on Sunday and get some chores done."

"Hae Jin feels a little left out," Min-ho stated.

"Left out? He's in the middle of everything."

"I know. I'm not sure why I said that."

"Well, when you figure it out, let me know. With his looks and his natural ability to lead, he won't ever lack for company if that's what he wants."

"You're saying he has a natural ability to lead?"

"I said that. I don't say things I don't mean."

"All right. Next time, will you at least come watch us play basketball?"

"Sure. If it will make you feel better, then I'll do that."

"I think it will definitely make things better."

"Awesome."

"You have excellent English."

"I also speak Chinese, Japanese, French, Italian, Spanish, German—you know, all kinds of stuff."

"That might come in handy when we play against the Germans again."

"Hmmph. *Those* guys."

"You don't like them?"

"If I don't, I have my reasons."

"Because you don't say things you don't mean."

"You learn fast. I'll bring you a plate of lasagna Sunday night."

"Really?"

"Yes."

"Nobody I know can make lasagna."

"You know somebody now."

"I just realized that. Wow."

"How's your hand?"

"It's good. Physical therapy is driving me crazy, though."

"I feel for you. When I went through that with my foot, I could barely walk afterward. It's worth it now, but at the time, I just wanted the pain to stop."

"Yeah. I guess you do know what that's like."

"Just get well. I need to get back to my normal life."

"Do you know how weird that sounds—that somebody wants to leave gaming behind to get back to their normal life?

Usually it's the opposite; they want to leave their normal life for the glamorous world of gaming."

"So far, I haven't seen any glamour."

"You haven't been to a tournament yet."

"You honestly think Hae Jin will let me play? He has no idea what I can really do, you know."

"I think he understands that now."

"I'm not sure that's true, but I'll take your word for it."

"Take his word for what?" Hae Jin walked in as Min-ho stood and stretched.

"That you know what you're doing," Min-ho poked Hae Jin in the ribs.

"That's not what I said."

"It really isn't what she said," Min-ho admitted. "She did say you had a natural ability to lead."

"Does everything you hear come right back out of your mouth?" I asked him. He laughed before sobering. "Manta's foot was crushed in an accident a few years back, so she can't put too much pressure on it. She can't run or jump, so no basketball for her," Min-ho explained.

"Crushed?" Hae Jin frowned at me.

"I have scars," I shrugged.

"And lots of titanium holding bone fragments together," Min-ho said.

"Let me see this."

"Hey," I drew my foot back as he knelt to reach for it.

"Pics or it didn't happen," Min-ho teased.

"Pics I have," I said, lifting my phone and sorting through

photos. "See, here's the X-ray after the surgery." I handed the phone to Min-ho, who showed it to Hae Jin.

"That's serious," Hae Jin frowned at the picture. "You have that much metal holding it together?"

"Yes. Swimming is the only exercise I can do that doesn't aggravate anything. I can't wear heels anymore because of all this, too. Not that I mind all that much."

"No basketball for Manta," Hae Jin handed the phone back.

"Yeah. Bummer," I said in English.

He snorted a laugh.

"There's a first," I said. "I don't think I've seen you crack a smile before now."

"Shhh, you'll scare it away," Min-ho whispered, making me snicker.

THE REST OF THE TEAM WAS ALREADY OUT THE DOOR AND heading for the basketball court Saturday morning when I called Hu Lin to pick me up. I was waiting at the sliding glass doors into the complex when an old Toyota pulled up outside. A woman got out of the driver's seat, went around, opened the passenger-side door and pulled a young girl out, then dragged her toward the door.

She rang the bell to be let in, holding the girl up by one hand gripped around her upper arm. The girl couldn't be more than twelve, I decided, when Hu Lin's Escalade pulled up beside the Toyota.

Opening the door from the inside, I walked out, only to have the woman shove the girl in my direction. "Tell Shi-joon he has to babysit. I have to work," she yelled, letting the girl fall to the concrete as she rushed to climb back into the car and drive away.

"What the?" In three steps I was at the girl's side and kneeling down to help her up. The moment I looked into her eyes I knew—the girl was sick.

Really sick. As in running a high fever and on the verge of collapse sick.

"Hu Lin, call the hospital," I shouted as he opened the car door and stepped out.

Phone in hand, he rushed to my side. "Ong Charities Children's Hospital," someone answered.

"Hello, this is Ong Rae-Rae," I took the phone from Hu Lin. "I have a very sick girl here, who needs medical attention fast. We'll be there in less than fifteen minutes."

"Yes, Chairman Ong. I'll alert the emergency department."

Hu Lin lifted the girl and carried her to the car; I got into the backseat with her. Hu Lin drove quickly and expertly to the Children's Hospital Ong Charities had built in Seoul, to find out why someone had dumped a sick child on the doorstep of Black Skies Gaming.

CHAPTER 3

R***ae-Rae***

"Rape victim. Severe infection. Dangerously high fever. Might not make it."

Those words, from various doctors and nurses, raced through my mind as I struggled to make sense of everything I'd witnessed so far.

"I think she's related to Shi-joon somehow, but I can't say that for sure," I told the police detective who'd arrived at the hospital to take a statement. "All I know is he's out with the rest of the Black Skies team, playing basketball. I didn't think to ask where that was. The woman who dumped the girl at Black Skies headquarters only said she had to go to work. She drove a 2008 blue Toyota Corolla, license number on the front 33 6844."

The detective blinked at the complete description I gave

but didn't remark on my memory. Instead, he told me he'd run the plate number and try to track down Shi-joon.

"That woman knew the girl was sick, and rather than bringing her to the doctor, decided to hand her to Shi-joon to babysit," I repeated. "I don't trust her at all in this. Please find Shi-joon first and ask him about the relationship. After all, this is a rape victim, and we don't know whether the woman was involved, do we?"

"True enough," the detective rubbed the back of his neck.

"If you don't feel comfortable placing a guard outside the girl's room, then I'll hire guards myself," I added. "Something is off about all this; I can feel it."

"Chairman Ong is seldom wrong," a physician stepped up beside me. "The girl is still in danger of succumbing to the infection. She must have been ill for days before she was brought here."

"Doctor Oh," I nodded to him. He gave me a smile. "You cut your hair," he observed.

"Unavoidable in the circumstances," I said, without further explanation.

"Tae-hyun said something of the sort."

"Well, he's not getting lasagna this weekend, unfortunately," I told Dr. Oh. "This has taken precedence, as you might imagine."

"Understandable."

"I'll find Mr. Shi-joon," the detective promised, pocketing his ballpoint and walking away.

"I'll call in three guards," Hu Lin offered, peeling away

from the wall outside the girl's room. "They'll run fingerprints on the girl to get her name and information."

"If that woman shows up, I swear I may have to pay out a huge settlement after I hit her a few times," I muttered. "She dragged the girl out of the car and just dumped her on the sidewalk."

"Nothing a normal parent or caregiver would ever do," Dr. Oh agreed. "If you want, we can find a comfortable chair in the nurse's lounge, or you can sit in my office; I won't need it until later today."

"I'll stay here with Hu Lin until we can get to the bottom of this," I said.

"I'll find something for you to eat," Hu Lin said, giving me a nod.

"There are vending machines, and the cafeteria should be open," Dr. Oh called out.

"He'll do fine. He's had to run after me for nearly eight years," I sighed.

"He wouldn't have it any other way," Tae-hyun arrived and dropped a hand on my shoulder. "You're our baby sister, Rae-Rae. The really, really, rich one."

"Right."

"How's the girl?" Tae-hyun asked Dr. Oh.

"Struggling," he sighed. "We have to wait to see whether the antibiotics will do her any good. For now, we're throwing everything we have at this. She should have been hospitalized days ago."

"What happened?" Shi-joon came running down the

hallway.

"First, tell us who she is," I held out a hand to steady him as he came to an abrupt stop.

"My half-sister," he panted. "Kim Mai-an."

"We ah, have things to tell you," Dr. Oh began. "Please, come into the room and we'll do our best to fill in the details for you."

"DID YOU BRING HER HERE? WHAT ABOUT THE BILLS?" SHI-joon whispered.

"You don't have to worry about any of that; this is Ong Charities Children's Hospital. Anyone admitted is treated free of charge," Dr. Oh explained patiently.

"But if my mother and stepfather are involved in this, or are convicted of neglect—Manta, I don't have the resources to take care of her afterward," he brushed tears away.

"Shi-joon, stop worrying, all right?" I patted his shoulder. "All that will be taken care of, I promise."

"But how?" he said.

"You don't know who you're talking to yet," I told him. "I just have to ask you to keep this a secret, okay?"

"Keep what a secret?"

"That she's really Ong Rae-Rae," Dr. Oh patted Shi-joon's shoulder. "If she says it's taken care of, then it's taken care of."

"Ong Rae-Rae? The real Ong Rae-Rae?"

"I had to cut my hair after one of my ex best friends signed me up to play in a professional gaming league," I said. "So far, I can't say it's been one of the better experiences of my life."

"What about the exhibition match? I don't want to leave Mai's side. Dr. Oh says she might not make it. I have to be here," he said.

"Then I guess Hae Jin will have to play Manta in your place," I said. "Whether he likes it or not."

"I need to call him," Shi-joon hung his head.

"Why don't you let me call him—or, better yet, I'll talk to Min-ho. He's a little calmer in these situations, I think."

"Hae Jin is the poster boy for calm most of the time. It's—I've only seen him lose his cool since, well," Shi-joon hunched his shoulders.

"Since he had to deal with a girl gamer instead of a guy gamer," I finished the statement for him.

"Then call Min-ho."

"Can I get his phone number? I don't have anybody's number on the team."

"We didn't give it to you? That was stupid," Shi-joon sighed. "Here's my phone," he unlocked it for me. "Call whoever you want."

"Then I'll try Hae Jin. If he doesn't cooperate, I'll hang up and call Min-ho."

"If they knew who they were talking to," Shi-joon said.

"And you can't tell them, okay?"

"I won't. I promise."

"Good. I'll go out in the hall to talk."

"HAE JIN, THIS IS MANTA," I BEGAN WHEN HE ANSWERED the phone.

"Manta, where is Shi-joon?"

"In the hospital room with his sister. She's really, really sick. As in she might not make it sick. He doesn't want to leave her side, so you may be stuck with me filling in for Shi-joon in the exhibition game."

"How did you end up there?"

"Well, someone dropped Mai in front of Black Skies Headquarters just as I was leaving this morning, and she collapsed. I got her to the hospital and I've been here ever since. I had to ask the police to help find Shi-joon, because I didn't have anybody's phone number."

Hae Jin cursed softly for a moment. "All right, do you need somebody to come get you?"

"I have a ride," I said. "Does this mean you want me back there tonight?"

"I do."

"Then let me get things settled here and I'll be on my way. You have my number, right?"

"I got it on the first day."

"Awesome. I'll get yours from Shi-joon's phone, if that's all right."

"Yes—it's all right." He sounded exasperated for some reason.

"Everything will be okay—or it won't. It's out of our hands now. All I can say is that the best pediatricians in Seoul are tending to Mai at the moment, so if there's any chance, then she's in the best place she can be."

"Good. Call when you're on the way."

"I will."

I hung up after that; I just felt too awkward to tell him goodbye—as if he were an old friend rather than someone I couldn't get a handle on for some reason. Most people I could read easily, but Hae Jin was certainly different in that respect.

"I think Hae Jin wants to give a lecture, so I'll be on my way," I told Shi-joon moments later. "I'll call for updates, and if you need anything, use this." I held out a credit card.

"I don't need it," he said.

"Just in case. It'll make me feel better," I told him.

"All right, but I won't use it."

"That's up to you. Hang in there, all right?"

I picked up Hu Lin on my way out, so he could drive me back to headquarters. I had no idea what Hae Jin wanted to say, so I prepared myself mentally for the worst I could imagine.

Shi-joon

"I can't believe this," I muttered. I had no desire to call my mother—not after she dumped Mai and took off when she knew my sister was sick.

As for my stepdad, well, if he wasn't involved in this sick mess somehow, I'd be very surprised. He was the one who'd kicked me out of the house ten years earlier—for being gay. My time with Mai since then had been very limited.

Until today, when our own mother decided that a sick girl wasn't her responsibility. "Thank goodness Rae-Rae was there," I covered my face with my hands.

"There's a reason they call her the Saint of Seoul," Dr. Oh put an arm around my shoulders. "If there's a way, Rae-Rae will find it."

"I hope there's a way for Mai, then."

"We're doing everything we can," Dr. Oh soothed. "Just hold on and stay close by her side. Keep talking to her—that seems to help."

"Thank you, Doctor," I said. "I really don't know what to do or how to act in this situation."

"Nobody expects you to be anything other than what you are," he said, giving me a smile. "Stop worrying about things like that and devote your energy to your sister. I think she'll need you more than anything else in the coming days."

Rae-Rae

"I just left the hospital. It'll take about twenty minutes to get there," I told Hae Jin.

"We'll have a meeting when you get back."

"Okay." I ended the call, wondering whether I should be worried or not. After all, I hadn't given Hae Jin any choice in the matter, but there really wasn't any other choice for Shi-joon to make—between family or a job—that might mean little if his sister died while he was killing imaginary characters.

"Is Shi-joon all right?" Min-ho asked the moment I walked through the door into Black Skies headquarters.

"He's terrified," I stated baldly. "His sister is barely hanging on. If the antibiotics don't work fast enough and her organs start shutting down," I shook my head. "If she'd been taken to the hospital a day or two earlier," I shivered, thinking about what pain Mai had suffered already, and what her body was dealing with now in its struggle to function and sustain her life.

"Do you know what's wrong?" Jun-woo asked.

"I don't. The doctors are trying to keep her alive at the moment. I think underlying reasons sort of take a backseat to all that."

No way did I want to blurt out that Mai had been raped—likely repeatedly—and then suffered damage that became infected then spread throughout her body. If Shi-joon wanted to tell his colleagues, that was his choice to make, not mine.

"Now isn't the best time for something like this to happen," Hae Jin stalked into the foyer.

"No time is the best time for this to happen," I whirled and glared at him.

"Yes, you're right, of course," he said in English, holding up a hand. "How is Shi-joon?"

"Devastated," I snapped. "How would you feel if a family member were in that situation?"

"Calm down, Manta," Min-ho patted my arm. "Your hair is fuzzed out like a spitting cat's."

"Spitting cat my ass," I hissed in English at Hae Jin. "You haven't dealt with doctors and nurses and a sick child all day. Have you?"

"No. I haven't." He lifted dark eyes to lock with mine; eyes that held a moment of haunted sadness. I almost felt sorry enough to take back my words.

Almost.

"We have to decide what avatar you'll play tomorrow," he sighed. "I want the team's input."

"If you give me a decent avatar, the Seahorses will strike it," I said without thinking. "Pick one to throw away, then let me play Empress Jade."

"Empress Jade is worthless," Minjun scoffed. "All she does is plant bombs that go off at unexpected moments."

"Then you've never fully explored Empress Jade," I shrugged at him. "Besides," I turned back to Hae Jin, "this is only an exhibition game, and my first time officially playing with the team. What could it hurt?"

"Our reputation," Si-woo grumbled.

"I'll make sure your reputation remains as clear and unsullied as it currently is," I said. My barb sailed right over his head; in the past, if there were any trouble caused for Team Black Skies, the twins were behind it one hundred per cent.

Min-ho ducked his head while a dimple appeared in his cheek. He knew, whether the twins did or not.

"If this doesn't work out in our favor, I'll fine you and ban you from competing in our first tournament," Hae Jin said. "We're done. Everybody, go to bed. We'll start practice at nine tomorrow morning. Get plenty of sleep; you'll need it."

HAE JIN

"Empress Jade," I tossed the folder with our original game plan toward the back of my work cubicle before turning to Min-ho.

"She did good work with Court Magician Oh. I hope she has something similar in mind with Empress Jade," Min-ho pulled my hassock forward and sat on it with a heavy sigh. "I got a text from Shi-joon; he says no changes for now. They're worried his sister won't make it through the night."

"And that will be the biggest blow, not only for him and ultimately for the rest of us, but at the beginning of preseason, too."

"I understand what you're saying," Min-ho raised a hand.

"But I stuck my foot in my mouth earlier with Manta, right?"

"Yes. She's witnessed this firsthand, while we haven't."

"True. Will she be able to hold it together tomorrow—if Mai doesn't make it?"

"Maybe we should consider canceling if Mai, well," Min-ho looked uncomfortable.

"Right. Let's hold off on that and hope for good news in the morning. If the worst happens, I'll talk to Team Owner myself."

"I think that would be best—to let him make the choice rather than taking it on yourself."

"Yeah."

"As for Manta, I've been watching her when she plays," Min-ho began. "Since I have to sit it out, I'm in a unique position to do so."

"And?"

"Every time, it's like the first time we watched her take on Minjun. She goes cold as ice. No expression, no emotion, nothing. It's as if the game plan is in place and nothing will sway her. Yes, she listens to what the rest of you are saying, but she doesn't let our emotions affect her play. I guess what I'm saying is that if my life were ever on the line and somebody needed to be cool and collected to save it, well, the person I choose could be Manta."

"I'm hurt."

"Don't be. If I could sit in your chair and let you observe her for a while instead, I think you'd see the same thing. As for learning the team's strengths and weaknesses, I think she already has all that mapped out."

"Too bad she hasn't done the same for the Seahorses."

"Maybe she has and we just don't know it."

"I doubt it."

"Wanna bet on the outcome tomorrow, if we play?"

"You're asking me to bet against my own team. I won't ever do that."

"I'll be watching closely, then, to see what happens."

"You do that. In fact, if you can record Manta's performance without her knowing, that would be even better."

"I'll look into that. It's not like we won't be televised, after all."

"Duly noted."

"I DON'T NEED MY FOOT TO PLAY," MANTA TOLD ME Sunday morning. "I may have sprained it swimming. The doctor is going to look at it to make sure the bones aren't affected, then I'll be back, all right? In the meantime, practice like normal."

"And normal means?" I struggled to hold back my temper.

"The team usually treats me as if I'm not there anyway. I only play avatars that nobody else cares about. In fact, just let Min-ho sit in my chair and play left-handed. It'll be almost the same thing."

"If I find out that you're skipping practice on purpose," I hissed into the phone.

"Take deep breaths. In. Out. You, too, can be calm and collected," she teased in English.

"Manta," I threatened.

"Oh, right. We're at the hospital now. I'll keep you posted." She hung up, leaving me frustrated and still feeling angry.

At least Shi-joon's sister had made it through the night. He'd called and said the doctors were beginning to have some hope that Mai could pull through.

"Come on, let's start practicing," I pocketed my phone and surveyed the gaming room. "We can do this, right?"

"Right," the twins said in unison, while giving high fives to each other.

Rae-Rae

"It's muscular, no bones involved," Tae-hyun said, pulling the X-rays off the light window. Tae-hyun wasn't only my orthopedic surgeon, he was the best foot and ankle orthopedic surgeon in South Korea. He stayed busy, so a weekend off was worth more than a hundred pounds of gold to him.

"I didn't mean to call you out on a Sunday, when you should be off work," I said, feeling guilty as hell.

"Rae-Rae, with everything else that's happened this weekend, this is nothing. Although I will say that you owe me lasagna sometime in the future."

"I swear I'll make it the first chance I get," I promised.

And then chili. Extra hot."

"You got it. I'll make extra so you can freeze some and have it whenever you want."

"Best thing I've heard today," he grinned at me. "The day we met in college was one of the best days of my life, and I'd freely admit it to anyone who asked."

"Awesome. Need anything else from me?" I asked him. "I'm thinking about stopping by Children's Hospital to check on Mai and Shi-joon."

"I think Dr. Oh and Shi-joon would be happy to see you—especially if you took them some lunch."

"Lunch it is."

"Stay off the foot as much as possible. I'll have somebody come in and wrap it for you. You can swim again in three days, unless the pain persists."

"Okay."

"Your weight and vitals are really good, Rae-Rae. That experimental drug is doing wonders for you. Still no side effects?"

"None that I've noticed, unless being grumpier than usual is a side effect."

"I think being grumpier is a side effect of almost killing yourself with work in Taiwan."

"Not that anybody there would actually notice," I employed my new level of grumpy. "They have no idea why I did that."

"Would you have it any other way?"

"I guess not."

"Good. I'll send in a nurse to wrap your foot. Remember what I said—no swimming for three days and stay off it if you can."

"You're the boss."

"Like I believe that lie for more than half a second."

"That's why I love you. You get me."

"Hu Lin gets me."

"And I'm happy for you."

"We know. I'm just teasing. You really ought to consider finding someone for yourself."

"If you think there's a man in this country—or any other country—who might be interested in me for me, then you're welcome to show them to me. Everybody else just sees the money."

"Or the power, or the prestige, or your lasagna."

"Unbelievable. Go away. Go home. Make Hu Lin happy."

"Who's driving you if Hu Lin takes me home?"

"Man-sik is coming, with Auntie Cheng. I'll ask them to take me by Children's on the way back to headquarters."

"Good enough. Don't wear yourself out, Rae-Rae. I mean it."

"I know. Same goes for you."

"I only do the improbable. You do the impossible. Two different things," he pointed a finger at me.

"Get out," I shooed him away with a hand.

I stood beside Shi-joon's chair as he held his sister's hand. She'd been intubated and was breathing with the aid of a ventilator, but Dr. Oh had already told me that things were looking marginally better for the twelve-year-old.

"She's trying to stay with me," Shi-joon's eyes were reddened from shedding tears and lack of sleep.

"I know." I rubbed his shoulders. "Don't worry about anything else, all right? Mai's the most important person right now."

"A detective came earlier—he said our mother has been arrested for neglect and maybe—other things too. Stepdad had a warrant already for selling street drugs."

He'd probably sold Mai, too, but I didn't want to voice my fears aloud. "So that's why there's a policeman and one of my guards outside the room, then."

"Yes."

"Don't go anywhere alone if you leave the room, all right? I'll have my guys go with you if you want to eat or get a shower or whatever. Tell Hu Lin if you want to clean up; he can take you to my apartment."

"Dr. Oh already offered to let me clean up at his place."

"Then whatever you want is fine. Just make sure Hu Lin or one of the other guards gets you back and forth."

"You're that worried?"

"I am. Don't worry, my guards can handle most situations. That's what they're trained to do."

"Why do you think somebody might come after me?"

"Why do you think they kept your sister away from the hospital?"

"Because," he hesitated and thought for several seconds. "We know stuff, don't we?"

"I'd say that's likely. Don't put yourself or your sister in danger until Stepdad is in jail."

"You think he did this?"

"If he didn't, then he knows who did; I'd bet a billion won on it."

"I want him dead," Shi-joon breathed angrily.

"I'd say you're not the only one. Let the police do their job, okay? Stay here with Mai—she needs you most."

"I will. If I leave, then I'll make sure a guard goes with me."

"Good."

"We're here," my Chief of Security, Gwan Man-sik, said as he and Cheng Li, his wife, walked into the room. Cheng Li was the one I'd call mother if I could; she'd been working with me since I was in college. I'd learned most of my cooking skills from her, too.

"Mai's just a baby," Cheng Li crooned as she sat on the chair opposite Shi-joon's. "How could this happen?"

Cheng Li, in her fifties, was a widow before she met and married Man-sik. She'd never had children with her first husband, who'd died in an accident while both were in their twenties. She'd never considered a second marriage until Man-sik came along.

"I can stay here with her if you need to clean up or stretch your legs," Cheng Li turned to Shi-joon. "Just take Man-sik with you. Rae-Rae says you could become a target if we're not careful."

"I'm beginning to believe she may be right," Shi-joon shuddered.

"Come on, let's get you fed and cleaned up," Man-sik tapped Shi-joon's shoulder. "I imagine you'll feel better after a bath and a hot meal."

"Go on, I'll get the guard outside to drive me to headquarters," I encouraged Shi-joon. "If you want, I'll send you an update after the match."

"That sounds good. Thanks, Rae-Rae. I can't imagine what I'd do if you hadn't helped."

"Don't worry about it," I waved off his thanks. "I should go now or I'll never hear the end of it."

HAE JIN

"Where the hell is she?" I cursed in English just as the gaming room door opened. Manta, her left foot wrapped in an elastic bandage, hobbled in.

"You're late," I hissed at her.

"I know. I'm sorry. Apologies," she dipped her head in a short bow to me.

"We'll be televised, are you wearing that?" I growled.

"I'll change. Give me ten."

"Make it five."

"You're the boss."

It took her seven, but she looked more like a gamer when she came back. Wearing an embroidered, purple silk top with a Mandarin collar over black jeans, she was as fine and slender as a king's *saingeom*. She'd pulled her hair into a purple-tipped topknot and wore hair sticks in the knot, giving her a mysterious air.

Even with the purple tips.

"I hope you don't need to warm up; we're about to go live in ten," I snapped as she took her seat and pulled headphones onto her head. She'd chosen to let the curve of the headset rest on her neck rather than the top of her head, so the topknot wouldn't be disturbed.

My body betrayed me again.

Snarling softly, I pulled out the chair to sit at my station at the table, which was right beside Manta's.

"Cameras are live," Min-ho's voice sounded inside my headset the moment I settled it on my head. "The fans are already in an uproar over Manta. Messages are piling up on the website."

"Good or bad?"

"Both."

"Of course."

"She isn't looking at any of them."

"Probably a good thing. The twins are eating it up."

"Because they love that kind of thing. What about Minjun?"

"Getting some backlash still from the championship game."

"How's he handling it?"

"Looks like he could chew wood."

"So can a carpenter ant."

"Do you expect him to contribute in this session? What if he freezes like he did in the championship?" Min-ho asked.

"He'd better do his job," I said. "If he messes up an exhibition game, how can we trust him in another tournament?"

"I'm not sure we can trust him at all."

"What's that supposed to mean?" I demanded.

"Something's off about him. He's not fitting in with the team like he used to."

"You don't think it's embarrassment after we lost the title?"

"At first I thought that, but things just don't feel—the same. Oh, two minutes. We have to go to work."

"Pay attention, then—to Minjun and Manta. I want a full report."

"You'll get it. Signing off, Captain. May the odds be in your favor."

Sneaking a glance at Manta before the game started, I caught a glimpse of what Min-ho had described to me before.

That look she wore—of icy concentration. As if anyone who might get in her way should prepare for a storm.

I almost wanted to ask what that look meant—and if it were directed at anyone in particular. I didn't.

Later, I was glad of it.

WITHIN THE FIRST TWO MINUTES OF THE GAME, WHILE THE rest of us were battling Seahorse team members, Manta ran a circuit through the gaming field while the least experienced Seahorse trailed after her.

He could barely stay on her trail, she was so fast, but, in my peripheral vision, I couldn't see that she'd attempted to throw one blast, bomb or power discharge in her pursuer's direction.

"What the hell are you doing, Manta?" I hissed into my headset.

"You'll see."

At that moment, Lady Jade passed Samurai Kusunoki, my avatar. Almost casually, Manta reached over and tapped a button on my mouse, causing my avatar to leap high into the air.

Outraged, I reached out to slap her hand, just as a series of bombs began to explode around the playing field.

Everywhere Lady Jade had ran, she'd laid a bomb. The thing was, Lady Jade's bombs could be set on a timer, but that option was basically useless. Nobody knew where or when an enemy avatar would be.

Except for Manta, apparently.

One by one, the Seahorse team was hit and either disabled or destroyed. It took forever as I blinked at the carnage on-screen.

In actuality, it took less than five seconds.

Only Minjun had taken a hit, but his avatar was still standing, although injured. The Seahorse team didn't have anyone left on the team to perform healing, leaving those injured as sitting ducks for Black Skies to destroy at their leisure.

"Whoa," the twins shouted in unison before going in for the kill.

The game lasted less than ten minutes, when it was supposed to last half an hour.

I turned to Manta, who slowly removed the headset and placed it on the table beside her mouse. What she'd done had required timing like I'd never seen before.

"What the hell were you doing?" I asked, dumping my own headset on the desk.

"We're on camera, remember?" She turned to me wearing a tight smile. Her lipstick was a deep purple—to match the dye in her hair and the tint in her glasses. Her mouth, a perfect bow, was enhanced by the dark color.

"Hae Jin, stand and bow. Everyone, stand and bow to the Seahorse team," Min-ho rushed to my side.

"Stand," I ordered, jumping to my feet. "Bow," I snapped, bowing to our opposition that were standing on the big screen opposite us.

"Thank you for the game," I said, once I'd straightened.

"The fans are going crazy," Min-ho breathed beside me as he flipped off the cameras and turned up the gaming room lights. "Nobody in their right minds will ever let Manta play Lady Jade again."

CHAPTER 4

Hae Jin

"I went through their gaming files and watched their matches," Manta told me for the fifth time. "They have habits. I exploited them. I have a headache. Can I go to bed now?"

"Go to bed," I waved a hand helplessly. "I just wish I'd known you could do this sooner. I'd have saved that trick for a tournament match. Now, every team will strike Lady Jade off the avatar list first thing."

"You think I can't work with any other character?"

"I have no idea what you can do. That's obvious by what happened in the match earlier."

"You could ask. Politely."

"Fine. I'll ask. Later. Go to bed. Take something for the headache."

"Thank you." She turned and stalked out of the Captain's office, her small shoulders tight with anger, fists clenched and steps stiff.

My phone rang shortly after she left.

"Shi-joon?" I answered.

"I saw the game," he said. That was—I don't know how to describe something that happened so fast."

"The Seahorses never knew what hit them," I admitted. "They were talking smack, too, before the match, once they learned Minjun was playing."

"I saw. Their Captain was saying with an inexperienced newbie like Manta and a failure like Minjun playing, we didn't stand a chance."

"I didn't see that one, I guess."

"I read some of the stuff to Mai. Doctor Oh says she can still hear me, even if she's unconscious. So I read to her and talk to her. I hope it's doing some good."

"I've heard that, too. Keep it up. She knows her brother's voice."

"Manta leveled that bunch of wannabees, didn't she?"

"In a manner of speaking."

"It was a good strategy, Captain. Keep the main team members occupied while planting doom beneath their feet. I'm glad I decided to watch."

I didn't tell Shi-joon that it wasn't my strategy. In fact, if Manta hadn't sent my avatar leaping high into the air, I'd have been destroyed along with the Seahorse Captain I was fighting at the time.

When my avatar touched ground again, it was to find the enemy dead at my feet. I was still reeling at the impossibility of it.

Habits. Manta said the Seahorses had habits. I knew they had a penchant for certain things, but I'd never gone that in-depth before.

Could Manta do the same with other teams?

I was afraid to ask. I always put her on the defensive, somehow, and that wasn't the way to get a team member's cooperation. *Let Min-ho find out*, I told myself. *She seems more comfortable around him.*

So why did that fact upset me?

Cursing, I rose and stalked out of my office, almost as angry as Manta had been.

Rae-Rae

"I can't swim for three days. The doctor said so," I explained to Min-ho as I poured a glass of milk for myself Monday morning. "I'm going to order breakfast delivery. Want anything?"

"What are you ordering?"

"Ham and cheese croissant from the hotel bakery. They're pretty good."

"I'll take one," Minjun shuffled in, yawning.

"Do they have espresso drinks?" Min-ho asked.

"They do. I'm getting a vanilla latte."

"Then I'll have a caramel mocha cappuccino and a ham and cheese croissant."

"I'll just order stuff for everybody," I said, tapping orders on my phone. "If they don't like coffee or the sandwiches, then somebody else will eat them. There," I said, finishing the order and putting in the address. "Should be here in less than half an hour."

"Who ordered food?" Hae Jin walked into the kitchen later as the rest of us ate around the oblong table set there.

"Manta. Yours is on the counter," Min-ho pointed in the right direction. "I said you liked vanilla lattes, so that's what you got."

"Still warm," Hae Jin sighed gratefully after biting into the sandwich.

"Website is still going nuts this morning," Jun-woo said. "Some of the pros with aliases want to know how those bombs were set to detonate at the right time."

"You know they're aliases how?" Hae Jin asked.

"Seen them before," Si-woo grinned. "If you watch carefully, they can't help but give themselves away. One of them is Werner from the German team."

"You're kidding?"

"Nope. Already digging to find out how it was done."

"I'll never tell," I said, stuffing the last bite of croissant into my mouth. "Unless he can beat me in a one-on-one challenge against an avatar I choose myself."

"Don't make that challenge," Hae Jin pointed at one twin and then the other.

"Damn. We were getting interested," Jun-woo complained.

"Manta, Dirk Werner is an elite gamer," Hae Jin rounded on me. "Maybe the best in the world. If it's him behind that alias, then you want nothing to do with him."

"You're the boss."

"Yes. I am. Thanks for the food." He crumpled the paper bag into a wad and tossed it in the garbage before grabbing his drink and leaving the kitchen.

"How did you do it?" Min-ho asked as we listened to Hae Jin clomp up metal steps to the second floor.

"Timing is everything," I quipped. "I have laundry to do."

HAE JIN

"Timing is everything? That's it?" I asked Min-ho.

"That's what she said. Then she went to do laundry."

"Is she using the washers here?"

"I think she left the building."

"Call her."

"Why?"

"I said so."

"Fine." Min-ho pulled his phone from a back pocket and dialed the number he'd gotten only the night before. Reaching over, I put the call on speaker.

"Min-ho?" Manta answered.

"Uh, where are you," Min-ho improvised.

"At home, doing my laundry."

"You kept your apartment? Where is that, exactly?"

"I don't have to tell you that, and I own the apartment. Of course I kept it. Why would I dump it for a one-year contract?"

"Most people would rent it while they were gone," I couldn't stop myself from joining the conversation.

"Now I know why you called. I didn't rent it because I don't like people touching my stuff. They might run off with my Peace Prizes."

"That's hilarious," I said in English. Get your laundry done and get back here. We have practice this afternoon."

"I'd get done sooner if I weren't dealing with nuisance phone calls. Are you offering to renew my car warranty, too?"

"That kind of talk will get you a fine, Miss Manta," I still spoke to her in English.

"You're the boss." The phone went dead—she'd hung up on me. *Us.*

"Let me know the minute she gets back," I told Min-ho.

"You're the boss."

"Don't start," I held up a hand. Min-ho opened his mouth to retort, then thought better of it.

As well he should.

Rae-Rae

"We've been tailing her ever since she sold this piece at the same pawn shop," Bak Jin-won tapped the evidence bag that held my mother's jade necklace—the same jade necklace that had disappeared shortly after her death.

Jin-won's image was on my laptop—he'd placed a video call to show me what he'd found. At least some of my mother's things were coming to light—my mother's other jewelry and valuables had disappeared a handful of years after her death, and none of it had been accounted for before now.

"How do you think this woman's involved?" I asked Jin-won about the suspected thief. "She wasn't old enough at the time to steal anything this valuable."

"We're just as confused. We did discover that she's living with an older man, though. He owns a small dry-cleaning business. We've tailed him, too, but he hasn't been anywhere or done anything out of the ordinary. This means we're still investigating where the piece came from and how the woman got her hands on it in the first place."

"Keep the pawn shop proprietor paid, and reimburse him for any expenses incurred," I sighed. "Make sure all the paperwork is done so we're covered."

"Don't worry. I've cleared it with my bosses at work," Jin-won assured me. "They want to solve these cases almost as much as you do."

"I hope this lead takes us somewhere. We've hit so many dead ends in the past."

"I know. I wish I could give this necklace to you, but it's evidence. Don't worry, we'll keep it safe and release it to you once we get to the bottom of this."

"Thank you. Please keep me informed if anything new comes up."

"You've done us so many favors in the past, Chairman Ong," Jin-won said, stuffing the evidence bag into a suit coat pocket. "This case is a pleasure to work."

I said good-bye and closed my laptop before going to the laundry room in my penthouse apartment. I was doing laundry, just as I'd told Hae Jin. *Really, why couldn't the man let up for even five minutes?*

My phone rang while I was folding socks. "I convinced the Flying Stars to take over Minjun's contract," Zhang Bao informed me. "Team Owner Wu Chang is more than happy to let him go. And I convinced Gu Han to take over as both alternate player and team manager. He only wanted a two-year contract, but he actually liked the idea. You know he wants to build his own team after this, don't you?"

"I suspected he might. Wu Chang has already fired Team Manager Chen Ling after he was arrested for gambling yesterday. Good work getting that done so fast."

"Hmmph. Easy mark," Zhang Bao said. "He just couldn't help himself. He'll be betting with his fellow prisoners soon, if he isn't already."

Hae Jin

"We're having a meeting in ten with Team Owner," I growled at Manta the moment she walked into headquarters pulling a rolling suitcase and carrying an over-the-shoulder tote filled with clean laundry.

"I'll hurry," she said, ignoring the dark look I leveled at her.

Eight minutes later she settled onto a seat in the meeting room, where the rest of us had gathered. Team Owner arrived three minutes afterward.

"I suppose you're wondering why Minjun isn't here this morning," he cleared his throat and began. "The Flying Stars offered to buy out his contract; they needed an experienced alternate and Minjun was the only choice because the other teams they approached turned them down."

This was news, but not unwelcome news in my opinion. Minjun no longer fit into the team and bad blood had roiled just below the boiling point since the world championships.

"What will we do in the meantime?" I asked. "If he's gone already and Shi-joon is still with his sister at the hospital?"

"I already have a replacement; he's coming to sign the contract later today," Team Owner smiled. "I think you'll appreciate this one—I was very surprised when he accepted my offer."

"Who?" Min-ho asked immediately.

"Gu Han," Team Owner's smile turned into a self-satisfied grin. "He has also agreed to act as Team Manager when he's not serving as alternate. He'll have a meeting with all of you when he arrives in two days. Your next exhibition game is in a week, so time is short to integrate him into the team before then. I also hope that the situation with Shi-joon's sister is better by that time, too. This way, we'll be back at full strength and able to present a united front."

"Gu Han?" Min-ho mouthed at me. I chewed my lip—neither of us expected to work with such a legendary gamer and character designer. He was thirty-three—a bit old for gaming, but word had it that he was still adept at it. I hoped those rumors were true, although it wouldn't take much to operate at Minjun's level.

"Thank you for convincing him to join Black Skies," I stood and bowed to Team Owner. "Gu Han will be a welcome addition to the team."

"I am just as pleased," Team Owner said. "Expect him in two days."

"Gu Han?" The twins mumbled right after Team Owner left. "Five years ago, he could take on any one of us."

"Maybe he still can," Manta said. "You never know."

"He hasn't been the same since his wife died," Min-ho remarked. "He didn't play or do anything for two years after that."

"I think we shouldn't bring up his wife, unless he talks about her first," Manta rose from her seat and stretched. "People grieve differently. Give him his privacy, please."

Everybody in the gaming industry knew Gu Fawn died of ovarian cancer. It had gone undetected until it was too late, and it had devastated Gu Han, who was at the top of his field at the time.

"That's a good suggestion. Everybody, leave that subject alone unless Gu Han talks about it himself."

"Yes, Captain."

"All right, we're a person short, but we still need to practice," I said. "Be in the gaming room in twenty."

"WHERE DID YOU HEAR THAT?" I SAID, STARING AT Min-ho.

"From a friend who follows the Shooting Stars," he replied. "They're releasing Minjun from his contract, after another player changed his mind and decided to sign on as their alternate."

"That's—unusual," I said, although it wasn't the first word that came to mind. "Did they find something on Minjun that they didn't like?"

"It isn't like there's not enough to find on him," Min-ho frowned. "If he insulted a team member right off the bat like he did Manta, that would be reason enough to let him go immediately."

"He does have a habit of opening his mouth when he shouldn't," I agreed tactfully. "Do you think any team will hire him if that gets out?"

"Doubt it. They all know what he did at the championships. Who wants somebody who will freeze at clutch time?"

"Sometimes I worry that he might have done that on purpose," I admitted.

"Why would he do something like that?"

"I don't know. I just get an odd feeling now and then," I said. "Never mind, we have Gu Han coming in two days. Any update on Shi-joon?"

"Says things are looking better, but his sister still isn't conscious."

"Is he getting enough rest and plenty to eat?"

"He says that someone has taken care of all that at the hospital, so I didn't pry."

"You think we ought to go for a visit?"

"Couldn't hurt. So far, the only one who's been there for him is Manta. He said she brought him breakfast early this morning."

"Then we can take a bag of snacks and some drinks," I decided. "And we'll see if he needs anything done for him."

"He may need clean clothes. I'll call and ask."

"Good idea."

Rae-Rae

"We're watching Minjun now," the NIS agent reported. "If

he's involved in the hacking ring, he's bound to meet up with somebody sooner or later."

"He won't meet with anyone important. Not yet," I warned. "Just keep tabs on him for now and investigate anybody he meets."

"We're on it."

"Thank you."

Zhang Bao had first brought this to my attention—that there could be connections between players in the gaming industry and an international hacking ring. The ring had already hacked into and shut down several big businesses plus a few government agencies, worldwide, before asking for exorbitant ransoms to remove the viruses they'd planted.

Zhang Bao had also taken the initiative to place me at the center of it all the moment he'd learned of the empty seat at Black Skies.

His friendship with Team Owner hadn't hurt, either.

"Next time, Zhang Bao, you get to be the hands-on person," I sniped after ending the call. Interpol had already been informed that we were working on the case from our end in South Korea. They were dealing with it in several other places, including Germany, the US and Italy.

I'd sneaked away from headquarters, claiming I needed to make a trip to the nearest convenience store, so I asked Hu Lin to drop me off on our way back. I'd load up with snacks for the team; enough to last them three days. It would last for two with their appetites, but that was the way things went at Black Skies.

With two huge bags filled with snacks, I walked into headquarters after Hu Lin dropped me off nearby.

"Are those snacks?" Min-ho strode toward me. Grabbing one of the bags, he began searching through it. "You just saved us some time," he grinned. "We're going to see Shi-joon and wanted to take snacks."

"Then take everything. The twins can buy for themselves," I said, handing the other bag to Hae Jin, who'd arrived at Min-ho's side. "If Shi-joon needs anything else, tell him to call me."

"You barely know one another," Hae Jin scoffed.

"Who got his sister to the hospital while the rest of you were playing basketball?" I asked as pleasantly as I could. "Honestly." I walked away in a huff.

"We don't have to pay for snacks," I heard Min-ho say as I left them behind.

HAE JIN

"One of Manta's friends did some laundry for me," Shi-joon explained. "Even ironed my shirts. I never iron anything."

"We know that about you," Min-ho teased. "Who's the friend? Anybody we ought to know?"

"She said to call her Auntie Cheng," Shi-joon shrugged.

"She makes the best kimchi I've ever tasted. She sits with Mai when I leave for meals or if I need a shower."

"Why are there guards outside?" I asked.

"Oh. Well, uh," our friend looked uncomfortable for the first time. "It involves why Mai is here to begin with. She didn't just come down with an infection. She was uh, assaulted."

I drew in a breath.

Assaulted. Probably sexual assault, although I didn't want to ask further questions. Shi-joon deserved to keep this secret —both for himself and for his sister.

"And the culprit is still at large, I'm guessing?" Min-ho thought to ask.

"Yes." Shi-joon studied his shoes for several seconds. It was likely that someone he knew was involved in this. My mind searched back to what I'd learned before—Shi-joon's mother had dropped the girl off at Black Skies Headquarters.

The girl was very ill already when that happened. Neglect suddenly entered the picture—the mother should have taken the girl to the hospital. Instead, she'd dumped her at Shi-joon's workplace, without making sure Shi-joon was there to take charge of his sister.

Shi-joon had a stepfather—one he didn't like. Things were becoming clear for me, and I didn't like what I saw.

Manta knows this already, I told myself. She was holding Shi-joon's secrets to her so tightly I doubted anyone could pry them loose. After all, she'd gotten the girl to the hospital and had likely saved her life in the process, while tracking down Shi-joon and contacting the police. Hence, the uniformed guard plus the plain-suited one stationed outside the door.

"Mai could wake any time—at least that's what the doctors say—that the infection is showing signs of improvement," Shi-joon said. "We're lucky she was brought here. The best doctors work at this hospital."

"I've heard that about all of Ong Charities' hospitals in the country," Min-ho agreed. "The staff are paid very well, and they don't have the pressure to do things that other hospitals demand that they do. Even rich people try to get in, but they're usually turned away since they can pay. The ones treated here are treated at no charge."

I felt a pang of guilt; how many times had my parents told me that they could set me up with Ong Rae-Rae, the one behind Ong Group and Ong Charities? I'd turned them down flatly every time. Since I was eleven, there was only one girl I wanted to meet, and I still didn't have a clue who she was.

After Mai was better, maybe I ought to write a thank-you note to Ong Rae-Rae and ask my mother to deliver it. She knew the woman, I didn't. They were good friends, from the way Mom gushed about her. "She always contributes to my charity ball," Mom told me.

Dad was more reserved, but even he had encouraged me to at least meet her once. I'd still refused. I didn't want anyone else's image clouding the one I had in my mind—and had held there for the past eighteen years.

A pale, fragile face, with a pretty bow of a mouth. If I ever saw that mouth again, I'd want to kiss it. I just knew I would.

What if she's married?

What if she's dead?

Those two questions plagued me and had for more than a decade. What would I do if I finally found her, only to discover that she was taken already?

Or had met an untimely end, as I almost did?

I shivered; Min-ho noticed.

"Someone disturb your grave in another life?" he asked.

"No."

"Is Gu Han really joining the team?" Shi-joon asked.

"That's what Team Owner says. He'll act as manager and alternate. Once you're back, then he can concentrate on being Team Manager."

"I never thought I'd get to meet him," Shi-joon sighed. "He still has a huge following."

"We have a huge following, too, remember?" Min-ho teased.

"I remember."

I wanted to ask Shi-joon about convalescent care for his sister after she was released from the hospital, but I didn't. For now, it appeared that Shi-joon was Mai's closest relative and the one responsible for her wellbeing. I hoped it didn't affect the future of either if he continued to play with Black Skies—we needed his talent and steady hands on the team.

"Someone has already offered to take Mai in while I'm

working," Shi-joon said, answering my mental questions. "Auntie Cheng and her husband have begged me to let her stay with them. They work for Ong Group and for Ong Charities, and they live here in Seoul, not far from headquarters," he added. "It will make it easier for me to see Mai and still be able to work with the team."

"You're her guardian now, aren't you?" Min-ho asked gently.

"Yes. It just happened that way. The legal papers are already signed."

"Shi-joon?" The soft, mumbled question came from the bed.

"Mai? Baby sister, are you awake?" Shi-joon was up and at her bedside quickly.

"Yes," her eyes cracked open. "Where am I?"

"In the hospital. Don't worry, everything will be fine."

"Okay." Her eyes closed, as if she were only waiting for Shi-joon's reassurance before sleeping again. Shi-joon brushed hair back from his sister's face before reaching for the call button to summon the nurse.

"She woke up for a few seconds and recognized me," Shi-joon told the nurse who'd appeared.

"I'll let the doctor know." The nurse busied herself checking Mai's vitals before leaving the room.

"That's a relief," I found myself saying with a heavy sigh. "Thank goodness things are looking better, now."

Rae-Rae

By the time Hae Jin and Min-ho arrived to tell us Mai had wakened for a short time, I'd already gotten calls from two people telling me the same thing. Auntie Cheng and Dr. Oh had both let me know that things were looking far better now than they had a few days before.

I was grateful.

TWO DAYS LATER, GU HAN ARRIVED AT HEADQUARTERS AND Mai was fully awake and aware of her surroundings. No mention of her mother and stepfather were made to the girl, and she didn't speak of them, either.

She wasn't ready yet to talk to anyone about what had actually happened. The police were still searching for the stepfather, though, and I hoped he'd be caught soon.

"This is Manta, our newest player, who is here on a one-year contract," Hae Jin introduced me to Gu Han.

"I watched the exhibition game with the Seahorses," Gu Han nodded to me. "I've never seen anyone play Lady Jade with such skill."

"I find her character more than interesting," I replied,

shaking his hand. "Plus, the element of surprise didn't hurt in the circumstances."

"I'd like to see more of what you can do," Gu Han said.

"Of course." I suppose it didn't hurt that Lady Jade was one of his character designs. Gu Han had a subtle touch when giving his characters hidden abilities.

"We're worried that Lady Jade will be stricken off the list of avatars by our opposing teams in the future," Hae Jin steered Gu Han toward the twins.

"She will," Gu Han agreed. "But there are plenty of other avatars with hidden skills we can exploit," he said.

"How's Mai?" I leaned over to ask Shi-joon, who'd left the hospital long enough to meet Gu Han.

"Great. She's talking and eating, although not much of either, right now," Shi-joon explained.

"I'm glad she's better," I breathed.

"Thank you," he said softly. "Auntie Cheng is already a perfect fit for Mai."

"I knew she would be. Don't worry about a thing," I added. "She'll be in the best hands possible. When the time is right, we'll bring in the psychologist to work with her."

"Can I meet her?" Shi-joon asked.

"I think she'll want to meet with you, too," I said.

"Good. Dr. Oh says if things continue to improve, Mai could be released in a week. She'll need plenty of care when she leaves the hospital, but Auntie Cheng says no problem."

"She's more than happy to take care of Mai," I said. "And

that means you can come back to practice and see Mai afterward. Things will work out."

"You may be able to come back next week?" Hae Jin was back and listening to our conversation.

"If the doctor says yes," Shi-joon replied.

"Good. Perfect. Let us know," Hae Jin grinned at Shi-joon.

CHAPTER 5

HAE JIN

"Shi-joon hasn't been back long enough to participate in the next exhibition game," I said during the team meeting. "He's still rusty, so Gu Han will fill in. The Firebirds aren't a team to take lightly; they took down the Harpies with no trouble in their first exhibition match."

"Do we have the avatar lineup yet?" Jun-woo asked.

"Gu Han, Min-ho and I are working that out," I said. "Don't worry, you'll end up with something you're comfortable with."

"Will I end up with something comfortable?" Manta asked.

"We haven't decided, remember?"

"Right. Sorry."

"You'll end up with Ladybug," Si-woo teased her. Ladybug

was a character kindergarten children played in a simplistic version of the game.

"Ladybug will not be an option," I glared at Si-woo. "Neither will we play Tom Thumb," I named the second most popular character among five-year-olds.

"Thank you," I heard Manta whisper.

"I heard that."

"Sorry," she almost sang.

I ducked my head to hide a half-smile.

SATURDAY BEFORE THE EXHIBITION GAME ON SUNDAY arrived, and basketball was on the agenda again.

"You're going. You can chase loose balls," I told Manta, whose lower lip was certainly leaning toward a full pout. "And stop pouting. You can do your laundry some other time."

"You're the boss." The moment she turned and stalked off, I found myself wanting to call her out for her impertinence.

That could lead to all sorts of problems, I knew, so I clenched my fists instead and waited for her and the others to change before loading up and driving to the court. We had an indoor court reserved today; it was raining hard outside and the rain was as cold as it could be in late February without freezing.

Everybody arrived dressed for the weather; Manta wore a purple down jacket, a woolly hat and a scarf. "You look like an

Oompa Loompa," Jun-woo laughed at her purple jacket, scarf and hat.

"We Oompa Loompas get the job done," Manta sniffed and climbed into the van ahead of him.

"Are we going for lunch afterward?" Si-woo asked.

"That's the plan," I said.

"Great. I want hotpot."

"We'll see." Dealing with the twins was often like dealing with third graders—they were self-serving in the extreme.

Half an hour later, everybody piled out of the van and headed for the front doors. Inside, our basketball court reservation was checked while a small crowd of people gathered nearby; they recognized the team and probably wanted autographs.

"Is that Gu Han?" I heard somebody whisper as we walked past without engaging them.

"Why can't I ever get Lee Hae Jin to look at me?" a female voice whined. I deliberately didn't look in that direction, choosing to stare straight ahead.

"Manta Ray is shorter than I thought," a male voice spoke. I choked back a laugh.

"*Though she be but little, she is fierce*," another male voice quoted Shakespeare.

Manta has a fan, ran through my mind. I mentally reminded myself that she needed to be on the website more; every team member was required to have a regular presence and interact with fans. Manta had done little in that respect since she'd joined the team.

We shut the door behind us, keeping the onlookers outside when we reached our reserved court. Jackets, scarves and hats came off and were tossed or laid carefully on the bleachers on one side.

Manta, still dressed in a thick sweater and turtleneck with jeans and leather sneakers, stood at the sidelines while the others grabbed basketballs off a rack and began to shoot practice balls.

"I'm supposed to chase after all those?" Manta looked at me incredulously as balls went bouncing everywhere after hitting the backboard.

"That's your job."

"Wow," she said in English, shaking her head. "Sadistic, much?" Without waiting for my answer, she began picking up the nearest balls and lobbing them toward the first empty-handed teammate.

"Here," I held out my hands. She tossed a ball to me and glared while she did it. I took a shot from just inside the side-line. Made it, too, on my first try.

After fifteen minutes of shooting, we were ready to play. By that time, Manta was worn out from chasing balls and sending them back to us.

"Where are you going?" I asked as she headed for the door.

"To get water," she said.

"Ask the front desk to send some in for all of us," I told her.

"All right."

Rae-Rae

"Will you send water to court number three?" I asked at the front desk.

"Sure thing. One or two bottles each?"

"Make it two."

"You're Manta, aren't you?"

"That's what they tell me."

"I saw your exhibition game."

"Pure luck," I said in English.

"That's not what some of the experts are saying. I read one article that says you're the one to watch this season."

"Well, that may be rather optimistic."

"I like to think he's right."

"Stranger things have probably happened," I said, making him laugh.

"The water will be delivered in a few minutes," he said. "Can I have your autograph?"

"If you insist." I signed the piece of paper he slid across the desk.

"Good luck with the season," he said after I returned the paper to him.

"Thank you."

"Water is coming," I announced when I got back to the basketball court.

"I hope you got more than one bottle for each of us," Hae Jin said, toweling his face during a break.

"I asked for two. If that's not enough, I'll bring in the fire hose."

"Two should be fine."

"Awesome."

"You speak English like an American."

"I know. I have a doctorate in languages from Seoul National University."

"Seriously?"

"Yes."

"That still doesn't explain how you speak English without a Korean accent."

"My grandfather liked old American movies. I learned from watching them. He was especially fond of John Wayne, Clark Gable and Jimmy Stewart."

"You're kidding?"

"Nope." I didn't add that his movie collection was on video tape and had been stored at the house in Busan after his death. I'd watched the tapes during sleepless nights in the attic of that house, using an old combination TV/VCR player.

"What was your favorite John Wayne film, then?"

"*The Quiet Man*," I said promptly. "I could do an Irish accent after watching that one."

"How old were you at the time?"

"Seven."

"You baffle me."

"I baffle a lot of people."

"Will you two stop speaking in English? I can't understand a thing you're saying," Min-ho complained, swatting at Hae Jin with his towel.

The water arrived then, so the team gathered around the employee who'd brought it to get a bottle. The rest was set on the bleachers for later.

I grabbed a bottle for myself after the others were done and sat nearby, drinking water. Chasing balls was thirsty work.

Once our time was up, we put on our coats and hats, then left to have lunch. We ended up at a hotpot restaurant that had very little in the non-spicy department.

Even so, I had some chicken that needed soaking in soy sauce to become edible and was still a bit hungry when we left the restaurant.

"Are you okay? You didn't eat much," Shi-joon whispered as we loaded into the van.

"I'll get something else later," I said.

"I'm having dinner with Mai and Auntie Cheng tonight. Want to come?"

"Sure."

"I LIVE UPSTAIRS—IN THE PENTHOUSE," I EXPLAINED TO Shi-joon as we rode up the elevator with Hu Lin. Hu Lin had come to pick us up.

"Don't tell me—you own the building?"

"I do, but keep it to yourself."

"I will. Who'd believe me?"

Two minutes later, we stood outside the door of Auntie Cheng's and Uncle Man-sik's apartment. I was surprised when Dr. Oh opened the door for us.

"Shi-joon," Dr. Oh hugged Shi-joon warmly. Well, that was a relationship I hadn't seen coming.

"It's good to see you, Dr. Oh," Shi-joon grinned when the Doctor let him go.

"Mai is doing very well," Dr. Oh took Shi-joon's hand in his and led him toward the kitchen.

"I think we just got left out," Hu Lin grinned at me.

"Well, in this case, I really don't mind," I said. "Shi-joon needs that support, I think."

"Auntie Rae-Rae," Mai smiled when I arrived in the kitchen.

"Look at you, all pretty and everything," I told her.

"Auntie Cheng got this for me," Mai twirled in her new dress.

"She has good taste."

"Rae-Rae didn't eat much at lunchtime," Shi-joon said. "They took us to a hotpot restaurant, and there wasn't anything she could eat."

"Haven't they learned to be more careful?" Auntie Cheng complained. "Want some milk before dinner?" she asked me.

"A small glass."

Dinner was traditional Chinese, with egg foo young added at the last minute because Auntie Cheng knows I love it.

Most of the time, I think Shi-joon and Dr. Oh held hands under the table. I didn't care and neither did anybody else.

"I like egg foo young," Mai decided, as we cleared dishes off the table. I helped load the dishwasher; Hu Lin and Man-sik washed what needed handwashing, letting Auntie Cheng, Shi-joon and Dr. Oh send Mai off to bed.

"At least she can trust those two men," Man-sik sighed as we finished in the kitchen. "She's wary around any man she doesn't know and trust."

"Understandable," I agreed. "Who knows what may have happened to her? The psychologist should be setting up an appointment for next week."

"We heard from her. She's setting up a meeting with Shi-joon and us first. Then she'll meet with Mai."

"I heard that her stepfather may have left the country. I sent out some notices to various places to watch for him getting off boats and such. He didn't get on a plane, of that much we're certain."

"If there's any justice in the world, he'll be arrested fast," Man-sik growled.

"I feel the same way."

"She's in bed," Shi-joon came back to the kitchen with Dr. Oh. "If you don't mind, Dr. Oh will drop me off at headquarters," he went on.

"Not a problem. Hu Lin, looks like it's you and me," I said.

"Not a problem," he repeated my words with a grin.

Hae Jin

"Where is Shi-joon?" I asked Manta when she walked into the building.

"He found a separate ride home," she said.

"Curfew is eleven," I began when Shi-joon walked through the door.

"I'm here with three minutes to spare," Shi-joon grinned at me. "My sister is fine; the doctor says so. I rode home with him, by the way."

"Practice starts at ten tomorrow morning," I said. "Go to bed. Now."

"You're the boss," Manta and Shi-joon said in unison.

"Be glad I'm in a good mood," I called after them. Shi-joon ran lightly up the steps; Manta followed slowly behind. Only then did I wonder if the day's activities had aggravated her foot.

She'd tell me, surely, I rationalized.

Except she might not. We didn't have the kind of relationship that encouraged a free exchange of information.

That may have been the first time I considered how to go about fixing the rift between us.

"PUT IN BOTH AVATARS YOU PRACTICED WITH," I TOLD Manta. "The other team will decide which one you end up with."

"You're the," she began.

"Can you at least paraphrase?" I winced.

"You're the grand high poo-bah," she said in English. I snorted a laugh. "I'll end up with Jo-jii," she added, naming the lesser of the two characters she'd practiced with.

"Yeah, I figure you will."

"Someday, will you trust me with more than a hundred won and a secondary character?"

"I guess we'll have to see."

"Right."

"Just follow the practice game plan."

"You're no fun." She put on her headset so she couldn't hear my reply.

"If it saves the match, I'll allow you the leeway," I said, knowing she wouldn't hear. It probably wouldn't stop her, either. Even in the short time he'd been with us, Gu Han had noticed that Manta went all in every time she played. She'd been assigned some of the worst avatars, too. I had a feeling that if she'd been given Lady Bug to play, Manta would make the opposition feel her presence before her character died.

Jo-jii was like a walking virus; he could kill the health points of any character if he came close enough. The trouble was, most players couldn't get him close enough to another avatar without getting Jo-jii killed.

Manta was fast enough and clever enough to do it. She'd even taken out my avatar—twice—during practice.

"Stay alive," I sighed in Manta's direction before taking my seat and putting on my headset.

"Live in ten," Min-ho began the countdown.

"Everyone, do your best," I said before the match began.

The Firebirds came out fast, attacking everywhere at once. Just as Gu Han and I expected, they came after the stronger avatars, ignoring Jo-jii. Manta drained her first victim's stamina, drawing some attention from the team captain.

"Take him out while his health points are low," I snapped at Jun-woo, who was closest. Manta, who'd zoomed out of reach, was suddenly back when one of the Firebirds threatened Jun-woo's avatar. She hit him, too, taking his health points down to nearly nothing.

Si-woo rushed in to help his brother; together they eliminated two of the Firebirds while Jo-jii disappeared into the trees and tall grass of the landscape.

"They're weak with only three players," I snapped, "take the initiative."

Gu Han joined me as we went after the Firebirds' captain and their second-in-command. Their third team member joined them, forming a triangle. "Jun-woo," I ordered, when it looked as if Gu Han and I were about to be overwhelmed in a three-on-two fight.

Jun-woo and Si-woo were rushing toward us when Manta appeared right at the center of the opposing triangle. Health points drained out of all three avatars at once. "Attack," I shouted, swinging my virtual blade as quickly as possible.

Less than fifteen minutes, from start to finish, the game was ours.

"You have to be fast," Manta shrugged without looking at me. She'd waited until the three remaining players were focused on Gu Han and me before zooming in-between two opposing avatars and draining health points.

She'd taken out the first two players that way, too, by moving in so quickly they never saw her coming.

I couldn't recall anyone ever winning a game with Jo-jii before. Hell, I'd never seen anyone play that character in anything close to an official match.

"Jo-jii will be off the list from now on," Shi-joon's hand fell heavily on my shoulder. "If you thought you were punishing her," he leaned in to whisper, "I'd find a different way next time."

"I wasn't," I said as he moved away.

Was that what I was doing? Punishing her? If so, why? At first, before she was introduced to the team, I'd been worried that Team Owner was thinking of replacing Min-ho. He and Manta were adamant that my thinking was very wrong.

Somehow, I knew Manta wasn't kidding when she said she was leaving after her contract was up.

"The website is blowing up," Min-ho placed a bottle of water in my hand. "Somebody has already slowed down the recording so they can see Manta's movements."

"What are they saying?"

"That her hand skills are exceptional. We knew that already; we just didn't know that we knew."

"Yeah." I rolled my shoulders. "If she can do this with a secondary character, what would she do with a top tier avatar?"

"No idea. What are you going to do, Captain?"

"Keep feeling her out, I guess. This way, the opposition will worry about any character she plays."

"True. Just be careful that you don't dampen her enthusiasm."

"Huh?"

"I'd get tired of being assigned the dregs," Min-ho patted my shoulder. "Really tired, actually."

"I thought you'd be happy to make your competition suffer."

"That's not my competition. I believe her when she says she's leaving when her contract is up. She's not kidding, Hae Jin. Something in me is convinced that her talent wasn't meant for gaming."

"Then why is she here?"

"I don't know. Maybe you should ask her."

"Maybe I'll ask Team Owner instead."

"Good job skirting the issue." Min-ho walked away. "Don't forget to post on the website," he called out.

"That goes for everybody, including you, Manta," I raised my voice over the din in the gaming room. "Everybody—get on it now."

"SHE WAS RECOMMENDED BY A COLLEGE FRIEND," TEAM Owner said as his assistant set a cup of coffee in front of me. "Said she was really good. I wasn't sure he knew what he was talking about, but I decided to give it a try."

"There wasn't a resume or anything?"

"Just a contract. He was very specific about the one-year deal. Said she'd refuse if it were longer."

"Is there a way I can talk to your friend?"

"Can you speak Chinese?"

"No."

"Then you'll have to ask Manta. Has she refused to answer your questions? If so, I'll talk to her."

"No—no, nothing like that. I just wanted to see her resume if there was one."

"Is there anything else?"

"I was thinking about taking the team out for a meal."

"Go ahead. Don't go crazy with the alcohol."

"Of course."

Rae-Rae

"We're going out for a team dinner," Hae Jin sat next to my chair at the gaming desk. "What can you eat? I don't want to see you picking at your food again because it's too spicy."

"What's on the list of choices?"

"Do you like Japanese?"

"I love Japanese. The question is whether the twins like Japanese."

"They picked last time. Min-ho, Shi-joon and I like Japanese."

"Awesome."

"Be ready to go at six tonight."

"Dress code?"

"Business casual or thereabouts."

"Can the twins even do that?"

"If they're forced to, and only when free food is involved."

"I see. You know I can't drink, don't you?"

"Why is that?"

"Only a little will render me unconscious. Don't try to slip me anything, either. I can usually smell it, but just in case, I have an app on my watch that calls an ambulance if I lose consciousness."

I didn't add that it called my bodyguards, too. He'd find that out if it ever happened.

"Good to know," Hae Jin nodded. "See you at six."

Hae Jin

I was unprepared for Manta's appearance at six; the rest of us had gathered near the front doors waiting for the team van to pick us up. Manta walked toward us wearing a caramel-brown leather double-breasted motorcycle jacket that looked as if it had been designed specifically for her, and black designer jeans with low-heeled boots.

Her hair was in a tight topknot this time, where the purple tips swirled around the outside, lending a mischievous air to her outwardly calm demeanor.

"*Daebak*," Min-ho breathed beside me.

"Settle down," I warned, although I'd been thinking nearly the same thing, only in English.

"Is that real?" Jun-woo reached out to touch the sleeve of Manta's jacket.

"It's real, you idiot," Si-woo elbowed his brother. "Where'd you get it?" he asked.

"I ordered it," Manta said.

At least Si-woo didn't ask how much it cost, although I knew he wanted to. Something like that would be priced in the thousands in the States, I knew that much. Perhaps Manta came from a wealthy family and that's why she didn't want to give out too much information.

I wasn't familiar enough with the rich and famous of South Korea—I'd spent too much time abroad. My parents might know better than I would, but how could I ask them when I didn't even know her real name?

Maybe an introduction?

No—they'd think I was actually serious about some sort of relationship, when nothing could be further from the truth.

Maybe if I gave them a heads-up beforehand?

That could work. I'd say it was to satisfy my curiosity. They'd wanted to meet my teammates before, but I always refused, giving one excuse or another to keep family and team separated.

In this instance, though, if Manta had anything to do with the wealthy of Seoul, then Mom would likely know better than Dad.

I'd get that worked out somehow, but it would involve getting Manta alone, and then making up some excuse to drop by my house when the parents were home.

With that in mind, I climbed into the van last and shut the door. Our driver took off toward the Japanese restaurant, and I was looking forward to the evening out.

Just as she'd said, Manta refused to drink. I had to tell the twins three times not to give her anything.

"I can't drink," Manta explained after their third try. "I'm really too sensitive to alcohol; it's similar to an allergic reaction."

She'd ordered a steak and lobster stir-fry, sharing more than half of it between Shi-joon and Min-ho, who were happy to add it to their plates.

So why was I feeling a bit left out when it wasn't offered to me? *Maybe I should have arranged to sit closer*, I thought. Shi-joon and Min-ho sat on either side of her, so they'd gotten first choice.

Gu Han and the twins didn't get any, either, I reassured myself as I watched her eat. Her table manners were neat and precise; she even ate her stir-fried rice with chopsticks rather than a spoon, like some of the others did.

"Where did you learn gaming?" Gu Han asked Manta directly.

"A friend wanted me to learn so we could play together. I'm more familiar with CTF type competitions."

"Capture the Flag? The hacking tournaments?"

"If that's how you want to describe it, then yes."

Min-ho turned toward me, an incredulous expression on his face. "Hacking?" he mouthed at me.

"So this friend taught you how to play?" Gu Han continued his questioning.

"He showed me the basics. I beat him within a week, and he hasn't played against me since. We've played together," she was quick to add. "We take on challengers now and then."

"What avatars do you play?"

"This and that," she hedged. She didn't want us to know for some reason. "I've played most of the top tier avatars at one time or another. I won't step on any toes here," she promised.

"I don't think you should concern yourself with that," Gu Han told her. "I'm speaking as the manager here, and not a teammate. You have a gift, Manta. I'd like to see it fully explored."

"I'd say that's up to you and Team Captain," she replied. "I'm only here for a year. I don't intend to play professionally for longer than that, so take that into consideration."

"You don't intend to play at all?" Shi-joon asked.

"Not professionally. No."

"So a friendly game isn't out of the question?"

"If I have time."

"You really have another job?" I asked.

"Yes. Right now, I'm on a leave of absence from that job."

"What job is that?"

"I can't tell you."

"Can't or won't?" I asked.

"Both."

That was a strike against her being from a wealthy family—perhaps. I was still trying to wrap my head around the fact that she'd somehow participated in CTF. I didn't have the skills necessary for that kind of tournament.

"Manta has secrets," Jun-woo pointed his chopsticks at her. "Bro and I will figure this out, just wait and see."

"You're welcome to try, just stay out of my room," Manta warned.

"Stay out of her room," I snapped as the twins exchanged a speculative glance. "You'll be fined for even thinking about it."

"Fines will be doubled if you actually try," Gu Han backed me up.

"There's nothing in there," Manta said. "I just don't want anyone digging through my stuff."

The twins pretended to back off; I knew they'd still try if an opportunity arose.

"We have an appearance scheduled next week at an electronics store opening," Gu Han announced. "New team uniforms are coming from a sponsor; shoes are coming from a second sponsor. Be sure to wear what you're given."

"What size did you order?" Manta asked. "Nobody talked to me about a team uniform and shoes."

"I asked Minjun to check sizes and turn those in before he left," Min-ho said, before realization dawned. "Oh," he breathed.

"They won't fit," Manta sighed. "Guaranteed."

"Is it too late to get something else?" Min-ho asked.

"I'll find out," Gu Han promised. "Manta, don't worry, we'll find something for you."

Minjun had done his last misdeed against Manta before he'd been shipped to another team and then released from his contract. We'd be scrambling to find similar shoes and an outfit that wouldn't completely match with the others.

"The fans will have something to say, for sure," Shi-joon observed.

"True," I agreed. "Let's think about this. Min-ho, how's your signature using your left hand?"

"Barely legible."

"It'll have to do; they want all of us to be there. Gu Han, you won't have a uniform either. Have you taken that into account?"

"That will be understandable, since I just joined the team.

I'll be there as Team Manager anyway, so I can dress differently."

"I'll ask Team Owner to contact the sponsor tomorrow," Min-ho said. "Maybe they can do something in the time we have before the signing."

"Thank you," I told him. "If there's a way, I'd like to present the team as a whole, Gu Han included."

"I'll find out."

CHAPTER 6

H*ae Jin*

"They can do two extra uniforms, but they'll have to do Manta's and mine as a separate, custom request. That means we have to show up at their workshop this afternoon," Gu Han informed me after he'd met with Team Owner.

"I can drive you," I offered. I had a Jeep Grand Cherokee parked at headquarters; I seldom got to drive it, though.

"I have a lunch appointment with a friend. He'll drive me over and bring me back," Gu Han said. "Take Manta."

"All right."

"Take me where?" Manta walked into the kitchen where Gu Han and I were talking.

"I have to get you to the sponsor's workshop so you can

be measured for a custom uniform this afternoon. Be ready to go around one."

"Okay."

"You're not going to argue?" I asked.

"Why would I argue? I hate driving."

"Good to know," I said.

"Casual dress?"

"That's how I'm going."

"Good to know."

"You have a smart mouth, missy," I said in English.

"Is that a compliment? If so, thanks. If not, well, you're the boss."

"That. That right there is what I'm talking about," I called after her, still speaking in English.

"I love you, too," she flung back at me in English.

"Liar," I shouted.

"You started it," she yelled back.

I turned back to Gu Han, who'd obviously understood the entire conversation and was now trying to keep a straight face.

"I started it," I said in Korean. He laughed.

"You have an apartment in Seoul, don't you?" I said, trying to start a conversation with Manta while I drove us to the fitting appointment.

"Yes."

"Which you own."

"Yes."

"Is it close to Black Skies Headquarters?"

"It's more than half an hour away."

"There are coin laundries closer. Why do you go home to wash your clothes?"

"Because I can relax there. It feels normal."

"You don't feel normal at headquarters?" Once those words were out of my mouth, I realized I'd opened myself to criticism.

"Everything I do at headquarters is evaluated, scrutinized, critiqued and discussed, while my input regarding personal status or preferences remains minimal," Manta said, her face turned toward the passenger-side window. "I realize Gu Han is a known quantity, but really, look at the preferential treatment he gets in contrast to my treatment, which is closely akin to someone who may be infected with plague."

"I don't think it's that bad," I countered.

"You asked the question. If you didn't want an unvarnished answer, then lead with that next time."

"I retract the question. Feeling normal is important to you. Understood."

"Awesome. If I buy a new mattress, can I use it at headquarters? The one I have is flat, a little hard, and definitely lumpy."

"I don't have a problem with that."

"Thank you."

"Do you plan to get new bedding, too?"

"Yes; the pillows are flat and the comforter is faded."

"Those things are up to you to change if you want; there's nothing in the contracts about keeping those or the towels provided."

"That's a relief. I hate those gray sheets and towels." I glanced over at her; she was already pulling up images of sheets and towels on her phone.

"Min-ho suggested that the team could cook together as a PR event a while back," I said while Manta's hand hovered over a set of sheets and a matching comforter.

"That sounds good," Manta mumbled as she placed an order for the full set in gold stripes and went looking for other colors.

"Do you have any suggestions on what to cook that would be simple enough for even the twins to make? I highly doubt they have suitable skills in any kitchen."

"If you'll let me fix that excuse for a kitchen at headquarters, we can do it there," she said, choosing another sheet set in blue stripes.

"You'll fix it?"

"If that's permissible. I get depressed every time I look at that ancient microwave. Don't even get me started on the hot plate. That thing is a fire hazard. Besides, we can install a gas cooktop and a separate electric oven," she said. "Gas is important on top, but the oven can be gas or electric. Of course, a new sink and faucet are a requirement. Since I've been here, the only person who's cleaned it is me."

"I'm still wondering why and how you're willing to install a kitchen."

"Self preservation," she replied. "Do you know how unhealthy cup noodles are?"

"I'll discuss it with Gu Han and Team Owner."

"Thanks."

I pulled into the parking lot of the studio where the team uniforms were designed and made. Gu Han pulled in right next to my SUV.

"Good timing," I said when we got out of our vehicles. "Let's get this done; we need to practice afterward."

"What, no nap?" Manta asked.

"I hope you're kidding," I frowned at her.

"I'll nap during the ride back."

"What if I ask you to drive so I can nap?"

"Then I'll drive. I hate it, though."

"Wow. That makes me feel safe," I replied in English.

"Do you think I'd put myself in danger just to make you feel uncomfortable?" Manta asked. "I assure you, that's not my intention."

"I'll drive. End. Of. Story," I said.

"I love you, too," she snapped in English.

"I've heard that before," I snarled back. "Come on or we'll be late."

Rae-Rae

Hae Jin sat on a chair provided by an assistant, his arms crossed over his chest and a glower on his face as Gu Han was measured first.

"Oh, you're so little," the tailor gushed as he measured me at the chest, waist and hips. His hands touching me brought Hae Jin out of his snit for a moment as he locked eyes with the man. I could have told him the tailor was gay but didn't feel it was my place to out anybody, so I kept my mouth shut.

"Don't worry, we'll have the uniforms ready by the weekend," the tailor promised after getting my measurements written down. "The shoes for Mr. Gu shouldn't be a problem. Miss Manta's shoes *will* be a problem. I suggest a plain white pair until a special size can be ordered for her."

"As long as the uniform matches," Hae Jin muttered.

"I'll have the uniforms delivered to the address on the invoice," the tailor promised.

"Thank you," I dipped my head to the man.

"Let's go, we have practice," Hae Jin grumbled, grabbing my arm and hauling me toward the door.

Once inside his SUV, I dug around in my purse for granola bars. "Want one?" I held out an extra for Hae Jin. It was polite to offer whatever one was eating to any companions.

"If you'll unwrap it," he said, backing out of the parking space.

"Okay." I unwrapped the top half so he could bite into it.

"Feed it to me," he said, pulling out into traffic.

"You're kidding."

"I'm not."

"Well, here." I held the bar up to his mouth. He took a bite out of it and chewed energetically. "Let me know when you want more." I set his aside and unwrapped my own granola bar.

"Another bite?"

"Here you go." I pulled more of the wrapper down so he could get another bite of the bar.

"Where did you get these? They're better than what I usually get."

"From an all-natural bakery," I said. "There are no preservatives. A friend picks them up for me."

"You have friends?"

"Do you want the rest of this, or should I feed it to the birds?"

"I'll eat it."

"Good choice. Want the last bite now or later?"

"I'll take it now. Do you have water?"

"I have an unopened bottle of water."

"Can I have some when I finish the granola bar?"

"Yes." I may have rolled my eyes when I said it, but he wasn't looking at me anyway.

After he was fed and watered, I finished off my granola bar. "Do you have any transmittable diseases?" I asked, holding up the half-empty bottle of water.

"None I'm aware of."

"Awesome." I uncapped the bottled and drank from it. "Next time, I'll bring you an extra bottle."

"But what if it isn't enough? What if I need part of yours, too?"

"Can you please make these decisions ahead of time? I can only carry so much stuff in my purse, you know."

"Do you plan your thirst ahead of time?"

"Yes. That's why I brought a bottle of water. For *me*," I said with emphasis.

"But you had two granola bars."

"For emergency rations," I pointed out.

"Then consider me an emergency that could require an extra bottle of water."

"Of course. You're the boss."

"You know drinking after someone is like sharing a kiss," he said.

"I really want to hit you right now."

"But you said you loved me."

"Oh, my God," I said. "Didn't they teach you about sarcasm in school? If not, then your education in the US is woefully inadequate."

"Sarcasm? I thought it was snark," he replied, a half-smile forming on his lips. I decided that his mouth was far too sexy to be his. It should have been given to someone who'd find a better use for it.

"Oh, no," I said. "Sarcasm is a bit on the mean side. Snark is witty but not nasty."

"Thanks for clearing that up," he grinned. "I thought both were plain nasty. Turns out, I was wrong."

"From now on, I'll clearly define my terms so you won't make mistakes going forward."

"See that you do. I expect a full, written report on any use of sarcasm or snark in the future."

"You may be sorry you asked for that."

"Since it's you, then I will surely regret it."

"See that you do," I pointed a finger at him and repeated his words. He laughed.

Hae Jin

"Dinner delivery." Gu Han carried two large sacks of takeout into the kitchen after I'd ended practice for a meal break.

"Sweet and sour chicken," Gu Han handed Manta her meal after reading the contents of the first container.

"*Xiè xie*," Manta told him thanks in Mandarin. Other meals were handed out as labeled and we gathered around the kitchen table to eat. As usual, Shi-joon and Min-ho sat on either side of Manta before anyone else could take those seats.

Instead, I chose the seat opposite hers, with Gu Han on my left and the twins on my right.

"How's Mai?" Manta asked Shi-joon as she unwrapped her chopsticks and began to eat.

"Good. Auntie Cheng and Uncle Man-sik are taking really good care of her. I don't think she's eaten this well ever."

"Auntie Cheng taught me how to cook," Manta said. "Chinese is a specialty, but she can do almost anything else, too."

"How did you meet her?"

"While I was a student at Seoul National University, I volunteered at the orphanage where Auntie Cheng worked as a cook. Spent four years working a few hours every week, learning everything I could about feeding myself and other people."

"Sounds like you were both lucky," Shi-joon said, digging into his pork fried rice.

"I think so."

"You said you have a PhD from SNU," I told Manta. "You just said you spent four years there."

"I did. I started when I was sixteen. Blew through the lower levels and graduated with a PhD at twenty. I was particularly motivated at the time."

"I don't believe you."

"Then don't." She shrugged and went back to her food.

Gu Han's phone beeped with a text. "Look at this," he handed his phone to me after reading the message from Team Owner.

We have a new sponsor, the text read. *Osprey Technology and Robotics has not only offered to sponsor Black Skies, but has also donated new computers, keyboards and mice. These items will be delivered in two days.*

"We're getting the best the industry has to offer," Gu Han

raised his hand for a high five. I obliged, slapping his hand hard and grinning like a fool.

"What's this?" Min-ho took the phone to read the text. He was laughing and talking to the others before he'd even finished reading.

"Nice. I thought my keyboard was too slow anyhow," Manta shrugged at the news.

"You'll get your wish, then," I said, taking the phone away from Min-ho and handing it back to Gu Han. "Osprey is the best, with a hefty price tag to go along with it. Most clubs don't even dream about Osprey equipment."

"Then we got lucky, I guess," Manta said.

"Time to get back to work," I said, checking the time. "Three more hours and then you can discuss your luck."

RAE-RAE

Practice was worthless after dinner. I was tired and slower than normal, but fortunately the twins acted up so much that I didn't get yelled at by Gu Han or Hae Jin. Instead, I forged through the training exercises and was more than grateful when practice ended at nine.

"I'm thinking about a bottle of beer," Min-ho rose and stretched. "Anybody else want one?" Well, he could think about a beer—he wasn't training with the rest of us; he was only watching and helping Gu Han and Hae Jin police the twins.

"Have fun," I waved a hand before heading toward the stairs and my bedroom. My new mattress and bedding wouldn't arrive for three more days, and I wasn't looking forward to sleeping (or attempting to sleep) on my lumpy mattress for another three nights.

Originally, I'd planned to call my personal assistant and ask him to contact businesses for estimates to remodel and equip the kitchen at Black Skies but decided it could wait until the following day. I was just too tired to deal with it at the moment.

"Manta?" Hae Jin's voice stopped me before I could open the door to my bedroom.

"Hae Jin?" I turned to face him as he walked toward me.

"Order new bedding and mattresses for the entire team," he said. "Team Owner says it's past time those things were replaced anyway."

"Then I need to get preferences," I began.

"I saw what you ordered for yourself. Just get the same for everybody."

"But I ordered a gel mattress for cooler sleeping," I said, leading up to the price, which wasn't on the cheap side.

"Get the best price you can. Team Owner says we need decent sleep, and you're not the first to complain about this."

"All right. I ordered mine on my card. Will I be reimbursed?"

"Turn it in to finance; they'll take care of it."

"So, six more mattresses with bedding, then," I said, covering a yawn. "I hope I can arrange to get them all here at the same time."

"When is yours coming?"

"In three days."

"Try for that and let me know. I'll tell the others when we have a firm date."

"Okay." I opened my bedroom door to go inside.

"I'm still working on the kitchen thing—it's a good idea," Hae Jin said as I walked through the door.

"Thanks," I said. "Since I don't have to pay for my mattress and bedding, I can put that money toward the new kitchen."

"Whatever you want to do," he shrugged. "Team owner won't mind putting in a kitchen, but he doesn't want to spend too much all at once."

"Understood. Good-night." I shut the door before he could say anything else.

Hae Jin

She was tired and I'd just stood there, babbling like a fool. Only now was I beginning to wonder at her willingness to put money into the kitchen, but decided to ignore those thoughts after only a few seconds.

A new kitchen would be nice, and if somebody didn't

mind cooking once in a while, that would be even better. Shi-joon said Auntie Cheng was an excellent cook; if Rae-Rae was decent, that would be a huge plus for the team.

How long does it take to get a kitchen remodeled? I wondered as I walked toward my bedroom door. The thought of sleeping on a new mattress with fresh bedding didn't upset me in the least, either.

"TOMORROW WOULD BE GREAT. YOU GOT THE measurements, right?" Manta spoke on the phone while she walked into headquarters the following morning after her swimming exercises. "Yeah, that's perfect. Thank you," she spoke in Korean before hanging up.

"All the beds will be here day after tomorrow, and the bedding will be delivered tomorrow. Kitchen will be done tomorrow," she blinked at me briefly while shoving her phone in a back pocket of her jeans.

"Huh? That was fast," I sputtered. "How did you manage that?"

"I have friends in the business," she shrugged. "They gave me a nice discount, too, on all of it."

"How much of a discount?"

"Forty percent."

"You're kidding."

"No. They're good friends."

"They must be, to offer that kind of deal."

"They're doing the install, too, so we only have to worry about washing sheets before they go on the beds."

"I'm betting the twins won't bother," I blurted.

"I'm not taking that bet."

"Have you had breakfast?"

"I was thinking about ordering something, but I'm tired of eating breakfast sandwiches. I really want to make myself a rolled omelet, but that will have to wait until I have a stove and cookware. Oh, I need to order cookware and dishes." Pulling out her phone, she began tapping on it.

"I'll order breakfast," I said as she took a seat at the table in the kitchen to flip through sets of pots, pans and bakeware.

Twenty minutes later, breakfast arrived. I'd ordered omelets for everyone, who'd arrived after running their required three miles. I'd gotten up at my usual early hour to get my training and running done, and had finished long before they did. Only Manta rose at close to the same time to go swimming, and usually took her morning shower at the hotel spa afterward.

"New beds will arrive the day after tomorrow," I announced as the team ate. "Bedding will be here tomorrow, and I hear the new kitchen may be here tomorrow as well."

"When is the stuff from Osprey coming?" Min-ho asked.

"Two days is what Team Owner says," Gu Han replied. "We'll be getting a new set of uniforms too, that will reflect the new sponsors."

"So we'll only wear these new uniforms once before the new ones arrive?" Shi-joon asked.

"Yes," Gu Han told him. "We'll probably change colors, too, so the new sponsor will stand out. I hear they've made a major investment in the team. I hope they're black; the gray we have now is all right, but it's not my favorite."

"Finish your breakfast," I ordered after checking my watch. "Get cleaned up and be in the practice room in an hour."

There was some grumbling from the twins, but they left the table with the others. Manta shook her head at the mess several had left behind, then went to get the wastebasket to drop the trash into before wiping down the table.

"We need a cleaning crew," Gu Han remarked as he helped Manta clear off the table.

"We've had three," I said. "The twins convinced all of them to quit."

"The twins need to be fined for making a mess," Gu Han grumbled. "That ought to straighten them up a little."

"You're in charge of that," I said.

"Then I will be happy to hand out the violation notices and dock their pay."

"You have my full admiration and support," Manta bowed her head to Gu Han. "Fighting." She raised her fists in the standard gesture of encouragement after lifting her head.

My phone pinged with a text message, as did Gu Han's. "Schedule's out," Gu Han held up his phone.

"Who do we play first?" I asked.

"The Germans," Gu Han frowned as he checked the list.

"Damn," I muttered.

"I don't think I ought to be playing a secondary character against those guys," Manta spoke in English. She gave me a deep frown after swiping the last corner of the table clean with a wet cloth.

"We've been ah, discussing that," Gu Han admitted.

"Awesome." Manta rinsed the cloth in the sink and draped it over the divider to dry. "I'll be in the practice room at the required time." She stalked out of the kitchen, heading for the stairs.

"I guess we should include her in the discussions," Gu Han shifted uncomfortably.

Rae-Rae

"Were they waiting for the afterlife to tell me anything?" I fumed, tossing the hand towel over the rack in my bathroom. Were they going to dictate which avatars I could play for the entire year? After what I'd been through so far, nothing would surprise me.

Also, what sadist had set the final competition from the previous season as the season opener this time? The Germans cheated to win; I knew they'd gotten inside information from Minjun. I wondered if they'd approached anyone else on the team for inside information since Minjun's exit.

A text pinged my phone; Bak Jin-won had found another piece of my mother's jewelry—a ruby bracelet made by a famous designer. I'd have to find time to meet with him and learn the details; he'd spent a small fortune getting the bracelet away from a shady pawnbroker, so I arranged for payment before heading downstairs for practice.

Hae Jin

"Prince Indigo," I told Manta when she walked into the gaming room. "And Princess Opal." Both were on the low end of the elite avatars available, and neither were a choice of any teammate. Certainly, they weren't an option considered by anyone on the German team.

"I designed both of those," Gu Han grinned at Manta.

"I've played both," Manta nodded. "Nice work."

"Thank you."

"Which do you want to start with?" I asked.

"I'll go with Princess Opal first."

Gu Han and I had decided to wait and see what Manta could do with both avatars before pointing out some of the hidden features built in, in case Manta had already explored all their capabilities.

After all, she hadn't missed anything in the other avatars she'd played already. Gu Han had bet me that Manta hadn't discovered that Princess Opal was ambidextrous and had a second, hidden blade that could be summoned with a small spell.

There was only ten thousand won riding on the bet, which was roughly the equivalent of eight dollars and fifty cents in US currency.

The trouble with Princess Opal being ambidextrous, however, lay in whether the player was capable enough to operate both the avatar's hands at the same time. If Manta knew about Princess Opal's talent, would she be able to handle it at all, or even use it to her advantage?

Once the team was settled in their seats and ready to go, the training session began.

Gu Han lost the bet.

"Go away."

I'd taken the seat next to Manta in the meeting room, where she half-lay on the sofa, her face covered by a magazine after we'd eaten lunch.

"What are you doing?" I asked instead.

"Working."

"Sleeping," I accused, reaching for the magazine.

"Lunchtime isn't over yet."

"It isn't," I conceded, moving my hand away.

"Then why are you bothering me? Why not one of the others?"

"They're not hiding under a copy of Gaming Moments."

"Does the magazine have something to do with your being annoying, or are you merely annoying for the sake of being annoying?"

"I wanted to know how you figured out Princess Opal's hidden talent."

"Do you need to know this in order for your life to be complete and fulfilling?" Manta pulled the magazine off her face and glared at me.

"You weren't sleeping," I accused.

"You were the one who said I was sleeping."

"You weren't working, like you said you were."

"I was."

"Doing what?"

"Solving a riddle."

"You're joking."

"No. The Joker jokes. The Riddler riddles. Get your Batman villains straight, dude," she said in English.

"All right, what's the riddle?" I sat back, waiting for her to flounder before making something up.

"How does a woman, too young to commit the crime herself, end up with stolen goods from a murder victim killed twenty-three years ago? The woman had no connection to the victim, and neither did any of her relatives. Did she just stumble across the stolen items one day and decide that, rather than taking them to the police, she ought to try selling them first?"

"Well, that wasn't the answer I was expecting," I admitted.

"What did she do with the money?"

"No idea. Nothing was purchased and it wasn't put in a bank anywhere. Maybe she's carrying it around in her purse, but that could be dangerous. It's a lot of money."

"Is she married and trying to get away from her husband?"

"She is married, but there's no evidence that she's unhappy with her circumstances."

"Trip to Bermuda?"

"Doesn't seem to be the traveling type."

"Kids?"

"None. Although," Manta tapped her chin and appeared thoughtful for a moment. "I'll get back to you on that."

"I think this may be the strangest conversation I've ever had with a woman."

"What's the strangest conversation you've ever had with a man? Never mind, don't answer that."

"Where are you going?" I asked as she moved around me to slide off the sofa.

"To check on a couple of things before you start slave driving again."

"You have ten minutes."

"Right. Gotcha. All that."

I watched her walk out the door and head for the stairs while Min-ho sidled up beside me. "Most women wouldn't have passed up the chance to flirt with you," he said. "You sat right next to her, too, which isn't like you in the least. Maybe she's gay."

"She isn't," I said, although I didn't know how I knew it.

"I don't get that vibe either, but I still don't understand why she doesn't appear interested. Maybe you're just not her type."

"I'm not for everybody," I said, although it bothered me that Min-ho had pointed out Manta's disinterest.

"Huh." Min-ho slapped my back with his left hand and walked away.

"I still don't know how she knew about Princess Opal," I mumbled to myself. The topic had changed quickly and my brain had latched onto the new problem.

"I'll either find out or I won't," I philosophized and headed for the training room. I considered calling out Manta if she were even a minute late for afternoon practice. After all, she needed to feel uncomfortable in exchange for the hard-on she'd given me earlier.

RAE-RAE

I played Prince Indigo during the afternoon session. In some ways, he was better than Princess Opal—a stronger avatar at the outset, but Princess Opal was far more subtle and talented, in my opinion.

During rest breaks, I imagined how I might make Zhang Bao pay for getting me into this mess to begin with; he needed some comeuppance for making me deal with the twins' shenanigans.

"We have two hours after dinner to be on social media representing the team, and then we can have the rest of the evening to ourselves," Shi-joon grinned at me after we stopped for our evening meal.

"Great. I've discovered that the average age of the website's online visitor is fourteen," I said. "What should we do, help them with homework?"

"Can you do math?" Jun-woo leered at me.

"Maybe. Who wants to know?"

"Min-ho, will you supervise Manta's online presence tonight?" Hae Jin spoke up. I wanted to smack his arm for it, but held back the urge.

"What do you want me to watch for?" Min-ho asked.

"Make sure she's only answering approved questions."

"Right. Because the inappropriate and unapproved ones go straight to Mr. Hae Jin," I snapped. "I can get my own dinner, thank you." I headed for the hallway that led to the outside door, pulling my phone from a pocket on the way. Hu Lin was nearby; I could get a ride to a restaurant somewhere —a place where I didn't have to stew in misogyny while I tried to eat.

"Where do you think you're going?" Hae Jin caught my arm before I could get through the sliding glass doors.

"To a restaurant where I don't have to listen to a bunch of people assume that I don't have two brain cells to rub together," I snapped at him. Jerking my arm away from Hae Jin's grip, I fled Black Skies Headquarters, the sliding doors clicking shut behind me.

CHAPTER 7

Hae Jin

"She isn't stupid, Hae Jin," Shi-joon muttered. He refused to look at me while he said it, too, his arms crossed tightly over his chest as if he were holding back vital information.

"She's not answering her phone," Min-ho said after ending his tenth attempt to reach Manta.

"I'll get back to you later," I pointed a finger at Shi-joon.

"She's only five minutes late," Gu Han attempted to defuse my temper. "It may be difficult to find a restaurant to serve her in the amount of time she has."

"If she's not here in ten, I'll fine her."

"Because you're so strict at fining the rest of us." Shi-joon dropped his arms and stalked out of the kitchen.

"I'll talk to him," Min-ho ran after Shi-joon.

I suddenly felt like an idiot. Why—*why* was I treating her so radically different than the rest of the team? Would I have warned any of them about inappropriate questions? That subject was covered sufficiently in the rules, which Manta hadn't neglected to read.

The team captain was notified of anything appearing online that wasn't acceptable, and in turn, I'd make the decision whether to ban the visitor from the site or give a warning. Any threats were relayed immediately to the police.

"Sorry I'm late," Manta walked in, wearing a cranberry jacket she hadn't taken with her on her hasty exit from headquarters.

"Don't worry about it," Gu Han held up a hand while slashing a warning look in my direction. He wasn't going to let me upset her again; I could read his intention clearly.

What he didn't know was I'd already started to think in a more rational manner and had no intention of upsetting Manta again if I could help it.

"Everybody, man your computers and log onto the team website," Gu Han exercised his authority as Team Manager. "Any questions, ask me."

Through the course of the next two hours, Manta received eleven marriage proposals, six condemnations and eventually, a question about math homework. I suspected the twins asked some of their fans to do it. Manta, unfazed, told the fan the answer, but also told them they'd have to show their work to prove the answer.

I asked Gu Han to screenshot the question so I could

double check it. Later, after fumbling my way through forgotten college algebra, I found the answer was correct.

Manta's fan base was getting established, looked like, and there were plenty of people praising her for her performances so far. Half her fans wanted tips on playing the game; Manta answered a few and said she'd try to do a quick video how-to on Empress Jade the following week.

Still worried? Min-ho texted me as I read through some of Manta's replies.

Not answers from her, I confessed. *I still worry about the assholes who might threaten her.*

We all worry about that—for the entire team, Min-ho responded. *The twins get plenty, although nothing tonight.*

We're still in preseason, I reminded him.

You're right.

"Time's up," Gu Han announced. "Finish off your last responses and log out."

Manta set down her headset and stretched before rubbing her neck. Shi-joon approached her and bent down to say something. I couldn't hear his words, but Manta nodded, then rose and followed him toward the stairs.

"Whose room will they end up in?" Si-woo whispered in my ear.

"Shut up," I snapped at the younger twin before heading for the stairs myself. I caught up with them just before they slipped inside Shi-joon's room and slid in right behind them.

"If you're going to join this conversation, then you can

contribute," Manta said, crossing arms over her chest and lifting her nose in the air.

"Contribute to what?" I demanded, only now second-guessing my choice to join in uninvited.

"We want to redecorate the room Mai is sleeping in at Auntie Cheng's," Shi-joon said. "It was used for storage before and doesn't have anything my sister might like in her bedroom."

"Oh."

"Auntie Cheng asked us for help because she wants it to be a surprise, so Shi-joon is the best resource we have on what Mai likes," Manta shook her head at me and sighed.

"She likes purple," Shi-joon said.

"That's a good place to start," Manta nodded. "Make yourself useful," she swatted at me. "Look for purple comforters and sheets. I don't think we ought to cover the room in purple, but bedding and a rug might not overpower everything else."

"Having a threesome?" Jun-woo opened the door and leaned into the room.

"Shut up and get in here," Manta said. "You can help, too. We're trying to find stuff to redecorate Mai's new bedroom. She likes purple."

Jun-woo, looking somewhat ashamed, shuffled into Shi-joon's room, his shoulders sagging. Right behind him came Si-woo, his brother, and after that came Gu Han.

Phones came out, as did questions about favorite anime characters and such. Manta wrote a list of what could be found where, as suggestions were made and decisions reached.

"She needs clothes, too, but I'll help with that," Manta tapped more information into her phone.

"What about school?" I thought to ask.

"We're still working on that," Shi-joon said. "She needs to meet with the psychologist, first, so we'll know if she's ready for school or if she ought to have private lessons for a while."

The others still thought Mai had been beaten. I figured that may have been part of the attack against her, but sexual assault was first and foremost in my mind.

"Have they caught the ones who did this?" Gu Han asked.

"Not yet. They're still looking."A grim expression crossed Shi-joon's features. "The police are worried that the main perpetrator may have left the country."

Manta turned her head away when Shi-joon made that statement. Likely, she thought the same as I—that the refusal to take Mai to the hospital in a timely manner had allowed the perpetrator to get away. Without Manta's quick action in getting the girl to treatment, the charges would have been upgraded to murder.

"This is enough for now," Manta announced, holding her phone list aloft. "Shi-joon, do you want to send this to Auntie Cheng, or would you like me to do it?"

"You do it," he said. "I have a call to make."

"All right. Everyone," Manta addressed the rest of us, "your new bedding will arrive tomorrow. If you want sheets washed before the new beds come the day after, then be prepared. Also, the kitchen will be off-limits tomorrow while new appliances and such are installed. That is all."

Manta scooted around me and walked out of Shi-joon's room. "When did she learn to take over?" Gu Han whispered while the others dispersed.

"No idea."

"Are we getting a toaster?" he asked after thinking for a few seconds.

"Don't know. Shall we ask?"

"Sure. I haven't really had a decent conversation with her yet."

Following Gu Han, we walked two doors down to reach Manta's room. Gu Han knocked on the door.

"Questions?" Manta asked after finding us outside.

"Toaster?" Gu Han grinned.

"Commercial grade six-slice. Also a mixer, coffee maker, espresso machine and electric tea kettle. Probably other things as well. If you want to add to the list, now's the time."

"Can we come in and talk?" I asked.

"You're the boss." She moved aside so Gu Han and I could enter.

"Close the door, please," Gu Han said once we were inside.

"All right." She shut the door and pointed toward the two chairs near the window in her room. "Please have a seat. Do you want tea or instant coffee?"

"I'm good," I waved off the offer, as did Gu Han.

"What do you want to know, then?" she asked, sitting on the edge of her bed.

"Was Mai sexually assaulted?" I asked. "I get the feeling that she was."

"Yes," Manta dropped her eyes. "You cannot discuss that with anyone outside this room. It's for Shi-joon's and Mai's sake, not mine."

"Understood," Gu Han raised a hand to reassure Manta. "My next question is merely to quell any rumors, all right? Is there anything between you and Shi-joon?"

"Huh?" Manta looked at Gu Han as if he'd lost his mind.

"The twins will cause trouble if they think there's the slightest thing there," I said.

"Are they willfully stupid?" Manta snorted. "I mean, the fact that Shi-joon and a certain doctor sat outside in said doctor's vehicle necking for five minutes last night should have been a dead giveaway, yet here are the twins, going as fast as they can in the *wrong* direction."

"Doctor? Male or female?" Gu Han thought to ask.

"Definitely male. Shi-joon isn't trying to hide anything and has told me as much. He gave me permission to answer your questions if either of you asked. Kudos to the twins, though, for being blind as well as brainless."

Gu Han muffled a guffaw. I turned my head to hide my amusement.

"If I were you," Manta went on, "I'd keep this information away from the twins for now. Shi-joon doesn't need more trouble than he already has, all right?"

"I think we can all agree on that much," Gu Han nodded soberly. "I'll work on this problem with Hae Jin. Perhaps a reasonable solution can be reached."

"I'd appreciate it," Manta said stiffly. "I think the rules as to how the team handles one another's personal information could be improved," she added.

"I'll entertain suggestions," Gu Han told her.

"Just go online and read the excerpts from Ong Group's employee handbook. Lots of good stuff to be found there and can be utilized as is. Modifications must be approved by Ong Group's legal department."

I stiffened at the mention of Ong Group; Dad had already admitted to using most of the handbook that Ong Group had facilitated in their worldwide holdings. Well, Dad and Mom knew the owner. I didn't.

"Thank you for the information." Gu Han rose and nodded to Manta. "I look forward to having a six-slice toaster."

"Many people do," Manta smiled. "Good-night."

AFTER LEAVING MANTA'S QUARTERS, I REALIZED I STILL hadn't done what I'd intended, and that was to offer an apology. *You have her phone number, idiot*, I chastised myself. Settling on the side of my bed, which sunk farther down than it should have, I sent a text to Manta, saying I wanted to apologize and promised to treat her and the others the same.

I'll accept your apology, and look forward to being treated the same, she replied and left it at that.

I should have thanked her for ordering new beds for us; I hadn't realized how bad my own bed was until I paid attention to it.

Rae-Rae

The kitchen builders and remodelers arrived shortly after I returned to headquarters following my swimming exercises the next morning. With drawings and measurements in hand, they began tearing out what already existed and cleaning up the space before the others got back from running.

"Not wasting any time, I see," Gu Han stood next to me and watched while boxes and crates were pulled off the truck and hauled into the kitchen area.

"They have one day to get it finished," I shrugged. I didn't tell him that I'd promised a huge bonus if it could be done in a single day.

"Will the sounds of drills and hammers interrupt practice?" Hae Jin now stood beside Gu Han.

"I don't think it will be overly bothersome if we wear our headphones," I told him in English. "I think any discomfort will be outweighed by the benefits of a new kitchen."

"I hope you're right."

"Time will tell, I suppose. Besides, tomorrow is going to be extra busy, with the new computers and beds coming, you know."

"All the more reason to get a full day's practice in today," Hae Jin countered.

"Okay, *kkondae*," I said. Gu Han snorted a laugh.

"Practice starts in twenty," Hae Jin checked his watch and gave me a stern look.

"Of course it does. I will be there," I told him. He squared his shoulders and walked away.

"Is it all right if I order a footstool for my computer station?" I asked Gu Han. "My feet dangle all day since they don't reach the floor. It's tiring."

"Go ahead. I'd have done it already if you'd said something before."

"I never know when the right time is to say anything," I sighed.

"Hae Jin means well, he just doesn't know how to handle a mixed crew. He's used to dealing with guys only."

"Okay."

"Our next exhibition game is on Tuesday of next week," Gu Han reminded me. "We have the signing on Saturday, and that will take all day. I'm sorry to say that we'll have practice on Sunday rather than giving everyone the day off."

"Understood. Will I play either of the latest two characters?"

"I'll discuss that with Hae Jin and get back to you."

"All right. I should go brush my teeth before we start practice."

The call from Zhang Bao came in while I was brushing my teeth. "We have a lead on the hackers in France," he told me.

"Let me know when you want me to let the dogs out," I said.

"I'll let you know."

BY THE END OF THE DAY, THE WORKERS HAD EARNED THEIR bonus and Black Skies had a brand-new kitchen, complete with sink, stove, dishwasher, new microwave and refrigerator, double ovens, cabinets and food storage space.

"Look at this," Min-ho grinned as he opened cabinet doors to check the space inside. "I didn't know this was possible."

"Cookware and a load of groceries are coming tomorrow," I said. "Mr. Hae Jin will write a new set of kitchen rules."

"Mr. Hae Jin has no plans to do so," Hae Jin said.

"All right. The first time somebody steals your blueberry yogurt, you may change your mind."

"I delegate responsibility for rule writing to Manta," Hae Jin pointed a finger at me.

"Fine. Do you want to approve everything before the rules are posted?"

"Of course."

I tapped my phone and sent him the rules I'd put together the night before. "There you go. The individual baskets for each person's food and drinks will arrive with the other stuff tomorrow. This way, everybody gets the same space in the fridge, with their baskets labeled. The rest of the fridge will be devoted to team stuff, like bottled water."

"You even sent pictures. Cool," Min-ho stretched to peer over Hae Jin's shoulder. *Face it, Hae Jin is just tall*, I reminded myself. I felt like an elf standing next to him most of the time.

"Time for practice," Hae Jin looked up from his phone.

Well, there was no getting a compliment from the man.

Hae Jin

"What would you think about having a strong avatar as a backup for Manta?" Gu Han asked as we waited outside later for dinner delivery.

"I wouldn't mind, as long as it could help the team win. She also would need extensive practice with the character before I'd allow it."

"Have you seen anything yet that she couldn't play?" Gu Han didn't look at me when he spoke. The weather was almost icy outside, and we'd pulled on thick jackets to wait for the delivery driver.

"No." I dropped my gaze and studied my shoes—I'd pulled

on a new pair of Nikes that morning and decided they were comfortable enough.

"I'm thinking about letting her try Storm Harper," Gu Han sighed.

I went still. Storm Harper was the avatar Gu Han designed specifically for his wife, who was now deceased. Nobody else was allowed to play the character, and Gu Han had never released Storm Harper to the gaming industry.

"You're thinking about it?" I said after several moments passed.

"As a very limited release."

"You mean to Manta only?"

"For now. We've held her back long enough, don't you think? Storm has good and bad points, just as any other avatar does. I'd like to see what Manta can bring out of her."

"What about you?" I turned toward Gu Han. "I only hesitate because," I didn't finish.

"I know. I wouldn't have brought it up if I hadn't thought carefully about it."

"Then the decision is yours. I reiterate, though, that Manta must meet both our requirements on the new character before we allow it to be played."

"I didn't want to release it until the regular season starts. Preseason can continue as is."

"That's reasonable enough."

"When can we tell her?"

"Next week—after the next preseason game."

"That sounds fine." The delivery driver pulled up on his

motorbike beneath the portico and parked before pulling bags from the insulated box on the back of the bike.

Splitting the heavy bags between us, Gu Han thanked the driver and followed me into the building. This would be our first meal inside the new kitchen, and I greatly anticipated the changes.

"Chicken and beer," I held bags aloft.

"Chicken only in this bag," Manta said, opening one of the sacks and removing the first full container of chicken.

"Woah, real plates?" Si-woo breathed as he held a glass plate aloft.

"Careful, don't break anything on the first night," Min-ho warned, indicating that Si-woo should set the plate back on the wide island, which had taken the place of the old table the team had previously used.

"Real chopsticks and forks, too," Jun-woo held up his set of stainless utensils.

"All of which go in the dishwasher after you're done," Manta said. "So we can have clean dishes for next time."

"You'll have to remind them," Shi-joon pretended to whisper at Manta.

I set the boxes of beer on the counter next to the sink, for those who wanted it. Manta was the only one not interested, as it turned out. What I hadn't failed to notice was how close Shi-joon and Manta had become. *He's gay*, I reminded myself. *That doesn't stop me from feeling just a tiny bit of jealousy*, I realized. Why did I want that easy, teasing manner that he had with her? There was no explanation for it.

None.

"Manta, do you have a pair of white athletic shoes?" Gu Han asked after dinner was finished and the team sat around the island sipping the last of their beer.

"I do."

"Good. The new uniforms will be here tomorrow. Make sure to try everything on to see that it fits. Everyone, we'll be loading onto the team bus Saturday morning at seven-thirty, to arrive at the electronics store by nine to do the signing. Nine to five, with a break for lunch. I'll be sure to have drinks and snacks for all of you during the day. Manta, if you need anything other than what we have, be sure to tell me," Gu Han instructed.

"I'll be fine as long as there's something available," Manta said.

"Can you get more of those granola bars?" I asked.

"How many do you want?" Manta turned her gaze toward me.

"Enough for Saturday to start with? The one you gave me was really good."

"I can ask the bakery. Someone will have to pick them up if they have enough."

"I'll drive you," I said.

"I'll let you know."

"What granola bars?" Shi-joon asked.

"They're organic, baked fresh and have no preservatives or artificial colors," Manta told him. "I like the oatmeal chocolate chip, but they have several kinds."

"Another thing to talk about is the fashion photos of not only the whole team in uniform, but each team member, dressed differently," Gu Han said.

"I hate dressing in a suit," the twins said in unison.

"I'll wear a suit if you'll wear a dress," Manta offered the twins.

"Now there's an idea," Jun-woo began.

"No," Gu Han said sharply. "Manta, don't put ideas in their heads—they're not smart enough to recognize sarcasm. We'll be meeting with a fashion director, a photographer and a makeup crew in two weeks at their studio before the regular season starts. They will make suggestions on what each of you should wear for these photos. Remember, these will go into the team booklets and the tournament programs, just like the team photos will."

"What will we do tomorrow while the new computers are installed?" Min-ho asked.

"We can choose between basketball or some other activity," I suggested.

"Or, we can make an appearance at a PC bang," Gu Han said. In Korean, bang meant *room,* and was the simplest way to name a PC café.

"Not only can we get some practice in, but we can do some PR work by playing with some of the fans there."

"Do you have a place picked out?" Shi-joon asked.

"Go-Go Gaming and Cyber Café," Gu Han smiled. "An old friend owns it, and he's been asking for an appearance ever since he heard I was joining the team. We're scheduled to arrive at ten tomorrow morning. Dress casually but appropriately. I've already cleared this with Team Owner."

"Are we taking the team bus?" Min-ho asked.

"Yes. There's no way to hide it, so anyone in the area will be able to see it," Gu Han replied. "Be ready for a crowd."

"What about crowd control?" I asked. "Or will we have people standing all around us while we work?"

"My friend says he has employees ready to handle that."

"I hope he knows what he's doing," Manta sighed. "I'm going to bed. Don't forget to clean up your own mess before you leave," she added, placing her plate and utensils in the dishwasher before heading for the stairs.

MANTA WAITED IN FRONT OF ME THE NEXT MORNING TO board the bus. Her purple-tipped hair was pulled into a neat bun atop her head and tied with a purple ribbon. She wore a purple shirt and jacket over black jeans and black and purple Brooks athletic shoes. With hands shoved in her jacket pockets to keep them warm, I watched as the amethyst drop earrings she wore dangled delicately from her ears.

"Are you warm enough?" I leaned down to ask softly.

"I'm okay," she said, hefting a purple tote bag higher on her shoulder. "What about you?" She turned back to glance at me.

"I'm fine. This jacket is made of wool and did great when it was cold in Boston."

"This thing is fleece lined, but I think maybe they should have added a second sheep," she said, tapping her purple denim jacket.

"So the problem is just not enough sheep?"

"I think so. What are your thoughts?"

"In the interest of peace and prosperity, I'll go with not enough sheep for five hundred, Alex."

She snickered, surprising me. Most people around me wouldn't get that joke. "Did you check on the granola bars?" I asked.

"They're baking us five dozen. We can pick them up tomorrow afternoon, if that's okay," she said.

"Sounds great. Did you get one kind or an assortment?"

"I asked for an assortment, so everybody can decide what they like the best when we order again."

"Good idea," I absentmindedly patted her shoulder. "Is one tomorrow afternoon all right? We can wait and go to lunch then and pick up the bars on the way back."

"You're willing to be seen at lunchtime—with me?" Her eyes widened.

"Stranger things may have happened. I can't recall. Come on, shorty. Get on the bus," I said, gesturing for her to move forward.

"I'm going, don't be so hasty," she said, walking toward the open door after the twins had dawdled there for five minutes or more.

I found myself smiling as I boarded the bus behind her.

"THIS IS BIGGER THAN I THOUGHT," MIN-HO SAID AS THE bus pulled up outside the PC bang. Just as he spoke, six students began shouting and waving outside our windows.

"This is your fault," Manta teased me. "They're your fans, I can tell already."

"How can you tell?" I lifted an eyebrow at her. "They're not waving signs."

"Yet," Min-ho said, rising from his seat to get a better look.

At that moment, another ten or so joined the first six. The new arrivals were waving signs, three of which had *Lee Hae Jin* written in colored markers on them.

"Told ya," Manta drawled in English while poking at my arm.

The other six signs bore an assortment of Min-ho's name, the twins' names, Shi-joon's and Gu Han's.

"I'm the only one who can get to the door without being accosted," Manta grinned.

"Uh, no," Gu Han said when five more ran up, all chanting "Manta, Manta, Manta."

"Then Hae Jin has to get off first," Shi-joon teased. "Since his fans showed up first."

"I'm not sure that's how we should sort this out," I argued.

"We need to take care of Min-ho, since he's injured," Manta pointed out. "What about surrounding him as we walk in? I don't want anyone grabbing his hand when we get off the bus."

"Good point," Gu Han agreed. His phone rang; he answered it. "We have guards coming, courtesy of Osprey Technology and Robotics," he announced when the call ended. "They'll be here soon."

He was right; moments later, six guards lined up on both sides of the bus door to keep us safe while we walked into Go-Go Gaming. "Let's go," Gu Han ordered the moment the way was cleared. We walked past the six guards, who fell in behind us and followed the team inside the building. Once there, we were led to six empty cubicles stationed together for our practice session. The guards set up outside that perimeter to make sure we were kept safe.

"Remind me to send a thank-you letter to Osprey," Shi-joon set his jacket over the back of his gaming chair and sat down.

Still, fans streamed into the building, and stood outside the allowed perimeter to wave signs and chant their favorite players' names. I took the cubicle between Manta and Shi-joon, before Min-ho could grab it. Instead, he took the one on Shi-joon's other side.

"We'll be posting the game on the big screen in front of you," Gu Han walked down the aisle behind our chairs with the owner. "There's a waiting list to play against you already."

Behind us and past the security guards, fans snapped

photos with their phones and tapped messages on social media and to their friends.

"Do you want to start with Lady Jade?" Gu Han asked Manta.

"That's fine," she said, lifting her headphones and settling the top curve against the back of her neck.

"Look at how cute she is," someone pointed out in the crowd.

"Hae Jin is right beside her. How can you ask for more?" someone else gushed. *Time to put on my own headphones and ignore the crowd*, I told myself. Manta had already turned into her icy alter ego, as if nothing fazed her. A part of me wished for that icy control, as if the rest of the world had ceased to exist. I wondered how she did it, too, but thought it would be too nosy to ask.

"You'll be introduced to your opponents first," Gu Han's voice sounded in our headsets. "They'll give names, ages and a brief rundown of their gaming experience and level," he went on.

We were introduced to the first five players, who ranged in age from thirteen to twenty-six, most of them mid-level gamers who'd been playing for at least five years. Not a low-level elite gamer in the bunch.

"Have they played together before?" Manta asked.

"No. They were picked by a drawing."

"Doesn't sound too fair," she pointed out.

"Should we play one-on-one, then?" Shi-joon asked.

"How about I play Ladybug?" Manta asked.

"You're kidding?" I huffed.

"Then switch team members. Two of us go play with them, and vice-versa."

"That I can live with," Gu Han laughed. "Hang on, I'll hold another drawing to see which players get to switch. They can choose which of you plays with the other team."

A shriek went up from the other side after they learned what was planned, and then two of the opposition came over. One changed seats with Jun-woo, the other with Manta.

"My dream just came true," the thirteen-year-old grinned as he took Manta's seat.

"Which character will you play?" Gu Han leaned down next to the boy.

"Captain Blizzard," he replied, his face threatening to split, his grin was so wide.

"Manta is about to unleash Lady Jade against us," Shi-joon pointed out.

"I'm aware," I replied dryly. "That means we need to target her first thing and hope nothing else goes wrong."

I discovered that Manta and Jun-woo hadn't wasted their time in talking to their new teammates. They came out swinging against us, leaving Manta free to run. I went after her at the first opportunity but ended up chasing her around the field.

Jun-woo was battling his brother and Shi-joon together, convincing me to ask my two new teammates to tackle their counterparts from the opposition.

Yes, I realized seconds too late that the strategy employed

had served to scatter the team rather than presenting a united front against the others. Bombs laid by Lady Jade began detonating with regularity while I commanded the team to regroup near the center.

"I'm on Manta," Si-woo said, directly disobeying my order.

Behind us, I could hear the crowd screaming, even through the headphones. Si-woo fell victim to one of Lady Jade's bombs. "Don't go after him," I told Shi-joon. "We're still alive and somebody has to come against us. We fight together now, or we'll lose."

Jun-woo led two of his three new cohorts against us, just as I predicted he would. He couldn't stay still for long, especially when I'd left his brother in the weeds to die. "Pick the attackers apart," I told my crew.

Two of the new players from the opposition died quickly, while Jun-woo picked off both of our new players. That left him fighting me and Shi-joon, until Lady Jade ran in. Lady Jade wasn't much of a fighter in close quarters; I killed her quickly while Shi-joon dispatched Jun-woo.

We were prepared to celebrate our victory when the last of Lady Jade's bombs detonated beneath us.

The only player left standing was the least experienced newbie from Manta's team, but it counted as a win for them. The crowd of fans went crazy behind us, their screams deafening as we removed our headphones.

The last player standing from the other team was raising his arms in victory, as if he'd killed all the other players himself. As a training exercise, it was a complete failure. From a PR standpoint, it was a rousing success.

We played several more games with attendees chosen from the crowd, and each time, two different members of the team were chosen to switch with two of the new players. We learned some of our shortcomings that day, and Gu Han took notes. At the end of the day, we loaded onto the bus, exhausted.

Manta slept the entire trip back to headquarters.

CHAPTER 8

R***ae-Rae***

"Chinese Undersecretary of Defense Chen wants a meeting with you," Zhang Bao informed me by phone Friday morning after I got out of the swimming pool.

"I don't want a meeting with him."

"He's putting a lot of pressure on me."

"What kind of pressure?"

"He didn't mention arrest exactly, but," Zhang Bao said.

"Great. Where is he?"

"Beijing."

"I can only give him a few minutes this afternoon. Is he okay with a video call?"

"He'd prefer an in-person, but I suppose a video call would be better than nothing."

"It's a video call or nothing," I mumbled. "I'm not in the mood to see his face in person. Really."

"You know what he wants."

"Why should I waste time or distance on him? He's only one of many who messed up, and what he wants help with I can't do anything about. That's out of my hands."

"He doesn't understand that."

"You mean he doesn't *want* to understand that. If he gave the initial order, then maybe he *should* be losing his eyesight, along with the others."

"Rae-Rae, I was never initiated, you know that. Please don't give me more information than I should have."

"Fine. Forget I said anything. How do you skirt around the fact that the main culprit is your own adopted brother?"

"We no longer speak," Zhang Bao admitted. "Father has all but disowned Lóng Hàoyǔ. He's had no contact with us after the accident."

"It wasn't an accident. You know that."

"I know that now—after he used me for bait to get to you."

"I hope Mister Undersecretary understands that if I have to pull you out of North Korea a second time, things will not go easy for him," I huffed.

"I am grateful that you are my friend, Rae-Rae."

"Maybe you should come back and do your work in South Korea."

"I have considered that many times, but Father refuses to come with me, and he is no longer young in years. If the

Undersecretary insists, I could be banned from the country with no way to legally visit Father."

"I know. This is a mess, no matter how I look at it. I'll be speaking with the Undersecretary this afternoon, one way or another."

"Thank you."

HAE JIN

"The new bed is so comfortable," Shi-joon took a seat at the kitchen island, a cup of coffee in his hand. "I slept like a baby."

"Wait until you see the new equipment," Gu Han arrived in the kitchen wearing a huge smile. "It's amazing."

"Beds are nice," the twins walked in together, followed by Min-ho. "We approve." Both held thumbs up to indicate their approval. "Somebody even washed our sheets and laid them on our beds."

"That would be the new cleaning crew," Gu Han told them. "Don't upset them or make them quit—especially if you like clean sheets and a clean kitchen."

"Did you sleep well, Hae Jin?" Min-ho asked, taking the seat next to mine.

"I did. I wasn't aware how bad the old mattress was until I slept on the new one."

"I tend to get hot at night—this one fixed all my problems," Gu Han admitted. "I'll buy one for myself next time."

"Where's Manta?" Shi-joon asked. "Usually she's back by this time."

"Manta had to take an annoying phone call," Manta walked in and overheard the question. "It wasted ten minutes of my life."

"Who wasted ten minutes of your life?" Si-woo teased, helping himself to a breakfast sandwich.

"The Undersecretary of Defense in China," Manta snipped.

"Yeah, right," Jun-woo laughed. "If you're going to make stuff up, at least say it's the actual Secretary of Defense in China."

"I really hate that guy," Manta said. "He knows better than to call."

"There's one sandwich left if you want it," Gu Han told Manta. "Eat it; we start practice in twenty."

"This is the nicest system I've ever used," Shi-joon leaned back from his keyboard with a happy sigh. "The response time is exceptional."

"Team Owner's here," Gu Han entered the gaming area at a near-run. "Everybody, to the meeting room and hurry."

"What's up?" I rose quickly from my seat to follow Gu Han.

"Seahorses got hacked early this morning, but you didn't hear that from me."

"SOME OF YOU MAY HAVE HEARD ALREADY THAT THE Seahorses got hacked this morning, around six-thirty," Team Owner said. "Not only did some of their data get wiped, ransomware has scrambled what's left of their system. They have a team working to release their files, but so far, no progress has been made."

"Will this happen to us?" Si-woo asked.

"According to the designers and technicians at Osprey, our new system is built to repel ransomware. In all their experience, none of their computers have ever been infected. Let's hope that remains true."

"How much are the hackers demanding from the Seahorses to release their files?" I asked.

"Half a million, US."

"The Seahorses don't have that kind of money," Gu Han stated flatly.

"Everybody knows that," Team Owner replied.

"Do you find it odd that the Seahorses have played more top tier teams than anyone else so far this preseason, including several outside the country?" Manta asked. "I know they only released excerpts from those international games online. Did the hackers access the records of their opponents' information in what was wiped or stolen?"

I jerked my head around to stare at Manta. "I don't know the answer," Team Owner admitted. "I'll try to ask—discreetly, of course."

"What would you do—if you were in charge of this investigation?" I asked Manta.

"Look closely at team members and anyone else with access to their computers, to see if anyone allowed easy entry into their files. Ransomware generally scrambles everything. Why would the hackers be interested in seven preseason games—if that information is what was stolen or deleted?"

"Before you speculate too much, let's find out whether that information was taken," I frowned at Manta.

"Wanna bet?" she mouthed at me.

"TELL ME WHAT YOU THINK," I SAID WHILE DRIVING Manta to the bakery to pick up the granola bars she'd ordered for the team.

"Did Minjun know anyone on the Seahorse team?"

"Before he played with Black Skies, he was on the same team with one of their players," I replied. "Why?"

"I had a bad feeling about him from the beginning, and it wasn't just because he's a misogynist."

I winced when she said that word. At times, I worried it could also be applied to me. "Should I ask around to see if Minjun has been out drinking with his old teammate?"

"Couldn't hurt, I guess. If he's involved in this mess, it's because he doesn't have a regular paycheck anymore and is willing to do whatever for whomever."

My phone rang; I tapped the button on the Jeep's steering wheel to answer Min-ho's call.

"Minjun just got arrested for selling Choi Dae-in's login information to hackers," Min-ho said right away. The call was on speaker, so Manta heard it, too.

"Any word on the hackers?" I asked while Manta nodded; she wanted to know as well.

"Nothing. Minjun claims he doesn't know who they are; just that he got a message offering money for the information, so he took Dae-in out for soju."

"Thanks for the information," I told Min-ho. "We'll talk when I get back." Ending the call, I glanced at Manta in the passenger seat. "You scare me," I told her. Another call came in—this time, it was Team Owner.

"Is Manta with you?" he asked quickly.

"She's here."

"Manta," he began, and then started speaking in Chinese. I didn't understand anything he said.

"We'll stop by Seahorse Headquarters on our way back," she promised, then nodded to let me end the call.

"We're stopping by Seahorse Headquarters?" I asked in English.

"Yeah."

Lunch was a quick sandwich at the bakery, before taking our box of granola bars and loading into the Jeep for the drive to the Seahorse base. Team Owner was there waiting for us when we arrived, as were two NIS agents, one of whom recognized Manta.

He was discreet and didn't give her identity away, though. I'd started a list in my head as to what Manta's day job actually was. NIS agent or tech was at or near the top, now.

Neither Team Owner nor I were allowed into the Seahorse gaming area. Both NIS agents and the Seahorse Team Owner went inside with Manta. Ten minutes later, they were back. The agent who knew Manta was finishing a phone call as she walked toward Team Owner and me.

"They have a strong lead on the hackers, now," Manta sighed. "Can we stop on the way back for some milk or juice? I'm a little thirsty," she said.

"The team will pay for whatever she wants," Team Owner said. "I'll see you back at headquarters."

"I CAN'T HANDLE BUBBLE TEA," MANTA SAID AS SHE SIPPED her milk through a straw.

"I've learned to like it—Min-ho doesn't recognize any cold, non-alcoholic drink that isn't bubble tea," I said. "If I guess what your day job is, will you tell me?"

"Sure," she laughed.

"So, are you an NIS employee or agent?"

"No. Sorry. The Seahorses have most of their files back, though, and it didn't cost them anything."

"What will happen to the employee who handed his login to Minjun?"

"I don't know. That's team business, not my business. They will be changing all their passwords, et cetera, very soon, I think."

"Should we change ours?"

"That's up to you, Gu Han and Team Owner. Did Team Owner tell you not to tell the others that I was involved in any part of this?"

"He all but threatened my life."

"Okay."

"You're okay with someone threatening my life?" I pretended offense.

"You said he all but," she pointed out. "That doesn't include your life."

"Nitpicker."

"Grump."

I laughed before I could stop myself.

"YOU GET ONE GRANOLA BAR FOR A SNACK; THAT'S IT," I warned the twins, who were perusing the box of freshly-baked goods. "The rest are for tomorrow and Sunday."

"Is it all right if I take fifteen minutes to return a phone call?" Manta asked as she headed for the stairs.

"Yes, but hurry. I'll extend the break for everybody until then."

"Thanks. I'll hurry. I don't want to talk to this guy anyway."

RAE-RAE

I hurried up the stairs; the Chinese Undersecretary of Defense was waiting irritably, no doubt, to make my life more of a tangled mess than it already was.

Tapping on my laptop, I entered his number to begin the video call.

"I was hoping to see you in person," the Undersecretary didn't bother with a greeting.

"I have no patience or sympathy for those who can't be bothered with manners," I said. "What do you want? I have ten minutes to give you today."

"Where is the flower?"

"I have no idea. Ask Lóng Hàoyǔ; he had it last."

"You know it disappeared."

"Then it is protecting itself. I don't know what happened."

"He is completely blind, now, and going deaf."

"Again, I know nothing of it and had nothing to do with that."

"Several others are also dealing with the same illnesses."

"I wish I could offer sympathy, but I can't and won't. The scrolls say clearly that to harm the Lotus is to harm oneself. I suspect anyone who had anything to do with the decision to bring harm anyway is now suffering in some manner."

"I am going blind," he thundered, slapping his hands on his desk.

"I can't help you," I snapped. "I had nothing to do with that. Even if I could help you, I wouldn't. This is what you get for attempting to force government restrictions on a mystical source. You're trying to control something that can't be controlled. Now, what happened to the real Monks of the White Flower, huh? Did any of them survive the tender mercies of your forebears?"

"How dare you accuse them—or me," he shouted indignantly.

"Prove me wrong."

The screen went dark—the jerk hung up on me. Well, that might buy me a week of peace before I heard from him again. If he were going blind, he'd do anything in his power to keep his sight. I hoped he'd learned not to attack me, however, unless he wanted to deal with something worse than blindness.

I'd certainly learned not to trust him or anyone else who belonged to the current Monks of the White Flower. They were the reason my left foot had been crushed—after one of them had stomped on it when I was in an automobile accident.

Zhang Bao hadn't spoken to his adopted brother once since the idiot had broken my foot. Nor had his father, who was appalled by his adopted son's behavior.

I certainly wasn't planning to speak to him—or any of the others who were now going blind, deaf and who knew what else.

The actual White Flower was capable of vengeance, it appeared.

I didn't mind a bit.

I made it back downstairs for practice with a minute to spare. "Call done?" Min-ho asked.

"Yeah. Turns out he just wanted to complain and then hang up on me."

"Got a boyfriend?" Si-woo leaned around Min-ho to tease me.

"I'd slice my wrists if that guy was my boyfriend."

"Seems a bit drastic," Hae Jin frowned.

"You haven't met the guy."

"Does your uniform fit?" Gu Han arrived to herd us into the gaming room.

"It fits," I answered with a heavy sigh.

"What's wrong with it?" Hae Jin asked as he took his seat next to mine.

"The uh, zipper is a little low on the jacket," I confessed.

"You can wear a scarf or a turtleneck if it's uncomfortable," Gu Han said.

"Thanks. Since we're sitting down to sign, I really wasn't looking forward to a bunch of teenage boys looking down my top while I sign their stuff. What? It's a girl problem, okay?" I gave Jun-woo an exaggerated pout.

"It's the kind of girl problem we like," Si-woo grinned beside his brother.

"Of course it is."

"Twins, shut it," Hae Jin ordered.

"I'll fine you next time," Gu Han threatened the twins. "This is your teammate, not a pin-up poster."

We stopped for dinner at seven, and Gu Han let us have the rest of the evening off. "If I weren't so tired, I'd go out for steak," I raised arms above my head and yawned.

"I'll drive," Hae Jin offered. "Steak sounds good. Anyone else?"

Shi-joon, Min-ho and Gu Han joined Hae Jin and me. "How about Philippe's?" Gu Han asked while Shi-joon placed a call.

"Philippe's is a good choice," I agreed.

"Doc, how about Philippe's?" Shi-joon spoke into the phone. "We'll be there in about twenty."

"Doctor Oh is joining us," Shi-joon grinned as he stuffed his phone in a pocket.

"The boyfriend apparent," Gu Han teased.

"It happened that way. I don't mind that you know."

"The twins, on the other hand," I shook my head and closed my eyes.

"I looked at the handbook you recommended," Gu Han said. "I think we should incorporate everything that pertains to us. It will protect Shi-joon and everyone else in the long term, if we deal with relationships in the future."

Hae Jin

"What does Team Owner say about using that manual?" I asked. I felt guilty that I hadn't looked at the handbook Manta recommended, but if Gu Han liked it, then it was good enough for me.

"He's going through it now. We'll know early next week."

"Manta?" Shi-joon said, causing Manta to open her eyes and turn around in her seat.

"Huh?"

"My mother pled guilty to neglect and child endangerment," he said. "They're planning to ask for a five-year sentence, since the injuries and illness were so severe."

"I talked to the prosecutor," Manta said. "She says there's been no communication between your mother and the other parties."

"I'm not surprised."

"If I hear anything else, you'll be the first to know."

"Thank you."

We drove beneath the canopy outside Philippe's; I let the valet have my keys and we walked inside. Doctor Oh had arrived just before we did; Shi-joon gave him a warm hug before introducing him to the rest of us.

"Why didn't you tell me he was Mai's doctor," I whispered to Manta as a server led us toward a table.

"Not my tale to tell," she shrugged. "That story belongs to Shi-joon."

"If we end up at a wizarding school, will you be my secret keeper?"

"You want to end up at a wizarding school?"

"Maybe. Who wants to know?"

"I'll take the small prime rib, cooked medium rare," Manta ordered.

"I want the large prime rib, cooked medium rare," I said. Once again, I'd managed to beat Min-ho to a seat next to Manta, but he'd merely taken the seat on her other side. Gu Han sat across the table from me, while Shi-joon sat in the middle and Doctor Oh got the other end.

"Side dishes?" the server asked.

"Caesar salad and baked potato, please," Manta said.

"I'll have the same," I handed my menu to the server.

I ended up with part of Manta's extra prime rib; Min-ho got the rest. She did eat most of her Caesar salad and gave half her baked potato to Gu Han. He'd ordered steak and lobster, so he didn't need the extra prime rib.

"I'll take the check," Doctor Oh held out his hand after we'd finished eating.

"Are you sure?" Manta asked him.

"Yes," he smiled at her. "I owe you, I think."

Doctor Oh drove Shi-joon back to headquarters. Manta fell asleep in my Jeep's passenger seat, only waking with a start when I shut off the engine in the parking garage.

"I'm awake," she announced, awkwardly opening the door to let herself out.

"Who are you trying to convince?" Gu Han laughed at her.

"Me, mostly. Are you convinced? Do I sound convincing?"

"Come here, you," Min-ho draped an arm over her shoulders and pulled her toward the backdoor into headquarters. I almost snarled at him.

"You'll have to move faster," Gu Han fell into step beside me. "Shi-joon says she's definitely single, but," he shrugged.

"What else does Shi-joon know?"

"No idea."

"Are we ready for tomorrow?" I ignored Min-ho walking through the door, his left arm still around Manta's shoulders.

"Osprey is sending their guards again. We almost didn't get in and out of Go-Go Gaming without them."

"What do you mean, almost?" I demanded. "We'd have been trampled without them."

"You're right."

Rae-Rae

"These hackers are slippery," Zhang Bao told me. "By the time the authorities found their base of operations, it had been cleaned out and abandoned."

"That didn't take long," I said.

"Do you suppose they were expecting someone to look into it?"

"I couldn't use the bloodhound software, since I was called to Seahorse headquarters," I explained. "So I couldn't tag specific hackers. I could only tag their base. Did you hear from our favorite Undersecretary?"

"No and I am grateful."

"I'm surprised—and grateful. I doubt we've heard the last of him, though. He's developed the same maladies that your former family member has."

"I hate to say it may be deserved, but," Zhang Bao didn't finish.

"Yeah. How can I get the message across that I had nothing whatsoever to do with any of that?" I asked. "He still doesn't get it."

"Don't worry about it anymore tonight. Get some sleep. You sound tired."

"Only because I am."

"Good-night, RR."

"Good-night, ZB."

Hae Jin

Manta squinted at the pouring rain beyond Black Skies' portico Saturday morning. "Who had flooding on their bingo card?" she asked.

"Don't worry, you won't melt—you're not sugar," Si-woo taunted.

"I'm not worried about that. I'm worried about kids standing in the cold rain," she made a face at him. "If Go-Go Gaming was an indication, they'll be lining up outside the electronics store."

I watched her disappear inside headquarters for a few minutes before reappearing, just as the bus pulled up.

Manta wasn't wrong about people standing in the rain; when our bus pulled into the parking lot, there was already a line outside in what had become a steady downpour. What I hadn't expected was to see employees from a rental agency erecting tents and awnings to cover the crowd, while store employees handed out hooded rain ponchos.

"Osprey sent ponchos," Min-ho said, as visitors donned ponchos the moment they were handed out. Sure enough, each poncho bore the bird emblem that represented Osprey Technology and Robotics.

The driver took us to the back of the store, where our guards waited at a door next to the loading dock. If the weather had been fine, some of the crowd would have followed the bus. In a downpour, the crowd waited for ponchos and shelter from the rain on the opposite side.

I maneuvered along the bus aisle until I stood behind

Manta. "Those concrete steps to the back door are steep and wet," I told her. "Be careful walking up."

"I'll do my best." She looked up at me. "Do you have your umbrella?"

"The driver has a box full."

"Okay."

"Be careful getting off the bus and climbing those steps," the bus driver said as he opened the door for us. Two guards with umbrellas waited outside the door for us to disembark.

Gu Han led us off, grabbing an umbrella from the box at the front of the bus on his way. The rest of us followed suit, although Manta had her own purple umbrella stuffed inside her purple tote bag.

Once we were off the bus, the guards carried the bags of snacks we'd brought with us; the store was providing coffee, bottled water and soft drinks.

"Welcome," the store manager waited inside on the loading dock as we walked into the back of the store. "We've already got a crowd waiting, even in the rain. I was surprised when Osprey sent the tents and ponchos. We'll be mopping wet floors all day anyway."

"Way to think about yourself, dude," Manta said softly in English beside me. I casually draped an arm around her neck and pressed fingers against her mouth. "Hmmph," she muffled past my fingers.

"Baby girl," I leaned down to whisper in English against her ear, "Don't poke the bear." The electronics store was a subsidiary of a huge conglomerate, and one we didn't want to offend in any way.

Manta rolled her eyes but she didn't respond, so I reluctantly moved my hand away from her mouth. It wasn't until later that I noticed the perfect print of her mouth in purple lipstick on the fingers of my left hand.

ONCE WE WERE SHOWN TO THE SIGNING TABLE PLACED AT the center of the store, the manager proceeded to tell us everything we should and shouldn't do at a signing, which we already knew.

"He'll ask us to promote sales of something he's trying to unload, next," Manta mumbled.

"And, if you could mention that we're having a two-for-one sale on last year's computer monitors," the store manager boomed, "that would be great." He gave us two thumbs up and a huge, false smile.

I was beginning to think I owed Manta an apology. Their computer monitors from the year before weren't the best and had plenty of problems. No way was I asking fans to spend their hard-earned money on those things.

"Those monitors are crap," Min-ho breathed on my other side. "No way I'm telling people to buy them."

"We're about to open the doors, get ready to ramble," the manager misquoted the last phrase in English, attempting to copy US boxing announcers. When the man strode away to open the doors, Gu Han asked for our attention.

"It isn't our job to sell substandard equipment," he said quietly. "So don't. Instead, you can tell the fans to feel free to shop the store, or even, "Welcome to Lightning Electronics."

"Best advice, ever," Manta sighed as the doors opened and the crowd flooded in.

CHAPTER 9

Hae Jin

"Next time, we're bringing seat cushions. Those folding chairs were used as torture devices in the Middle Ages," Shi-joon complained as we loaded onto the bus after the signing.

"I feel the need for pain patches," Min-ho said.

"I'll buy," Manta told him. "My neck and arms hurt."

"We can have them delivered to headquarters," Gu Han offered, tapping on his phone. "Dinner first?"

"And alcohol," Jun-woo said.

"Manta has to come to every signing from now on, just to interpret and talk sign language," Si-woo said. "I had no idea what those people from Thailand were saying."

"You could always learn a second language," Manta pointed a finger at him.

"Me?" he mouthed, tapping his chest with a finger.

"Another candidate for retiring on Venus as a short order cook," Manta sighed and took a window seat. "Please say we'll go someplace that has something not spicy on the menu."

"That's our goal," Gu Han replied.

"Thank you," Manta sang.

I took a seat across the aisle from Manta—everybody else had taken their own row, although Min-ho sat in the row in front of Manta, and Shi-joon sat in the one behind her.

"Will there be parking available at the restaurant?" Manta leaned over in her seat to ask me.

"If not, the driver will drop us off and pick us up."

"Will he be able to eat something?"

"He likely ate before showing up to get us this time," Min-ho turned around to tell Manta.

"Good idea," she nodded. "I'm just not used to traveling by bus everywhere."

"And you hate to drive," I teased. "How do you get anywhere?"

"People take pity on me and drive me around."

Shi-joon snickered at Manta's statement.

"We're here," Gu Han announced as the bus pulled to a stop outside a popular restaurant.

"Come on, pitiful, time to eat," I said, rising from my seat.

"THEY HAVE A FEW WESTERN DISHES ON THE MENU," Gu Han said, handing a menu to Manta.

They did have a few—spaghetti, a sirloin steak and a burger with fries. "I don't order steak unless it's one of their specialties," Manta sighed, striking off one item immediately. "I'm too picky about my spaghetti sauce, so burger it is—unless they make it with hot spices."

"There are grilled tiger prawns," I suggested. "Ask them to leave the spice off."

"Do you think they'll have garlic butter?"

"They'll have garlic. Ought to have butter."

"I'll ask about the burger and the prawns." They assured her they could do both without making them spicy. I overruled her and ordered both items when she decided on the burger.

"Someone will eat what you don't," I reassured her. She ate half the burger and one tiger prawn. The team shared the rest, and both were good.

"I'll order the tiger prawns next time," Gu Han enjoyed what he'd gotten. "I don't always want them spicy."

"I need a pain patch and my bed," Shi-joon rubbed his back as we walked outside after our meal. The bus was already parked at the sidewalk and waiting for us.

"I just want to be horizontal. The rest will take care of itself," Min-ho said.

The ride back to headquarters was quiet—even the twins were subdued after a long day and several bottles of beer. I wanted to ask Manta if her neck still bothered her, but once again she was bookended by Min-ho and Shi-joon, so I didn't ask. Rumors would start far too easily if I showed too much interest.

Why are you showing interest? A small voice inquired.

Maybe because she hadn't shown interest in me. Was my ego that fragile? I'd spent the day fending off too many girls and quite a few women who did their best to touch me while I signed their posters, shirts and other memorabilia.

More than a few males had done the same to Manta, and the others had their own troubles keeping fans from getting too close. I was glad we didn't have another all-day signing scheduled for the rest of the season.

"You know how to put a stop to that, don't you?" Manta had teased me in English during a break.

"How?"

"Stop being handsome."

"Seriously? That's it? I thought you'd say to tell them I'm gay or something."

"Nah. Some people see that as a challenge."

I smiled at the memory from earlier. It was a funny story to tell my mother, who'd love hearing that at least one female had called me handsome, and I hadn't insulted her in exchange.

"You still want me to stop being handsome?" I leaned forward to ask Manta as we lined up to get off the bus at headquarters.

"I never said I wanted you to. I said it was the only way to stop everybody from touching you at the signing."

"So, you don't want me to stop being handsome?"

"Why would I do that? I wasn't touching you. You're like the Mona Lisa in the Louvre. Look but don't touch."

"Maybe I wouldn't mind," I mumbled.

"Huh?"

"Nothing. I'm nothing like the Mona Lisa and I don't want to live at the Louvre."

"You might not get a lot of conversation from your companions there, and I've heard they're not into gaming, so probably a good plan."

"Come on, off the bus," I pointed ahead.

"You're the boss."

"Get in bed early," Gu Han ordered once we were inside headquarters. "We've lost a day of practice, so we'll start at ten tomorrow morning and end when I say we will."

The twins complained all the way up the stairs. "Like they're not going to text their friends and play WoW for the next three hours," Manta shook her head at their antics.

"Here are some pain patches," Gu Han caught up with us on the stairs and handed a package to Manta.

"Thank you. My neck is teched out. Did Shi-joon and Min-ho get some already?"

"We're covered," both walked up the steps ahead of us.

"Need help getting patches on your back?" Manta asked Shi-joon.

"You will not be looking at his back," Min-ho said brusquely, before I could say the same thing. "I'll help him and he can help me."

"Whatever works," Manta shrugged.

"Why did you offer?" I whispered to Manta.

"Because Shi-joon's boyfriend is less likely to be jealous if I help him," Manta replied.

"Oh. I didn't think of that."

"And now that you have?"

"Maybe it still bothers me, but to a lesser degree."

"I thought it only concerned Min-ho."

I pinched the bridge of my nose—I hadn't meant to let that truth out. "Are you concerned about Min-ho?"

"As a friend."

"Ohhhh," I faked an arrow hitting my chest.

"Calm down," Manta swatted at me with a hand. "You're overreacting. I'm only here for another nine months. It's dangerous to get involved, don't you think, when I'm only going to leave at the end of my contract?"

"But you said you have an apartment here in Seoul."

"We travel in different circles, remember? Otherwise, you'd have known of me before, I think."

We'd reached the top of the stairs, so she turned left to reach her dorm while I turned right to get to mine. *Baby girl*, I promised, *I will find out who you are before you go*.

Rae-Rae

"The soonest I can come to Busan is next Wednesday; my

schedule is full until then," I told Jin-won. I didn't add that it would take that long for me to adjust to seeing the house-that-was-a-prison where I'd spent the first sixteen years of my life.

Most of which I'd spent living in the frigid attic.

"Why do you think that woman is digging in the yard around the house?" I asked.

"I have no idea," Jin-won replied. "This is the first time we've seen her go near it, but it set off all our alarms. How would she know about the connection between that house and the jewelry she's been selling, unless someone told her?"

"You've checked for health issues and doctors' appointments, then?" I asked.

"Yes—for her and her husband. There's nothing out of the ordinary."

"Maybe we should look at this another way," I said. "We know who was likely behind the original theft. What if they never sold the jewelry? What if they've kept it as a macabre savings account in case they needed money someday?"

"We keep an eye on all visitors and communications that come and go from those three."

"But what about anyone they speak to inside their prisons?"

"I'll ask for copies of camera recordings around their cells immediately."

"Please do. The statute of limitations on some of their crimes is set to run out in two years. If I'm right, there's still one witness out there somewhere. What if they've figured that out, too, and they're hunting him now? It will take funds to get that done for them outside the walls."

"That's too frightening to contemplate," Jin-won shuddered.

"All the more reason to keep an eye on this. There's more here than just fencing stolen goods from twenty-three years ago. I can feel it."

"Anything else before I hang up?"

"Yes. Can you get a list of all the guards who work around those three? Plus anyone else who might come in regular contact? Then, let's check to see if any of those people have connections to our jewelry seller. It's too bad she doesn't have email or social media accounts."

"I'll get on that right away."

"If you need help from the Blue House, let me know. They owe me a few favors."

"I'd say that's true enough."

"Keep me advised." I ended the call with a weary sigh. "Damn. This just keeps getting more complicated," I moaned, covering my face with both hands. Perhaps it was time to go looking for a certain kidnap victim, whose name I'd refused to accept in order to keep both of us alive.

"Needle in a haystack," I breathed. "Go to bed, Rae-Rae," I admonished, although sleep was now a long way off and I knew it.

Instead, I answered a text from Zhang Bao, who was also sleepless and asking for a game to let off some steam. I played Madame Dragonfly and he played Silver Mountain King.

Together, we destroyed all comers until we were tired enough to sleep.

Hae Jin

Your grandfather is in the hospital, my mother texted me. *Just a slight scare with his heart. They're giving him fluids and putting him on medication. He should go home in a day or two. Call him tomorrow if you have time.*

Grandpa was eighty-seven, so it wasn't a surprise that if his heart hiccupped, they'd rush him to the hospital. *I'll call him in the morning*, I replied to my mother. Grandpa was an early riser, so I'd talk to him after I was done with my exercises.

Grandpa lived with my mother's oldest sister and her husband. Almost all their kids were grown and working outside the house, although one still lived at home. Grandpa liked playing chess with my cousin, and usually had at least one game loaded on the chessboard waiting for the next turn.

Lee Do-yoon would probably inherit most of Grandpa's legacy when the time came, but none of the rest of his grandchildren minded. Grandpa had already given away much of what he had, so artwork and keepsakes made up the bulk of what remained. Do-yoon had an affinity with Grandpa that none of the rest of us had.

"They're so much alike," my mother said often enough.

I didn't need any of Grandpa's valuables. A keepsake or two would be nice, but I'd prefer to wait another ten or fifteen years to get it. Grandpa was the only one who'd argued with my parents about sending me to America.

"We need to find out who did this to our Hae Jin," he'd shouted. "And make them pay."

"The others are dead," my mother had wept, speaking of the four other kidnap victims who hadn't survived, even when the ransoms had been paid. "If they find out he's alive and still living at home, they'll come after him again."

Even now, I didn't know which ones to side with, although my father had put his foot down and off to America I went. Whether those two bitches looked for me afterward I'd likely never know; I was packed and flown out of South Korea quickly.

I had two reminders of those three days I'd spent with my abductors; a school sweater with my name tag cut off it, and half of a train ticket from Busan to Seoul. On the back of that train ticket, a small girl had written in neat hangul, *Keep this. It's important*.

There were strange lines bordering the torn center of the ticket, both curved and straight. I wondered often whether they were a part of other writing on the remaining half of the ticket but had no way of knowing.

You can't tell what you don't know. Those words, along with two small fingers at my lips, kept me from telling my name that night. Why was she worried about knowing my name? *Or my knowing hers?* Was it only a childish worry, or was there something I couldn't fathom going on?

"Give it up," I told myself in English. I'd worried the subject to death and hadn't arrived at an answer no matter how many times I'd tried. Too, I'd done my best to recall the escape from a dusty attic in a forgotten house and neighborhood. Whatever drug they'd given me had made most memories of that night more than elusive.

Had my parents at least taken me to the hospital, the type of drug might have been determined, but they were rushing me out of the country instead, in an effort to save my life. Whether that effort was misguided remained to be seen.

Cousin Do-yoon now worked for the NIS. Perhaps it was time to ask him to look into all this for me—or whether it was even possible for him to do so. With that thought at the back of my mind, I began undressing for bed. Morning would come too early as it was.

"HERE. I BOUGHT TWO, IN CASE YOU WERE UP AND around." Manta handed me a large vanilla latte when she came back from swimming Sunday morning.

"It's still hot," I felt the heat of the drink through the sleeve over the paper cup.

"Got it just down the street. Enjoy." She shuffled toward the stairs.

"Uh, thanks," I said in English. At least I could enjoy a decent latte while listening to Grandpa talk about chess and what was going on at the hospital. I tapped his number while walking up the steps to my dorm room. Do-yoon answered the call.

"Cousin," I said. "Nice to hear your voice. Where's Grandpa?"

"In the toilet. How's everything with you? Still playing with cartoon characters?"

"Shut up," I told him amiably in English. He laughed.

"While I have you on the phone," I said, shutting my dorm room door behind me, "Can I ask a work-related question?"

"Your work or mine? I confess, I don't know anything about your work."

"Yours, goofy," I said. "Is there a way you can get into the records of those kidnappings that happened eighteen years ago?"

"You don't want anything do you? Those records are kept secret, and only a select few are allowed to get into them," he told me. "If I asked, I might get special permission, but they'd definitely ask why I wanted to see them. If they got even a whiff of your connection to all this, they'd never leave you alone."

"I was afraid of that," I sighed. "If that ever changes, let me know, okay? I have questions."

"As do I, but I can't display more than a passing interest

in this or they'll start looking into why. Your dad would have a fit if he found out."

"Yeah, Dad would have a fit. So would Mom."

"I like the lasagna your mom serves once in a while, so I'd like to remain on good terms with her," Do-yoon admitted.

"Here's a tip," I said. "Mom doesn't make that lasagna. Some friend of hers makes it, and she won't tell who it is."

"So we just need to find this friend, eh?"

"Looks that way. In the meantime, don't let her know we're investigating this, or we won't get any more."

"My lips are sealed."

"That's my boy."

"I'm only three years younger than you, so I'm not your boy."

"I'm the oldest. You're my boy."

"Stuff it. Grandpa, Hae Jin is picking on me," Do-yoon covered the phone with a hand.

"Hae Jin, stop picking on your younger cousin," Grandpa said.

"I was only teasing him, Grandpa."

"What's this about you looking into that kidnapping?" Grandpa had heard the previous conversation, along with the pretend fight.

"Grandpa, I just want to find the truth," I complained. "Not only about what happened, but who helped me that night. I couldn't have gotten away from those two women by myself, no matter what Mother thinks."

"Do-yoon and I believe you," Grandpa said. "But the information we can get leads us nowhere."

"You've looked into this before, haven't you?"

"I did, but I can't tell you who helped me. Back in the day, honest prosecutors were hard to find."

"I've heard that before," I agreed.

"I'll give you what I managed to get," Grandpa hesitated for a moment before telling me this.

"What is it?" I asked.

"Security camera recordings of two train passengers from Busan to Seoul, on the night you came home," he replied. "I have that and a few other things I'd like you to have," he added. "I'll have Do-yoon drop them off tomorrow afternoon."

"What format is the camera recording?"

"I had it transferred to one of those thumb-things."

"I can work with that. Thank you, Grandpa. You're the best."

"YOU SEEM DISTRACTED," GU HAN TOLD ME AT LUNCHTIME.

"I talked to my grandfather this morning. He's in the hospital," I said. I didn't add that what we'd discussed was the thing distracting me.

"Sorry to hear that. Is he all right?"

"He'll probably go home, soon. Just something with his

heart that gave everybody a scare. He's eighty-seven, so everything gives us a scare."

"Do you need a couple of hours to go visit?" Gu Han asked.

"We ought to practice," I sighed. "My mind wasn't on the game this morning."

"Don't worry about it. I couldn't get the twins to focus, either. If I let everyone go at seven tonight, will you have time to visit your family?"

"I'll text my mother and find out."

"Manta has food in the slow cooker for tonight," Gu Han said as I tapped a message to Mom.

"What is it?" I asked.

"Some kind of beef—it smells amazing."

Just then my mother texted that I could take dinner to my grandfather and Do-yoon. "Maybe Manta has enough to send three servings home with me," I said.

"Madame Dragonfly and Silver Mountain King made an appearance last night for the first time in a long time. Destroyed everybody who challenged."

"Anybody would hire either in half a nanosecond if they went public," I sighed.

"Ever play against them?"

"Min-ho and I took them on about a year ago. Got our faces slapped for our efforts."

"I've thought about playing them, but didn't have anybody who could play with me at the time," Gu Han said. "If they show up again, want to play them together?"

"Sure. We have to be available the next time they're online, though."

"True. Go ask Manta if she has extra food for your grandfather and cousin. I'll bet she'll make do."

"SOMEBODY ON THE TEAM COOKS?" DO-YOON ASKED AS I set the bag of food down on Grandpa's small table inside his suite.

"I tasted it before she packed it up—it's amazing. This is the beef," I tapped the first container, "and this is rice to go with it."

"Smells good," Grandpa walked in using his cane.

Do-yoon set out bowls while I opened containers and dipped rice for us. Once Do-yoon tasted his food, he was in love.

"Good," Grandpa nodded over his bowl. "Haven't had this in a while. Your great-grandmother used to make this."

I had no memories of Great-grandmother; she'd died when I was two. "I'm sorry I missed this," I said, stuffing more beef and rice in my mouth.

"Same," Do-yoon agreed.

Rae-Rae

"Auntie Cheng taught me," I said, when Min-ho asked me where I'd learned to make what the rest of the world referred to as Korean beef. Auntie and I had added our own twists to the old stand-by, though.

"I'm glad you learned to cook from Auntie Cheng," Shi-joon said. "This way, my chances double on getting a good, home-cooked meal."

"I've been craving this for a while, so I stopped to pick up the beef at the market this morning," I said.

"Does this mean we'll get more good stuff when you get a craving?" Gu Han asked.

"Probably. I almost made egg foo young, too, but decided it might be too much. One more thing," I said. "Do you know when our next day off is?"

"Probably Wednesday," Gu Han said. "It's right after our next preseason game, so it could be a good time to take a day off."

"Got plans?" Shi-joon asked.

"I need to go out of town for a few hours," I shrugged. "I have some personal business in Busan."

"If you need help, just ask," Shi-joon said.

"Nah, go spend some time with you know who."

"I'll help," Min-ho offered.

"Can you make kimchi with your injured hand?"

"No."

"You should probably stay here, then."

I was grateful the twins had eaten two bowls of food each

while the rest of us were still serving ourselves, and then went out. I figured they'd find trouble somewhere if it didn't find them first.

"Have you studied the Zebras' gaming habits yet?" Gu Han turned the conversation to team business.

"I've looked into it."

"And?"

"Without their second-in-command, three members of their team are relatively useless. He calls the shots instead of the team captain."

"Wow," Min-ho grinned at Shi-joon.

"It's only natural to go after the apparent leader first," I said. "He may be familiar with what his second intends to do, but he doesn't direct the others."

"Interesting. Will it be to our advantage to go after their second first?"

"Let me go after him. If I can keep their second busy enough to take him away from issuing orders, I think the team might fall apart after that."

"You scare me," Min-ho teased.

"Nothing scary about this. I'll make sure he's too busy to keep up with the other players, that's all."

"You may draw one or two of their team to chase after you," Gu Han observed.

"Then that leaves four on three, possibly, for the rest of you. How is that a problem? The more dangerous they think I am, the better the odds get for the rest of you."

"Have you checked the website lately?" Min-ho asked.

"Not since Friday."

"The visit to Go-Go Gaming has gone viral, and three of the participants have posted vlogs about their experiences playing with the team. It was a huge PR success," Gu Han smiled. "Team Owner is very happy."

"I'm glad he's happy. I hope we don't have to do it again for a while," I said, suddenly feeling weary.

"We're too busy getting ready for the new season," Gu Han said. "But when the season ends and everybody is rested, we'll certainly put a trip together."

"Hear that? You get to do it next time," I patted Min-ho's arm.

"Can you stay?" Min-ho asked.

"Nope. This is your job, not mine. I have my own job waiting when my contract is up."

"A part of me understands that," Shi-joon sighed. "Another part of me wants things to be different."

"You lived without me before. You can do it again with no trouble," I told him.

"I feel mistreated," Min-ho complained. "I want to trade off one of the twins instead."

"Stop that," I said. "That isn't why I'm here."

"Why are you here?" Gu Han asked.

"My friend from China signed me up and told me afterward," I replied. "He and I will have a showdown when this is over."

"How was he able to do that—sign you up?"

"He's best friends with Team Owner, that's how."

"Now I get it," Gu Han's nod was exaggerated.

"How much trouble is he in?" Shi-joon grinned.

"About neck-deep," I replied. I rose from my seat at the island and began gathering dishes for the dishwasher. Shi-joon got up to help, and Min-ho did what he could with one hand. I needed to contact Jin-won about going to Busan on Wednesday and set it up with a bodyguard to fly there with me.

HAE JIN

"Are you ready to see this?" Do-yoon asked as he loaded the file from the thumb drive onto his laptop.

"Yeah." I clenched and unclenched my fingers in trepidation. *Would I see her—the girl who'd gotten me away from my captors?*

"Here we go," Do-yoon said with a breathy sigh. The camera was situated high above the train seats on the right side of the frame. When the recording began, there were only a few passengers deboarding before the next passengers arrived.

Then, I saw them.

Us.

She and I.

My hand went over my mouth to stifle an unwelcome sob. She was so small, compared to the eleven-year-old me.

"Hang in there, cousin," Do-yoon rubbed my back. "That's really you—and really her, I suspect."

I couldn't answer, I could only nod my assent.

"You were still wobbling because of the drug, I think," Do-yoon said, separating himself from his professional persona. "She's leading you to your seat, see?"

What followed was a four-hour train ride from Busan to Seoul, while I, exhausted and under the influence of some unknown drug, slept with my head in a small girl's lap. Do-yoon and I sped through much of the trip; he said that the most interesting part of the recording was near the end, anyway.

"What is it?" I asked.

"You'll see." He stopped it at a certain point, and then ran the images through in slow motion.

I gasped. Before my eyes, I watched as the girl, her long braid falling over one shoulder, leaned forward and kissed my cheek shortly before the train pulled into the Seoul station.

"Whuh-why?" I breathed.

"No idea. Maybe she knew she'd never see you again. I don't know."

"Please say that's not true. I really want to find her."

"Without going public with this, which will upset your parents, there's really no way to do that."

"If there's anything in the files at the NIS," I argued.

"We've already had that conversation, remember?"

"Yeah."

"If anything can be done without revealing important

information, I'll do it," Do-yoon reassured me when the recording ended. "Just be patient, all right?"

"At least we know she's real," I sighed.

"She's real, Cousin. Really real. You didn't make her up or hallucinate her. Come on, Grandpa has your box of things ready. I've kept a copy of this thumb drive, just in case," he added.

"Good. Thank you."

"They're still out there," Do-yoon paused for a moment. "Those women who abducted you and killed the others. There's only a few years left on the statute of limitations since the crime took place before 2007."

"Unless we're lucky and they died during that time," I said. "Which isn't likely."

"I'd say that's true. And in all this time, there hasn't been a single shred of evidence to lead us anywhere. You may have been the only chance the authorities had of ever finding them, and that crime was never reported."

"Don't remind me. I feel guilty enough just for surviving, when the others didn't. What do you suppose they did with the ransom money? It was all in cash."

"No way to tell, as no trail was ever found," Do-yoon shook his head.

"At least one other person out there may know more about my kidnapping," I said.

"Who?"

"A little girl." I held the thumb drive aloft.

"Who is now an adult and hasn't come forward in the past

eighteen years. Do you suppose they found her?" Do-yoon asked the question that often troubled me.

"I hope not. I hope she's happy and healthy somewhere, without that worry hanging over her head."

"Me, too, Cousin. Me, too."

CHAPTER 10

Rae-Rae

We have the woman who sold your mother's jewelry under surveillance twenty-four-seven. If she speaks to anyone, we'll know. Also in the process of getting lists of guards and surveillance camera recordings from the prisons, but having some difficulty with authorities in charge. Will have available information ready for you Wednesday at bureau office in Busan—Jin-won.

I took several deep breaths to calm myself. This was the closest we'd come to locating these offenders for the other—and far worse—crimes they'd committed in the past.

Kang Dong-hyung was already serving a life sentence, but I wanted him to pay for all his crimes, not just some of them. As for Go Ha-eun and Go Ah-eun, they needed life sentences for murder, too, instead of only ten years for attempted murder.

If I found out they were still plotting against the only child left alive after their kidnapping and ransom plot—*calm down*, I told myself, drawing in deep breaths and slowly releasing them.

They had one vital piece of evidence that I didn't, and that was the actual name of their last kidnap victim. His family had to be wealthy, I knew that much, or they'd never have bothered with him.

I'd discreetly checked and rechecked through the years, but nothing had ever been said or even mentioned in passing about a wealthy family who had a member kidnapped around the age of ten to twelve.

The text had come from Jin-won while Hu Lin was driving me back to headquarters after my swimming exercises.

"Want coffee?" Hu Lin asked.

"Is the Pope Catholic?"

Want a latte? I texted Hae Jin.

Is the Pope Catholic?

His reply made me laugh.

"What's funny?" Hu Lin asked.

"I never thought I'd meet somebody who'd be on the same wavelength at times," I confessed.

"You met a man who makes you laugh? Wait until Tae-hyun hears this."

"It's nothing serious and certainly nothing to be concerned about, okay? We don't have that much in common at the end of the day."

"If you ever get engaged again, Tae-hyun and I have to

approve of your choice," Hu Lin sniffed. "He was always suspicious of Choi Soo-ho, even though they were friends and roommates in college."

"Then he had better judgment than I did," I admitted. "I still feel stupid that I didn't see the problems with his family or with him until the last minute."

"His brother and sister will be in jail for a while. Soo-ho was the only one not involved in all the criminal activity."

"Probably because they didn't trust him," I sighed as Hu Lin pulled into the drive-through of my favorite coffee shop.

"I still can't believe he's the one who called off the engagement," Hu Lin said as we waited our turn to give our coffee order.

"Water under the bridge. The least he could have done is talked to me in person. Instead, he asks for the ring back through an attorney—like it's my fault that his brother and sister are criminals."

"If he suddenly wanted to see you, would you agree?" Hu Lin asked.

"He no longer has any right to speak to me. The answer is a flat and emphatic no. I am done with him and anyone connected to him."

"Little Sister, he isn't worth wiping your shoes on," Hu Lin sighed. "Probably never was. Three large vanilla lattes and three heated croissants," Hu Lin placed our order.

I thought about telling Hu Lin that Hae Jin had called me baby girl two days earlier. Just those words had sent a shiver through me—the good kind rather than the opposite. I was probably reading far too much into that simple phrase, so I forced myself not to tell.

HAE JIN WAS STANDING OUTSIDE AS IF HE WERE WAITING for someone when Hu Lin dropped me off. He drove off, too, before Hae Jin could get a closer look.

"Who was that?" Hae Jin asked as I handed him a latte and a bag containing his croissant.

"My number two best friend, Hu Lin."

"Who's your number one best friend?" Hae Jin frowned at me.

"Number two best friend's husband, Tae-hyun," I replied honestly.

"I don't know what to do with you," Hae Jin said, sipping his latte.

"Were you hanging around out here because you were having coffee withdrawal?"

"Maybe. Who wants to know? Does Hu Lin take you swimming every day?"

"Usually. It's on his way to work."

"What does he do?"

"He works in security. His husband is a doctor."

"So that's why he drives a black SUV."

"Probably. He has a pair of dark sunglasses to match."

"Come on, you, you look cold," Hae Jin headed for the front door just as another car pulled up.

Full of girls.

"Hae Jin, Hae Jin, Hae Jin," they chorused with the windows rolled down.

"That must get annoying after a while," I said as the front doors shut behind us.

"You have no idea."

"Remember—stop being handsome," I teased.

"Shut it."

"You're the boss."

HAE JIN

Before the day was over, the twins had been fined for causing a disruption during team practice. They didn't think it would happen. They learned Gu Han wasn't kidding.

I was grateful to him; the rest of us, Min-ho included (and he wasn't even practicing), had had more than enough of their roughhousing and stupid jokes.

Manta hadn't said a word, but her face was pale and the areas around her eyes and mouth looked pinched—as if she wanted to fire both twins and be done with it.

The twins, grumbling, went out to eat together, leaving the rest of us to eat without them. "What a worthless day,"

Shi-joon complained, leaning forward and resting his forehead on the kitchen island.

"Delivery or go out?" Gu Han asked.

"Go out," I raised my hand.

"I'm with Hae Jin," Min-ho said.

"Manta?" Shi-joon asked.

"Let's go out—just not where the twins went."

"That's a given," Min-ho agreed. "Let's get a cab so we can drink and not drive."

"I can drive us back," Manta sighed. "If someone else will get us there. I won't be drinking," she reminded us.

"Can I pay your friend to drive us in his SUV?" I asked Manta.

"He'd probably do it—as long as we don't make a habit of it. I'll owe him lasagna, though."

"I vote we owe him lasagna if he'll drop us off and pick us up," Gu Han said.

"Let me see if he's available," Manta pulled out her phone and sent a text.

Several minutes later, we were getting dressed so Manta's friend could pick us up and take us to a restaurant nearby.

"Just keep in mind I can't carry anybody up the stairs, so manage your drunkenness accordingly," Manta said as we walked out the door to load into her friend's SUV.

"Just leave me on the floor downstairs," Min-ho laughed. "If I'm that drunk, I won't care."

"Everybody, this is my good friend Hu Lin," Manta introduced us as we loaded into the SUV. "Hu Lin, this is Gu Han, the team manager, team captain Hae Jin, and vice-captain Min-ho. Shi-joon and Hu Lin have already met."

"It's nice to put faces with names," Hu Lin nodded at us. "I usually drive Manta to her swimming exercises, and every now and then she'll talk about the team. All good—except for the twins occasionally."

"We're not talking about them tonight," Gu Han admitted. "Thank you for driving us. It's been a long day."

"Not a problem. Everybody in and buckled up? Good. Let's go."

"TRY NOT TO OVERDO IT ON THE ALCOHOL TONIGHT—WE have a preseason game to get through tomorrow evening," Gu Han warned everybody when we took our seats at the restaurant.

"Ohhh, I wish I could order the coq au vin," Manta studied the specials on her menu.

"Doesn't the alcohol cook off?" Shi-joon asked.

"No. You'd have to carry me out of here," she replied. "I'll just order the fish."

"You don't get to eat French cooking?" I asked her.

"Only the non-alcoholic stuff. I like fresh-made tomato soup."

"Can you make it? I love tomato soup and grilled cheese sandwiches," I said.

"Absolutely."

"It would be best to do that before the regular season starts," Gu Han pointed out. "We have roughly one game per week scheduled for the next six months, and we'll be traveling a lot of the time. After that, we start quarterfinals, semis and finals. I intend to see this through to the end, so count on the full eight-and-a-half months."

"Logic cracks opens a window so we can face reality," Manta sighed. "I feel exhausted already."

"You feel exhausted because the twins wore us out today," I said.

"Yeah. You're right."

I had the sudden urge to put both arms around her, and that had never happened before—not with any woman. Instead, I asked a question that had recently popped into my mind. "What do you think of the pool at the hotel where you swim?"

"It's okay. Nothing great, and sometimes the guests just go off and leave their kids there, even that early in the morning."

"There's an Olympic-size pool at the athletic club where I train," I said. "If you're interested, I can take you in as a guest to get your exercise some morning. It may be cheaper to swim there than at the hotel."

"Are kids and drunks allowed?"

"No drunks. Kids only if they're training professionally."

"Nice," she said. "Will they let Hu Lin drink his coffee and read his newspaper while I swim?"

"I think they'll be all right with that."

"I'll buy him a membership if they're not," Manta said. "A couple of times, I've had toddlers dive into the deep end right in front of me. There's a lifeguard, but both times I got to the kids before he did."

"You won't have that problem where I go, I promise."

"Might be nice not to deal with that."

"Want to come tomorrow?"

"Want to ride with Hu Lin?"

"Sure. What time do you normally leave?"

"Five-thirty."

"I'll be ready."

I WALKED OUTSIDE AT FIVE-TWENTY-FIVE THE FOLLOWING morning, right behind Manta. Hu Lin was waiting outside, and the interior of his vehicle was already warm.

"I like this," I said, climbing into the backseat as Manta got into the front passenger seat. "No waiting until my car heats up," I clarified. I gave the address to Hu Lin, who nodded and took off.

"I know you," the desk clerk smiled at Manta. "Lee Hae Jin never brings a guest. Welcome to you and your friend. There are two tables with chairs at the pool; he's welcome to take one of them."

"Thank you," Manta accepted her day pass and followed the directions to get to the pool.

"I'll see you up front in about an hour," I told her before heading off for my Krav Maga lesson.

"Thanks."

"So, the Captain of Black Skies brought a guest, eh?" Trainer Park, my instructor, caught up with me. "A girl," he leaned in to tease me.

"Shut up. She was swimming at a hotel pool, and it was becoming hazardous."

"In what way?"

"Kids jumping into the deep end in front of her," I shrugged.

"That's dangerous. Don't they have a lifeguard?"

"A slow one."

"She won't get that here. Not that I watch your competitions or anything, but Manta knows how to take down the opposition."

"I've ah, noticed."

"I recall somebody complaining about her right after she joined the team."

"Before I knew better."

"My sister is in love with her."

"Your sister needs to back off. She's not gay."

"My sister says it only makes the conquering sweeter."

"Oh, for Christ's sake. Manta isn't somebody who needs conquering."

"I'll pay you to introduce them."

"No. That's just creepy, dude. It's like your brother paying you to introduce me."

"I don't have a brother."

"Thank goodness."

"Will you introduce Manta to me?"

"If she decides to buy a membership, I'll introduce you as my trainer, but that's it. Besides, her friend Hu Lin works in security. I think if you get too friendly, he might have something to say about it."

"Hey, expert in Krav Maga, here," he grinned.

"I haven't asked Hu Lin what his talents are."

"Hu Lin was the army champion for two years in a row in Krav Maga," Hu Lin stepped out of the men's room just ahead of us. "Hu Lin provides security to some of Seoul's most elite Chairmen and CEOs. In case you were wondering. Also, this wouldn't be the first time that someone has offered to introduce Manta to a gay sister. Manta always says the same thing."

"What's that?" I asked.

"That she doesn't mind having a new friend, but ultimately, they're both doomed to disappointment."

Trainer Park laughed out loud.

"Let's go watch Manta swim," Trainer Park grinned.

"Are you suggesting we cut training today?"

"First and only time?"

"What the hell. Hu Lin, wait up."

"I like this," Hu Lin smiled as a server set a cup of coffee at his elbow, then placed a latte and a cappuccino in front of me and Trainer Park.

My eyes were glued to Manta as she went through a second round of laps doing the butterfly stroke. "She's like an otter, the way she cuts through the water," Trainer Park said absently, lifting his cappuccino to drink.

Manta was dressed in a black, knee-length tech suit, and wore a black swim cap on her head. Goggles were over her eyes; I could smell the chlorine from our table, so she was wise to protect her eyes like that.

On the far side of the pool, another swimmer was also doing laps. She'd catch up to Manta now and then, only to fall back again.

"How does she stay focused?" Trainer Park asked Hu Lin.

"She's thinking. Her body is on automatic," Hu Lin explained. "That's the closest I can come to describing what she's doing."

At the second table across the pool, someone was timing the other swimmer with a stopwatch. That didn't keep their eyes from wandering to Manta now and then.

"What's she thinking about?"

"She has some personal business to take care of in Busan tomorrow," Hu Lin explained. "That's probably what she's thinking about. Once she gets out of the pool, her mind will be on the preseason game tonight."

"Does she need anyone to go with her tomorrow?" I asked.

"Tae-hyun and I are going with her. There's a restaurant we really like there."

"You think she'll get a membership here?" Trainer Park asked.

"We'll know when she gets out of the pool."

Twenty minutes later, Hu Lin lifted a towel off the chair next to his and walked to the side of the pool. Manta climbed out and took the towel from his hands, wrapping it around her slender body.

"So, what's the verdict?" Hu Lin asked as she walked toward the table.

"I like it. No interruptions and I could turn off the worry that some kid would just drop out of the sky," she said. "Take my card and go get both of us a membership."

"What about Tae-hyun?"

"If you think he'd like one, then by all means." She turned and headed for the women's showers and locker room.

"Your question has been answered," Hu Lin fished in his pocket for a credit card. "Maybe I'll take one of you on next time."

"I'm willing," Trainer Park agreed. "We'll see what the military has to offer."

WE FOUND OUT HOW HUNGOVER THE TWINS WERE WHEN we got back to headquarters. "Si-woo threw up five minutes in; his brother after eight minutes," Gu Han described their run that morning.

That resulted in both getting hauled to a hospital for an IV and electrolytes. "They don't smell the best," Gu Han whispered as Shi-joon and Min-ho helped the twins up the steps to their bedrooms.

"What will we do if they're unable to play tonight?" Manta asked.

"Forfeit is the only option. I can only replace one of them. We don't have a second alternate."

"What if we had a second alternate?" Manta asked.

"Can you get him here in the next hour? I want to see what he's got," I said. I wasn't putting much hope in somebody off the street, but rather than forfeit, we could tell the person to hide in the weeds while the rest of us took care of business.

Manta pulled out her phone and dialed. "Hey, Little Brother," she said. What are you and Chin-mae doing tonight? Okay, want to play with Black Skies as an alternate?" She held the phone away from her ear as jubilant shouting began.

"They're excited," she said after asking one of them to come as soon as they could. "One will stay and handle the appointments; the other one will be here in an hour."

"Appointments?" I lifted an eyebrow.

"They're veterinarians," Manta explained. "But they've been gamers since middle school. You'll see."

"WE DREW STRAWS," CHIN-MAE GRINNED WHEN HE arrived and was introduced. "In-Su was disappointed, but he'll survive."

"We're about to put you to the test; I hope you don't mind," Gu Han told him.

"I don't mind. It's an honor just to try out," Chin-mae smiled. "We play whenever we can, and sometimes we bug big sister to play against us. She designed both our characters, you know."

"We didn't know, but we'll see how they stack up. Are they approved?"

"Certified," Chin-mae said. "But we're the only ones cleared to play them. Big sister won't release them to the public."

"That's something else we didn't know," I cast a doubtful glance in Manta's direction. I hadn't envisioned her in the role of character designer.

"Come with us, then, and show us what you can do," Gu Han led Chin-mae toward the gaming room.

"Cool," Chin-mae breathed when he walked in and got his first glimpse of Black Skies' gaming den.

"Sit down and get your character loaded up," Gu Han directed. "I'll get Shi-joon back down here."

Gu Han left the room while I stood behind Chin-mae's seat, watching. He tapped in his gaming codes, and the computer buffered for a few seconds before his character appeared.

"Cloud Emperor?" I said, my voice almost a squeak. "You play Cloud Emperor?"

"In-su plays Cloud Empress," Chin-mae grinned over his shoulder.

Both those characters were widely known in gaming circles. They were tough to beat by the normal crowd, and even some pro players had trouble with them when they played together.

Then it hit me. "You're sure Manta designed those characters?"

"We begged her to do it," Chin-mae confessed. "We asked for a married couple. She asked male or female. We decided on one of each."

"Cloud Emperor?" Gu Han was back, with Shi-joon right behind him. "Manta, is this your work—really?"

"They begged me," she said, as if it were an everyday occurrence.

"Nobody can code like Manta," Chin-mae said.

"Telling all my secrets?" Manta asked.

"Oops, sorry," Chin-mae apologized.

In half an hour, we'd filled Chin-mae in on our opponent and began our first training exercise. The longer we worked, the happier Gu Han and I were with Chin-mae's performance.

If he hadn't gone to veterinarian school, he could have

been a professional gamer—except his current profession was likely a better one for his future.

"Don't get any ideas—he's just on loan," Manta came to stand beside me. "They do a lot of good at their clinic, trust me. Gaming is a hobby, and one they enjoy. I don't want to put a damper on anything they love, and animals are at the top of their list."

"I get it," I said. "Really. There are only so many spots for pro gamers."

"And only so many people who are cut out to be veterinarians. How long can most people sustain a pro gaming career? Until they're thirty, maybe? After that, only so many can manage a team, or train others. What will you do when the time comes?"

"I already promised my dad I'd take over the family business."

"Awesome," she said in English. "Little Brother-in-law already has an established career—that he and Little Brother chose together. Little Brother has been through a lot, and Chin-mae helped him get through it. I couldn't be prouder of those two."

"Someday, you'll have to tell me that story."

"When my contract is up, just ask. So, are we going with our two alternates, Captain?" Manta asked me.

"Yes. Even if the twins rise from the dead this afternoon, they'll sit this one out because they knew better than to drink that hard last night."

RAE-RAE

Gu Han went with the excuse that the twins had food poisoning. Which was true if you counted alcohol as a food.

The Zebras did just as I thought, sending two of their weakest players chasing me. Chin-mae was smiling a huge smile when he and Hae Jin managed to take out their second-in-command, and then, while I dispatched the two running after me, they and Gu Han destroyed the Zebras' captain.

It took twenty minutes, but Chin-mae was ecstatic. He was on the phone with In-su afterward, laughing and talking about the game. Gu Han loaded Chin-mae down with team T-shirts and memorabilia and told him he'd get a check in the mail for playing. Chin-mae tried to refuse the money, but Gu Han wasn't having it.

After Chin-mae went home, Gu Han turned to me. "You designed Cloud Emperor."

"Yeah. And Cloud Empress. Because my little brothers wanted a married pair."

"Is there anything else that you're not telling us?"

"Plenty, I'm sure."

Gu Han laughed.

"How did they meet? Your little brothers?" Shi-joon asked.

"In elementary school. Chin-mae's parents are wonderful people. When Chin-mae was twelve, he told them he loved my little brother. They were okay with that. In-su and Chin-mae have been together for a long time and weathered a lot of storms during those years."

"I wish I'd had parents like that," Shi-joon sighed.

"Same here."

"What about your parents?" Hae Jin asked.

"Dead," I said. "Little Brother is actually step-family, but he's all I have. We're closer than a lot of blood-related siblings."

"So you have a stepfather? Or stepmother?"

"*Had* a stepfather. He's dead, too. In fact, that's why I'm going to Busan tomorrow; I need to check on the house Stepdad left Little Brother. Looks like somebody has been poking around where they shouldn't, so we'll be working on security measures."

"Want something to eat?" Gu Han offered. "We can order or go out."

"Pizza," Min-ho grinned. "I can eat that with my left hand."

That's how we ended up at a pizza restaurant a few blocks away, talking over two large pizzas.

"Stepfather had a mistress. She's In-su's mother," I explained after Shi-joon asked about growing up with In-su. I told him we didn't even know about each other until Little Brother was in his last year of high school, after Stepfather was murdered.

By In-su's mother.

"I told you he's been through a lot. He didn't even know who his father was," I said. "His mother foisted him off on a cousin and her husband, who mostly ignored In-su. Without Chin-mae's friendship and willingness to stick with him no matter what, In-su would have had a terrible childhood."

"What about his father—when he was still alive?"

"Stepfather was famous for ignoring children, especially those he was responsible for. Trust me when I say it wasn't entirely a bad thing. He was a horrible parent."

"Did you have any kind of relationship with him?"

"None. We hadn't spoken to one another since my mother died. Not even once."

"When did your mother die?"

"When I was four. Let's talk about something else, now. Okay?"

Hae Jin

I wasn't the only one with a messed-up childhood. Manta and her little brother had dealt with a lot growing up. At least they'd found one another eventually. I had more questions for her, but she'd shut down the moment she was asked about her mother.

A sore spot, no doubt.

"Are we going to the gym tomorrow?"

"Of course. My flight doesn't leave until ten. Plenty of time to get my exercising done first. Hu Lin can drop you off at headquarters afterward, before we pick up Tae-hyun and go to the airport."

"I still want to go," Min-ho complained.

"If I take you, then I have to take everybody," Manta told him.

"Sounds like fun. I haven't been to Busan in ages," Gu Han said.

Manta pulled out her phone and placed a call. "Can you get me four more tickets round-trip to Busan tomorrow? I can hold. You guys can go have fun while I'm talking to the security people, okay?" Manta informed us while someone on the other end put her on hold. "Then we can go to Tae-hyun's favorite restaurant. They serve really good seafood."

The person on the other end came back on the line. "We're set up? Yes, they'll have their IDs and everything with them when we get there. Thank you.

"Everything's arranged," Manta ended the call and put her phone away. "We'll get a second rental car, so you can go sightsee while I deal with business. Tae-hyun is from Busan originally, so he can show you around."

"We can't all fit in Hu Lin's SUV," I pointed out. "I'll follow in my Jeep and leave it at the airport."

"Nice," Manta held up her fist for a fist bump.

CHAPTER 11

Hae Jin

I looked at the box of things Grandpa had given me. It sat on a chair inside my dorm room—I still hadn't opened it. In my opinion, the most important thing Grandpa had ever given me was the thumb drive—the one that held the images of a little girl and me riding a train from Busan to Seoul.

A part of me wished I could explore Busan on my own—the one and only time I'd been there during my lifetime was after my kidnapping and I'd been unconscious for most of it. Another part of me was grateful I wouldn't be there on my own when I saw it as an adult.

"Tomorrow starts early," I reminded myself aloud. "Brush your teeth and go to bed."

THE TWINS STILL WEREN'T UP WHEN WE LEFT headquarters for the airport Wednesday morning. "Everybody have their ID?" Manta asked before we loaded into two vehicles for the trip. Her friend, Tae-hyun, had taken a taxi to headquarters and arrived shortly before we returned from exercising.

Once we were assured that everybody had what was required to fly, Hu Lin drove out first, with me close behind in the Jeep. Once we'd parked in covered parking, we walked into the airport and to the ticket counter.

"Yes, I have four additional first-class tickets under Kim Hu Lin," the airline employee said when Hu Lin presented his ID. "I just need to see the IDs and enter the information."

The rest of us stepped forward and presented our IDs while Gu Han mouthed, "First class?"

"The airline owner's wife is a good friend of Manta's," Tae-hyun leaned in to inform us. "She owes Manta a few favors. We're getting our tickets free."

"It *is* good to know people," Min-ho grinned.

Once our IDs were checked, the ticket agent began issuing tickets—after a quick word from Hu Lin. I wondered what he'd said to the woman, until I found I'd been seated next to Manta on the flight.

I wasn't upset that he might be attempting to matchmake, and that had never happened in my lifetime.

"We have a hotel room rented as a sort of meeting and resting place during the day," Tae-hyun said after we were seated in first class on the plane. "We can join Manta for dinner there, after she's done with her security company. The restaurant we're going to has a nice view of the Diamond Bridge. It's amazing at night, with all the lights on."

"I've never seen it," I admitted.

"We're on the last flight back to Seoul, so we'll get back after midnight tonight," he went on. "I'm glad I'm working the late shift tomorrow."

"Early lunch when we get there?" Manta asked.

"I'm all for that," Tae-hyun agreed.

"I could eat," Hu Lin patted his stomach.

"This is going to be fun," Shi-joon said from his seat behind mine. He and I had gotten window seats; Manta and Gu Han had the aisle on our side. Opposite us, Tae-hyun and Hu Lin sat, and behind them was Min-ho and an empty seat.

"Baby girl?" I leaned over to speak to Manta in English.

"Huh?"

"Are you comfortable? Are you sure you don't want the window seat?"

"I'm fine," she said, patting my arm. "Enjoy the ride."

At that point, a flight attendant came through offering us drinks and snacks before we took off. Manta asked for tomato juice with no ice and a bottle of water. I asked for the same, except I wanted ice in my tomato juice.

"Is it too early for beer?" Min-ho quipped.

"Not on this trip," Tae-hyun leaned around the edge of his

seat to reply. Min-ho asked for an imported beer and leaned back in his seat with a contented sigh.

"The flight is only a little over an hour," Gu Han answered Shi-joon's question. "Don't eat too much—we'll have lunch in Busan."

"That's right—I'll take you to some great restaurants, I promise," Tae-hyun said.

"I LIKE OYSTERS IF THEY'RE COOKED PROPERLY. THIS IS MY favorite," Manta offered me part of her lunch plate of fried oysters and squid.

I tasted it. It was good, if I could get around the fact that it was oysters—and *squid*.

"First thing she wants every time we come here—oysters and squid," Tae-hyun teased Manta.

"There's nothing wrong with that," Manta said, lifting another oyster with her chopsticks and biting into it.

"How did you guys meet?" I asked Tae-hyun.

"Manta and I were best friends in college, even with the age difference," he grinned. "We lived in an off-campus dormitory, down the hall from each other."

"That was before I met either of them," Hu Lin broke in. "Tae-hyun's mother still sees Manta as a daughter, but she also calls me son," he shrugged and grinned lopsidedly.

"We were never together that way, and you know it,"

Manta pointed a finger at Hu Lin. "Tae-hyun and I are friends. I don't know how anybody could think otherwise."

"Lots of people want Manta as a daughter. She's just picky who she accepts," Tae-hyun put an arm around Hu Lin. "Your dad, for starters."

"Yes, my father would love to have her as part of the family."

"Don't go there," Manta held up a hand.

"What's the problem?" I asked.

"My father wants grandchildren, and I'm an only child. I don't know how many times Tae-hyun and I have told him that when the time is right, we'll look into it; he always talks about Miss Manta."

"He might have a harder time getting grandchildren even if I were his natural born daughter," Manta sighed.

"Why is that?"

"She was engaged, once. The guy turned out to be an absolute jerk," Tae-hyun explained. "I think she's afraid to get involved with anybody else."

"We're not here to discuss my love life, or the lack of one," Manta told him. "No questions," she pointed at me and the others, who'd suddenly stopped talking among themselves.

"Your escort is here," Hu Lin's voice broke into the quiet that ensued.

"Good. I trust you can get the check?" Manta asked, standing up.

"I still have your card."

"Awesome."

I watched her walk away until she reached a dark-suited man who stood at the edge of the restaurant's main dining room. They spoke briefly and then left.

"She'll be fine," Tae-hyun reassured Hu Lin.

Perhaps Hu Lin was reassured.

I wasn't.

Rae-Rae

Bak Jin-won led me to his car outside the restaurant. "The woman is working the counter at her husband's dry-cleaning business today, so we don't have to worry about her coming to the house while we're there. She's still under surveillance, in case she leaves for any reason."

"Are the groundskeepers still coming on a regular basis? I don't want her to see any signs that we were there and become suspicious."

"Yes. In fact, one of our agents is now working that crew."

"Good. What are the agency's thoughts on what she's looking for?"

"Has to be valuable or incriminating—maybe both, don't you think?"

"I can't ignore that possibility, either. Did you bring a metal detector?"

"I did. We'll do our follow-up search today. She's concentrating on the ground at the back side of the house, mostly beneath the largest tree."

"The roots of which could have pushed anything out of the way in the past twenty-four years."

"True enough."

It took forty-five minutes to get to the house. A truck belonging to the professional groundskeepers was parked in the driveway. Jin-won pulled in behind it. "Our guy is here by himself today. He'll help us dig so it won't be noticed if we find anything."

"Chairman Ong," the Agent walked around the house dressed in a groundskeeper's uniform. "I have the metal detector in the back, whenever you're ready."

"I'm ready," I told him.

"Let's go," Jin-won agreed.

"These are the holes she's dug already," Jin-won pointed at five different spots. One was in the center of a grassy area beneath the tree; the other four were either at the base of the tree in a ringed flower bed or in an adjacent flower bed where the digging wasn't as obvious.

"Have you run the metal detector over the area beneath the tree?" Jin-won asked the agent.

"I got hits in several places, some stronger than others."

"Let's start with the strongest," I said.

"Here." He led us toward a flower bed that was farther away from the tree.

"This flower bed wasn't here twenty years ago," I said, as

the detector started beeping. "In fact, this tree was only a sapling when my mother died."

"Want to dig here?" Jin-won asked.

"Of course."

Hae Jin

Busan was noted for its temples. The one Tae-hyun showed us was built at the edge of the sea. *Haedong Yonggungsa Temple* is a Buddhist temple which signified the absolute and limitless power of *Gwanseum-bosal*, the Goddess of Mercy.

"The Goddess of Mercy is known to keep you from harm if you call her name," Tae-hyun came to stand beside me as I stood at the base of her statue. "There are several stories of her appearance here at this temple."

"I was pulled away from harm once, when I was little," I confessed. "Maybe I had help I wasn't aware of."

"Maybe you did."

I couldn't have predicted it, but I found myself liking Manta's friends. I learned from Hu Lin that Tae-hyun was not only an excellent orthopedic surgeon, but he'd done the surgery on Manta's crushed foot so she could walk again. I suppose that if your best friend in college turned into an orthopedic surgeon, there could be benefits attached to that friendship.

"What can you tell me about Manta's ex?" I asked.

"She won't ever have anything to do with him again," Tae-hyun answered. "He turned out to be the worst kind of idiot, and I'm glad he was the one who asked for the ring back. She might have decided to stay with him, and that would have been a mistake."

"What happened?"

"His older brother and sister were involved in criminal activities, including murder, bribery, you name it. He thought Manta was involved in turning them over to the NIS, when she wasn't aware they were being arrested."

"So he didn't mind that his siblings were criminals, just that Manta may have had something to do with their arrest?"

"That's it," Tae-hyun agreed.

"He really is the worst kind of idiot."

"Manta hasn't looked at any man seriously since then. We keep hoping that will change. She needs someone strong beside her, who will tell her to slow down now and then. She has a tendency to work herself into exhaustion."

"Will she ever tell us her real name?"

"If you worked at it, you could probably figure it out on your own. She doesn't like to lie and sometimes, when she says something outrageous it's probably true, as unlikely as it may sound."

"You mean like working with the NIS to help find hackers?"

Tae-hyun tried to hide a smile but couldn't quite achieve it. "Most people don't even see that side of her," he barked a laugh. "You're one of the fortunate ones."

"I swore I wouldn't tell the others," I admitted. "I guess it's safe to say it to you, though."

"It is—to either me or Hu Lin. And, if I could give you our phone numbers, please call us if she needs help—especially if she's not feeling well."

"Where can I find friends like you two?" I asked. "I've never had friends that good."

"You don't understand—this friendship works both ways. Manta will move heaven and Earth if either of us need anything."

"What's the biggest thing she's done for either of you?"

"How about I tell you what she did for the guy who got her onto your team?"

"What did she do for him?"

"She was instrumental in getting him out of North Korea, after he'd been kidnapped and taken there."

"You're kidding?"

"Not kidding. She saved his life. This is what he did to repay her. She may kick his ass when this is over. Just know this; Manta doesn't fool around when lives are on the line."

RAE-RAE

"This is the first batch that disappeared," I sighed, staring at the jewelry box that used to sit inside my mother's closet.

We'd dug it up, and found it wrapped in plastic beneath a flower bed, where a tree root had pushed it.

"This could explain where part of it was, but this is the first time that we know of that our jewelry fencer has dug in this yard," Jin-won said.

"I'd say you're probably right," I agreed. "The women involved in this would have found a safer, easier solution after a while. I'd say this information came directly from one of them. Nobody else would have known about this location, I think."

"Then we need to look at who she's been communicating with, and that leaves guards and other staff at the prisons," Jin-won said, stuffing his hands into pants pockets. "I'd like to go pick her up now, but that could ruin the entire investigation."

"We need to cover this hole as if it had never been dug up," I said.

"I can do that," the agent said. "Don't worry about a thing. I was planning on putting fresh mulch down anyway."

"Thank you. Jin-won, will you take this jewelry box to NIS headquarters to catalog and photograph the contents?"

"I'll send you copies as soon as we have it done," he said. "Where do you need to go from here?"

"Let me see," I said, pulling out my cell phone. "Can you drive by the dry-cleaning business? I don't need to stop; I only want to see it for myself."

"Of course."

Hae Jin

"How about we meet at the hotel?" Tae-hyun spoke to Manta over the phone. She'd finished with the security company and could join us now.

"We're at the temple, so it will be a while for us, too. Just put your feet up and make phone calls. I know that's what you're going to do anyway, except for the putting up your feet part. Order a snack from room service if you want."

"We can pick her up at the hotel," Tae-hyun ended the call. "She sounds a little tired—probably from having to deal with this mess."

"What was the problem?" I asked.

"Somebody was digging up the yard," Hu Lin shrugged. "Weirdest thing ever."

"Just randomly digging?"

"Looks that way. I'm sure they'll increase security somehow—maybe add more cameras or something to catch whoever's doing this."

"Let's go find the others so we can head back," Tae-hyun said.

"They'll be looking at the water, I'd bet on it," I said.

SURE ENOUGH, MANTA WAS ON THE PHONE WHEN WE GOT to the hotel room. She had an empty milk bottle on a small table next to her chair, and a wrapper from a snack she'd eaten.

"Get everything fixed?" Hu Lin asked her.

"We're putting in more surveillance equipment," she said after ending her call.

"Where should we go now?" Gu Han asked.

"I've been here before. You choose," she rose from her seat. "Want a snack? We can get room service or go downstairs."

"I'd like a drink at the bar," Min-ho said.

"Then let's go downstairs and talk about where to go while doing that," Tae-hyun agreed.

"I'll take some tomato juice with lime, some olives and a celery stalk," Manta poked Tae-hyun's arm with a finger.

"Let's go."

"Is that as close to a bloody Mary as you can get?" I teased her in English.

"Yes, sadly enough."

"No, no, you have to speak Korean," Shi-joon said. "Not all of us are fluent in English."

Tae-hyun translated for him. "Four years training in the US at Johns Hopkins," he grinned. "Manta and I were in the same English language class in college. She was seventeen at the time and got me through the whole course. After that, my English was good enough and my grades were good enough to get me into Johns Hopkins' Orthopedic program."

"The Head of the English Language Department was one of the people who wouldn't let me test out of the classes," Manta explained. "For the first two years, anyway."

"Manta never spoke in class. I thought she was just really shy," Tae-hyun said. "One day we had a guest lecturer from the US. The Department Head told the class he'd take all of us out for a steak dinner if anyone could converse in English well enough to satisfy a famous American scholar like our guest.

"I really wanted that steak dinner, and there probably wasn't a student in the classroom who didn't want to show up the Department Head, but we were all too afraid to open our mouths. Manta asked me how bad I wanted steak. I told her I hadn't had steak in a long time.

"What would you like to talk about? Manta stood right up and asked the guest, in the best English I'd ever heard from a Korean.

"One of my specialties is American politics," the guest speaker replied. Well, we all thought we were dead in the water. Hardly any of us knew anything about American politics. Manta proved all of us wrong. They started talking about Richard Nixon, went into the rule of law, and I was completely lost after that. Manta not only held her own, she made the guest laugh several times. If I hadn't seen it myself, I wouldn't have believed it. We got Korean beef for dinner, and the guest spent most of the meal discussing politics and a lot of other things with Miss Manta."

"I still hear from him," Manta said. "He's the editor of a

big newspaper, now, and anytime there's anything in the news concerning Asia, I get an email."

"The Department Head changed his tune on letting Manta test out of English classes after that," Tae-hyun chuckled.

"I think it's because Dan Hillyard told him that most Americans couldn't discuss American politics on that level either," Manta smiled. "In English or Korean."

"Is she really that good?" Min-ho whispered to Hu Lin.

"Hmmph," Hu Lin replied.

"The Blue House has me on speed dial," Manta quipped.

Everybody laughed except Tae-hyun and Hu Lin.

Was this what Tae-hyun meant earlier—about Manta's outrageous truths? Was anybody on speed dial for the Blue House?

I wondered if Tae-hyun would tell me if I asked.

"Where are we going from here?" Tae-hyun changed the subject. He and Hu Lin offered several tourist attractions, including a fountain and several beaches.

"I would like to see a nice beach," Gu Han said. The others agreed.

"How about Gwangalli Beach?" Tae-hyun asked. "It has a view of Diamond Bridge, and the restaurant where we're going for dinner isn't far from there."

"I'll rent a beach chair," Manta said.

"I'll sit next to you and buy your drinks," Tae-hyun teased.

"I WASN'T EXPECTING THE WEATHER TO BE SO NICE," I SAID as several of us settled onto our rented beach chairs and watched the water wash up on the sand in front of us. The others had opted for a walk along the beach before getting a chair for the afternoon.

"Sixty-eight degrees. Perfect napping weather," Manta yawned as we made ourselves comfortable beneath a rented umbrella.

"What would you like to drink?" Hu Lin asked.

"Water," Manta said. "I've had too much other stuff already."

My phone rang; I looked at the caller ID. "Looks like the twins finally woke up," I said before answering the call.

"Where are you?" Si-woo demanded.

"Busan."

"Huh?"

"We went to Busan for the day. We'll be back tonight."

"We're hungry."

"Hold on." I covered the phone with my hand and looked at Manta. "They're hungry," I said, shaking my head.

"And they're telling you this because?" Manta asked.

"If I'm right, they blew all their money on alcohol the other night."

"Oh. Now I get it. Tell them to text me what they want and I'll have it delivered."

"Did you hear that? Manta will have food delivered if you tell her what you want."

"Hot pot," I heard Jun-woo in the background.

"Which restaurant?"

"Gong's," Si-woo said.

"All right. I'll text when it's on the way," Manta said.

"It'll be there soon; we'll let you know. Anything else?" I asked Si-woo.

"That's all for now."

"Good, because I'm hanging up."

"The unmitigated gall," Manta sighed in English.

"Tell me about it." I shoved my phone in a pocket. Manta scrolled through her own phone and made a call to Gong's. She ordered hotpot from Gong's and a bucket of chicken from a nearby restaurant, plus four bottles of beer.

"Maybe that will hold them until we get back," Manta said, before sending both online receipts to Si-woo.

"You're too generous," I said. "It wouldn't hurt them to starve a little after causing the team so much trouble."

"Then my suggestion is this; find another alternate to put on the payroll full time for a one-year contract, with the possibility of an extension. Make sure Team Owner explains that the twins' unreliability is the reason for hiring another alternate, not Min-ho's injury. If that doesn't make them start sweating, then they're impervious to job insecurity," Manta said.

"Have you ever run a business?" I asked her. "You're beginning to sound like my father."

Tae-hyun started laughing. Manta swatted his arm and told him to shut up.

"I'M GLAD WE'RE DRESSED WELL ENOUGH TO GET INTO THE restaurant," Gu Han said softly as we were led to a table later.

I wasn't sure we would have been, if Tae-hyun hadn't been with us. The host recognized him when we walked in and handed us off to an employee to get us seated immediately.

"What are you getting?" I asked Manta.

"King crab," she replied. "It's my favorite thing at this restaurant."

"They have king crab?" I didn't bother to open my menu.

"They do. It's amazing."

"What's good with it?"

"Anything they have."

The entire table ended up ordering king crab. As usual, Manta handed part of her order to Hu Lin and me. I hadn't had king crab since I left Boston, and I missed it.

An hour-and-a-half later, we were back at the airport to fly home. "Not a bad day," Gu Han sighed. "Better than what I had planned, for sure."

"I could get used to first class," Shi-joon admitted, when we were called to board first.

The others were tired but happy. I noticed Manta looked tired and haunted after she returned from the restroom.

"What happened to put that look on your face, baby girl?" I whispered next to her ear.

"Ancient history," she mumbled, dropping her eyes.

Rae-Rae

"What happened?" Hu Lin pulled me aside.

"They found the woman behind a restaurant. She'd been stabbed," I said.

"Dead?"

"Barely hanging on. She's our only lead at the moment," I said. "They've arrested her husband as the chief suspect. The last bit of information is this—the money from the sale of my mother's jewelry can't be found anywhere."

"The same MO as before?"

"Yes. If there's anything pointing to that man and his two bitches, it's this. We really need to find the surviving kidnap victim—if he's still alive."

"You think he is, don't you?"

"That's the only reason those three would come out of retirement, I think, if someone can still point a finger at them for those deaths—and ultimately for treason."

"They're calling for us to board," Tae-hyun approached us. "You'll have to finish your discussion later."

"Yeah," I said. "Let's go. I'm depressed enough for one night."

I walked onto the plane behind Tae-hyun with Hu Lin behind me and took my seat next to Hae Jin. "What can I do for you?" he leaned close to ask.

"Nothing, unless you can turn back time," I said.

"I'd do that for myself, too, if I could."

"Did you read the Lady of Shallot when you were in High School in the US?"

"I did."

"Have you ever had that feeling—as if you're viewing everything in a mirror and it's all shadowy and backward from what it should be?"

"Many times."

"That's how I feel too much of the time," I said.

"Stop fretting," he reached over and patted my hand. "Things will work out, I swear."

"I hope you're right."

"Yeah. Me, too."

HAE JIN

Manta talked with Hu Lin and Tae-hyun outside the building for a little while after we got back to headquarters while the rest of us went in to find our beds. I thought about staying with her but decided not to after Hu Lin gave me a small hand motion to go inside.

She was safe enough with her friends; I was tired and facing an early morning. When I closed my dorm room door behind me, and before I turned on the lights, I saw a faint glow coming from the box Grandpa had given me. Feeling my way along, I reached the carton and opened the flaps.

Inside, I found a small, white carving emanating the light I'd seen. Lifting it in my hands, I discovered Grandpa had given me a palm-sized carving of a white lotus blossom. It appeared to be jade, but in the near-dark, I couldn't say that for certain.

I'd never heard of authentic jade glowing in the dark, either, so there was a good chance it wasn't jade.

Using the carving to light my way, I walked to the side of my bed and turned on the table lamp. The carving was pure white and seemed to be a natural substance, but I wasn't an expert. The carving itself was quite fine, so I decided to put it on the bookshelf near the bed. Likely its only value to me was that it came from Grandpa.

I'll ask my cousin about it when I see him next time, I decided, before undressing and going to bed.

CHAPTER 12

Rae-Rae

"We found a tracker on the truck our agent drove from the groundskeeping service," Jin-won told me as I dressed to leave headquarters Thursday morning.

"Are you going through all those employees, now?" I asked.

"We are. Our surveillance team lost sight of the woman yesterday evening, somehow, and didn't catch up with her again until she'd already been stabbed."

"I have a request," I said. "Two, actually. First, find an excuse to transfer the woman to Ong Charities Hospital in Busan. Next, I want somebody to go over every inch of that yard with ground penetrating radar. I'll cover the cost."

"I'll get that started by this afternoon."

"Good. Keep me updated on the woman's condition and

let me know if anything else is found in that yard."

"We're working our way through the records of all prison employees surrounding our ultimate suspects," Jin-won told me. "The authorities wouldn't release video of the interactions between them and our targets. If there's anything in their employment information, we'll find it. I'll add two more NIS agents that I trust to the case, so we can get through this faster."

"Thank you."

I ended the call and headed for the door; I didn't want to make Hae Jin late for his Krav Maga lesson and I needed some time in the pool to think on these most recent events.

Hae Jin and I climbed into Hu Lin's SUV and buckled our seat belts.

"You heard from security, didn't you?"

"Yeah. Busan just got more complicated," I sighed as Hu Lin drove away from headquarters.

"Complicated?" Hae Jin asked.

"Since somebody attempted to dig up the yard, we decided to see whether there was actually something to find. Something may have come to light—we'll know more later," I said.

"It does sound complicated," Hae Jin agreed. "Now I'm curious. Will you keep me updated?"

"If possible."

Hae Jin

"Want to show us what you have?" I asked Hu Lin as he and Manta received their new ID cards identifying them as current members at the athletic club.

"Go ahead," Manta told him. "Nobody gets hurt, okay?" She pointed a finger at both of us.

"We got it," Hu Lin grinned.

"Right. I'm off to swim," she waved a hand and headed for the pool.

Hu Lin followed me to the gym where Trainer Park and I met for Krav Maga lessons. Trainer Park was excited about sparring with Hu Lin.

At first.

And then he got his ass handed to him and had to admit that somebody was actually better than he was.

"Thanks for the workout," Hu Lin told Trainer Park and me before heading for the showers. I finished cleaning up at roughly the same time, so we went to find Manta afterward.

"Get your thinking done?" Hu Lin asked her.

"Some of it," she said. "Enough for now, anyway. Tomorrow, I have to get my purple tips redone, so no swimming for me," she leaned around the edge of her seat to tell me.

"I can drive myself," I said. I didn't add that I'd miss our daily ride together.

But I *would* miss it.

Cousin Do-yoon called when I reached my dorm room. "What's up?" I asked in English.

"I'm being transferred to the Busan office," he told me. "Something weird is happening there, and I was specifically requested by a regional chief."

"Is it interesting work at least?"

"It's looking that way. I can't give you any information, but it's something I'd want to investigate if I were given the choice."

"Good for you. Will Grandpa be able to survive?"

"Mother will look after him," Do-yoon snorted. "He can always come for a visit if he wants, and it's a short flight if I get a day off."

"When are you leaving?"

"Tomorrow."

"Got time for dinner tonight?"

"Maybe."

"I'll send a text."

"Sounds good."

A tap sounded on my door. "Gotta go—somebody's at my door," I said. Do-yoon hung up. "It's open," I called out.

Gu Han walked in. "I have a question," he said.

"What's that?"

"Do you suppose Manta could get permission to play both Cloud Emperor and Cloud Empress?"

"LITTLE BROTHERS WOULD BE OVERJOYED," MANTA SAID. "But I'm the only one they'll allow to touch either of those characters."

"Not least because you designed them, eh?" Gu Han smiled at Manta.

"Something like that."

"How much practice might you need to play either or both?" I asked.

"Little to none. I know them inside and out."

"We have one more preseason game on Monday," Gu Han said. "We'll go with one of your previous avatars in that game, and then start the regular season in two weeks with your choice of one or the other against the Germans."

"A sound strategy," Manta agreed.

"Good. Let's get practice started, then," Gu Han said. "The Pandas will be tougher to beat than the Zebras," he added.

"I'll get the others down here," I said. "For now, let's keep this information between us."

"Agreed," Gu Han nodded.

"I'M HAVING DINNER TONIGHT WITH MY COUSIN, WHO'S being transferred to Busan tomorrow," I told Manta later. "Want to go? He doesn't like spicy, either."

"Don't you want to spend time together?"

"It won't hurt to have somebody else there to keep us in line."

"Oh. Is that what it's called?"

"If you don't want to," I said.

"No—I think I'd like to go. You know, to see if your family is like you," she pointed at me.

"Is that an insult?"

"No. You're just—wary of strangers, I think."

I didn't reply, but realized she was right. I didn't warm up to anyone right away—and never had. Not since I'd been kidnapped at eleven, anyway. "I am like that," I agreed. "Be ready to go at eight."

"Okay."

"Lee Do-yoon, this is Manta. Manta, this is my cousin, Lee Do-yoon."

Do-yoon bowed briefly to Manta, who did the same. Manta and I took our seats at Do-yoon's table but Do-yoon only took his eyes off Manta when I caught him staring.

We talked about things that didn't matter, mostly, including the cost of rent in Busan. Do-yoon said his company was paying his rent while he was on assignment there, effectively skirting the fact that he worked for the NIS.

He did say he worked in insurance fraud, though, which was one of his past jobs for the NIS.

"Not the most fun job, I imagine," Manta said.

"It can be rewarding, I guess," Do-yoon grinned. "Depending on who ends up on the winning side."

"True enough," Manta laughed.

After dinner, I waited with Do-yoon for his car at the valet station. Manta was going to drive my Jeep since I'd had two glasses of wine with my steak.

"I'll trade you," Do-yoon said out of the blue.

"Trade me what?"

"Jobs. You go to Busan and I'll work with Manta."

"No, thanks. I like where I am."

"All right. I'll remember you said that," he told me. His car arrived and he got in with a wave before driving off. I walked down the sidewalk where Manta waited for my Jeep.

"He won't be far away," Manta absently rubbed my back. I went still; I'd never allowed any woman to touch me like that.

I'll only allow it from this *woman*, I told myself, after realizing I liked her touch. "You're a safe driver?" I asked for perhaps the tenth time.

"I haven't had an accident yet—not when I was driving, anyway."

"Now I'm worried because you're due."

"Shut up. Don't jinx us."

The Jeep arrived; we got in and fastened seat belts. "You do remember how, don't you?" I teased.

"You're cruisin' for a bruisin'," she said in English, then put the Jeep in gear and drove away from the restaurant. I laughed.

Rae-Rae

"Wow, you're still in one piece," I blinked at Hae Jin after parking in the garage next to headquarters.

"Your driving is passable. Barely," he said.

"Right."

"I'll even let you drive again sometime."

"Damned by faint praise," I made a face at him.

"What other kind of praise is there?"

"Inconceivable."

"I can quote all of *The Princess Bride*, thank you."

"You think I can't?" I shot back.

"Maowwidge," he said. I had to stop walking I was laughing so hard. "Come on, baby girl," he said, lifting me in a fireman's carry and hauling me into the building. I laughed the whole way.

Hae Jin

Why hadn't I met Manta earlier? I asked myself. She was turning into a good friend, with the possibility of being more.

That thought no longer worried or frightened me. She'd laughed and slapped my back a couple of times while I carried her, which made me laugh, too.

After dropping her off in the kitchen, I'd gone upstairs to my dorm room to get ready for bed.

That's when Do-yoon called me. "Did you miss me already?" I teased.

"Hah," he said. "There's something that's bothering me," he went on. "Actually, it's not bothering me. And, since nobody has said anything about this to me, especially about keeping my mouth shut, I don't feel obligated to keep the information from you."

"What information is that?"

"Who Manta really is. Do you want to know?"

I went still. "Her best friend told me yesterday that if I worked at it, I could probably figure it out for myself."

"Well, that's true," Do-yoon agreed. "My question now is, why is she a member of your team? I'm guessing there's more to this than what's on the surface."

"What are you talking about?"

"The one other time that I'm aware of that she went undercover, it was to rescue a Chinese national from the tender clutches of a kidnapper in North Korea. At the time, I'd have said the guy was dead meat. She pulled off the impossible."

"Her friend told me about that, but he didn't give details," I said. "He also told me that anything she says that sounds outrageous could be true."

"Like what?"

"She joked that the Blue House has her on speed dial."

"Ah." I could envision Do-yoon wincing.

"The Blue House has her on speed dial?"

"I'd say that's true."

"Who the hell is she?"

"Do you think you can continue to treat her the same? This is important, Hae Jin."

"I'll treat her the same, I promise."

"Then keep your promise. She'll notice if you don't."

"Tell me who she is."

Still, Do-yoon hesitated for a moment. "Ong Rae-Rae," he breathed, as if the name held holy reverence. "I think it's a good thing your parents never show pictures of you, and that you go by Grandpa's last name," Do-yoon went on, while my brain and body turned numb. "She'd have known who you were immediately. She owns thirty percent of your father's company, you know."

"Why do you think she's here—on the team," I said, forcing my brain to work.

"Have you heard of all the hacking going on—of major corporations and governments worldwide? It's on the news," he said.

"I've heard a little," I hedged.

"I think it has to do with that. All those countries are stops for your tournaments. Last year, the tournaments and hackings occurred too close together to be coincidences. I'm telling you this in strict confidence, and it's not something you can share with anyone else."

"Is this why she was called to the Zebra's headquarters after they were hacked?" I asked.

"You were there?"

"I was in the building. I didn't see what she did."

"Then that confirms my thoughts on the matter. She's working this case undercover, probably at the request of the previously mentioned Blue House."

"Why would she be the one? How would she be the one to do this?"

"You probably don't know because it's not common knowledge, but Ong Rae-Rae built Sea Eagle Security and Osprey Technology and Robotics from the ground up. More than half the patents Osprey holds are for her personal designs. As for Sea Eagle, world governments contract with them to provide security measures. Now are you getting the big picture?"

"Damn, cousin, this is scary."

"Have you noticed anyone who hangs around there regularly? If so, then they're probably a personal bodyguard."

"Oh, my God," I said in English, pinching the bridge of my nose. *Hu Lin*. The friend who drove her to her swimming exercises. The one who went with her to Busan, along with his husband. Hu Lin was guarding Manta.

"You've noticed, haven't you?"

"He drives us to the athletic club and back. She introduced him as a friend."

"I've heard that—that her closest bodyguards are also good friends. Tonight was the first time I've been personally introduced to her, though. Probably a good thing, or her radar would have gone off immediately. She may have done a background check on me anyway, so she could already know I'm not just an employee of an insurance company."

"I'd say it's a good thing all around that neither of us has been introduced to her before," I muttered.

"I would love to work with her," Do-yoon admitted. "Can you imagine working next to somebody who's that capable and tech savvy?"

"I do work next to her," I growled.

"I hope you appreciate it," Do-yoon sighed. "I just want to know how she got that guy out of North Korea without causing an international incident."

"What do you suggest—since it appears she's working undercover on that hacking thing?"

"Try not to give her any grief," he said.

Where was your advice at the beginning? I found myself thinking. She really wouldn't think twice about leaving at the end of her contract. Min-ho's job had never been in danger. Not from her, anyway.

"Why don't more people recognize her?" I asked.

"She cut her hair, and dyed part of it purple—two things Rae-Rae would never do. I'll send a couple of photographs. She looks different, cousin."

My phone dinged as two photographs were texted to me. "Huh?" I breathed, looking at a woman in an aqua evening gown, her hair nearly to her waist. It was taken by a professional photographer, no doubt.

In the photograph, she was beautiful, and appeared taller

than she was. The other photograph was a shot of her as Chairman of Ong Group, opening a new factory.

"I can see why nobody would think it's her," I agreed as I studied her hair, pulled back as it was in an elaborate braid.

"Her hair is her signature," Do-yoon sighed. "I think she probably suffered when it was cut off like that. I have to finish packing; I'm leaving on the first flight out tomorrow morning. If you have questions, let me know."

"Okay. See ya."

The moment the call ended, I searched through my phone for the numbers Tae-hyun had given me. I wasn't sure I could treat Manta the same as before, so there was a way to get around that without implicating my cousin.

"Tae-hyun," I said when he answered the phone. "You said I could figure out who she is if I worked at it?"

"Did you work at it?"

"I guess I did."

"So you know, now."

"I guess I do."

"I'll tell her. She won't be upset. Just—keep this to yourself. By the way, Park Shi-joon already knows. Rae-Rae is the one who got his sister into Ong Children's. Her Chief of Security and his wife are taking care of Mai now."

I wanted to curse under my breath. Of course Shi-joon knew, and that upset me for some reason. "She appreciates your candor," Tae-hyun interrupted my thoughts. "I hope this doesn't drive a wedge between you."

"I don't want that, either," I confessed.

"I'll let her know you figured it out," Tae-hyun said. "It'll be okay."

Rae-Rae

"I was worried about him finding out at the end and getting upset," I admitted to Tae-hyun. "Is he?"

"Upset? I don't think so. He called me, I think, because he was worried you might be upset."

"I was wondering whether I should just tell him and ask him to keep it to himself. I mean, Shi-joon has known for a while."

"I told him that Shi-joon knew. I think he may have been upset that somebody else knew before he did."

"If that's the only reason, I can live with that. The only two I worry about on the team are the twins. They're trouble-makers, and it wouldn't surprise me if they sell the information if they learn of it."

"Have you discussed this with my husband?"

"I have. I thought he was going to march into headquarters and threaten them afterward."

"We both know Hu Lin likes to handle things head-on."

"Yes, we do know that. Isn't that why you married him?"

"Little Sister, where is your mind?" Tae-hyun laughed.

Hae Jin

"Where are you going to get your hair done?" I asked when Manta shuffled into the kitchen at five-thirty Friday morning.

"My hairdresser, who knows all and sees all," she replied.

"Do you think she can cut my hair? I've needed a haircut for two weeks."

"If you want. She's very talented—and close-mouthed."

"Even better. Usually when I go, I have people who stare," I said.

"No fun. If you want to try it, then you're welcome to come with me."

"Thank you. And uh, thanks—for not being upset about," I waved a hand.

"I was thinking about telling you, but I was worried you'd be upset that I waited until now," she said. "We're good."

"I sort of understand," I said.

"I'll take sort of."

"When are we leaving?"

"As soon as Hu Lin gets here. There he is," she said as Hu Lin's SUV pulled up outside.

"Your hairdresser works this early?"

"I'm the only one she gets up this early for. She gets paid well and gets off extra early every time."

"I feel privileged."

"Well, you should."

"I was teasing."

"Me, too."

We walked out of headquarters and loaded into the SUV. "He's getting a haircut," Manta told Hu Lin.

"Have you been to Ong Group's main headquarters before?" Hu Lin asked me.

"I haven't."

"We'll go in from Rae-Rae's private entrance."

"Somebody has a private entrance?" I pretended to be shocked.

"Shut up."

"Thiwat will likely be waiting to ambush you."

"Who's Thiwat?"

"My Chief Personal Assistant. He's Thai. We speak Thai most of the time. Will you feel left out or think we're discussing you? If so, we can do Korean or English, your choice."

"He knows about this?" I asked.

"Thiwat knows almost everything, as do my CEOs. Okay?"

"They have to know," Hu Lin said. "If they can't find Rae-Rae for any reason, they tend to panic. And then they call me. If I can't find Rae-Rae, we would all be in trouble."

"What would you do to them?" I frowned at Manta.

"Not me. President Pung Chung-hee."

I barked a laugh. Hu Lin shook his head. "You think she's

kidding. After President Pung has a fit, the American Secretary of State would have a heart attack."

"Why?"

"I don't want to talk about it," Manta said.

"Don't ruin her day," Hu Lin warned.

Forty minutes later, we pulled into a private entrance to an underground garage. "Have a guest today?" a guard asked as we stopped at a checkpoint.

"Yes, this is Lee Hae Jin," Manta introduced me.

"Nice to see you again, Chairman Ong," the guard tipped his hat.

"Good to see you, Kwang-sun," Manta told him. Kwang-sun grinned widely and waved us through.

"We just passed a test, didn't we?" I asked.

"I knew he was smart," Manta told Hu Lin. If she'd given anything except the guard's correct name, I had no doubt we'd be surrounded by security now.

Just as Hu Lin said, someone waited outside a hair salon in the basement of Ong Group, vibrating with impatience as we walked up.

"I have sixteen contracts for you to sign," the man Hu Lin identified as Thiwat spoke in Korean.

"Let me get in the chair and I'll look at all of them."

Thiwat relaxed a little when Manta took the handful of papers away from him and began reading while a middle-aged woman muttered over her hair.

"The hotel only knows enough to throw chlorine in the water," Manta sighed as the hairdresser started combing through her hair. "I did change my swimming location. That's one of the reasons."

Manta's hair was trimmed and then the tips were re-dyed while she signed all but one of the papers brought by her assistant. "I don't like conditions three and four on this one," she handed one back by itself. "The rest are good to go."

I think Thiwat was grateful only one contract didn't pass muster. He bowed to Manta and left.

Hu Lin's phone rang; he answered. "She's having her hair done," he told the caller. "Tell her what?"

"Who is it?" Manta asked.

"Zhang Bao."

"What does he say?"

"That the Chinese Undersecretary of Defense has left his post. Word has it he's headed to Korea."

"The absolute last thing I need," Manta complained. "Ask ZB to send particulars in an email if he has them."

Hu Lin passed on the message, then hung up.

"Uh, should I pretend I didn't hear that?" I asked, as the hairdresser pulled the cape off Manta and helped her out of the chair.

"It doesn't matter," Manta said, motioning for me to get into the chair next. "You'll only be more confused if I try to explain any of that."

"Just be aware that this man may be desperate—enough to try to grab Rae-Rae," Hu Lin said in English. "You're good enough at Krav Maga to stop that from happening, I think."

"Will you notify President Pung?"

"Already working on that," she said, sending a text on her phone. "The Undersecretary will be followed if he lands at the airport."

I settled onto the chair and a cape was draped over me and fastened at the neck. "Nice hair," the hairdresser said, as she ran her fingers through it. "Thick, too. Hard to cut?" she asked.

"Sometimes," I admitted.

"That's okay. How much off?"

"About here," I indicated a length just below my eyebrows using a finger.

"Okay."

"ZB says the Undersecretary left early this morning, according to his informant."

"It could take a little while to get here from Beijing."

"Then we'll hope for a short reprieve."

"Your hair looks great," Manta told me when the cape came off. The hairdresser had styled it for me, too, pushing it back and off my forehead.

"Do I pay for my cut?" I whispered to Manta when the hairdresser went to the back of the salon to get a broom.

"I've already paid for both of us and I always contribute to her kids' college funds on their birthdays," Manta said. "You're good to go."

"Thanks," I said.

"Want breakfast?" Hu Lin asked.

"He's hungry," Manta laughed. After thanking Manta's hairdresser, we left the salon and headed back to the parking garage.

"What do you want for breakfast?" Manta asked as we buckled into our seats in Hu Lin's SUV.

"I want rolled omelet," Hu Lin replied.

"Are there supplies at my house? Or your house?"

"Auntie Cheng will have what you need," Hu Lin said.

"I'll call and ask for whatever she has."

"We're going to Auntie Cheng's?" I asked.

"No, we're going to my place."

ANOTHER UNDERGROUND PARKING GARAGE AWAITED US, and I learned quickly that the building we'd parked under belonged to Manta. The elevator took us to the top floor and opened into the penthouse.

On our way to the kitchen, we passed a glass cabinet that held honors and awards. At the center was a large photograph of Manta. Or rather, Ong Rae-Rae. In her hands she held two Peace Prizes. On either side of the photograph were the cases containing the actual Peace Prizes themselves.

"Holy God," I breathed.

CHAPTER 13

H*ae Jin*

"The first Peace Prize was for bringing water to drought-ridden countries in the interior of Africa," Hu Lin explained while Manta put grilled pork and rolled omelets together. "It was a massive undertaking and had to have agreements with every country the pipeline passed through. Plus desalination plants in all of them."

"One country is growing fair trade crops with their share of the water," Manta said as she cracked eggs. "They weren't even a part of my original goal of providing potable water to the drought-ravaged, but they have forward-thinking people in charge of their government. It's amazing what can happen when their main objectives aren't greed and crime."

"The other Peace Prize is for the fifty-plus schools and hospitals Ong Charities has built in poor countries," Hu Lin went on. "They're training the next generation in those places to create better living conditions for future generations, and how to best use their resources to bring that about. Much of their educational focus is to train their own future teachers and doctors."

"You can't hand them a fish to feed themselves if they don't know how to cook it," Manta sighed. "They can't deal with the wide world when they don't know much about it."

"Or if they don't know how to make sushi," Hu Lin teased.

"Some of us don't eat raw fish," she shook a finger at him. "Here." She set plates of food in front of both of us. "Rolled omelets, just like you wanted."

One bite and I knew why Hu Lin wanted this for breakfast. It was good. We were even served vanilla lattes that Manta made for us with her own espresso machine.

"Tae-Hyun and I used to live in the building before we bought a house," Hu Lin said. "Half the time we'd be here for breakfast."

"You said you wanted a house," Manta pointed her chopsticks at Hu Lin.

"The house is wonderful. Having to cook breakfast ourselves isn't."

"You can hire somebody," Manta said.

"Who do you think we'd trust to do that? It's hard enough to find somebody decent to clean."

"They just have a hard time trusting people to invade their privacy," Manta sighed. "If Auntie Cheng didn't supervise the cleaning crew here, I'd feel the same."

"Find us another Auntie Cheng and we'll hire her. Or him."

"I'll add it to my to-do list."

"I'm kidding, Little Sister."

"Are you still building schools and hospitals?" I asked.

"Yes, but only two sets this year. Before we spend the money and effort, we have to make sure the area is stable enough. It would be an endless headache if we just dropped a school and a hospital into lands where warlords and dictators are fighting over territory. It wouldn't last five minutes, and these are teachers and medical professionals that we have to protect."

"Is there anything you can do in those places?"

"We partner with several organizations who go in to provide temporary care," Manta explained. "As for schooling, if the parents are fighting, there's not much chance of teaching the kids anything."

"You're talking places where they hand out guns to kids and train them to be guerrillas, aren't you?"

"Yes. It's horrific."

"Rae-Rae is a special ambassador to the UN, because she's been in too many of these places and had conversations with too many warlords and dictators," Hu Lin said. "The Security Council leans on her a lot."

"You're starting to scare me," I told her.

"It's just coincidental knowledge. I've talked to these people to try and find a way to compromise—to get medical care and food to their people. Most of the time, they can't come to an agreement on anything. If food and medical supplies are sent in, most of that disappears quickly, either sold off for money to buy guns or used for a warlord's own enrichment rather than the benefit of the general population."

I considered how the normal person on the street in any country I could name never even thought about this stuff. Many had no idea it even existed.

"People have their own worries," Manta almost read my mind. "They have their own kids to feed and their own bills to pay. The reason why I think about it is this—consider that the Earth is a single body. Consider that the body is fighting off infections, in the guise of wars, civil unrest, epidemics and genocide. If you don't try to take care of the entirety, soon enough the infections will take over the healthy parts, too. It's all connected."

"Except some people will argue until they die that it isn't true," I said.

"And then planes fly into buildings," Hu Lin shrugged. "That's when people discover that the world is getting smaller every day. Something that was a long way from you yesterday could be on your doorstep tomorrow."

"I think we've worried him enough, when he only came for a haircut and breakfast," Manta said. "Take a deep breath. In. Out. Clear your mind. We have imaginary swords to wield and imaginary characters to fight today."

We rode down the elevator in silence, then walked through the back door into the underground parking lot.

That's when Manta and Hu Lin grabbed my arms and jerked me back inside the building.

"Something's not right," Manta breathed, pulling out her cell phone and tapping a code into it. An image appeared on the phone screen, showing us the parking garage. I blinked—the image began to move, as if it were...

It was. The image was one shown to us by a flying drone. "There," Hu Lin pointed at Manta's screen. Three men crouched next to the guard's station just inside the entrance. The drone passed them unseen and flew inside the small kiosk itself.

"He's alive," Manta said as we saw the guard crumpled on the floor. "Police are on their way. What's your choice, Hu Lin?"

"Somebody could get hurt," Hu Lin muttered.

"Somebody already has. Jeong Gon's head is bleeding."

"Let's give them a rest, then."

"What?" I whispered. I was ignored. Then, I watched in shock as all three men fell over, as if they'd been hit by invisible gas.

"We have five minutes. Where are the police?" Manta asked as Hu Lin jerked the door open and ran through it.

"Two minutes," Hu Lin flung over a shoulder and sprinted toward the guard station. "I can't run," Manta told me. "If you want to help Hu Lin, go ahead."

I ran after Hu Lin, while Manta walked behind me. Hu Lin already had two culprits' wrists zip-tied by the time I arrived. He did the last one while I called an ambulance for the bleeding guard.

"NICE, THEY'RE SPEAKING RUSSIAN," MANTA SAID AS THE three men woke and began talking among themselves while the police investigated the scene and Jeong Gon had his head wrapped by paramedics.

"What are they saying?" I asked. "Are they Russian?"

"I doubt it—their Russian sucks. Accent sounds faintly Chinese. Oh, here's the NIS," she said as three agents drove up in a car and got out. "I'd send you back to headquarters, but they'll want to talk to all of us."

"What should I say?"

"Just answer questions honestly."

"Oh."

I shoved my hands in my jacket pockets. My left hand came in contact with something I hadn't put there. Drawing it out, I found the jade lotus flower I'd gotten from my grandfather in my hand.

Except it was now the size of a large marble and not glowing.

What the hell? I blinked at it for several seconds before putting it back. Too many strange things had happened in the space of half an hour and I had no explanation for any of it.

Not least of which was Manta handing a thirty-centimeter drone armed with tranquilizer darts to the NIS agents and showing them three spent tranquilizer darts supposedly pulled from the three culprits who'd attacked Guard Jeong.

My cell phone rang; Gu Han was calling. "We're answering questions for the police," I said truthfully. "Someone got attacked and we're witnesses. We'll explain when we get there."

"I'll let the others do speed drills," Gu Han said and hung up.

"Did you see the drone fire the darts?" One of the NIS agents came to me and asked.

"It all happened so fast," I said. "I really didn't."

"Not surprising. Chairman Ong says this is new technology," he explained.

"Well, I've never seen it before," I agreed. Nearby, Hu Lin struggled to hide a smile.

"Baby girl, you look pale," I said after Hu Lin dropped us off outside headquarters.

"I feel that way, too. I hope the twins didn't drink all the milk. I need something."

"Let's go find out. I'll order some if they did."

They hadn't, so I poured a glass of milk for Manta and watched while she drank it. It was nearly lunchtime anyway, and I'd ask Gu Han to give her a break until our afternoon session.

"She just got upset—probably by all the blood. They hit the guy on the head," I improvised to the rest of the team while Manta went upstairs to lie down for a little while. "Then, the police came and asked us what we saw, so that took a while."

"Is the guard okay?" Shi-joon asked.

"He went to the hospital," I said. "The three who attacked him were sent to jail."

"Nothing exciting like that ever happens when we get our hair cut," Jun-woo complained.

"Like you'd know what to do if it did," Min-ho countered.

"Stop arguing," Gu Han ordered. "I want to remind all of you that the fashion photographs will be taken next Wednesday, so get your outfits ready or be prepared to wear what they find for you to wear."

"Time to get the tux out?" Shi-joon teased me.

"Only if you're getting yours out, too. I hate those things."

"I remember. They stuck you in one last year anyway."

"If I ever see another contract that gives free reign to promote my person in images, etc., I will remove that with an indelible marker."

"I guess this is why Manta wanted to get her purple redone now," Shi-joon said.

"Now that you mention it, it makes sense. If she hadn't said something I would probably have gone without a haircut," I admitted. "I'd put those pictures right out of my mind."

"I have an appointment on Monday," Shi-joon said. "Dr. Oh is ah, choosing my outfit."

"He wants his honey to look good," I leaned in close to Shi-joon's ear to whisper. Shi-joon blushed deeply. "I know who Manta is," I added. "She knows I know, so you don't have to be secretive with me."

"Thank goodness," he sighed. "I thought I would freak at first, being the only one."

"Don't freak," I said, patting his shoulder and moving away. "I don't need a player freaking for any reason. Okay?"

"You didn't freak?"

"Maybe at first. I've had bigger freak-outs since then, I promise." Not least of those was a jade-like carving that appeared to shrink at will—and glow and not glow at will.

Don't forget the relocation at will, I reminded myself. I hadn't put that thing in my pocket.

No. Way.

I'd taken my jacket off earlier and left it in my room. The marble-sized lotus carving was now in my pants pocket.

I hadn't put it there, either.

I was beginning to wonder if the thing was something Grandpa had given me, or if it was something that merely showed up in a convenient place. It was certainly doing its best to follow me around, now.

Your duty is to protect the Lotus, breathed into my mind.

I was supposed to protect a marble?

The human Lotus, it corrected me. Manta's image swam into my mind, stilling my breath.

Now you know. Do not willfully fail in your duty, as the last one who carried me did.

"Hae Jin? You okay?" Shi-joon waved a hand in front of my face.

"Oh. Sorry. I was lost in uh, thought," I said. *I was busy talking to a marble*, I added mentally.

I am the Companion Stone, sometimes called the White Flower, it sounded offended.

Right. Companion Stone. Why me?

Because you are the one the Lotus needs.

Rae-Rae

"We think there may have been a body buried there at one time, but it appears it was removed and a flower bed installed," Jin-won informed me. "Two finger bones were found, one with a ring on it. Things like that can get missed, especially if the site is dug up at night."

"Can you get DNA or anything from it to make an identification?" I asked.

"We're working on it now. We also found one other cache of jewelry, but there were only a few things in the ceramic container."

"Ceramic container?"

"A teapot," Jin-won said. "A Japanese piece, I think, from the occupation."

"Sounds right, if we're talking about my stepfather and his family. They cozied up to the Japanese during that time."

"I'll send photos of what was inside it—the pieces may be older than what your mother had, I think."

"So it could have been there for a while?"

"It's possible."

"You know if you try to point at the three in jail and say they murdered somebody, buried the body in the yard and then moved it, they'll pin the blame on my stepfather, since he's dead and can't deny it. We both know he wasn't smart enough to kill anyone himself. He relied on someone else to do the dirty work and preferred they leave him out of the loop. Plausible deniability, you know."

"Until he's dead and becomes the scapegoat," Jin-won agreed.

"Yes."

"Have you told your little brother?"

"Not yet. I don't want to worry him unnecessarily. He had nothing to do with any of this, that much is certain."

"I agree. And as of now, the fewer people who know, the better."

"How's the woman?"

"Improving some at Ong Charities' Hospital."

"Good. I really want to hear what she has to say about all this."

"If the ones behind this are who we believe, the moment she wakes up she'll be in terrible danger."

"I know. We may have to move her again if that happens. What about her husband?"

"Not talking. We're going through his residence and dry-cleaning business looking for evidence, but so far we've uncovered nothing, including any of the money she got from the sale of jewelry."

"Or any other jewelry, I suppose," I said dryly. "Does he own any other property, or does anybody he's related to or is friends with own other property? There has to be something somewhere."

"We'll check everything. I'll get my two new employees to start working on that end of things."

"Keep me posted, all right? I want to know about it, no matter how remote the possibility. We're missing something, I swear. Do you have the logs from before she sold the last batch? I want to know if she even stopped at a gas station to use the restroom."

"I'll send those to you tonight."

"All right. Thank you."

"Manta?" Hae Jin tapped on my dorm room door. "Food is here."

"On my way." The last thing I wanted was to eat right then, but I had to or I'd collapse during afternoon training.

"Did you not rest?" Hae Jin frowned at me when I opened the door.

"Phone calls," I mumbled. "What's for lunch?"

"I ordered chicken-rice soup for you."

"Thank you. I don't think I can handle more than that."

"Upset stomach?"

"It's on the sour side."

"Hu Lin texted me and said you need to eat something. He said bland is best."

"He's texting *you*, now? Do I need to separate you two or something?"

"Come on. Just eat slowly. Okay?"

MANTA FORCED HERSELF THROUGH AFTERNOON PRACTICE, although Gu Han and Min-ho kept an eye on her. Even when she didn't feel well, she managed to beat the twins in a practice game.

Twice.

When Gu Han stopped practice for a dinner break, that's when she started vomiting. At least she made it to the downstairs toilet before anything came up.

I sent a flurry of texts to Hu Lin, who mobilized immediately and was on his way to pick her up.

"Her friend says she needs fluids, so he's picking her up to take her to the hospital," I told Gu Han. "I'll go with her," I added when Min-ho opened his mouth to say the same thing.

"Come on, baby girl, just walk out the door with me," I

coaxed as I helped her up from the floor of the toilet. "Hu Lin is waiting for us."

What happened once we were out the door shocked me; Hu Lin lifted her in his arms and ran toward the SUV's back door. "Drive," he snapped at me as he loaded Manta into the SUV and got in beside her.

By the time I was in the driver's seat and had my seatbelt buckled, Hu Lin was already on the phone with Tae-hyun, giving him Manta's temperature and other vitals.

"Little Sister, do you have a headache?" Hu Lin asked. He had to lean in to hear Manta's reply. "She says a headache started about an hour ago," Hu Lin answered Tae-hyun's question.

"Tell Hae Jin to drive at best possible speed before it gets worse."

"Where are we going?" I asked.

"Ong Charities Hospital. Do you know where that is?"

"Yeah. I do." I switched lanes and picked up speed to get there.

"MIGRAINE," HU LIN EXPLAINED ONCE MANTA WAS hurried to a private room and hooked up to an IV. A drug was administered quickly once that happened, and they worried electrolytes into her.

"Does this happen often?" I asked.

"No. The attack on the guard this morning was probably the last domino in a full set that was making her anxious," Tae-hyun arrived and rubbed Hu Lin's back gently. "There are some things happening that go back to a trauma experienced in her childhood. Anything to do with that—and the ones who caused it, can bring on a migraine."

"Can I sit with her?"

"Yes. She trusts you. If she didn't, you'd never have seen the inside of her kitchen."

Two more guards showed up who I didn't recognize, but Hu Lin did. He stationed both outside Manta's door, then followed me inside her room.

"Tae-hyun gave her a sedative, so she can sleep while the medication works," Hu Lin told me. "If you need to go back at any time, let me know. I'll have someone drive you."

"I'll stay."

"She'll be here all night."

"I'll stay."

"All right."

I texted Gu Han, letting him know that Manta had a migraine and would be getting fluids and medication during the night. He texted back, telling me to keep him posted about her status.

Then, the text from Do-yoon came. *I've seen part of THE FILE*, he wrote in English. *I can't tell you anything or I'll lose my job. All I can say is STAY CLOSE TO MANTA. You could be in danger if you don't.*

My hands shook as I pocketed my cell phone after reading

the message. *Stay close to Manta*, he'd said. *You could be in danger if you don't*. No doubt it was because she was always guarded.

What the hell was going on?

My kidnappers are still out there, I reminded myself. *Have they found me? Were those men who attacked the guard this morning coming after Manta—or after me?*

"Baby girl," I murmured, reaching out and taking Manta's left hand. The IV was in her right, and I didn't want to touch that. Instead, I leaned in to kiss her free hand before setting it down gently and patting it. *Thank you for protecting me*, I told her silently. *You and Hu Lin*.

RAE-RAE

"How's the headache?" Tae-hyun stood over me at daylight the following morning.

"Have you had any sleep?" I squinted up at him.

"I got some sleep in my office. Hu Lin is still there on my sleeper sofa. Man-sik is here, and Hae Jin is asleep on your sofa. How's your headache?" he repeated.

"Not there," I sighed. "Thank you for knocking it out so fast."

"Good. I'll have someone bring breakfast."

"I feel empty," I confirmed.

"As long as it's not nausea, I'm happy."

"Ask them to bring breakfast for Hae Jin, too."

"I will. He can have coffee. You can't."

"You're no fun."

"You can have coffee tomorrow if the headache is completely gone."

"Thanks. Swimming tomorrow, too?"

"If the headache is gone. Just take it easy today. Nap or read. And eat."

"You're letting me go home?"

"If you eat your breakfast."

"She'll eat her breakfast," Hae Jin came to stand beside Tae-hyun, arms crossed and wearing a stern expression. "I hesitate to take her back to headquarters, though."

"Then take her to her place. Auntie Cheng will make sure she eats."

"Will Gu Han let you off? You can't have slept that well on a sofa," I said, frowning at Hae Jin.

"I'll find out," he shrugged.

HAE JIN

"Two of her friends will make sure nothing happens," I reassured Gu Han. "I just want a comfortable bed in a quiet place. Who sleeps at hospitals anyway?"

"Shi-joon is saying the same thing," Gu Han admitted. "Go ahead—get some sleep but I want both of you here tomorrow, ready to practice for this last preseason game."

"Don't worry," I said. "We'll be rested and ready to go."

HU LIN DROVE US BACK TO MANTA'S BUILDING. AT LEAST the crime tape was down and two guards manned the kiosk this time. We parked and entered the building without incident, and I met Auntie Cheng for the first time when we arrived in Manta's penthouse home.

"There are three other bedrooms on this level," Auntie Cheng told me. "You can take your pick. Rae-Rae's is down the hall from the kitchen; the other three are to the left of the elevator. The main house is one floor down, if you need more room."

"Main house?"

"This is basically the attic," Manta gave me a tired smile. "There's a greenhouse and a lawn to the right of the elevator, we just haven't shown it to you yet. I live up here because the main house is too much for just one person. Go to bed, Hae Jin. Auntie Cheng will show you the way and find pajamas for you if you want. I'm having a glass of milk and then lying down."

Auntie Cheng was a slender, half-Chinese, half-Korean woman with slightly graying hair and a no-nonsense attitude for the most part. She'd already sent her husband out to find pajamas and a fresh set of clothing for me; they were waiting in the bedroom she led me to.

"This is nice," I told her, taking in the large bedroom with an attached library.

"We keep these clean and ready to go; sometimes Hu Lin and Tae-hyun stay here after they've had dinner and too much to drink. The other bedroom down this hall used to be mine, before I married Man-sik and moved down a few floors."

"How's Mai?" I asked. "I heard she's staying with you and your husband."

"She's fine. Still reluctant to talk much with the psychologist, but that's a lot of trauma to deal with, I think. We're hoping things improve as time goes by."

"What about the ah," I hesitated.

"Still on the run. For now, Shi-joon has custody, since neither parent is fit to raise dogs, let alone children. The mother has already signed away her rights, and it looks like she may be in jail for a few years. They found evidence that she was helping her husband with his drug dealing, too."

"That's horrible. Thank you for helping Shi-joon and Mai."

"It's no trouble. We will keep Mai as long as Shi-joon lets us keep her. We don't have any children and at our age, it won't happen unless we adopt. This is like a dream for us—to have a child in the house."

"The one big piece of luck in this whole, sorry mess," I said. "Thank you for that."

"I want to thank you, too," she said, looking me in the eye. "For watching out for Rae-Rae. That eases my mind a lot."

"She has a way of growing on people," I said. "At the beginning, I would have said it was impossible."

"For you or for the team?"

"For both. I don't have women friends."

"Hmmph. Just one look at you and I can see why. I'll bet they pester you to death. Don't they?"

"You're very shrewd," I said. "Most of the time, I can see what they want from meters away and I just want to run."

"You found out Rae-Rae isn't like that, didn't you? Looks don't mean anything to her. It's what's in here," she patted her forehead, "and here," she patted her chest, "that counts with her."

"I did find that out. Most women are annoyingly obsequious. She let me know right away that she doesn't treat people that way."

"That's my girl," Auntie Cheng snorted a laugh. "If I could choose my first child, it would be her. My second would be Mai. It's funny how they came to me when I needed them."

"It may have been the other way around," I said, smiling at Auntie Cheng. I could understand why people spoke so highly of her, and it wasn't just for her cooking.

"Go to bed, you look exhausted," Auntie Cheng shooed me inside the bedroom and shut the door. I decided that I was officially an Auntie Cheng fan, too.

I EXPLORED THE LIBRARY INSIDE THE BEDROOM SUITE, which held a complete set of a popular web comic in paperback. The books had been published over a period of fifteen years, by an anonymous author.

I'd read the first five, but school had interfered with reading for pleasure, so I hadn't read anything past that. Here was an opportunity to catch up a little and read myself to sleep at the same time. Taking book six off the shelf, I set it on the bed, went into the spacious bathroom to take a shower and dress in pajamas, then settled on the bed to read.

Rae-Rae

I slept for several hours and felt hungry when I woke up. When I wandered into the kitchen, I found soup in a Thermos, plus egg foo young and broccoli with beef in the warming oven. Rice was ready in the rice cooker.

"Is that food I smell?" Hae Jin, wearing sweatpants, a T-shirt and a pair of borrowed slippers, came scuffling into the kitchen. At least he looked somewhat rested.

"Yes. Auntie Cheng left us all kinds of food. Soup is in the Thermos and the rest is in the warming oven and rice cooker. Help yourself."

"This is so good," Hae Jin stuffed broccoli beef and rice into his mouth.

"I love Auntie Cheng's broccoli beef," I sighed.

"It's my favorite. Oh, can I borrow some of the books in the bedroom bookcase?"

"You can have them," I said.

"But I don't want to bust up the set of *Dare Me*."

"Don't worry about it. Just take what you want."

"Remember, you said it," he shook a finger at me. "I had the hardest time getting the first five in the States. By the time I started reading them, all I could get was the Korean versions from my little brother, and then I only got the first five."

"You want the English versions?"

"I read in English most of the time—it's what I've done since fifth grade."

"I'll find you the English translations of books six through twenty-two," I said, nibbling on my last bite of egg foo young.

"I'd eventually like the entire set in English."

"I'll get it for you."

"What are you planning to wear for the fashion photo shoot?" he asked.

"That. Can they skip me and just let Min-ho do it?"

"Min-ho will be in it anyway, as an alternate this year. As a member of the main team, you have to do the photos. It's part of your contract."

"Which I still haven't seen," I complained. "Zhang Bao is in deep trouble when I see him next time."

"Is Zhang Bao the one who got you into gaming?"

"Yes." I made a face and slumped in my seat. Hae Jin laughed.

"Where's your closet? I'll help pick something out that won't look like a circus outfit provided by the photographer and his stylist," he added.

"Oh, crap, does that happen?"

"Have you looked at any of the past years' photoshoots?"

"No. I didn't think that was necessary."

"Come on, show me your closet."

"But what if I hate what you pick?"

"Then tell me you hate it. I promise to take that into consideration."

"Fine."

CHAPTER 14

H*ae Jin*

"This is amazing." I held up a floor-length aqua silk gown.

"I wore that to a charity ball two years ago. People will recognize it."

"Then show me what you haven't worn."

"Fine. That stuff is in the closet on the other side."

"Why didn't we start there?" I demanded.

"You said you wanted to see my closet. This is the one I use all the time."

We walked across the hall into what should have been the man's closet. It was smaller, that's how I knew. Several things hung from the rails, most of which were draped in plastic to keep them dust-free.

"What's this?" I pointed to something that appeared to be in parts or layers.

"That's a Chinese-designed gown, with a silk organza kimono to go over it," Manta explained.

"I want to see you in it. Don't argue—it has your signature purple as a base color."

"How do you know so much about this stuff?" she demanded.

"My roommate in undergrad was in fashion design. He's working with a big-name designer right now."

"And you survived that without being turned into a model?"

"Actually," I rubbed the back of my neck. "He was pissed because I went into the MBA program at Harvard rather than signing up to work professionally as a model. If I'd told my dad I wanted to do that, he'd have flown to the States the next day and personally whacked me."

"See, my advice to stop being handsome still stands."

"Do you want me to stop being handsome?"

"Not particularly."

"Then stop giving me that advice."

"Fine."

"Put this dress on." I peeled it off the hanger and handed it to her.

"Fine."

"Baby girl, I don't know what you've been saving that dress for, but it's stunning," I told her as she modeled it for me. "Wear that, please. If you don't buy extras of the pictures, then I'll buy them."

"I don't want this to be the only choice," she made a face at me.

"Then I'll find something edgy but casual, that shows you're a gamer," I said. "Got any ripped jeans and designer T-shirts?"

"Seriously? Ripped clothing?"

"What size do you wear? We can order from a department store and have it delivered to headquarters."

"I have to buy from the teen section," she mumbled.

"Then we'll look at what they have." I pulled out my phone and started scrolling through a popular local website to buy clothing.

"No ball caps," Manta complained as my fingers hovered over a black cap with a popular logo.

"And you called me a *kkondae*," I complained. "All right, no ball caps," I agreed after she shot me an accusing look. I ended up buying a pair of black ripped jeans with a purple half-T-shirt that would look adorable on her. "You can wear this outfit with your black and purple Brooks."

"Thank goodness something I have already passes muster," she complained.

"That Chinese dress is amazing," I said. "You already had that, too."

"Are we done, then? What are you wearing? Please say

you'll wear a black turtleneck sweater and do your hair like it was done yesterday."

"I can do both those things—if it makes you happy."

"I'll be happy."

"Good."

"Fine."

"Are you hungry?"

"I was thinking about dinner."

"Good. I want dumplings."

"I love dumplings. Where can we get some?"

"I know a place but I don't have a car."

"I have a car."

"Let's go. I'll drive."

"Should I change?"

"You look fine."

"Then it's on you if you're embarrassed to be seen with me."

"Same."

"These are good," Manta sighed before biting into a second dumpling.

"Min-ho brought me here not long after I joined the team. These are our favorites."

"Will he be upset that we came without him?"

"It would be easier if we just don't tell him."

"Tell him what?"

"Exactly."

Before we finished eating, Manta called Hu Lin. "Want dumplings?" she asked.

"We need three orders of dumplings to go," she said after ending the call. "He was just thinking about what to do for dinner. You don't mind dropping them off at their house, do you?"

"I don't mind," I said. I didn't add that I enjoyed her company, and driving let us talk longer without too many distractions.

Once we had the dumplings bagged up and were back in the car, Manta sent me toward the same addition where my parents had lived their entire married life together. It turned out that Tae-hyun and Hu Lin lived just a quarter of a kilometer away from my parents.

I didn't tell Manta that, however. She knew my parents, and they knew her. And, as Do-yoon had said, Rae-Rae owned thirty percent of the stock in my father's company. I decided to ask him about it the next time I had dinner at home.

"Nice house," I said as we pulled into the driveway.

"Tae-hyun used to drive by this house and dream of owning it someday. After he and Hu Lin got married, they bought it," Manta told me. "Want to go in or just drop off food and go?"

Hu Lin walked out the front door when Manta spoke. "Let them eat in privacy," I said. "You should go home and rest some more."

"Thanks for the food," Hu Lin grinned as Manta passed the bag out the passenger-side window.

"Good dumplings," she said. "I think you'll want to go back."

"Then we'll all go together," Hu Lin said.

We left when Hu Lin carried the food in the house. Manta leaned back in her seat with a sigh.

"Tired or happy?" I asked.

"Both."

I thought about telling her that this was the first time I'd ever been out with a woman who I felt comfortable with—one that I actually wanted to be with.

"Thank you for taking me out of the house," she said while my thoughts chased one another. "Usually, I lock myself in and become a hermit—or that's what Tae-hyun says, anyway."

"There's something we should consider, as much as I dislike it," I said.

"What's that?"

"We left headquarters together. If we go back together, then the twins won't let it go."

"I hate rerouting my life because of those two miscreants," Manta said flatly.

"Same here, but they have access to the Internet and don't use the privilege wisely."

"True. And if they ever figure out who I am, things could go sideways fast, as far as public scrutiny goes."

My parents wouldn't mind a bit if I were caught in any sort of scandal with Ong Rae-Rae, real or otherwise, I reminded myself. *Would I mind?* I asked myself instead.

Maybe.

Maybe not.

"Why don't you drive this thing back to headquarters tonight, and say you borrowed it from a friend?" Manta said. "The twins may ask where this vehicle came from, and if they find out it's mine, they'll start speculating immediately."

"I can work that out and say it belongs to my cousin," I agreed. "Since he's out of town, he won't need his car. He wouldn't mind owning a Cadillac XT5, even if it is white."

"What color does he prefer?"

"Red."

"Of course. Just leave it parked next to your Jeep and give Hu Lin the keys. He'll get everything back where it belongs."

Manta's phone rang. She studied her phone before answering. "Jin-won?" she said, then listened carefully to what the caller told her.

"All right. Thank you for the information," Manta said after only a few minutes. "If anything new develops, please let me know."

"Who is Jin-won?" I asked while a wave of jealousy threatened.

"The guy who's in charge of security in Busan. While they were figuring out why somebody was digging in the yard of Little Brother's house, they found two finger bones. One had a ring on it. They've determined that the bones were that of a female who disappeared around 1922 in that neighborhood, and the teapot with the jewelry they found not far from the bones are from that same era. They figure it happened during the Japanese occupation of Korea. It *is* known that the people living in the house at that time were *chinilpa*—Koreans collaborating with the Japanese during the occupation."

"That's crazy," I said. "Somebody was digging for that? How did they even know it was there?"

"Oh, they weren't looking for that."

"What were they looking for?"

"Some of my mother's jewelry, which was stolen after she died."

"Did they find it?"

"No, but Jin-won and I did. The NIS has it now."

"This—this is the riddle you said you were trying to solve, isn't it?"

"You remembered? Good job."

"Why did you turn it over to the NIS? Shouldn't you hand it to the local police instead?"

"Well, at the moment this is speculation. How good are you at keeping secrets, Hae Jin?"

"I'd say I'm one of the best."

"Awesome. When I was nineteen, I was stabbed by the woman in charge of that house and her sister, when they found out they couldn't get their hands on the money left to me by my maternal grandparents. Actually, that money was the only reason I lived as long as I had back then.

"Those two venomous spiders and the criminal jackass CEO of Ong Group at the time who pulled their web strings to get them to do his bidding, were eventually thrown in jail for that crime and for others they'd committed. The crime I want to keep them in jail for forever until their bones are nothing but dust, is that of the kidnapping and murder of four teens from wealthy families.

"For that crime, there has never been a single shred of evidence found. I haven't stopped looking for that evidence even a second since I was ten years old. I *know* they're the ones behind it, I just can't hand over physical evidence."

By the time I knew she was talking about the kidnappings —of which I was the last victim—I'd pulled over and stopped the SUV to listen.

"How do you know they're the ones," I demanded, sounding nearly breathless.

"Because there was a fifth victim."

"Huh?"

"This is the secret you need to keep, Hae Jin. Wherever he is, his life is in danger. I'd bet nearly everything I have that they've figured out he's still alive and can possibly identify them. If they're not hunting him down already, then they will be soon."

"*How do you know* there's a fifth victim?" I demanded.

"Because I pulled him away from those two bitches and got him out of Busan on a train to Seoul, that's how. He was tied up and gagged in the attic of that same house in Busan. You cannot say this to anyone else. I think only three people at the NIS are even allowed to know this right now."

"Why don't you know his name?"

"I refused to let him tell me. It was too dangerous. Both our lives hung in the balance that night, plus I had to live with those bitches. I hoped he could get away and live a decent life. Back then, I couldn't have guaranteed my survival from one day to the next."

"Did you give him any clues at all? If he wanted to find you?"

"I gave him half the train ticket I bought."

"What about the security cameras on the train?"

"By the time I hacked into the system, they'd already taken and likely destroyed those images."

"Where's the other half of the train ticket?"

"In a file with the NIS."

Damn, I thought to myself while Manta tapped on her phone.

"See—here's a copy of my half, front and back. Look at the date."

My hands shook as I took the phone from her. Just as she'd said, the date on the ticket matched that on my half.

On the back, though, was what made my breath catch and my heart stop for several seconds.

The straight and curved lines on the back half of my ticket would no doubt line up perfectly. She'd written her name vertically in English. It read:

Ong

Rae-

Rae

"Do you have photographs of those women?" I asked when my breathing returned to normal.

"Here. They're on the Internet, too, you only need their names."

Go Ha-eun and Go Ah-eun, dressed in prison garb, stared back at me from those photographs. They'd aged nearly twenty years since I'd seen them last. I'd never known who they were before. "What about their mastermind?" I asked.

"Kang Dong-hyung," she said, pulling up a recent photo. "Currently serving a life sentence for multiple murders, graft, bribery, theft, you name it. I want him to have those kidnappings and murders added to his list of crimes, though. If we don't find evidence to tie those bitches to those crimes, they'll get out in about two years. I think that's why they're desperate to find that last victim and get rid of him—before he realizes he's in trouble."

My mind raced—I wanted to speak with Grandpa. I wanted to talk to Do-yoon. And then I wanted to talk to my parents, but how and what would I say to them?

"I ought to get back to headquarters," I said, putting the SUV in gear and pulling onto the street again.

"You probably do. It's nearly eight, and the twins will be having a gossip fest if you don't show up soon."

"When will you get back?" I asked, as if my life hadn't turned upside down in the space of ten minutes or less.

"I'll see you at the athletic club tomorrow morning. Hu Lin will drop me off afterward."

"What about that Undersecretary guy?"

"No word on him. I figure his cronies in North Korea may have given him a free pass through their territory. He could show up here any time, although he'll probably be forced to get a guide by that time."

"Why does he need a guide?" I asked.

The jade carving in my pocket answered. *Because he has harmed the Lotus and continues to be a threat. We have punished him with blindness.*

What about those two women who stabbed her, then? I asked.

They do not know what she is. This one knew and brought harm anyway.

So anybody can harm her, as long as they don't know?

We must consider this.

Please do.

"He's going blind," Manta answered my question after much consideration. "But that's not your worry."

The hell it's not. "Do you think those three who attacked your guard yesterday were sent by him?"

"He has connections everywhere, legitimate or not."

"Does he have connections to those people who stabbed you?"

"Now that's an interesting thought." Manta lifted her phone and began tapping again.

"What are you doing?"

"Checking to see whether he's had an influx of money lately."

"Can you do that?"

"Not legally."

"I don't want to hear that."

"Hear what?"

"Nothing. I heard nothing."

"You're too cute for your own good. Here's my take on the whole thing. If somebody is coming after me with ill intentions, I will do whatever it takes to stop them. Wouldn't you?"

"Can't you call the police?"

"And tell them what—that the Chinese Undersecretary of Defense has it in for me and may be traveling through North Korea to do it?"

"Well, that does sound far-fetched."

"So you don't believe me either?"

"No—I believe you," I said. *Mostly because a jade carving keeps showing up in my pocket, lighting up whenever it feels like it and changing sizes to suit itself.*

Oh, and did I forget that it talks telepathically, too?

"Here's your building," I said.

"Don't bother going into the underground parking area. Just let me out by the front door. I'll be okay once I'm inside."

"Baby girl," I started to argue.

"Really, I'll be fine. Just let me out at the front door, then go straight to headquarters, okay?"

There is no danger close by at this time, the carving informed me.

"Fine." I drove into the half-circle drive in front of the building and stopped to let Manta out.

"See you tomorrow morning," she said, gathering her purse and phone before letting herself out of the SUV.

I watched her walk through the front door of the building after tapping on her phone for a moment. She had an electronic code to enter the place. I wondered if she'd trust me enough to let me have a code, too.

Hauling out my phone, I told it to call Do-yoon.

"Calling Lee Do-yoon," the SUV informed me, making me jump. "You are on a secure call to NIS Agent Lee Do-yoon. Connecting now."

"What the hell?" I muttered.

"You are on a secure network. Your call cannot be tapped while inside this vehicle," the SUV answered me.

"Like my phone could be tapped," I scoffed.

"Your phone has been compromised," the SUV said. "We suggest you either have it debugged or get a new one. Contact Chairman Ong for further details."

"Hae Jin?" Do-yoon's voice came over the vehicle's sound system.

"Do-yoon, my phone has been tapped, first off. Second, I found out who saved me when I was kidnapped. Don't worry, I'm driving Chairman Ong's SUV and it has a secure phone line so I can talk to you."

"Who saved you? It was Ong Rae-Rae, wasn't it?"

"How did you know?"

"She has too much information on the fifth victim for it to be otherwise. I read it in the file."

"She told me some other stuff that's happening in Busan—at the house where she used to live, I think."

"That's the case I'm currently working," Do-yoon admitted. "I can't tell you anything, though. Sounds like Chairman Ong told you plenty."

"I know more than I did."

"Did you tell her who you are—really?"

"No. She doesn't know that I'm a Sang, or the fifth victim. I was too terrified to tell her. She did say that the fifth victim is probably in danger because there's activity with the people whom she suspects of the kidnappings, although they're in jail."

"We are trying to verify that."

"She told me about the bones found in the backyard of that house."

"Unconnected to this case, as it turns out."

"Yeah."

"Anything else?"

"She told me the Chinese Undersecretary of Defense may be traveling through North Korea to get to her—he has some vendetta against her or something."

"What? Bloody hell," he said in English. "Is she closely guarded at all times?"

"Mostly," I hedged.

"Make sure. If anything happens to her, the President will have a fit."

She will be guarded, the jade carving informed me. *Reinforcements will arrive soon.*

Rae-Rae

"A sighting on the border of North Korea and China," my CEO of Sea Eagle Security informed me. "What troubles me is that he appeared to have at least thirty guards with him."

"How were they dressed?"

"All in black, with black face coverings."

"He pulled the best fighters from the monks," I sighed.

"What?"

"Nothing. I think I know who his guards are, that's all, and they don't belong to the Chinese military. He's hoping to take me by surprise." I didn't add that it was his only hope of taking me at all.

"Do you want extra guards?"

"I have enough. If we add more, it will be too obvious."

"If you change your mind, I have a hand-picked crew ready to go."

"Thank you. I'll let you know."

"Sea Eagle?" Hu Lin asked as I ended the call. He'd shown up at my condo five minutes after I'd gotten back.

"Yeah. The Undersecretary has thirty guards with him and they won't be friendly if they show up."

"Are they moving together or blending into the landscape?"

"They're trained to blend in." I didn't add that they would have had better talents in that respect had they been selected properly, rather than by an interfering faction of the Chinese military.

I'd never met a *real* Monk of the White Flower, so I could only rely on the transcripts I'd read in the archives. Those only alluded to the talents and capabilities of an actual Monk. There was no real proof.

Likely, the Undersecretary had somehow been charged with finding the human Lotus, should he be born during his lifetime.

So he could control him.

Nobody was forward-thinking enough to imagine the human Lotus could be born outside China—or as a female.

The Undersecretary was only looking for one White Flower. He hadn't bothered to read the texts which said that every true Monk of the White Flower would have his or her own White Flower.

It gave them advantages that others wouldn't have as they protected the Lotus.

Yes, I was supposed to have a small army of Monks to protect me. What I'd gotten instead was an encyclopedia full of lies, brief access to their archives (which they couldn't read), and then a smashed left foot when they found that the vehicle accident they'd orchestrated to kill me didn't go as expected.

Many of them were now going blind and deaf. I had nothing to do with that. The one White Flower carving that they'd managed to keep had somehow disappeared, too. I'd meant what I said when I told the Undersecretary that it was protecting itself.

They'd done too many awful things to warrant its stay. "I'll make sure the other guards are on high alert," Hu Lin said, breaking me away from my thoughts.

"Thank you. I'm worried about the rest of the team, though."

"I can put individual guards on them if you want."

"That sounds good. Be discreet, all right?"

"I will never be otherwise. Do you want someone to stay with you tonight?"

"Not necessary. Go home to your husband. I'll see you early tomorrow morning."

"Okay. Those dumplings were outstanding, by the way."

"I'll send you the address of the restaurant."

CHAPTER 15

H*ae Jin*

"I received a notice that a phone being used in my car had been tapped," Manta told me, handing me a new phone box. "This one is made by Osprey. They'll have a much harder time getting into it."

"How do I move all my contacts and information?" I asked as we walked into the Athletic club with Hu Lin.

"Just set them side-by-side. A screen will pop up on the new phone asking if you want to transfer information. Tap yes. It'll take a few minutes, but you'll be good to go after that. I suggest accidentally dropping the old one in the toilet afterward."

"Eww. Can I drop it in the pool instead?"

"Well, it is a more sanitary solution, I guess. For a fee, I might even retrieve it for you."

"You want a fee?"

"I'm teasing."

"I was about to ask if that's how you made your first million," I teased back.

"By retrieving lost phones in pools?"

"Everybody starts somewhere."

"I don't like where it's going."

"How did you make your first million?"

Hu Lin stifled a snicker.

"Is that funny?" I demanded.

"I'll tell you how I made my first billion," she said. "In dollars, not won."

"How?"

"Investments."

"If she gives investment advice, take it," Hu Lin whispered next to my ear. "Tae-hyun and I paid cash for our house after we did that."

"Hu Lin, go give Hae Jin and Trainer Park some pointers," Manta said as we came to the hallway that led to the pool. "You can stop by afterward and drop your old phone in the water if you want," she told me.

Trainer Park asked Hu Lin to teach him a particular throw during practice. He and I learned it together; Hu Lin was a good instructor.

"How long have you been working out?" Hu Lin asked after we'd showered and dressed. "You're in excellent shape."

"I've been doing some kind of training since I was twelve. I got into Krav Maga when I was in the army, and just continued once I got out."

"Did you play sports in the US?"

"I did—basketball and baseball, mostly. Football to me has always meant what they call soccer."

"Come on, we have to go get Manta Ray," Hu Lin said. "We can have a soccer discussion later—when you have time for lunch."

When we got to the pool, we found Manta having a discussion with two people—one of which was the coach for the young woman who trained at the same time Manta swam. The other, a man, I didn't recognize.

Neither did Hu Lin, and he was in battle mode the moment he saw them. Following right behind him, I almost ran to keep up with Hu Lin, who looked as if he were about to tear into two people.

"I honestly am too old and have no desire to compete professionally," Manta said, as if she'd already repeated that statement at least twice.

"Is there a problem?" Hu Lin arrived at Manta's left side. I took the space on her right.

"We're only trying to convince her she has talent," the man said.

"This is her identification," Hu Lin pulled a leather ID holder from his pocket and presented it to the man. "I'm her bodyguard. If there are further questions, please contact me." He handed over his business card as the man and woman stared at what was obviously Ong Rae-Rae's actual ID.

"Our apologies, Chairman Ong," the woman bowed first. The man quickly followed. The ID was handed back to Hu Lin quickly and both exited the pool area.

"Inconceivable," Manta sighed and raked fingers through her wet hair.

"You keep using that word," I said. "I do not think it means what you think it means," I quoted The Princess Bride. Manta laughed, which was exactly what I hoped for.

"Go get showered and dressed. We'll have coffee while we're waiting," I told her. "I parked next to Hu Lin outside."

"All right. I'll be quick."

WE'D NEARLY REACHED OUR VEHICLES IN THE PARKING LOT when Manta's and Hu Lin's phones began beeping.

"Get her back," Hu Lin ordered as he studied his phone screen. I pulled Manta farther away while she reached out for Hu Lin.

"What's going on?" I hissed against her ear.

"Somebody has either tagged your Jeep—or worse."

"Worse? How do you know it's my Jeep?"

"Because Hu Lin's SUV is wired to send a signal if anybody

tampers with it. Our phones will pick up anything dangerous within five meters," she said.

"We need the bomb squad," Hu Lin walked quickly toward us. Manta dialed and reported our location to someone at the NIS.

Ten minutes later, they were on the scene with a bomb disposal truck and a squad of trained personnel. I watched as an explosive device was removed from the underside of my Jeep.

"This doesn't make sense," Manta told Hu Lin. "I can understand trying to kidnap a team member to coerce me, but this? This is just crazy."

"We're collecting all the security camera images around the parking lot to determine who did this. Also, we'll take the Jeep in for further inspection," an NIS agent came to speak with us.

"He has another vehicle—keep it as long as you want," Manta plucked the keys from my fingers and handed them to the agent.

"What other vehicle?" I asked as the NIS agent walked away.

"You can drive mine. It will send your phone a text if anybody touches it."

"I'd prefer that you drove it," Hu Lin nodded to me. "It has special security measures."

"Tell everybody yours is in the shop so you're driving your cousin's car," Manta patted my arm.

"It's for the best," Hu Lin agreed. "When does your practice start? If we don't leave soon, we'll be late."

That's how I ended up riding with Hu Lin and Manta, while my Jeep went to the NIS for further inspection.

"TOMORROW NIGHT WE'RE PLAYING THE HARPIES," GU Han announced as we took our places in the gaming room. "While we've defeated those who've beaten them this preseason, they've gotten better recently. As you know, two of our players didn't get practice yesterday, so we have to make up for that today and tomorrow. Understood?"

"Understood," we chorused.

"Good. Manta, I'd like you to play Lady Jade tomorrow night."

"Okay," she said.

"I don't want the Germans to have any idea what we're about to spring on them for our first game of the regular season," Gu Han continued. "Therefore, going forward, every team member will remain silent on which avatars will be used in that game—is that understood?"

"Understood," we chorused.

"Nothing will be said or repeated on any strategy we will employ, and nothing about our training methods will be leaked to anyone. Is that understood?"

"Understood," we shouted together.

"During the next two weeks, before and after our arrival in Germany, journalists and bloggers will be seeking you out, asking for hints as to how we're going to deal with the German team. They will also ask about the health and well-being of our team members and any personal information they can squeeze out of us. You will have no comments. Is that understood?"

"They're asking already?" Min-ho breathed.

"Yes. I've refused more than twenty calls since yesterday, after a rumor leaked that two of our members were sent to the hospital." His gaze landed on the twins, who had the decency to lower their eyes. "Do I need to remind you two that you went to the hospital together before that, because you didn't know when to stop drinking? None of your teammates ratted you out."

"Sorry," they muttered in unison.

"What did you tell them?" Manta asked Gu Han.

"I said you had a headache. I wasn't lying. I also said Hae Jin went along to pay your hospital charges. That was the lie I told. You should check the messages on the website, however. I understand there's a buildup of questions for you."

"Right."

"Your post about how to make the most of your avatar was very well received, Manta. Good work following up on that."

"Thanks."

"All right, gear up; we'll get started."

"You can't eat if you're lying down," I told Manta. She'd taken the sofa in the meeting room while we waited for dinner delivery and lay flat on her back with eyes closed.

"Shhhh, don't rock the boat," she mumbled.

"What's wrong?" I asked, concerned immediately.

"Slight stomach upset," she breathed.

"Baby girl, please don't get sick again." Reaching out, I placed a hand on her midsection and stroked it lightly with my thumb. Her phone dinged with a text message. "I'll get it," I pushed her back down gently before taking the phone from her hand.

"What does it say?" she asked.

"Somebody named Lee Chan says that they've spotted CVIP at train station in Seoul. Two guards with him. Bought tickets to Busan. Will keep under surveillance."

"I was worried about that."

"What?"

"That the new enemy would fall in with the old ones. I should let Jin-won know he may have company coming."

Maybe I ought to let Do-yoon know, too. It couldn't hurt.

"Your hand is nice and warm. It feels good," she told me.

"I was worried you'd think it was a nuisance."

"What's going on?" Shi-joon walked in and stopped short when he saw my hand on Manta's stomach.

"Nothing to be concerned about," I said, moving my hand away. "Her stomach is a little upset."

"Dinner's here," Shi-joon said softly. "I can take Manta's upstairs if she's not feeling good."

"If you'll bring our food upstairs, I'll get her to her room."

"BABY GIRL, YOU DON'T WEIGH ENOUGH," I SAID AS I GAVE Manta a piggyback ride upstairs.

"I weigh more than I used to."

"We'll talk about that later."

Had I dreamed about carrying her? Too many times in the past eighteen years. I still had trouble convincing myself that the one who'd saved me from my kidnappers had been right under my nose for the past three-and-a-half months.

You should tell her, the jade carving warned.

You're not my conscience.

I should be.

Shut up.

"ARE YOU SURE YOU FEEL LIKE SWIMMING?" I ASKED MANTA the following morning.

"I'm okay. I got plenty of rest last night. Thank you for taking care of things," she said.

Even without makeup, her pretty mouth tempted me as she gave me an earnest gaze.

"If I hadn't done anything, Shi-joon would have."

"As much as I like Shi-joon, he's not as willing to argue with me."

"Does that matter?"

"It does to me."

"I'll remind you of that the next time you're wrong."

"I never said I was wrong, only that you were willing to defend your position."

"Is that what you meant? That you just want an argument, rather than admit you're wrong?"

"And guys complain that women twist their words," Manta shook her head in a gesture of exasperation.

"I'm teasing you," I reached out to pinch her cheek lightly.

"Right. Come on, Hu Lin is here."

When we walked out of headquarters, we found someone else in Hu Lin's SUV, sitting in the front passenger seat.

"This is Chung Dan-bi," Manta introduced the newcomer after climbing into the back seat with me. "She'll sit and watch me swim while Hu Lin smacks you and Trainer Park."

I introduced myself to Dan-bi, who was tall, stocky and looked as if she could easily trade blows with Hu Lin.

"How's the baby?" Manta asked Dan-bi.

"She's fine. She's with Ma-ri's mother this morning."

"Dan-bi's wife is a pediatrician," Manta told me with a smile.

"Chairman Ong lets me work part-time nowadays, so I can take care of our little girl," Dan-bi said. "It works out great for us."

"How old is the baby?" I asked. It was the proper question.

"Nine-and-a-half months. She's adorable."

"See?" Manta showed me a picture on her phone. In it were Dan-bi, the wife and baby, all smiling.

"A perfect family," I nodded, giving Dan-bi a smile.

"My wife will tell you different if it's her time to get up in the middle of the night."

"I'm not even getting in that argument with you," Manta waved a hand and laughed.

"Hah. You know Auntie Cheng will sleep during the day just to get up at night if you ever have one," Dan-bi said.

"She probably would," Manta agreed. "But there are other, necessary things that must happen first."

"Tae-hyun and I have already volunteered," Hu Lin said.

"Huh?" I blurted. "Wait a minute."

"I am not asking for volunteers," Manta snapped. "I'm not over the hill yet, or even close."

"Ma-ri says you should consider freezing your eggs."

"What?" Manta and I said in unison.

Dan-bi exchanged a glance with Hu Lin and both started laughing.

"I think I've been had," Manta told me in English.

Unknown Location

Hengduan Mountains, Southwest China

First Monk Kija

"We have forced out the last of the pretenders from the servants' village down the mountain, First Monk Kija," Second Monk Gi reported. "The footpath to the monastery is now secure and hidden. The trail has been obscured. The imposters will not find a way to return."

Second Monk Gi stood before me, dressed in the traditional silvery-gray of the Monks of the White Flower. This color aided in our becoming invisible to normal eyesight, and enabled us to move, unseen, among normal populations. At his side he wore a blade such as we all carried, except his denoted his rank on the pommel, just as mine did.

"Good," I replied to Gi's report. "Has Seer Sung-won been successful in his search for the Lotus?"

"Not yet."

"How has this one survived?" I mused. "Any other, without training, would have gotten themselves killed somehow."

"Our Lotus and Seer Sung-won have been correct so far—that our help would be needed now, rather than in the past," Gi reminded me.

"He has given us this assignment. We belong to this Lotus, now. If you had regrets, you should have spoken before."

"I do not have regrets. I have trained for this and have been committed to this Lotus ever since I learned that the Monks of the White Flower in this place were murdered and their jade carvings, save one, appeared in our dimension. We have eliminated anyone we found here who was currently involved in that charade."

"Eliminated as we were commanded," I agreed. "Very well, have the Monks prepare a meal and report to me if Sung-won has seen anything new. We will move on his advice."

"As you say, First Monk Kija." Gi bowed to me and left to inform the others.

Hae Jin

"What's wrong, baby girl?" I asked softly after we were dropped off at headquarters by Hu Lin and Dan-bi. We both carried lattes and bags with heated croissants.

"I feel strange—like somebody's watching," she gave me a troubled gaze. "It's not comfortable."

"Has this happened before?" I leaned down to speak softly to her.

"Not since I moved out of the house in Busan."

Those two bitches had watched her like a hawk—when she wasn't hiding from them. I'd learned that from Hu Lin. He and Tae-hyun knew the most about those years of Manta's life. At least they were willing to answer my questions, which I greatly appreciated.

I worried, though, that they'd be angry if they learned I had another reason to ask those questions about Manta's jailers.

That's how I'd come to see them—as kidnappers, murderers, and jailers. As for the man who pulled their strings, I'd already imagined the many, terrible ways he and his henchwomen might die.

"Anything I can do?" I asked Manta.

"I can't think of anything. Let's sit down in the kitchen and finish our coffee and croissants."

The team came in from their morning run while Manta and I talked and drank our coffee. Manta offered to make breakfast for everybody, most of whom ran upstairs for a hurried shower so they could get back for a fresh-cooked meal.

"I never get poached eggs," Gu Han breathed a happy sigh after finishing his plate of food.

"My favorite," Manta told him. "Except I like mine with ham or bacon instead of kimchi."

"I like them with avocado, too, but we didn't have any," Gu Han grinned.

"I'll ask somebody to make a trip to the grocery store," Manta said.

"You can have time after pictures tomorrow if you want to go yourself."

"Call."

"Call." Gu Han gave her a fist-bump.

"Lady Jade will never see the light of day during the regular season games," Shi-joon speculated after we laid waste to the Harpies. "They even knew it was coming and still didn't have an answer."

"Manta is officially the player to watch this season," Gu Han announced after checking the rankings boards. "Germans are still the number one team, but we're not far behind in the number two slot. All that could change depending on our first game, since it's against them."

"Have you already assessed their team play?" I leaned over in my chair to ask Manta.

"I've been watching them all preseason," she said. "Along with studying their avatars and moves from last season."

"Are you ready to play in front of a live audience?"

"I think so."

"Have you ever had a live audience before?"

I should have known better. Really. She lifted her phone and tapped for a few moments. My phone was bombarded with messages as she rose from her chair and stalked out of the gaming room.

The first message was a video of Chairman Ong giving a presentation to the United Nations in New York and speaking in several languages to answer questions afterward.

Numerous other speeches and presentations were listed, some at major universities worldwide and others at government agencies around the globe.

Manta was no stranger to an audience. I should have known that already.

"Stay in or go out to eat?" Gu Han asked.

I sent a message to Manta, since she'd gone upstairs to her room.

I'll go with the consensus, she replied.

Looks like we're going out, I texted back.

I'll be down in a minute.

She arrived dressed in a black hoodie and jeans. "We're taking the van," I told her.

"Okay. Where are we going?"

"Barbecue."

"Cook your own?"

"Yes."

"What happened to going out so you didn't have to cook?"

"Come on, it'll be fun."

"Who's cooking?"

"I don't know."

"So it's not you, then?"

"I don't cook."

"I'm not eating anything the twins cook."

"Probably a good idea," I nodded. "Come on, the van's here." I pulled her toward the door. We loaded into the vehicle and our driver steered us away from headquarters.

Rae-Rae

When we pulled up outside the barbecue restaurant, Hae Jin took my elbow and helped me out of the van. Before they disappeared, I saw two men standing nearby, dressed in silvery tunics, pants, and calf-high boots.

The color of their tunics and pants had gone from a silvery gray to midnight blue in the space of a second, before they disappeared before my eyes.

I knew I'd seen them.

Where did they go?

Were those actual swords and scabbards belted at their sides?

More importantly, who were they?

My phone chimed with a text from Jin-won. *Our three escaped from prison*, he wrote. *No known locations. Guards killed. Vehicles stolen.*

"What's wrong?" Hae Jin asked. Only then did I realize I was gripping his sleeve as if my life depended on it.

Holding up my phone, I allowed him to read the message. "Fucking hell," he snarled in English. "Where's Hu Lin?" he asked, this time more softly.

"On his way," I said after tapping a code on my phone. "Come on, we can't stand out here on the sidewalk like mindless tourists." Grabbing his wrist, I pulled him toward the door of the restaurant.

Two shots rang out.

I heard them before the bullets left the gun. Turning, I held out a hand while others still hadn't heard the sound of gunfire—and obviously hadn't reacted.

Hae Jin

I didn't hear the gunshots until they were fired. Manta reacted seconds ahead of that time. Everything went still. There was no slowdown to a stop—everything went dead, as if the atoms that made up everything stopped in their tracks.

Including the people.

Why wasn't I affected?

Because I am with you, the jade carving informed me. *The Lotus has acted. You will be a witness and a helper if she needs it.*

Manta walked away from me, crossing right in front of a car that only a moment ago had been traveling swiftly down a busy street. Even the lights failed to brighten the area before the vehicle; the light beams had also died.

Across the street, I saw a man with an illegal pistol in his hands. His stance was that of someone in the act of firing a gun. I moved, then, to follow Manta; she was walking right into the line of fire.

The backups have arrived, the jade carving said in what sounded like smug satisfaction. *They had doubts about a female Lotus. I think their minds may have changed quickly.*

"Huh?" I mouthed like an idiot, while the air grew thick around me and several men dressed in gray appeared behind Manta, their swords drawn.

Manta walked right up to the gunman and plucked two bullets from the air, as if she'd done that very thing dozens of times. She then removed the gun from the gunman's hand.

When she turned, the men in gray bowed to her.

"Here," she handed the gun and bullets to the one closest to her.

"Lotus, what do you wish done with this one?" a second gray-clad man asked, indicating the gunman.

"Can you take him away for now? I'd like to question him later."

"Of course. We will contact you."

"Do you have a phone?"

"We do not. We are not from ah, your dimension."

"I'm not surprised. The ones from this dimension only want me dead."

"We will pass a message to you through the one who holds the flower from this world."

"Who is that?"

"Him," the man turned and pointed right at me.

"Hae Jin?"

"Yes—that is what he is called, according to the flower he holds. He also bears the sigil from your meeting long ago—when he was rescued by you."

"What?"

"We understand from the flower he bears that he was

kidnapped long ago and was rescued by the young Lotus. You should not have had your talents so young, yet you used them to save his life."

"Hae Jin, we will have words," Manta snapped at me. "Come on, we have to get this guy out of here and put things back as they were."

Walking quickly, she grabbed my hand and hauled me toward the sidewalk where we'd initially stopped. Once there, she waved a hand again and things went right back to normal.

Until then, I hadn't noticed the absence of sound or the stillness of the air. A cool breeze touched my cheek as Gu Han yelled for us to hurry up or we'd lose our table.

"Fucking hell," I muttered under my breath, while Manta slapped my arm to get me moving.

CHAPTER 16

H*ae Jin*

"Later," Manta breathed beside me as questions crowded my mind. Yes, the jade carving had said *Lotus* to me.

Several times.

Had it meant anything?

Not until now. We reached our table; I hadn't realized I held Manta's hand in a near death-grip until she shook me off and told me to sit.

I sat, feeling numb and foolish at the same time. Was the gunman aiming at Manta—or at *me*?

Now, *I* wanted to question the gunman. Had he been sent to kill one or both of us? He'd fired twice; Manta had plucked two bullets from the air.

Do-yoon had told me to stay close to Manta. Did he know about *this*?

"Hae Jin?" Manta said.

"Huh?" I leaned toward her to hear better—there was a terrified buzz in my brain that wanted to interfere with all my senses.

"Breathe in and out. Slowly." Her hand gripped mine under the table and squeezed. "Everything is okay. We're okay. Got it? Keep breathing in and out. Go slow. Count your breaths if it helps."

In. Out. *One*.

In. Out. *Two*.

Eventually, that method returned my breathing and my heart rate to normal, although my appetite had all but deserted me. Manta coaxed me to eat more whenever my hand stilled and I found myself staring into space.

When we left the restaurant, I saw Hu Lin standing next to a flower bed, as if he were waiting to get in. Manta nodded discreetly to him, after which he peeled away and left.

For a moment, I felt as if nausea would overwhelm me. Manta touched my hand and things felt almost normal after a few seconds. The ride home was nothing more than a frightening blur. Manta followed me upstairs at headquarters and I was grateful. When nobody else was around, she pulled me into her room and shut the door quickly.

"HE JUST SAW AND HEARD SOMETHING HE WASN'T expecting. His stomach is upset, that's all," Manta told someone on the phone. "He's lying down already. Yes, I have a heating pad. All right, I'll do that. Thanks, Tae-hyun."

A few minutes later, I had a warm heating pad on my stomach and it felt good. "How's your head?" Manta asked as I blinked up at her.

"Confused," I mumbled.

"Tell me what you want to know—if you're feeling up to it."

"How? The jade carving keeps saying you're the Lotus, but I don't even know what that means."

"I didn't know what it meant either—not for the longest time. The ones posing as the Monks of the White Flower on Earth were supposed to find and teach me. Since they weren't the actual Monks, they withheld everything until they didn't have a choice. They've been trying to kill or disable me ever since."

"Who are they?"

"Well, they're under the supervision of the Chinese Undersecretary of Defense. He's going blind and probably deaf, too, along with several of those posing as Monks. They're the ones who crushed my foot. I guess their new disabilities are some sort of punishment for harming the Lotus."

She reached out and placed a gentle hand on my forehead. "No fever," she said, taking her hand away. I almost protested aloud when her hand left my skin—it felt good just to feel her touch.

"Why do they want to hurt you?"

"Because I won't cooperate with them. They want to use whatever I can do to further their own political agenda. That's not what the Lotus does."

"You just scared the hell out of me," I breathed. "What would they ask you to do if you did cooperate with them?"

"Use your imagination. I'm sure they've already imagined quite a lot. Plus, it pisses them off that the Lotus isn't Chinese, as has always been in the past."

"Baby girl, is that how you got me away from those women?"

"I didn't know I had it until that night. If it hadn't manifested, we'd both be dead."

"I'm sorry I didn't tell you before," I lifted a hand and rubbed my forehead. "My grandfather managed to get a copy of the security camera recording from the train ride that night. I have a copy and my cousin who works for the NIS also has a copy. I don't know how much Grandpa had to pay to get it back then."

"I know about Do-yoon. He's working with Jin-won in Busan. He probably told you who I am, didn't he?"

"Yeah. Don't be mad. Please."

"I'm not mad. Well, I'm a little upset that you didn't tell me who you were at first. Also, you're not obligated to tell me your real last name, but there were no Lees among the very wealthy during the time of your kidnapping."

"Oh, man," I whined in English. "You're gonna hit me for sure."

"Why?"

"Because my parents know you."

"Really."

"Do-yoon says you own thirty percent of Dad's company."

"Your name is Sang. I may hit you for real. I spent the first two weeks here going over Sang Group's company budget. If I'd known your name, I'd have made you suffer through it, too."

"Dad asks you to go over the budget?"

"How else are we gonna catch the ones trying to embezzle from the company? His presidents and vice presidents know better than to try to hide that crap in their budgets and year-end reports nowadays."

"You don't go easy on them, do you?"

"No. There's no reason for your father to support gambling habits, mistresses or vacation homes for people who earn a decent salary. The ones at the bottom deserve the biggest raises, percentagewise. If the ones on top are eating up the profits, there's less you can spend on the ones who actually do the work."

"I can see why a lot of the big names in Korean businesses don't like you."

"Does that include you, Mr. Sang?"

"I never said that."

"You don't mind if your lowest-paid employees can't afford rent and food at the same time? Would you like to go with me someday and check out the places where the lowest-paid employees of your father's main competitors live?"

"Is this something I need to know?"

"If you intend to take over your father's business someday, I think so. Plus, you're talking to somebody right now who owns more stock in Sang Group than the actual Sangs."

"What?"

"Your family owns twenty-seven and one-half percent of the stock. I have thirty. I keep trying to sell some of it back to your father. He refuses it every time."

I pinched the bridge of my nose. "Sang Group has shown record profits in the past five years," I mumbled.

"I know. I'm at every stockholders' meeting."

"I think I owe you an apology."

"For what?"

"For sympathizing with President Ho when he said he got his ass chewed by a major stockholder last year."

"How well do you know him? He'd love to dip his hands into some of those profits you just talked about. Last year, he presented an idea for appliances with a certain type of microchip in them. What nobody else in the meeting knew was that those were knock-off chips manufactured cheaply by a fly-by-night enterprise and charging nearly as much for them as the originals manufactured by a Japanese firm. Not only would Sang Group face charges from the Japanese company for stealing their design, the knockoffs weren't meant to hold up under the workload of a normal household. I trashed the entire project. He still has a job because I didn't have time to dig into how much he intended to make on the side for doing business with a company that disappeared overnight."

"I still like the idea of what those appliances were meant to do," I said.

"Fine. Design a chip that will hold up that's cost effective, and I'll support that idea. People don't need to add twenty percent on top of their appliance budget just to buy a microchip that will fail after eighteen months or less. Remember, you could be talking about those low-paid employees who can't afford rent and food at the same time."

"You scare me."

"I scare a lot of people, including the Undersecretary of Defense in China."

"I should go back to my room—I have a lot to think about."

"No problem. I think the others are all in bed by now. Get some rest. I need to go question a man about a gun."

"Cousin, I don't think I can handle this. It's like I'm dealing with two people. One is friendly and caring; the other is a cutthroat businessperson who won't tolerate mistakes."

"Your father is like that, too; you've just never been exposed to the other side of him. You lived outside the country for fifteen years, Hae Jin. You were too busy getting degrees to keep up with much that goes on in Korea's business world. Ong Group and Sang Group are two of the best paying business concerns in the country. People will fight to get an entry job at either place."

"I think I learned tonight that an MBA from Harvard doesn't come close to getting me ready to take over Sang Group."

"What makes you say that?"

"The corruption, for one thing."

"Wherever there's money, you'll find corruption, or at least the attempts at corruption. Greed is everywhere, cousin. Chairman Ong is right to cut out that kind of cancer the moment it appears."

"I wasn't expecting," I began.

"Your vision of the girl who saved you has transformed, hasn't it? That girl turned into a business-savvy woman who won't tolerate corporate thievery—one who believes in paying people what they're worth and providing health care benefits and other necessities. If that troubles you, then shake her hand, tell her thank you for saving your life when you were eleven and let it go. I'll ask her out when I'm done with this assignment."

"What?" I sputtered.

"I mean it, Hae Jin." Do-yoon hung up before I could say anything else.

Rae-Rae

"He wasn't expecting you to be there. His target was your companion," First Monk Kija informed me. "He still doesn't know who you are, and if you don't plan to eliminate him, we believe it is better that it stays this way."

I was still trying to come to terms with the fact that I now had actual Monks of the White Flower at my back, rather than the imposters who'd never offered so much as a morsel of food or any help with an enemy.

"What do you normally do with people like this?" Second Monk Gi asked.

Closing my eyes, I let my shoulders droop. "I check them into a prison in an inhospitable country," I confessed. "Like Russia, Saudi Arabia, or Turkey."

"Ah. Those places. That sounds suitable," Kija agreed.

"Get rid of his gun and the bullets," I said. "I'll leave him in a Turkish prison."

"The gun has already been destroyed. Build the gate; we will help you deliver him to his new home."

"I remember the first time I built a gate," I sighed while moving my hands and casting the mental net to bring two locations together by a mind bridge. "I was fourteen and trapped by bullies at school. I built a gate to the nearest police station, led them through and then closed it, leaving them there. I shouldn't have done it, but they never bothered me again after that."

"You should have had protection from the Monks long

before that," Kija told me. "We don't understand how you learned so much on your own."

"I can't explain it either; I just figured it out by myself. It's ready," I stepped back from the gate with a sigh. Let's take him through."

CHAPTER 17

Hae Jin

I drove myself to the athletic club on Wednesday morning—in Manta's SUV. I felt guilty as hell doing it, too. I hadn't bothered to leave a message for her, either, which made it worse.

She came in with Hu Lin, who stayed with her rather than working out with Trainer Park and me. We ended up back at headquarters at the same time. I noticed the dark circles under her eyes and the fact that she appeared to be exhausted.

Not a good day for pictures, and that's what we had scheduled for the afternoon.

"You look tired," Shi-joon told her when he came into the kitchen later.

"I spent half the night checking somebody into a five-star

Turkish prison," she quipped. Shi-joon chuckled while I went cold.

The would-be shooter was now in a Turkish prison. For real. How had she done that? The question that burned in my brain, however, was this—was his target me, Manta, or both of us?

You were the target, the carving informed me. *The others tell me this.*

Others?

The other jade carvings held by the Monks. Each Monk receives one when he joins the ranks. The Lotus saved your life—again. You should be grateful, yet you are not.

I thought she was just a regular girl, not—this.

Had she not been this, *as you say, you would be long dead. Is that your desire?*

Of course not. But, I stopped in mid-thought.

You're thinking of refusing me. Of refusing your place among the worthy. You may do that, of course—it is your right.

But what happens then?

I go to someone else. My *choice at the moment is Do-yoon. I am special, you see. I am the White Flower reserved for the one who loves the Lotus. In the past, I have been held by mostly women, but also by a few men. It matters not the gender, only that they care deeply for the Lotus. You are wavering, but it is still your choice to make.*

Does she use—whatever it is she has—to win in gaming? I asked. *Does she cheat?*

If she cheated, as you so bluntly put it, her character would never die in a game. No. She does not cheat. She uses what she has naturally to compete with you and the others. A Lotus is, by nature, always fair-minded.

I don't think I can do this, I said.

Then take some time to be sure.

How much time do I have?

I will give you until the end of the regular season. If you can't decide by then, I will make the choice for you, in the best interest of the Lotus. She deserves better than someone who cannot decide, don't you think?

Yeah. I guess she does.

Had she been this indecisive about saving your life, you'd be dead. We are done speaking for now.

I'd never been called an idiot by a piece of jade before, but that had changed.

Because I am *an idiot*, I reminded myself.

"Is there something I don't know?" Shi-joon looked from me to Manta and back again after a protracted, painful silence.

"Apparently we're not speaking," Manta tossed her paper coffee cup in the trash and rose from her seat at the island. "No good deed goes unpunished," she tossed over a shoulder as she headed for the stairs.

"Somehow, I think this may be your fault," Shi-joon sighed as he studied me.

"It is. I don't know how to fix it, or if it can be fixed."

"There's a problem," Min-ho walked into the kitchen.

"What problem?"

"The number of hotel rooms we have in Berlin."

"HOW DID WE END UP WITH ONLY TWO ROOMS?" GU HAN demanded.

"Someone changed the reservation without our knowledge," Min-ho snarled. "Probably Minjun, in his last act of maliciousness."

"We need to check all our reservations, then, to make sure he didn't sabotage any of the others," I said. "We can sleep three to a room if we have to."

"Except for Manta," Gu Han pointed out.

"Are all the rooms taken?" Shi-joon asked.

"They are. We're staying at the tournament location, as are a ton of fans. There are no other rooms to be had, and a very long waiting list."

"What about other hotels nearby?" Manta walked into the room.

"The closest ones are booked up."

"I'll find something," she said.

"I don't want us staying in separate hotels," Gu Han said.

"I'll find rooms for all of us. When do we have to leave to have photos taken?"

Gu Han checked his watch. "In two hours."

"I'll have something by then." Manta turned and stalked out of the kitchen.

Shi-joon and I fist-bumped. We would have something by then, or we weren't gaming with the real Ong Rae-Rae.

It took less than an hour. We had three penthouse suites in a nearby hotel that would sleep all of us, including three private bedrooms in each suite—courtesy of Osprey Technology and Robotics.

"Whoa, do you see this?" The twins were looking through photos of the rooms booked for us—they were lavish in the extreme and designed for wealthy clients and big-name politicians. "We can sneak girls in," Si-woo whispered loudly to his brother.

Manta, who'd brought the news to us, mimed throwing up at Si-woo's words. Shi-joon laughed.

"I'm not staying in the same room with the twins," I said.

"Me, either," Shi-joon agreed. Manta rolled her eyes; she'd pay even more money not to stay in the same room with the twins.

"I'll stay with them," Gu Han cast a searing glare in the twins' direction. "And I'll watch them every second."

"I can help Gu Han," Min-ho said. "Since I have my own plane ticket to Berlin."

"I'll reimburse your ticket, just for helping Gu Han," Manta told him. "I think Osprey will spring for your travel expenses to all the other locations, if you're there to help with the team."

"Yes!" Min-ho breathed, pumping a fist in the air.

"Everybody, it's almost time to leave for the photoshoot," Gu Han announced while still glaring at the twins. "Get ready to go; the bus will be here in forty."

"HAE JIN'S POSTER WILL SELL OUT LIKE IT ALWAYS DOES, BUT this one—I think this one should be very popular."

The photographer showed us digital copies of the photoshoot afterward. The photo he'd loaded to show us was that of Manta, dressed in the Chinese-designed gown I'd chosen for her to wear.

They'd used an electric fan to cause the filmy kimono over the dress to billow out, while Manta posed against a backdrop of sea spray at an oceanside.

It was a photo fit for the cover of a glossy fashion magazine, yet here it was, being used for gaming booklets and poster sales.

"I'll buy one," Min-ho mumbled beside me.

I refused to admit it, but I'd likely end up with at least one for myself—framed.

"We'll have these posters printed and ready for sale in Berlin," the photographer assured Gu Han. "I understand there will be four games taking place there?"

"Yes. First, Second, Third and Fourth place will face opponents in the city of the previous year's winner," Gu Han explained. "Except First and Second will face each other this year, rather than other opponents like they have in previous years. This means that Fifth place will also play their first opponent there."

"Sounds like somebody has it in for you—or they really favored Fifth place for some reason."

"We can't second guess the gaming committee," Gu Han replied. "It's our job to face our opponent, just as it is in every game."

"Of course."

"If there's nothing else, I need to take my crew to dinner; they're starving by now."

We were—the shoot had taken longer than usual, and it was now after nine, even with two photographers working at the same time.

Manta had taken three snack breaks while we were there, and passed out granola bars, bottled water and disposable toothbrushes each time to the rest of us. If she hadn't, the hunger complaints would have been heard all the way to the Blue House.

"I think I'd like to go home and order take-out," I heard her tell Gu Han. "The rest of you can go out if you want. I can also get a ride for myself, so you won't have to drop me off."

"Headquarters or your home?" I asked, earning an angry glance from Manta.

"You can go to your home if you want; practice won't start until tomorrow afternoon," Gu Han replied.

"I'll call a friend to give me a ride," she said, pulling out her phone.

I wanted to stop her. I wanted her to come with me or let me go with her. *Why?* Hadn't I already done my best to burn that bridge?

Is it because your kidnappers have broken out of prison and are still hunting you? the White Flower asked maliciously.

I hoped that wasn't the case but couldn't deny that it was a big part of my current worries.

"I'll meet you at the door," Manta spoke into the phone and walked away from me. Reflexively, I reached out to grasp her hand as she walked past. She turned, the phone still at her ear, shook off my hand and walked away.

RAE-RAE

"I need a flight from Busan to Seoul," I told Thiwat. "For Lee Do-yoon. No, he doesn't know he's coming yet. But he will."

"Why does he need to come back tonight?" Hu Lin asked as he drove his Escalade into the parking garage beneath my building.

"Because it isn't just Hae Jin we have to worry about. It's his entire family, too. Those assholes won't leave any of them alone until they have Hae Jin and he's dead."

"I'm almost at the point to let him survive on his own," Hu Lin growled.

"You might think differently if you wake up tomorrow and Tae-hyun has grown enormous horns overnight," I said.

"We'll deal with it like we have all our other problems," Hu Lin said philosophically. "Horns can be sexy, too."

"You know what I mean. Hae Jin has no idea how to deal with any woman, let alone one who's smart, rich, and all sorts of other things."

"You mean like saving his ass, past and future?" Hu Lin asked.

"I suppose that's true."

"He thought everything was perfect, as long as he was in charge."

"Don't tell me what I've already figured out for myself." My phone rang; it was Jin-won calling me back.

"Jin-won, I have something to tell you, and you will and won't like it," I began.

"What's the verdict?" Hu Lin asked once I got off the phone with Jin-won.

"He's sending Do-yoon back and asking him to take charge of a detail of guards and agents that he and I will put together to protect the Lees and the Sangs," I said. "Although Do-yoon may convince Hae Jin to allow him to act as his personal guard. They can share a room while we're traveling, and he's authorized to carry a weapon if need be."

"How do you think Hae Jin will react?"

"I think Do-yoon can do any convincing that needs done. These aren't nice people and never have been."

"How will Hae Jin handle the fact that you let his secret out?"

"I'm more worried about his parents, but he'll be mad enough. Look at it this way; he was already stepping away from me. This will give him an excuse to make it permanent. Besides, only a select few at the NIS will know of a fifth victim until this gets resolved."

"To save his life. And the lives of his family."

"Yeah. Tell Tae-hyun to cross another name off his list of hopefuls. I won't ever get the chance to marry. Or have a boyfriend, looks like."

"Want something to help you sleep tonight? I can call Tae-hyun."

"I wish I could say yes. With the way things are, I have to say no. Find two extra guards to put on duty downstairs and then go home to Tae-hyun."

"I'll leave my SUV here and have Dan-bi take me home," Hu Lin said. "In case someone's paying attention to whether I'm guarding you or not."

"Good idea. I'll see you tomorrow around eleven."

"Call me if you need anything."

"Okay."

Hae Jin

"Cousin, are you drunk?" Do-yoon asked after I answered his call.

"Tipsy," I replied. "Why are you calling?"

"I'm calling from the airport in Busan. I'm coming home tonight. I've been coordinating with a detail of guards and agents, who will be assigned to our family members in Seoul."

"Huh?" My mind, fogged as it was with alcohol, couldn't grasp what Do-yoon meant.

"I'm taking you as my assignment," Do-yoon continued. "It's not just you in danger after the suspects escaped from prison. They'll go after the family, too, me included."

"What?" Now I was beginning to see through the fog. "But," I said.

"I wasn't the one who outed you. She said I could blame her for everything you're going to be mad about. In her defense, she's right, and in her other defense, I agree with her."

"Because they'll come after Mom and Dad, too."

"That's right. These aren't good people, Cousin. They'll do anything to destroy the evidence against them, including the elimination of your entire family."

"Fucking hell," I said in English.

"They're calling my flight," Do-yoon said. "I'll see you tomorrow morning. Don't go anywhere alone, all right? I'll be home in two hours, and I have to explain things to my family and yours when I get there. Call if you need anything, all right?"

"I will. Thanks, Cousin."

Do-yoon disconnected, leaving me sitting on my bed, more sober than when I'd first answered his call.

I never imagined they could come after me. Maybe they assumed my disappearance at eleven meant I was dead. Now that I'd come back to Korea, they'd learned otherwise and were now searching—in fact, had already found me once.

Manta took care of that problem for me, I chastised myself. She was also the one who knew these people far better than I did and had done what she could to protect my family. I hadn't imagined they'd need protection to begin with.

What would Do-yoon say to my parents? Would they try to send me out of the country a second time?

The perpetrators know you're alive. They won't mind traveling to find you; they're on the run anyway, the White Flower informed me. *As the Lotus imagines, the one who has gotten them out of prison will stop at nothing to achieve his goal, which closely aligns with theirs.*

And those goals are?

Find you and find the Lotus. Kill one and control the other. They have an army of false monks behind them to achieve this goal.

I couldn't recall feeling this helpless since I was eleven.

Rae-Rae

"There's already a security net around this building and around Black Skies' Headquarters," I told Zhang Bao. "Two witnesses say that during the prison breakout, they saw several men dressed all in black, with black face masks. Who else would know enough to get around the security measures of a prison?"

"Our dear Undersecretary," Zhang Bao agreed. "He must believe that these fugitives will help him reach you, somehow."

"He knows enough, I think, to understand that their goals can be aligned to his satisfaction."

"You want the Chinese Government to declare him AWOL and dangerous, I understand that," Zhang Bao sighed. "Except that they'll never admit that one of theirs has defected and become a problem unless they're forced to."

"Then I'll try finding him in other ways. While the three fugitives likely have enough cash to keep them fed for a while, I'm not sure the Undersecretary will be able to stay away from his phone or other technology like they can. If he gets online for more than three minutes somewhere, I'll find him."

"You're saying actual Monks of the White Flower are here?" Zhang Bao touched on the second part of my call.

"Yes. Just showed up out of nowhere when that jerk fired at Hae Jin."

"You think you can trust them?"

"I am cautiously optimistic."

"Then I hope things work out. You may need their help if you want to survive the Undersecretary's assault."

"Right. I don't know how many false monks he has with

him, or if all of them are Chinese or if North Korea may have beefed up his forces. They still want me dead."

"Because you're dangerous to them."

"Right."

"Feel like a game? Since you obviously can't sleep?"

"A short one."

"Good enough."

Hae Jin

"What are you watching?" I asked Gu Han at breakfast.

"Madame Dragonfly and Silver Mountain King played the French team captain and their vice-captain last night. Somebody recorded the game. It's amazing. Madame Dragonfly destroyed both of them."

"Let me see," I leaned over to watch the match on Gu Han's tablet.

"Silver Mountain King gets in trouble here," Gu Han pointed out. "That's when Madame Dragonfly kicks into a higher gear. I've never seen anyone play like that."

"I'm sure the character design has something to do with it."

"It does, but both combined is a deadly force. There's a huge pool of people placing bets on who Madame Dragonfly and Silver Mountain King actually are."

"It's illegal to gamble in Korea," I reminded him.

"But think of the honor and prestige of actually guessing," Gu Han grinned. "Once they're named, we can offer contracts."

I'd skipped Krav Maga, since I didn't have anyone who could go with me. I worried that Trainer Park might become a target for my kidnappers if they couldn't get to my family. I also hadn't heard from Do-yoon, but it was early yet. I wondered how I was going to explain having a cousin who was also a bodyguard going with me everywhere we traveled.

The Lotus has worked everything out with Team Owner. Do not fear, the White Flower informed me.

That's why it shouldn't have surprised me when Manta walked in, followed by Do-yoon, Hu Lin and a third guard named Man-sik just before lunchtime. Team Owner was right behind those four, to explain that Osprey Technology and Robotics was providing guards for the team.

"YOUR MOTHER ALMOST FAINTED WHEN SHE HEARD someone tried to shoot you," Do-yoon informed me. "It convinced her that she needed protection, though, so it was worth it."

"How did Dad react when he heard those three were probably my kidnappers?"

"Grandpa gave him a hard look, so your dad kept quiet for the most part."

"Did you give them the information about—Manta?"

"I said we knew who she was, but that was information we didn't have permission to share at this time."

"Were they upset about that?"

"Your mother kept saying, 'She's real?' Grandpa just snorted a laugh. I think I'd like to introduce Rae-Rae to Grandpa sometime."

"He'll ship her with one of us."

"That's fine by me."

"I need to talk to her," I admitted. "And I really messed that up."

"She's talking to me just fine."

"Shut up."

"Don't you have to go practice?"

"Shut up."

"WE HAVE RECORDINGS OF THE GERMANS' PRESEASON games," Gu Han held up a thumb drive. "While they took longer to win those games than we did, they won all of them. I'd like to show you the first game *Erzwinge Fünf* played against the French team," he added, shoving the thumb drive into his tablet to display it on the big screen. "*Les Chats Noir* put up a good fight but lost the game in the last three minutes. Take a look."

We sat through twenty-eight minutes of gaming, while

Manta fell asleep against Min-ho's shoulder. Min-ho didn't mind a bit, but Gu Han had hands on hips when the game ended and he paused the action.

"Manta," he stomped his foot, making her jump.

"Huh?" she mumbled, still half asleep.

"Give me a strategy for the Black Cats in their game against Force Five," Gu Han demanded.

"Oh. I can show you," she said, pulling out her phone. "I've already gone through all their games." She rose from her seat, tapped on her phone and images appeared on the big screen. "Here," she said, showing a segment at the end of the game, where the Black Cats had gathered to attack Force Five's captain. "They hadn't taken into account that Force Five's healer was still active. See—he heals their vice-captain here, and then those two jump the two fighting Werner. You all know what happened after that. If even one of those players had bothered to put the healer out of business earlier in the game, they wouldn't have faced this impasse and ultimate loss."

"Didn't you get enough sleep last night?" Gu Han asked her as she cut off the video feed.

"No. Sorry."

"Then, as punishment for falling asleep during a presentation, you have to show us the rest of Force Five's preseason games and strategize each of them."

"Fine. All right, team, here's their second game, against the *Nokken* of Norway," Manta pulled up her second set of video notes. "They get off to a bad start, letting Force Five eliminate their healer in the first three minutes," Manta lectured.

BY THE TIME MANTA FINISHED, WE'D GONE OVER EVERY preseason game Germany's Force Five played, the strategy employed against each team, the weakest players on each team, how Force Five exploited that knowledge, and their penchant for attacking healers.

"In most cases, we're dealing with healer-mages," Manta pointed out. "Force Five has a harder time against healer-warriors."

We had a healer-warrior—Shi-joon held that position. We needed to have somebody defend his back against the Germans; there was no question. In fact, when Minjun had frozen in the championship game, he should have been helping Shi-joon. He hadn't and we'd lost in the last three minutes, just as the French team did in preseason.

"Nice analysis," Min-ho told Manta as we took a break.

"I prefer being prepared when walking into an ambush," she said.

"You think the Germans are planning an ambush?"

"I can't say for sure," she hedged. "I do know they'll gather every bit of information they can get on our team and use it against us."

"I'd like to speak with you in private," Gu Han stopped beside Manta.

"I'm in trouble, right?" Manta asked.

"Come with me and we'll discuss it."

I watched as Manta followed Gu Han into the small office reserved for the team manager. He shut the door behind them. Surely any additional punishment wouldn't be heavy, or perhaps he was going to levy a fine.

Falling asleep, however, was nothing compared to what the twins had done in the past few weeks.

Maybe I could get information from one or the other afterward. With that in mind, I turned to other things.

RAE-RAE

"You're not in trouble," Gu Han held out a hand to reassure me. "What I want to talk to you about is which characters you'll play this season. I'd like to add a backup to Cloud Emperor and Cloud Empress."

"Which character is that?"

"Storm Harper."

"Uh," I was at a loss for words. Storm Harper was his wife's elite level avatar; she'd been a very capable gamer in her own right and he'd designed Storm Harper specifically for her.

"The choice is yours, obviously, but I think I'd like to see her play again—even if it's only one season."

"I would love to play Storm Harper," I said. "I think that's your finest work, honestly. I just don't want to do harm to good memories."

"That won't happen," Gu Han told me. "I don't think I'd trust anyone else with Storm Harper."

"Why are you telling me this privately?"

"Because I'd like you to train with Storm Harper privately. This way, if a situation arises where Storm Harper might help the team, I want to be able to bring her aboard as a surprise player."

"Because you think, just as I do, that eventually, they could nix both avatars I plan to use."

"Yes."

"Then there's something else you ought to know," I said.

"What's that?"

I told him about my suspicions concerning Chung Minjun, who'd likely been offered money by the German team to sell out Black Skies. He kept the information under advisement.

HAE JIN

"Well, Min-ho and Shi-joon can room together, Do-yoon and Hae Jin can room together, and Man-sik and Hu Lin can room together, to make room for the guards coming in," Gu Han sorted out sleeping quarters at Black Skies. "If anyone needs help moving things, everybody should pitch in."

The twins already roomed together, so they'd stay where they were. Gu Han, the twins and Manta were the only ones without new roommates.

I didn't mind sharing with Do-yoon, but I did ask if we could get another bed for each new roommate.

"Osprey has already made arrangements—beds will be here by the end of the day," Gu Han said.

"I was worried you'd kick me," Do-yoon teased.

"Hmmph. I may kick you anyway."

"Osprey has also bought memberships for each of you at a nearby athletic club, so you can get your exercising done there, either on treadmills or running their indoor track. The van will leave here every day at six-thirty. Unless you're leaving earlier for other types of exercising, be in the van or face a fine."

"Can we swim with Manta?" Si-woo raised a hand.

"Can you do at least thirty laps?" Gu Han asked.

"I don't think he can swim," Min-ho laughed.

"I think running is better for you," Gu Han said and that was the end of it.

"Come on. I want to see this," Do-yoon said.

"But," I argued as he pulled me toward Manta's room.

"I want to see what a security net looks like," he wheedled.

"You think she'll show it to me?"

"I hope so. Come on." He knocked lightly on Manta's dorm door before I could stop him.

"What are you two doing?" Manta answered the door dressed in pajamas and a wrap.

"He wants to see your security net," I said before Do-yoon could lay any blame on me.

"Oh. Come in. I'll show it to you."

"When did you have time to bring all this in?" I asked as I surveyed the setup she'd built atop a desk that hadn't been in her room two days before.

"None of your beeswax," she told me in English. "Anyway, this is what it looks like," she tapped a button and a three-sixty of headquarters popped up on all three screens, lit up overall by a grid of neon-green dots. "If anything human-size comes through, we get a signal. If a machine or an object of any size comes through, we get a signal."

"Any size meaning?" Do-yoon asked.

"Bullet size or less, even."

"So, if somebody shoots at us," I drew out the question.

"We'll know about it. Specifically, Man-sik will know about it, as will a select crew at Sea Eagle Security. We've placed the same type of security nets around both family homes and around my building. Other guards will be notified if those perimeters are breached. Is that enough for tonight? I'm really tired."

"Yes. We'll ask for more details later," I steered Do-yoon toward the door.

"Awesome. Good-night."

Rae-Rae

I had just crawled into my waiting bed when the call came from the Blue House. The President was on the phone, asking me why Undersecretary Chin from China would bring a small army into the country illegally and break three prisoners out of jails in Busan. I spent the next two hours explaining what I could safely tell him about our unwelcome visitors and the criminals who were now roaming the country.

"You don't look like you went to bed at all last night," Hae Jin accused me as he and I climbed into Hu Lin's SUV the following morning. Do-yoon followed Hae Jin into the back seat; Dan-bi had come to help Man-sik with the others later.

"I told you the Blue House has me on speed dial. I spent two hours trying to explain to the President why Chinese Undersecretary of Defense Chin would break three Korean criminals out of prison."

"What did you end up telling him?" Do-yoon asked.

"That Chin has a personal beef with me, and the three jailbreakers have a beef with Hae Jin. They're combining forces to get rid of both of us."

"What did the President say?"

"He offered military assistance if it's needed, since we already have the cooperation of the NIS."

"Are you taking him up on his offer?" Hae Jin asked.

"Not at the moment. We don't need to muddy the water. Anybody involved in this can be bought without our knowledge, don't you think? We don't need a larger number who might sell us out. You don't know Kang Dong-hyung like I do. Paying people to switch loyalties is his favorite MO."

"He's nearly seventy and on the run. How does he have the strength and stamina to do all this?" Do-yoon asked.

"Haven't you noticed that nasty people seem to enjoy good health? He's always been that way."

"Sometimes it appears that they live forever, too," Hae Jin offered his opinion. Hu Lin pulled into the parking lot of the athletic club, where a guard waved us into a specific parking space.

"He'll be watching the lot and has been since Hae Jin's Jeep was compromised," Hu Lin explained. "We've added some security measures to the bus, too."

"Good. Thank you," Do-yoon said with a sigh. "Come on, Cousin. Time to rip those muscles."

WE SWITCHED UP OUR COFFEESHOP ON THE WAY BACK TO headquarters, since we could be tracked by our habits. Besides, Go Ha-eun's specialty was poison, and I didn't want anyone else to die by her hand.

"It's gonna be a long eight months if these people aren't captured before then," Hae Jin said in English as we climbed out of Hu Lin's SUV.

"Yeah," I echoed his sentiment. "Osprey will provide secure transportation on their company jet for the team and our security detail," I told him.

"You've spent too much already," Do-yoon told me while patting Hae Jin on the back.

"What's your life worth?" I asked. "I have money. For me, this boils down to not letting those assholes kill again."

CHAPTER 18

H*ae Jin*

We were scheduled to fly into Berlin two days before the competition started. The games would take place over two days, with ours coming last. We had reserved seats to watch the other games before ours; it was a good opportunity to see what we'd be facing in later bouts.

The flight time was roughly twelve hours from Seoul to Berlin; at least we'd have better seats on Osprey's jet.

"You packed yet? Bus pulls out at four today," Gu Han poked his head through my open door.

"I'm packed. What about the equipment?"

"We have Osprey techs downstairs loading mice and keyboards into cases," he said. "All labeled with your names and team affiliation."

I'd never had this kind of VIP treatment. Ever. "Is this how the other half lives?" I asked Gu Han with a grin.

"I've never been this close to the other half. How would I know?" Gu Han shot back.

This is to protect lives, the White Flower told me. *Technology can be compromised if the enemy handles it*.

Manta was making sure our equipment was guarded and checked every step of the way. "What's for lunch?" I asked Gu Han, changing the subject.

"WE LEAVE AT SIX PM FROM SEOUL," THE MALE FLIGHT attendant explained to us after we'd loaded onto Osprey's jet. "We will arrive at roughly six a.m., Seoul time. It will be around ten p.m., local time in Berlin, the night before."

"I asked for Jeremy. If Alice were onboard, the twins wouldn't leave her alone," Manta whispered to Do-yoon, who sat beside her one row behind mine.

I thought about hauling him out of his seat and plopping him into the empty one beside mine, but I figured it would be too obvious. For now, I'd leave him alone.

Jeremy went through the flight safety spiel afterward, adding that anyone causing trouble aboard the aircraft would be "lovingly tossed from the nearest exit."

"Twelve hours," Do-yoon sighed. "And dark when we get there."

"Not much international travel?" Manta asked.

"Hardly any. I've been to Taiwan," Do-yoon shrugged.

"You should get out more."

He was cozying up to Manta, and friendly conversation was the easiest path to do just that.

Yes, I was in a snit.

Your fault, the White Flower sniped.

Shut up.

"YOU HAVE TO BE KIDDING ME."

Manta peered out her window after we'd taxied to a private gate at the airport in Berlin. We could see a crowd waving signs inside the airport, waiting for us to deplane.

"We have fans," I teased her. "Did you expect to come in without a single person knowing?"

"I was hoping it would be subdued," she sighed. At lease we couldn't hear anything yet; the jet's door hadn't been opened.

Man-sik took charge of our guards, which had doubled to six before we left Seoul. They were already on their feet and ready to escort the team through the airport to a waiting bus.

The gangway connected to the jet; the door was opened and we could hear screams and shouting.

"This is your fault," Manta rose to her feet. Do-yoon had already stationed himself near the door to protect us.

"My fault?"

"Too handsome, remember? If they don't have posters by now, they will have soon enough."

The photos we'd taken had gone live on the website the day before. She was probably right about the posters, too. Those and the programs for sale plus the booklets that were giveaways with early ticket purchases were probably being traded already.

"Freshen up your lipstick, baby girl," I reached out to tap her nose. "We'll be walking through a crowd in five minutes."

"Great." She slipped into a fashionable, deep-purple sequined jacket, then did her lips with deep purple lipstick and donned the purple-tinted eyewear she wore as Manta Ray. Her hair was already in a tidy topknot secured by hair sticks. She was adorable, but I didn't say it.

Maybe you should *say it*, the White Flower said.

Shut up.

"I'll walk out behind him," Manta pointed at me when Gu Han asked which of us would go after Shi-joon, the twins and Min-ho. He lined us up, intending to walk behind Manta, with Hu Lin walking last in line to protect us from behind.

"Smile and wave," Gu Han shouted over the increasing din as Shi-joon walked out the door first, followed closely by the twins.

The screaming went up significantly when I appeared, while airport security tried desperately to hold the crowd back behind roped-off lines. Signs bearing my name were everywhere, as were signs for all the others. A knot of fans began chanting Manta's name the moment she emerged from the jetway, and Gu Han's appearance drew shouts and applause.

As Gu Han instructed, Manta and I waved to the crowd and smiled at a sea of faces. Flashes from cameras and phones nearly blinded us, there were so many of them. I should have asked Manta to walk in front of me; I worried about her during the entire journey through the airport to reach our waiting bus.

Gu Han and Hu Lin will watch out for her, the White Flower said. Its words didn't reassure me as much as they should have.

"THE TECHS AND EXTRA GUARDS HAVE ROOMS JUST BELOW ours," Manta said as we settled into our penthouse suites. "And they can order room service if they're hungry. The only thing we don't allow is drinking while they're on the job. They can wait for a day off if that's what they want."

"At least our gear was delivered to us," I sighed. I'd already stowed my case inside the bedroom I shared with Do-yoon.

"I hope I can get used to the time difference fast," Manta slumped onto a white sofa near the massive windows.

"A warm shower usually helps me," Shi-joon offered as he took a chair opposite the sofa. "Traveling tends to make me tired anyway."

"I think a few laps in the pool might be nice," Manta said. Lifting the phone, she dialed the concierge. "Yes, I'd like to swim," she told him. "Is that possible this late at night? Thank you."

She replaced the phone in its cradle. "I can swim anytime I want," she held up a hand in an elegant gesture. "I only have to let them know and someone will be at the door to let me in. Now, I have to tell Hu Lin that he has to follow me down there."

"I'll come with you. I haven't been in a pool in who knows how long," Shi-joon grinned. "Come on, Hae Jin. You, too."

Hu Lin was waiting for us by the time we'd changed into swimsuits and the robes provided by the hotel. As promised, a hotel employee let us through the locked door into the pool area and promised to wait until we were finished.

Towels were waiting on a table nearby; Manta didn't waste time and dove in, then began with her usual butterfly stroke.

"She swims like a fish," Shi-joon sighed before pulling off his robe.

"Somebody else called her an otter," I said.

"Otter it is. Come on, the water looks great."

"I THINK I'M TIRED ENOUGH TO GO TO BED NOW," MANTA told me after we'd gotten back and taken showers. She'd already told Hu Lin to get some rest. He'd ordered room service and then went to bed. Manta ordered a fruit and cheese plate and ate lightly; Do-yoon, Shi-joon and I had sandwiches.

"Brush your teeth," I called after her.

"Like I wouldn't," she yelled back before going into her room and shutting the door.

"She's adorable," Do-yoon grinned.

"Huh?" Shi-joon and I turned toward Do-yoon at the same time.

"Metaphorically speaking," Do-yoon raised hands in surrender.

"Shi-joon, this is my cousin, Lee Do-yoon," I officially introduced him. "He knows who Manta is, too."

"A fellow conspirator?"

"Yes. Due to unfortunate circumstances, however."

"I'll explain later. For now, let's go to bed. We have to be wide awake and presentable for video recording at the game tomorrow at three."

"Today at three," Do-yoon corrected.

"Sure."

Rae-Rae

I wasn't expecting an audience, but the fans who stayed at our hotel had lined up outside the exercise room and the pool to watch the team the following morning. I was grateful that only a few sour glances from Man-sik kept them at a safe distance while I swam.

"You were right about the twins," Man-sik informed me after we were the only ones left in the elevator for the penthouse. "They sneaked out last night and drank with a table full of girls."

"Does Gu Han know?"

"It's up to you whether you want to tell him."

"I'll let him know before we leave to watch the first match. We won't know if there's damage done until we face Force Five."

"Have you taken that into account?"

"As much as I could. Don't worry about it—it's only the first game of the season."

"And a matchup with last season's champion."

"Yes. Don't remind me."

"Guard Hanuel wants a word with you before we leave."

"I want to talk to him, too." I didn't add that I also wanted a word with Kija and wondered if that would be possible or advisable. "Is Hu Lin finished beating up Hae Jin yet?"

"No idea. They're probably putting on a decent exhibition, though, for the adoring fans."

"All right. I'm heading for the shower. I'll see you later."

The moment Man-sik was out the door, Kija appeared from nothing. "We are watching," he said, giving me a slight bow.

"I was hoping you were here," I said. "If Undersecretary Chin is here with the others, things could go badly."

"If we find his false army, we can discreetly pull them away. The Undersecretary is nearly blind, now, and is next to powerless without someone to guide him."

"Kang Dong-hyung isn't powerless, as long as he has those two women with him."

"We will watch for those three as well."

"Thank you. Keep them alive if possible; I want to talk to them if they're captured."

"They surely know we are waiting for their appearance," Kija mused.

"Unless Undersecretary Chin hasn't told them everything," I said. "He wants the Lotus to do his bidding, and he doesn't share well with others."

"Would you ever do that—follow his commands?"

"I'd rather die."

"We will do our best to ensure that never happens." Kija bowed again and disappeared.

HAE JIN

"They were watched the entire time," Man-sik handed photographs to Gu Han of the twins having drinks with several women the night before. "The guard didn't interfere—he was told only to ensure their safety."

"Damn," I pinched the bridge of my nose. "Do we know if they said anything—wait, how would the guard know about our strategy and planning?"

"If this weren't the first game of the season, I'd send both of them home," Gu Han said, then added several curse words to his statement.

"If we had a second alternate with us, I'd make them sit this game out," I muttered. "Two rules broken right off, and if they said anything, that's a direct violation of orders that came straight from us and Team Owner."

They'd been told no drinking and no sneaking out. While I wasn't surprised, they'd gotten drunk with six girls and who knew what they'd said or which questions they'd answered?

"We'll know when we face the German team," Gu Han said. "Let's table this for now. I'll suspend them and their paychecks if they ever try this again, though."

"Come on, it's almost time to leave for the first match," I said. "Gather up the team and let's go."

"I THOUGHT THE SEQUIN OUTFIT WOULD BE HARD TO BEAT," Shi-joon shook his head when Manta arrived at the bus wearing a purple, fringed jacket and black, boot-cut jeans. She'd French-braided her hair, and the purple tips only showed at the bottom side of the braid. Four-inch amethyst drop earrings hung from her ears, lending her a graceful air.

"I want to know who did her shopping," Do-yoon sighed. "They know her pretty well, I think."

"Come on, get on the bus," I pulled Do-yoon's collar. "Stop staring," I lectured with a hiss.

"Manta, I want you," someone shouted nearby.

"Can I make a rude gesture?" Manta asked as she walked past me to climb the bus steps.

"No rude gestures, baby girl," I breathed against her ear.

"Crap."

I snorted a laugh and followed her aboard.

"THEY'RE RECORDING FOR A LATER BROADCAST," GU HAN told us as we were led to our reserved seats in the hotel arena. Cameras were recording Black Skies and Force Five during our arrivals; we'd be sitting across the aisle from one another during the first two matches.

Gu Han and Min-ho made sure to bookend the twins, so they wouldn't toss insults in Force Five's direction. We had a brief moment of calm before the paid attendees were allowed through the doors; the arena exploded with sound once the doors were flung open.

The large overhead screen came to life and cameras panned Black Skies' and Force Five's seats. Cheers went up from a blossoming crowd as more and more fans arrived to take their seats.

Manta was seated between Do-yoon and me, with Shi-joon between me and Min-ho. The other guards were seated behind us, keeping an eye on everything.

"Baby girl, did you bring your emergency rations?" I leaned in and whispered in English.

"I always bring them. Hu Lin and Man-sik have more if you're about to cave in."

"I'm all right. I just wanted to make sure you were okay."

"I'm okay for now. I promise. What are we doing for dinner between matches?"

"We're booked at a restaurant in this hotel—this reservation was made right after the schedules came out."

"Oh. Okay."

"Gu Han double checked it, just to make sure."

"Good."

"Have you seen this?" I asked, pulling out my phone and unlocking it.

"Seen what?"

"The shirts?" I showed her the picture I'd taken earlier of a group of fans who'd had their own Manta Ray shirts made. They looked really good.

"Well, look at that," she smiled at the photo. "It's really nice, and the manta ray is purple, too. Can we find out who designed them?"

"I think they'd love for you to ask," I said.

"Then I'll look for them. I really want one of those shirts."

"We'll find them. I'm sure they'll make themselves easy to locate."

"You're the boss."

"I am."

"The cameras are watching you two," Do-yoon hissed. Our images took up an entire, enormous monitor at the front of the venue.

"Fist bump?" I asked, holding up my fist.

"Sure." Manta bumped her fist with mine, then we did a simultaneous starburst with our fingers. The crowd laughed and cheered.

THE FRENCH TEAM DEFEATED NORWAY IN THE FIRST GAME, which came as no surprise. The Nokken couldn't compete well against France's speed and practiced strategies.

During the break, Gu Han was approached about an interview with Black Skies the following day, before we took on Force Five. He declined, saying we'd save our comments for after the game.

Questions were shouted at us by members of the media as we left the arena to go to the restaurant, but we only smiled and waved as Gu Han instructed.

"I'm glad we didn't have to talk to the media," Manta sighed as she took her seat at the table between Min-ho and me. Do-yoon had been beaten to that seat by Min-ho somehow.

"We don't need that distraction," Manta added.

"They always try to throw us off balance," Min-ho agreed. "I much prefer talking to them after the match. We will have evidence to back up our answers by that time."

"All the teams have been asked to do a short signing event tomorrow morning," Gu Han announced. "For the guests who paid for a signed poster, sight unseen, before the tournament. It will only last an hour," he added.

"You'll be busy," Manta bumped her shoulder against mine.

"I think that guy who wants you will probably be there," I teased.

"Has anybody ever been slapped at one of these events?"

"We're supposed to have security at the event," I said. "You don't want to be hauled off to jail, do you?"

"Well, that could cause an international incident," Manta observed.

"True enough," I agreed.

THE SECOND GAME BETWEEN THE US AND ARGENTINA WAS hard-fought, with Argentina's team pulling out a victory in the last few seconds. The crowd loved the excitement, and journalists were clamoring to speak with both teams afterward.

That gave us an easier way out of the arena, so we took it rather than staying to watch the Q&A. Our hotel was barely five minutes away, but a crowd of fans waited for us when we got off the bus.

"There's your shirt," I tapped Manta's shoulder, nodding toward three fans who all wore a Manta Ray shirt.

"Hu Lin," Manta turned and beckoned for her guard. I went with them as Manta walked toward the three in matching shirts.

I thought the youngest and smallest of the three would lose her voice, she shrieked so loudly when Manta approached and shook her hand. We could barely make ourselves heard over the noise of the crowd, whose excitement level skyrocketed when approached by two members of the team.

Manta signed all three shirts, got a business card to buy her own, and took photos with them.

Actually, I was included in the photos, which caused much screaming and sign waving. Hu Lin pulled us both away afterward; we waved and smiled at the crowd as we were hauled toward the hotel doors.

"Two Peace Prizes and I never got that kind of reaction," Manta deadpanned next to me as we walked into the relative quiet of the hotel lobby. I threw back my head and laughed.

"JUST SIGN OVER YOUR PHOTO, NOT ACROSS THE FACE," GU Han instructed the following morning as we prepared to leave for the signing event. "That's for the team posters. For individual posters, sign to the side if possible."

I knew the drill—I'd signed enough posters in my two years with Black Skies to know what should be done.

"Manta made a popular gaming blogger's newsfeed," Min-ho held up his phone. "They're talking about her and Hae Jin signing autographs and taking photos with a group of fans last night."

"Good or bad?" Gu Han asked.

"All good—they loved the finger hearts in the photos. They're comparing that to Werner, who insulted some of his fans on the way to his room last night."

"Good PR is always welcome," Gu Han sighed. "Come on or we'll be late to the signing."

We were dressed in our black uniforms bearing the team's signature lightning strike and featuring Osprey Technology and Robotics' bird emblem for the signing, just as we'd be when we took on Force Five at seven that evening. We even had an extra uniform in case the unexpected happened.

"Come on, shorty," I tapped Manta's shoulder as we headed for the door behind Gu Han.

"How can you tell?" Manta wrinkled her nose at me. "I think you're just too tall and can't judge shortness properly."

"Short *and* opinionated," I sighed.

"Tall *and* short-sighted," Manta countered. One of our guards snickered.

THE SIGNING WAS SET UP IN A HOTEL BALLROOM, AND BY the time we arrived, fans were already lined up, posters in hand.

Boxes of markers were set at each table for our use; we'd go through the entire box if we signed everything brought to us. I pushed my way through to sit next to Manta at the middle of our assigned table. Someone had hung a Black Skies banner behind us, which bore the names of our sponsors as well as the group photo we'd taken of the team in uniform two weeks earlier. Osprey provided the banner; Team Owner and his staff had arranged to send it to the hotel for display.

"Take your seats; two minutes," a tournament manager called out. In two minutes, the doors opened and we were inundated with fans.

RAE-RAE

Ten minutes of the designated hour remained and still the crowd hadn't thinned. Our only consolation was that Force Five would be just as weary as we were from signing posters.

Each team member had become accustomed to focusing on the fan in front of them, smiling and signing their posters. Those with team posters followed their poster down the table for each signature. If they also had an individual poster, those were signed when they reached that team member.

Hae Jin had more than his share of those. He laughed when my numbers began to rise as well. "Wait until next time," he grinned evilly.

"Right on, too tall and handsome," I sniffed and signed another poster.

"I've never seen Hae Jin laugh," a fan handed him her poster to sign.

"That's my job," I told her. "He's just too serious, so I get paid to make him laugh."

"Good job," she told me and handed me a poster of myself to sign.

"Nice," Hae Jin fist-bumped her, making her laugh.

Things should have gone that way the whole time, but that didn't happen.

It didn't happen because of who showed up near the end, and if things had happened even a millisecond later, we'd all be screwed.

She was there, waiting in line.

Waiting for her chance to strike.

Go Ah-eun, hiding a syringe behind a poster, was prepared to end Hae Jin's life with a lethal dose of her sister's special potion.

Something made me look up as the syringe was revealed. Go Ah-eun was fast; she had almost hit Hae Jin's hand with the tip of the needle when I forced time to stop.

Only Hae Jin wasn't affected; he jerked his hand away with

a gasp as Go Ah-eun stared, her eyes the only thing capable of movement.

"I see Undersecretary Chin wasn't completely forth-coming when he arranged this—now was he?" Reaching out, I gently removed the syringe from Go Ah-eun's paralyzed fingers. "Should I stick you with this, instead?" I held it up. Fear filled her eyes, then.

"So, you are afraid of dying. I always wondered about that."

"Lotus?" Kija appeared on Go Ah-eun's left, while his second-in-command appeared on her right and took her by the arm.

"Imprison her. Not only do I want to question her, I'd like to decide all their fates together, I think."

"We can do that."

"Can you put this in a safe place?" I held out the syringe.

"It will be done." He removed a metal tube from a pocket and slid the syringe inside

before capping the top.

"Can we put someone in her place?" I asked.

"Certainly." Kija brought one of his Monks forward. I pulled the poster from Go Ah-eun's hands and gave it to him. He nodded to me. Kija and his Second disappeared with Go Ah-eun.

Raising my hand, I was about to put time in motion again.

"Wait." Hae Jin, who'd remained silent during the entire episode, spoke now.

"Are you okay?" I asked him.

"Rae-Rae," he spoke my real name for the first time. Then, he gently cupped my face with one of his hands, leaned forward and kissed me.

The kiss was perfect, and left me wide-eyed and breathless when Hae Jin pulled away.

CHAPTER 19

Hae Jin

"I recognized her," I told Manta when we were outside a restaurant waiting to go inside for lunch.

"Good. If nothing else, at least one of them is out of our way. It's just like Undersecretary Chin not to give full disclosure on something like this. If Kang Dong-hyung finds that out, it'll be interesting to see which one ends up on top."

"Discussing the weather?" Min-ho arrived and draped arms over both our shoulders.

"Yes. Why aren't you? I hear it's the thing to do in gaming circles nowadays," Manta teased him.

"Our table is ready," Gu Han called out. Min-ho dropped his arms and we followed Gu Han into the restaurant.

I wanted my hands on Manta, but that would be too much. Unless I was mistaken, tongues could already be wagging about my penchant for sitting next to her. I'd gotten one taste, she hadn't pushed me away, and now I wanted more.

As for the Monks who'd taken my kidnapper, I wondered where they'd taken her, but that question would have to wait for later. Manta said she wanted to ask questions—maybe she would take me with her when that happened.

Because I had questions, too.

"If I order the petite filet with lobster tail, will you guys help me finish it?" Manta set her menu down.

"Do you even need to ask?" I told her. "Somebody at this table will eat whatever you don't. Besides, I'm ordering the ribeye with lobster."

"You did sign a lot of posters," Manta nodded. "You deserve a bonus."

"Are you ticklish?"

"Why do you ask?"

Min-ho and I tickled her from both sides at the same time. Manta giggled and tried to fend us off.

"Are you even adults?" Gu Han asked patiently when we stopped.

"It depends," I said. Min-ho barked a laugh. For as long as I'd been with the team, we'd never laughed this much or had as much fun when out together. Manta had helped us find a release we weren't aware we'd needed.

After lunch, we watched the third game, then went back to our hotel to rest a bit before taking on the Germans. We'd find out then whether our secrets were safe or if we'd been compromised by the twins' indiscretions.

The two who'd normally be acting up at this time weren't—the twins were unusually quiet. That worried me. Had they done something accidentally?

Or on purpose?

We'd find out when the match started.

"Give me your key cards and anything else in your pockets," Gu Han called out as he passed a bag around for what we carried. We'd be televised live and didn't want any bulges or anything else showing in our uniforms. "Your things will be guarded and kept safe while you're playing," Gu Han added.

Manta had already handed her things to Hu Lin, who was used to carrying for her. The only thing of mine that couldn't be passed over was the White Flower, and it had a mind of its own anyway.

"Let's go," Gu Han called out. With our guards beside us, we followed him out of the hotel.

This was the game most fans had come to see—a replay of the previous season's final. There was, however, one main difference; Manta had replaced Min-ho, rather than Chung Minjun, our alternate, who'd frozen in the championship game.

Or so most people believed.

"Are we ready for this?" Shi-joon asked me as we loaded onto the bus.

"If we're not, we've wasted a lot of practice time for nothing," I told him. "Manta and I will help if you need it."

"I know. I hope I don't need it."

The ride to the venue was quiet, with only a few whispers. We were all lost in our thoughts, preparing for the match. Manta sat beside me, her mouth set and a determined look in her eyes.

I wanted to tell her not to worry, but she'd faced worse enemies than this, one of whom she'd dealt with only a few hours earlier.

No matter what the outcome of this game, we'd leave everything we had on the screen for the pundits and gamers to discuss and replay.

WE WERE INTRODUCED FIRST AS WE TOOK OUR SEATS AT THE gaming consoles. The hometown crowd erupted, however, when Force Five took the stage. They were the favorites to take this match and Werner, their captain, wouldn't settle for anything less.

Werner was famous for handing out insults, but as he spoke in German, I didn't understand what he'd said before donning his headset.

Manta knew, though. I thought about asking her but held

back. Her face had already settled into its icy mask, and I didn't want to interfere with that.

The announcers presented the list of avatars we were dismissing from the German team. It was a standard list that gave them an edge if we let them play their first choices.

Then, the Germans' list went up, and there were gasps, not just from the crowd, but from our team as well.

Cloud Emperor and Cloud Empress were both on the list. Werner was laughing and saying something in German as we studied the list; I knew that somehow, the twins had likely released that information to someone during their drinking binge.

"Manta?" I mouthed at her.

"No worries," she mouthed back. "Play Samurai Kusunoki." Most of the time, he was stricken from the list since they didn't want to face me at my strongest.

"Black Skies, enter your avatars," the announcer called out.

As team captain, I loaded up Samurai Kusunoki. Shi-joon followed with his second-best avatar, healer-warrior Thunderhead. The twins put up their warriors, and then it was Manta's turn. Werner was out of his seat and shouting angrily when Manta loaded up Storm Harper.

The crowd, stunned at first, burst into deafening applause. Storm Harper hadn't been seen since Gu Han's wife passed. The announcers spoke excitedly, but nobody could hear them over the noise of the crowd.

Then, Force Five loaded up their avatars—they had no

surprises for us. "Everyone, remember your strategies. Manta, is there anything about Storm Harper you want to tell us before we start?" I spoke into my microphone.

"Just treat me as if I'm playing Cloud Empress," she said. "And if we take the upper hand, follow my lead."

"Get ready," I barked.

The countdown began, and then we were in it.

"YOU SEEMED PARTICULARLY MOTIVATED DURING THIS game, Manta Ray," a gaming journalist spoke during our interview following the game. "Can you tell us what inspired you?"

"I don't take it well when the captain of the opposing team calls me *dumme schlampe,*" she replied.

The journalist reddened at her words—Werner had apparently called her a stupid bitch. "If you check the recording at the beginning, it happens around the two-minute and twenty-seven second mark," Manta added. "If you can't hear it, you can read his lips easily."

"How would you reply to that insult?" A female journalist asked.

"I believe I gave him my reply. He lost. It's over."

I wanted to laugh. Werner *had* lost. Badly. Force Five had never taken a beating like the one we'd given them. The game ended in a little over seventeen minutes.

"Everyone is calling Storm Harper's return a triumphant one," the first journalist remarked. "What do you say to that?"

"I want to thank Gu Han for trusting me with her," Manta said. "And I hope I did justice to her character and capabilities."

"Will Storm Harper be on everybody's ban list from now on?" the female journalist asked.

"Probably."

"Lee Hae Jin, were you surprised that Samurai Kusunoki wasn't stricken from the list?"

"Very," I replied. "But I was happy to play my favorite avatar. I suppose I should thank Force Five for that."

The interview lasted for another half hour, then Gu Han rounded us up and pointed us out the door. Shortly after we loaded onto the bus, Man-sik and Hu Lin approached Manta for a private word.

She caught my hand when I started to move away. "Stay," she told me. Hu Lin nodded his agreement.

"The police have Undersecretary Chin in custody, but he's unconscious and in the hospital. Somebody had beaten him badly before he was found," Man-sik said.

"Probably Kang Dong-hyung," Manta sighed. "After he figured out he'd been lied to, and after Go Ah-eun disappeared while trying to attack Hae Jin during the signing. This means that Kang Dong-hyung is now in charge of Undersecretary Chin's army."

"Do-yoon has been on the phone with the NIS, trying to

clear the way for us to talk to Undersecretary Chin—while he's still alive," Man-sik explained.

"They don't expect him to live?"

"It could go either way at this point."

"Crap."

"So far, this is a standoff with the Chinese Government," Do-yoon joined the conversation. "China doesn't want anyone talking to their Undersecretary, and Germany doesn't want to interfere. Right now, the answer is no, and we're scheduled to fly back to Korea tomorrow."

Without thinking, I reached out to rub Manta's shoulders. We still had one other person we could question; I just didn't know where she was.

"Don't worry if we can't talk to him," Manta's shoulders sagged. I pulled her against me and held her tight. At least Man-sik and Hu Lin were blocking us from the others on the bus.

"Then let's go back to the hotel. I know you're tired," Man-sik said.

We took our seats after that; Gu Han promised us a team dinner when we returned to Seoul and everybody was satisfied.

THE FLIGHT HOME WAS TIRING—MORE SO THAN THE FLIGHT to Berlin five days earlier. Due to the time difference, it was the following day in Seoul. We ate a small meal and went to bed—after greeting fans at the airport and having more than a few follow our bus to headquarters.

We had an interview with local journalists scheduled for the following day, but all we wanted at the moment was to sleep away our fatigue. The only thing that would have made going to bed better for me was if I could've held Manta while I slept.

OUR INTERVIEW TURNED INTO A LIVE APPEARANCE ON A local television show, with fans in the audience. Manta almost hyperventilated.

Not because of the fans, but because someone could recognize her.

"When are you going to tell Mom and Dad?" I asked.

"Huh?"

"At least that we're working together," I said.

"I need an antacid," she muttered, holding a hand over her stomach. She and I were alone in the kitchen early the following morning, having our first coffee and waiting for Dan-bi to drive us to the athletic club for exercise.

Hu Lin and Man-sik had been given two days off to rest after the busy trip to Berlin. Do-yoon was still asleep in my dorm room.

"Don't you call this being proactive?" I asked. "Before they find out and demand to see us?"

"Will they do that?"

"You're making this into something more than it should be," I said. "You know them—they don't bite."

"This is different."

"How?"

"You're their precious son," she held out a hand in my direction. "They'll automatically think," she didn't finish.

"Think what?"

"I don't know. Forget I said anything. Come on, Dan-bi just pulled up outside."

TWO EXTRA GUARDS MET US AT THE ATHLETIC CLUB. ONE went with me to work out with Trainer Park, the other went with Dan-bi to watch over Manta. I was glad—after the incident at our signing in Germany, I'd become more aware of our surroundings.

And more concerned for our safety.

That morning, I gave the lesson to Trainer Park. I'd been working out in Germany with Hu Lin and was better as a result.

"I think we both need to work out with Hu Lin," Trainer Park sighed after I'd taken him down the third time.

"I'll ask him," I shrugged. I had money of my own if

paying for lessons would convince Hu Lin to train me. Dad had kept a portfolio of stocks for me since I was young; it was probably worth quite a bit by now, but I hadn't bothered to check.

"If we hurry to clean up, you think we can see Manta before she gets out of the pool?" Trainer Park asked with a grin.

"Hmmph." I stalked toward the hallway and the showers beyond, hoping for that very thing.

"HAVE A SEAT, SHE'S IN THE SHOWER," DAN-BI OFFERED AN extra chair at her pool-side table. I took it, although I felt disappointed that I hadn't hurried enough to see Manta's last few laps.

In ten minutes, Manta approached, dressed in faded designer blue jeans and a purple T-shirt, with hair tied in a purple-tipped ponytail with a purple bow.

"The real thing hardly ever wears purple," Dan-bi sighed, shaking her head.

"Who does her shopping?" I asked.

"Auntie Nari. She used to have Thiwat's position, until she retired. She's working part-time now as Manta's dresser. Nobody argues with Auntie Nari's choices—they're all good."

"Ready to go?" Manta asked when she reached our table.

"Yes." I rose from my seat and allowed Dan-bi to go first.

That way, I could put a careful hand over Manta's shoulders as she moved forward.

We drove out of our way to get lattes that morning, but it was worth it to enjoy some extra time with my girl.

"Have you seen the message boards?" Min-ho asked when he and the others got back from their exercise later.

"What's going on?" I asked.

"Mostly they've all got the video of Werner calling Manta names before the game started, and he's getting trashed—even by some of his own fans."

"Like he didn't deserve it," Gu Han said, shrugging out of his windbreaker and hanging it on the back of a barstool in the kitchen. "I think he's learned not to make Manta angry. Everybody, the news crew will be here in an hour to film the morning show for tomorrow. Please make yourselves presentable," he called out.

"Some people are shipping you and Manta," Min-ho leaned in to tell me. They've got stills from the video of you two talking before the games."

"Like that's a real reason to put people together," Gu Han complained. "I talk to all of you. Does that mean we're together?"

"That would be really weird," Min-ho shook his head. "Nobody would do that."

"People will put her with anyone she talks to," Gu Han said. "She's a woman in a man's world, so the rumors were set to fly the minute she signed with the team. I'm grateful she's with us and not somewhere else. Can you imagine facing her if she'd signed up elsewhere?"

"I wouldn't want that," Min-ho held up a hand.

"Neither do I. Don't feed the rumors," he said.

If Min-ho was fishing for a denial from me, leaving the way clear for him to approach Manta, he wasn't going to get it. Gu Han did give me a quick grin when Min-ho moved away, though.

If he didn't know outright, he was good at guessing.

The interview went well with the team; Gu Han did a quick tour of the gaming den and Shi-joon and I did a short demonstration on the big screen for those who weren't familiar with gaming.

"I think your success will bring a lot of new interest," the show's host observed. "I hear the German team was the one to beat, and you took care of that quickly."

"They have all season to correct their mistakes," Gu Han pointed out. "They're a talented team and no doubt will be in the finals again this year. We may face them again at the end."

"Your next game will be here in Seoul?"

"Yes—next weekend. We'll play the French team, who just upended Norway."

"Two tough teams in a row?"

"They're all tough teams. Nobody remains in this sport by playing badly."

The interview ended after that, the news crew packed up and we were back to normal. Or mostly normal.

Gu Han and I had business with the twins and Team Owner, however.

Rae-Rae

"The fact that nothing happened in Berlin may be an indicator that the German team is involved in the hacking," Zhang Bao said. "I haven't heard anything recently on Undersecretary Chin's condition, either, although there is a rumor floating around that he'll be replaced soon."

"I hope his replacement doesn't know about the Monks of the White Flower—or the Lotus," I said. "Are they still refusing to admit Chin's role in breaking three inmates out of Korean prisons?"

"Nobody appears to know anything about that," ZB sighed. "They're completely clueless—according to them. Where are the German team playing next?"

"New York," I said. "Prime hacking territory. I've arranged to send someone to watch for any activity."

"I have tickets for the games in Seoul. I'll be there next weekend," ZB announced.

"As a guest of Team Owner, no doubt."

"Of course."

"Then I don't feel obligated to buy you dinner."

"But the boss always buys."

"*Now* you remember that I'm the boss—when it benefits you in some way."

"Will you make a reservation for us at R'Ong's?" He wanted to eat at the restaurant I owned, which was located in the basement of Ong Group's headquarters.

"What day do you want to go? I'll make sure you have a table and dinner is comped."

"You're the best."

"Right."

"Will they have lasagna?"

"No idea, and I'm not asking them to change the menu just for you."

"Fine. We'll have steak and lobster if the lasagna isn't available."

"You do that."

"Why don't we take the team there?"

"Zhang Bao, what are you thinking?" I complained. "I'm trying to stay under the radar, here, and you want me to waltz into R'Ong's, where all the staff know me?"

"There is that," he agreed.

"Right. Go have a nice dinner with Team Owner. We'll entertain ourselves."

"Has anyone been punished for letting out information on Cloud Emperor and Empress?" ZB changed the subject.

"I think that's being decided now. They're in a meeting with Team Owner, Team Manager and Team Captain."

"Do you think they did it accidentally?"

"I can't tell," I answered truthfully. "Team Owner and the others can sort this out. I don't want any part of it. I have my hands full with more serious criminals."

"Too bad you couldn't talk to Undersecretary Chin."

"Who says I didn't?"

"Did you?"

"I'll never tell. The latest word is that he still has internal bleeding from the beating he took, and that may not turn out so well for him. There are now Chinese military guards outside his hospital room but he's too fragile to move, otherwise they'd have flown him back to China by now."

"That doesn't surprise me."

"Me, either. I should go; I think the meeting with the twins is over now, so we'll likely have a full team meeting before dinner."

"Enjoy," ZB said before hanging up.

Hae Jin

Team meeting in ten, Gu Han texted all of us. He'd be explaining the twins' punishment for releasing sensitive information on other team members and our strategy for taking on Force Five. It could have cost us the game if Gu

Han hadn't approached Manta with a third option for her to play.

In my opinion, it would have been just as bad as Chung Minjun's error if he'd frozen deliberately to cost us the final.

The twins claimed they couldn't recall giving out the vital information—they'd had plenty to drink, though. One of the women kept buying their drinks and they were too oblivious to think it was anything other than ordinary lust.

Heavy fines and a curfew were handed out by Team Owner, plus a warning that if they broke the rules going forward, they could lose their jobs.

Gu Han was incensed about giving away Storm Harper; he'd wanted to save that avatar for a later match that could prove tricky. Instead, the twins' foolishness had revealed all of Manta's avatars at once.

Now, every team would take those avatars into consideration when they faced us in regulation play.

Team Owner held Gu Han and me back after dismissing the twins. Once they were out the door, he asked a question.

"I know this upset you, Gu Han, and I'm sorry about that. How upset do you think Manta is about this betrayal?"

"I don't know. She hasn't said anything," Gu Han confessed. "She certainly took out her anger on Werner and Force Five after Werner called her a stupid bitch, though."

"He won't get even a slap on the wrist for that," Team Owner muttered, leaning back in his chair. "At least the message boards and websites are angry about it, too."

"For now," Gu Han sighed. "You know how easily they're

distracted. It won't surprise me if they turn on a dime when a new scandal breaks."

"And scandals can be manufactured," Team Owner agreed. "I understand your thinking on this. For now, let me know if there is bad blood between the twins and Manta. If they blame her for any part of this, they may find themselves searching for employment at the end of this season."

I'd remained silent during this last, private meeting. I was angry enough as it was so allowing Gu Han to handle it seemed the best course of action. If the twins did try to take it out on Manta—my fists curled tightly at the thought.

Better to let Gu Han handle that, too.

"The situation has been dealt with," Gu Han announced at our team meeting. "I can't give out the full particulars, as those are between the twins and Team Owner. I will say that this behavior can never happen again," he gave the twins a hard look. "It could cost us the championship for the second year in a row."

"Could've cost us *this* game," Min-ho breathed beside me. I elbowed him to keep him quiet. Manta had come in last and chose to sit on a chair farthest from those occupied by the twins.

I couldn't blame her; if I hadn't felt obligated to keep them under close surveillance, I'd have sat farther away, too.

"As for how this affects the team," Gu Han said, "For the next four weeks, Si-woo and Jun-woo will have a seven pm curfew. They will be assigned a guard whenever they leave headquarters or the hotel where we stay and will be required to eat dinner in their room. They will not be allowed alcohol during that time, either. Then, for the remainder of the season, they will not be allowed any personal interaction with fans, unless it's our required website communications, signings and team-sanctioned events."

Gu Han had been adamant about that stipulation, and I supported his idea when he presented it to Team Owner.

Cutting my eyes toward Manta, I attempted to gauge her reaction. Her pretty face was set in its mask, revealing no emotion. I wanted her to tell me how she felt about all this, because she'd never willingly give that away in public.

This is how she is in difficult board meetings, too, the White Flower informed me. *Those in attendance will never read her expressions; she won't give them that information—or that satisfaction.*

"Now, for the rest of you," Gu Han said, addressing the team as a whole, "punishment for this infraction has been set. In no way are you authorized to add to it or mistreat any of your team members going forward. Remember, this is a *team* and not individual factions. Anyone ignoring these instructions may also be punished according to the infraction. Are there any questions?"

Nobody spoke. "Very well, you're dismissed," Gu Han said. "Dinner will be delivered in an hour."

"I JUST NEED SOME MILK, SOME IBUPROFEN AND A SHORT nap," Manta told me when I caught up with her. "I have a slight headache."

"It's not a migraine, is it?" I asked, suddenly concerned.

"No, just a regular, tension headache," she said.

"Anything I can do?"

"No, but thanks for offering."

"Why don't you go lie down now, and I'll bring the milk and ibuprofen?"

"That—sounds nice. Thank you."

WHEN I MADE IT TO MANTA'S ROOM WITH THE BOTTLE OF ibuprofen and a glass of milk, I found Shi-joon already there, kneeling beside Manta's bed.

"I just wanted to see if she has a fever," he explained, holding up the digital thermometer.

"Does she?" I asked.

"It's a little above normal," he handed the thermometer to me so I could read it.

"Want me to call Tae-hyun, baby girl?" I asked her.

"Let's try the ibuprofen first. If the headache doesn't go away and my temp goes up, we'll call Hu Lin."

I set the milk and ibuprofen down on the bedside table and moved to help her sit up. "Were you close to anybody who may have been sick?"

"Maybe, I don't know for sure," she said.

"Here." I placed two ibuprofen in her hand, then held out the glass of milk. She took the medication and drank half the milk before handing the glass back to me. "If I'm sick, you two don't need to catch this," she warned. "Make sure you wash your hands and wear a mask next time."

"If you're sick, we'll do that," I agreed.

"I'll let Gu Han know," Shi-joon said softly. He patted my shoulder and left the room.

"Go to sleep, baby girl," I soothed, brushing hair away from her forehead. "Let the medicine work."

If the medicine doesn't work, I will call the Healer Monk.

Huh?

CHAPTER 20

Hae Jin

"If any other symptoms appear, or if a fever develops, call Hu Lin to come pick her up," Tae-hyun told me.

Shi-joon had spoken to his boyfriend the doctor, who'd then spoken to Tae-hyun. Tae-hyun called me shortly afterward for an update. I'd already told him that Manta's temp was back to normal and she was asleep.

"I will," I promised Tae-hyun. "I know you'll kick my ass if I don't."

He laughed, then said, "That's right. Or I'll just let Hu Lin do it."

"I'd rather you did it. I might actually survive that way."

"Good one," he said. "We'll talk later."

"Her doctor?" Gu Han walked softly into Manta's room and spoke in a whisper.

"Yes. He says unless she develops a fever, then the medicine she took should be enough. If that's not the case, we have to call back."

"We always take this risk when we do anything that involves meeting fans or dealing with the public," Gu Han sighed. "So far, nobody else has complained of a headache or fever, although I should check on the twins."

"I need to stretch my legs; I'll come with you."

"Bring the digital thermometer; we'll do a quick check on everybody."

"Twins first," I said.

"So they won't have time to fabricate an illness," Gu Han agreed.

SI-WOO WAS RUNNING A REAL FEVER; WE FOUND HIM ASLEEP on his bed while Jun-woo played WoW on a laptop. So far, Jun-woo hadn't developed a fever, but he could already be affected by whatever this was.

I checked on Manta again; so far, her temperature was still normal, so I drove her SUV when Gu Han and I took Si-woo to the hospital.

And, as Manta told us, we wore masks to limit our exposure. Si-woo was given an IV and something for the headache, the doctor told us it was likely a virus of some sort and to keep him hydrated. He also told us to wear masks whenever we were within six feet of Si-woo.

"Jun-woo probably has this, too," Gu Han sighed as we loaded Si-woo into the SUV and drove back to headquarters. "They may not be able to play the next game. How likely will it be to get two substitutes this fast?"

"I'll ask Manta. It's a weekend, maybe her little brother and brother-in-law can help us."

"Find out. We need to know how serious Manta's case is, too, if she has the same thing."

"I'll let her doctor know what they say about Si-woo. He can make a decision whether she needs an examination."

"I feel like I need to puke," Si-woo complained from the backseat.

I pulled over quickly; Gu Han helped Si-woo out of the car and he did puke—on the side of the road rather than inside Manta's expensive SUV.

Rae-Rae doesn't have the same thing, the White Flower informed me. *The twins were exposed to this during their drinking binge.*

"Thank goodness," I muttered aloud. "We just have to keep the rest of us healthy, then, and hope Little Brother and his husband can help."

"You talking to someone?" Gu Han asked as he helped Si-woo into the backseat.

"Myself, mostly," I lied.

"LITTLE BROTHER AND BROTHER-IN-LAW ARE COVERING emergencies for another clinic this weekend," Manta shook her head at me while we had coffee the following morning. "But I may have a lead on someone else. I feel fine this morning, and if Gu Han covers for one of the twins, then we only need one extra."

"Who is it?"

"Somebody who's been playing on Little Brother's team for about four months. Little Brother says he's really good, too, but so far, seems to shy away from in-person meetings."

"Then see if we can change his mind," I said. "Jun-woo woke with a fever this morning, so Gu Han sent him to the hospital."

"I'll try to find out who it is," she said.

"I have a question."

"What's that?"

"You said you may have been in contact with someone who could have infected you. Who was it?"

"Oh. Well. I uh," she hesitated.

"Tell me. Especially if I'm not going to like it."

"What kind of logic is that?"

"Tell me."

"I went to question Undersecretary Chin," she said rapidly in English.

"You went to a hospital?" I asked incredulously.

"That wasn't what I expected you to say."

"What did you expect me to say?" I demanded.

"Something along the lines of, 'Are you crazy?'"

"That goes without saying," I snapped. "What did he say?"

"That he underestimated Kang Dong-hyung. What he didn't admit was how badly he underestimated the evil that is Kang Dong-hyung. He thought his trained army of false monks would follow him to the end of the world. It turned out that all of them jumped ship the minute somebody made a better offer. What they won't realize until it's likely too late is that Kang Dong-hyung will sell them out just like he sold out the Undersecretary."

"Did you get anything useful from him?"

"Not directly. He's still trying to save his own skin, remember?"

"So he'll survive his beating?"

"I didn't say that. His doctors are doing what they can, but Kang Dong-hyung generally doesn't leave things to chance. I'm surprised Chin was alive when they found him afterward."

"Did you say anything to anyone else besides Chin?"

"And risk being overheard? No way."

"Did he ask you questions?"

"He tried. I shut him down."

"You think Kang Dong-hyung was listening in some way?"

"Nothing would surprise me about that guy."

"You suspect something, don't you?"

"The very fact that the Undersecretary is still alive makes me suspect something."

"You didn't put yourself in danger, did you?"

"I don't think so."

"I wish you'd told me you were going. I'd have gone with you."

"And that would be exactly the wrong thing to do. Right now, Kang Dong-hyung wants you out of the way. I wouldn't put you in that kind of danger for anything."

"When will you talk to the woman we captured?"

"Soon. For now, we'll let her think she may be left in a cell to rot."

"I want to come with you," I blurted.

"It won't be a pleasant exchange," Manta told me. "People like her and her sister can always find someone else to blame for their crimes and shortcomings."

"I know."

"There's something else I found out this morning," Manta said.

"What's that?"

"The virus that probably infected the twins is having a field day in Belarus right now."

"Oh. The country run by the guy who calls himself a dictator."

"Yeah. That guy."

"You think one of the people who drank with the twins is from there?"

"Maybe. Or has ties, perhaps. Or it could be completely random. I'm trying to find out, though. We're looking for security recordings and anything else that can give a better picture—literally and figuratively—of that impromptu drinking party."

"What are you looking for, specifically, baby girl?"

"Ultimately, ties between Force Five and whoever is pulling the strings on these worldwide hackings."

"This is an ant's nest, isn't it?"

"It could be. Interesting metaphor, by the way."

"Thank you. I'm glad you like it."

"You're welcome."

"Dan-bi's here," I said, glancing toward the front doors.

"Then let's go get our exercise."

RAE-RAE

"His name is Yi Ha-kun, and when I said you were my sister and played for Black Skies, he was very interested," Little Brother told me over the phone. "He wants to meet with the team, I think."

"Whatever is convenient for him," I said. "We can buy dinner, if that's agreeable to him."

"I'll find out," Little Brother assured me.

"Let me know what he says."

"I will."

"Little Brother will set something up for us," I told Hae Jin, who'd waited in Dan-bi's SUV while I finished the call.

We were on our way back to headquarters when the call

came in, so we sat idling in the vehicle outside while Little Brother and I spoke.

"I'll let Gu Han know," Hae Jin said as we stepped out of the SUV.

"Thanks."

"Have you seen any of the games he's played?" Gu Han called me into his office after breakfast and before training began.

"I only have two games that Little Brother recorded," I said. "Yi Ha-kun acts quickly and decisively in an attack, defends himself well and knows when to ask for help."

"Can we get him up to speed in three days?"

"I have no idea. Do we have other options?"

"Not at this point."

"Are we going to meet with him?"

"Yes." Gu Han had the look of a man backed into a corner. He would have to train with the rest of us, and two unfamiliar players could upset the balance we'd worked so hard to achieve.

My phone rang; Little Brother In-su was calling me back. "What's up?" I asked in English.

"Ha-kun says he'll be happy to meet the team at the Japanese restaurant near your headquarters, at seven."

"Thanks, Little Brother."

"No problem. Hope everything goes well."

"He'll meet us at the Japanese restaurant at seven," I told Gu Han, who nodded.

"I'll call for the van and order something for the twins' dinner beforehand," Gu Han said.

Hae Jin

Yi Ha-kun was nearly as tall as I was and drew glances from single women and a few married ones inside the restaurant. He dressed neatly in trendy clothing, none of which could be had cheaply.

What irked me the most, however, was where his eyes lingered—on Manta. When he was first introduced to her, he wore a rapturous look as he shook her hand—as if touching her had become his fondest dream.

I hadn't expected to be so angry about his reaction.

Was it jealousy?

The short answer was yes. Yes, I was jealous, and that was a relatively new experience—one I hadn't had until I'd met Manta and gotten to know her. Would she respond to his charm? He *definitely* had charm. He smiled easily, was intelligent and appeared to fit in well with the others.

Don't like him, I sent a silent plea to Manta.

As if she'd heard me, she touched my hand under the table, then linked her fingers with mine for several seconds. I could have wept, I felt so relieved.

"Come tomorrow morning at ten and we'll do a few practice runs," Gu Han told Ha-kun. "We should be able to tell whether things will work out after that."

"Of course," Ha-kun nodded. "Here, try this Kobe steak—it's delicious."

"Where will we put him if he works out?" Min-ho asked on the drive back to headquarters.

"I have a solution, but it may not be popular," Manta said.

"What's that?" Gu Han asked.

"I have a condo here in Seoul," she began. "Ha-kun can take my room at headquarters and I can drive in from home every day."

"I don't like that at all," I said.

"I'll have a guard nearby."

"I still don't like it."

"We're crowded as it is," Gu Han acknowledged. "Hae Jin, why don't you and Do-yoon go with Manta. Manta, will you have a guard staying with you?"

"I can arrange that," she said.

"Good enough. This way, we can spread out again, and won't have so many in close proximity to the virus."

I wasn't thrilled that Do-yoon would be coming to Manta's with me, but I wasn't willing to let her go alone. At least he knew who she was, so he wouldn't be shocked when he walked into her place.

"We need to get a uniform for Ha-kun if he fits in," Min-ho pointed out. "I think he may be able to wear mine."

"Then we'll work that out," Gu Han sighed.

EVEN GU HAN AND I WERE SURPRISED AT HA-KUN'S ability to adapt to the team's strategies. He was a quick, intelligent player who took cues from the situation at hand and reacted well in every instance.

At one point I exchanged a glance with Gu Han—Ha-kun was slightly better than Si-woo at dealing with singular combat, and Si-woo had more experience in the game.

"I want to hire him as a permanent alternate," Gu Han drew me aside after the second round of training exercises.

"After the twins' fuck up with Force Five, I think Team Owner will agree," I said.

"He already asked me to look for someone who could fit in," Gu Han confessed. "If Ha-kun says yes, I want to sign him on a temporary basis at first. If he works out for two months, the position will become permanent."

"Agreed," I said.

"Even if he stares at your girl at times?"

"My girl is *my* girl," I growled.

"I never thought I'd hear those words from you. Everybody in the gaming industry has you labeled as a confirmed bachelor."

"I know. Or they think I'm gay."

"Wasn't going to go there," Gu Han laughed.

"Does it bother you—that Manta and I?" I didn't finish.

"As long as you're discreet—and you have been so far—I have no problem with it. There's something else, too."

"What's that?"

"We've been offered separate condos on the same floor of Manta's building—by Osprey. They've been notified that our quarters are cramped, and so the offer is in if we want to take it."

"Do you know who she is?" I asked.

"No. Nobody has told me anything," he said. "Sounds like you know."

"Look, I shouldn't be telling you this," I admitted. "And frankly, you may have to carry this secret to the grave."

"This sounds more serious than I thought it was."

"It is."

"Then spill it."

"Manta is Ong Rae-Rae. She's going to kill me for telling you."

"OUR OWN CONDO?" MIN-HO BREATHED.

"That's what Osprey has offered. All of them are on the same floor, except for Manta's—she owns her own condo in the same building on a higher floor," Gu Han explained. "I'm putting it to a team vote—you'll be held to the same rules there as here, by the way. The twins won't move until they're no longer sick and contagious, but the rest of you can go tonight if you want. The condos are ready and waiting. Movers can be here while we're out to dinner."

"I vote yes," Shi-joon raised his hand. The vote was unanimous in favor of the move. This would certainly give Shi-joon more privacy, and also provide a thicker wall of security for the team, in case those who were looking for me attacked headquarters.

Manta was behind this, and it was a good move. Team Owner wasn't responsible for any expenses, and it would make me feel more secure. I only hoped that I could continue with the original plan and stay in Manta's penthouse with Do-yoon.

"I appreciate the thought behind the move," Ha-kun said when he arrived in the kitchen to pour coffee for himself. "The only worry I had was the lack of privacy."

"It is rather like a fishbowl here," Min-ho agreed. "I hear we're getting a refitted lounge for our gaming den," he added. "The equipment we have here will stay here. Osprey is putting our new den together today—they started right after Gu Han gave the word."

Leave it to Manta to move things along at the fastest speed possible. I liked that about her—that once she made up her mind, things happened quickly.

"You and Do-yoon are still stuck with me," Manta said when she brought her empty coffee mug in for a refill.

"You have two bedrooms?" Min-ho asked.

"I have more than two. My grandparents left me some money," she shrugged modestly. I wanted to laugh. Whatever they'd left her, she'd grown and multiplied it who knew how many times? Besides, she owned the whole damn building. She had as many bedrooms as she wanted to have.

She owns thirty per cent of Sang group, too, I reminded myself.

Stop thinking about those things. She cares for you. Let that be enough, the Companion Stone derided me.

I smiled, remembering the feel of her hand on mind. The moment when it inverted itself to match her palm with mine, I ducked my head to hide the flush that heated my face.

"You okay?" Manta asked in English.

"I'm fine," I mumbled.

"You're not getting what the twins have, are you?" Min-ho asked.

"He's fine," Manta rubbed my back. "I think he just choked on his coffee."

I'd feel better if I could hug you, I thought.

Manta actually choked on her coffee.

"Looks like it's going around," Ha-kun quipped and walked out of the kitchen.

"WE GET A DAY OFF THE DAY AFTER OUR NEXT MATCH," Min-ho sighed after we'd eaten all that we could at our favorite Chinese restaurant.

"I'm just happy we don't have to move our own furniture to the new place," Shi-joon observed.

"You'll each have your own kitchen, equipped with a coffeepot and a few basics," Manta said. "Try not to burn down the building."

"The key codes will be waiting for us at the front desk in the lobby downstairs," Gu Han said. "If all your furniture hasn't arrived yet, it will before long. They sent an army of movers to take everything except the twins and their belongings. According to the doctors, those two should be ready to move three days after our match."

"What about your office?" I asked Gu Han.

"I get a two-bedroom condo, so one of the bedrooms will be turned into my office."

"Is it a nice building?" Min-ho asked.

"I've been there because Auntie Cheng lives there," Shi-joon said. "My sister is staying with Auntie Cheng. The place is super nice; it has a pool and an exercise room in the basement, a party room that can be reserved, and underground parking with guards posted round the clock."

I recalled then that Manta's SUV was still parked at headquarters. We'd have to move it sometime soon.

"Don't worry about the car," Manta bumped my shoulder with hers. "Hu Lin has a spare key. It'll find its way home."

"Are you reading my mind or what?" I breathed against her ear.

"I thought you were reading mine, dude."

"Can we talk tonight?" I asked.

"If you want to."

"I want to."

"WILL THIS DO?" MANTA ASKED WHEN SHE SHOWED Do-yoon his bedroom. It was nicer than the one he had at home, but I didn't say that. It was decorated in soothing colors of brown, green and blue, had enough space for a king bed, a sitting area with a chair and a sofa, plus a large television hanging opposite his bed.

Near his sitting area was a nice desk and chair if he wanted to work or check his email. "This is great," he said, nodding his approval.

That meant I could have the same one where I'd slept before—the one with all the amenities that Do-yoon had, plus the separate library and reading room.

That suited me just fine; Manta had sent the books I'd requested to headquarters, but I'd been so busy I hadn't had time to read any of them. I hoped that would change; the reading room was the perfect place to relax and devour a book, with a small table that was suitable for refreshments.

"My stuff is already here," Do-yoon called out after opening the door of his walk-in closet.

"Hu Lin supervised the moving of your and Hae Jin's things," Manta said. "You got top priority, I think. Feel free to explore the rest of the house but be careful going downstairs; the A/C is off, so it isn't temperature controlled. Plus, if you're not familiar with where the light switches are, you could be fumbling in the dark."

"Downstairs?"

"This is the attic, where I live," Manta smiled at him. "The downstairs is the main house, but since I live alone, there's no reason to use the electricity needed to keep that behemoth powered up."

"This is the attic?" Do-yoon mouthed at me. I shrugged my reply.

"There are four bedrooms, a kitchen, an office, a sitting room and a few other things on this level," Manta explained. "Downstairs, there are six more bedrooms, a massive kitchen, formal dining, a ballroom and tons of useless space to wander around in. Most of it isn't furnished, either, since I don't use the space."

"Sounds like it takes up that entire floor."

"It does."

"Where's all that room on this level?"

"If you want to see, I'll show you."

"Yes, I want to see this," Do-yoon breathed.

He and I followed Manta toward the doorway and main elevator beyond. On the other side of that stood two tall, carved-wood doors.

Do-yoon and I gasped when Manta pressed numbers on a keypad and opened those doors. Lights blinked on, and my cousin and I stepped into a glass-walled and ceilinged wonderland filled with tropical plants and trees. Somewhere, water tinkled in a fountain, giving off a vibe of peace and calm.

"There are seating areas throughout the greenhouse," Manta said as she led us forward. "I'll give you the code and you can come here anytime; it's great for relaxing or having a nice lunch."

"Where are we going, then?" Do-yoon asked when we reached another set of doors, these made of glass but opaque because it was night.

"To the unexpected," Manta smiled at both of us before entering another code on a keypad. Once again, lights blinked on when she opened the doors, only this time, we found ourselves standing on a beautiful lawn, where fairy lights hung around the edges and in and around a few trees that had been set in planters on the building's rooftop.

"This is amazing," Do-yoon sighed. "I never thought this was here, and I've passed this building so many times."

"You can see Namsan Tower from that side," Manta pointed to her right. We walked in that direction until we could see around the massive greenhouse. Namsan Tower was indeed a part of the view from the roof.

"I just thought it would be a terrible waste if we couldn't get a good look at the tower on a nice night," Manta said. "So I asked the architect to build the top floor this way, rather than covering it all up with a penthouse that nobody would ever use half of."

"Why didn't you ask the architect to change the downstairs, then?" Do-yoon asked.

"Ah. Well, I was engaged to him at the time, and that's what he wanted. He got that floor; I got this floor."

"I think I'll ask for that story at a much later date," Do-yoon cleared his throat.

"Thank you. We don't speak, and, if I have my way, we will never speak to one another again."

A part of me which had tightened in anger now relaxed. It was over between them. If it hadn't been, I wasn't sure what I would do if I ever met the bastard.

"Hu Lin wants to rip his head off," Manta patted my back. "Come on, let me take you to your room."

"May I stay and wander through the greenhouse?" Do-yoon asked.

"Sure. Make yourself at home," Manta told him. "If you need us and can't find anyone, send a text. We'll come rescue you."

"Maybe," I muttered as I followed Manta through the greenhouse and into what she called the attic.

"You get the same room as before, unless there's a problem," she told me as we turned right to follow the hallway leading to the kitchen.

"No, I was hoping for that one. I love the library," I said.

"Your clothes should be in the closet already, and you and your cousin should have towels and toiletries laid out in your bathrooms. Auntie Cheng did that for you."

"I'll have to remember to thank her."

"Want something to drink?"

"What do you have? Do-yoon might share a bottle of

wine."

"Red or white?"

"White. Chilled sounds good right now."

"Okay."

She pulled a bottle of Chardonnay from the wine fridge and handed it to me. "You get to open," she said. A corkscrew was placed in my hand while she pulled a wineglass from a rack over the wine fridge. Then, she found an ice bucket and put ice and water in it to keep the wine chilled.

"For someone who doesn't drink, you know plenty about serving alcohol," I said.

"I have friends who imbibe. I just can't imbibe with them."

The cork came out with the usual *boop*, I poured for myself and put the bottle in the ice bucket. "Good," I nodded after taking a sip.

"I'm glad you like it—it's one of Tae-hyun's favorites. He's the one who stocks my wine fridge. He buys and Hu Lin delivers."

"Really?" I moved forward, crowding Manta against the counter.

"Yes."

I drank a generous swallow of wine before leaning down and kissing her. It was an extended kiss.

Manta went limp in my arms.

I learned that night how sensitive she was to alcohol, and also learned never to kiss her while I was drinking. I caught her before she fell to the floor.

CHAPTER 21

H*ae Jin*

After Tae-hyun stopped laughing when I admitted (over the phone) the embarrassing truth about Manta's unconsciousness, he told me not to worry too much.

"She'll wake up in a few minutes," he reassured me while I stroked her face with a shaking hand. "She'll be groggy, so don't let her walk anywhere unassisted until she's steady on her feet."

"The Chardonnay is good, though," I said. "She told me you're the one who buys the wine."

"A former patient owns a liquor store. He sells me what I want at a discount."

"Good to know," I said. "Oh, I think she's waking up," I

added, when Manta's head moved to the side and she made a slight noise.

"If there are unusual symptoms, call me back."

"I will. Thank you."

"No problem."

"Baby girl, are you gonna wake up for me?" I crooned softly. I'd laid her on the counter—it was the nearest flat surface—other than the floor—when she fainted.

"Hmmm?" Her hand moved upward, bumping into my hand when it reached her chin.

"Come on," I coaxed in English as I covered her hand with mine. "Wake up now and talk to me."

"Nooo."

"Somebody wants to argue when they're drunk," I teased.

"Go 'way."

"I won't go away. You're stuck with me, baby girl." Leaning down, I kissed her forehead. I'd learned my lesson about her lips—that I needed to brush my teeth and rinse my mouth after drinking before kissing her again.

A knee rose in the air. Eyes fluttered open. She struggled to focus on my face. "Huh?" was all she could manage at first.

"Now I know why they make non-alcoholic mouthwash," I grinned at her.

"You dodo bird."

"Congratulations. You have achieved second-grade level in insults," I laughed.

"Shut up. This is your fault." She rubbed her forehead.

"Headache?" I asked, suddenly concerned.

"Just a small one. It should go away if I eat something."

"Milk or a cookie? Milk *and* a cookie?" I'd seen a box of Scottish shortbread cookies on a nearby counter.

"I'll take milk and a cookie." She attempted to sit up.

"Let me help," I said, pulling her up and steadying her while she swung her legs around to drop off the counter's edge. "Sit here for a minute and I'll get milk and a cookie for you."

"I feel better now," she said after crunching into a cookie and drinking the milk I brought her.

"I'm sorry. I didn't realize that was the wrong thing to do," I told her.

"Well, it was a learning experience. For both of us."

"Having cookies and milk without me?" Do-yoon wandered into the kitchen.

"You don't know the half of it," I said. "Want a glass of wine?"

Manta snickered.

I WORKED OUT WITH HU LIN THE FOLLOWING MORNING, while Manta did her laps in the building's basement pool. She made breakfast for Hu Lin, Do-yoon and me afterward, and then we went down to the seventh-floor game room to see our new gaming den.

Huge, curved screens hung from the ceiling above an

open-centered, circular desk which held all our gaming consoles.

"This is nice," Min-ho nodded his approval. To one side, a bar and barstools were lined up, with a refrigerator and cabinets for snacks and drinks.

"No liquids near the gaming consoles," Gu Han announced as we surveyed our new workspace.

"I can work with this," Yi Ha-kun said with a smile.

"Then sit down and let's get to work," Gu Han announced. "We have a day and a half to prepare for our next match."

"When I shut my eyes, I can still see the game," Shi-joon complained when we stopped for the day.

"I'm starved," Min-ho declared.

"Dinner's on the way; we can eat in my kitchen or you can take your food to your own condo—just don't forget to clean up after yourselves," Gu Han said.

"We'll eat with Gu Han," I said, indicating myself and Manta. "We haven't had a chance to discuss anything other than gaming strategy all day."

Min-ho and the others agreed; we'd eat with Gu Han. Three kinds of fried chicken were delivered; Manta chose the non-spicy variety, as did I. The others went for the spicier versions, and we all found places to sit at Gu Han's table or at his breakfast bar.

"The twins are feeling a little better. Their fever has come down, but they're still contagious," Gu Han told us. "If you want to talk to them, then a phone call is the safest way for now. We have a nurse checking on them three times a day, and food deliveries scheduled. The last I heard, they were watching a drama series on television and sleeping through most of it."

"I'll send them a basket of treats," Manta said, scrolling through her phone. "Do they like fruit, or is it only chips and candy they want?"

"I'll split the cost with you," I offered. "They'll eat apples sometimes."

"Sounds good. I'll send apples, chips, candy and other snacks." She tapped in the address and the twins' names after choosing the items for the gift basket. "There, all done. They'll get it tomorrow." Manta shut off her phone.

"You're more forgiving than I would be," Min-ho sighed.

"It's over and they've been punished," Manta said. "Grudges get heavy after a while. I don't want to carry that load."

"A good attitude to have," Ha-kun acknowledged.

"THE UNDERSECRETARY DIED THIS MORNING," MANTA'S shoulders sagged as we rode the elevator up to her penthouse.

"His organs began to shut down yesterday and they couldn't get the internal bleeding to stop."

"What happens now?"

"No idea, really. I don't know if his replacement will know anything about me or the Monks. If he does, I can't say what his reaction will be where we're concerned."

"And we're still dealing with Kang Dong-hyung and his old and new army."

"Yeah."

The elevator doors opened into the small foyer outside Manta's penthouse. The doors into her penthouse opened once she entered the code; we walked in to find Do-yoon waiting for us.

"Jin-won says the woman who was selling your mother's jewelry in Busan has disappeared from the hospital," he informed Manta.

"No worries," she said and tapped her phone to bring it to life. "I have a tracking device on her."

"Thank goodness," Do-yoon sighed.

"Come on you two, let's get to work," Manta snapped, stalking toward her home office.

"WHERE THE HELL IS THAT?" DO-YOON, WHO WAS ON THE phone with Jin-won, his superior in Busan, stared at Manta's computer screen.

"It's a cleaning supply business in the suburbs," Manta said after checking her second computer screen. She rattled off the address, which Do-yoon relayed to Jin-won. "The corporation that owns it on paper doesn't exist," she added after researching the name and address.

"That doesn't make it suspicious," I mumbled sarcastically.

"Jin-won and his agents are on their way; they should arrive in fifteen," Do-yoon said.

"I'll connect my computer to his phone, so they won't be wandering around," Manta said and tapped in a phone number.

"That's handy," I observed.

"Ask him if he's still carrying the matchbox I gave him," Manta instructed Do-yoon.

"He says yes," Do-yoon said after relaying the message.

"Good. Tell him to open it with his left thumbprint the minute he's inside the business."

"He's on it," Do-yoon said.

"Good. Thank you."

"What's in the box?" I whispered to Manta.

"Mosquitoes."

"Huh?"

"I'll explain later."

The following fifteen minutes took forever. I felt as if I'd been holding my breath for hours when Do-yoon relayed the message that they were inside the building and the matchbox was open.

Suddenly, new images appeared on all three of Manta's screens.

Drone images.

I'd seen something similar one time before—in the building's parking garage after the security guard was attacked.

Mosquitoes.

Tiny drones. There was no other explanation for this. One had a view of Jin-won and his agents as they followed the images sent by Manta's computer. Two others had spread out and were traveling fast through the building, looking, no doubt, for possible ambushes.

We found what waited for Jin-won and his men—outside the room where Manta's tracker had located the kidnapped woman.

Quickly, Manta sent the images to Jin-won, who held his men back for a moment while they discussed a course of action. Manta sent her own suggestion; the small room in question was located in a far corner. For the moment, dim lights shone throughout the building.

You have night vision goggles? Manta sent a text.

Yes, came the reply.

Good. I'm about to turn out the lights and disable the CCTV cameras, so they can't see you coming. Do your own recording from this point forward.

Will do.

Manta tapped her keyboard; the building was suddenly left in darkness.

Now, attack from three sides, Manta suggested.

Jin-won followed her advice; we were able to see his movements thanks to the heat sensors on the mosquito following him and his agents. This wasn't any run-of the mill technology—this was sophisticated equipment designed precisely for this type of event.

Jin-won had also called for backup. According to his texts, which Manta had tapped into, additional agents and local police were arriving outside the building.

That's how a second batch of ambushers bearing pipes, bats and other weapons, were found and arrested outside.

The fight between Jin-won's men and the first batch was short but intense, leaving twelve men lying on the floor with zip ties securing hands and feet. Two of Jin-won's men were injured, but their injuries weren't serious.

Now what? There's no door, Jin-won texted Manta. *It's solid cinderblocks on the inside walls, and my backup says it's the same on the outside wall.*

There's a way, give me a minute, Manta replied, before tapping her keyboard again.

"What's that?" Do-yoon breathed as we received a larger, more detailed picture of the inside of the room.

"The tracker has climbed out of the victim's hair," Manta replied.

"Holy shit," I muttered. I blinked in amazement as the tracker scanned the interior of the room until it found the minutest crack where a doorway lay hidden.

Are you seeing this? She sent to Jin-won.

I see it, he replied.

It takes an electronic key, which we don't have, Manta said. *Is there anything handy to break through the cinderblocks?*

We have a forklift.

Try that. The body is against the far wall. Also, just break through the wall. I think there's enough evidence hidden in this room to hang all three of our culprits.

"What?" Do-yoon and I chorused.

"I think we found the place where they stashed those kids' bodies," Manta said, her tone grim. "If we're lucky, we'll find enough to put those three in jail forever."

I swallowed hard; this was the place I'd have been taken, before being cut up and scattered for the police to find elsewhere.

Like the other four had been.

In less than five minutes, Jin-won's crew had created a small hole in the wall, after which his men attacked the opening with the pipes and other weapons brought by those who'd waited to ambush them.

Meanwhile, Manta not only turned the dim lights back on, she somehow tapped into the grid and flooded the entire building with light.

"Forensic teams are on their way," Manta turned to me with a weary sigh. "Let's let Jin-won do his work. He'll text if he needs us for anything."

"I need a drink," Do-yoon sighed.

"The hard stuff is in the cabinet above the wine fridge," Manta told him.

"I want some, too," I said. "I may never sleep again," I added.

"Don't say that—we have a match tomorrow night," Manta reminded me.

"Yeah. Thanks for the update."

THE NEWS DIDN'T BREAK UNTIL AFTER WE'D FINISHED OUR match against Les Chats Noir from France. Manta played Cloud Empress, since they'd banned Storm Harper. While I'd have made the same choice the French did, it made little difference in the end. We won the game in twenty-one minutes and shook hands with the team afterward.

"LOOK AT THIS," I HANDED MY PHONE TO MANTA WHILE we waited for our food at an upscale restaurant. Do-yoon had sent me a link to the report coming from a Busan news service.

"The NIS and local police have found evidence from a shocking crime committed eighteen years ago," the news anchor reported. "While we have few details at the moment, an unidentified source has told us that evidence from the kidnappings and murders of four teens nearly twenty years earlier has been found. We will closely follow this investigation and report our findings to the public as soon as they become available."

"Wait until they find out those miscreants are on the street," Manta muttered, handing the phone back to me.

"Does this make us safer or put us in more danger?" I leaned close to Manta's ear to whisper.

"Potato, po-tah-to," she shrugged. "If they discover that I had anything to do with finding their cache of evidence, well, they love revenge almost as much as they love murder."

The Monks will be on high alert, the White Flower informed me.

Manta's phone beeped. Pulling it from her pocket, she stared at the screen. "*Wéi nǐ hǎo*," she answered the call in Chinese.

What followed was a rapid conversation in Chinese, which I couldn't follow. Manta hung up shortly after. "What's going on?" I asked.

"The ah, new Undersecretary wants a word," she sighed.

"Of course. And why not now, as opposed to in a month or two?" I said, employing my best snark.

Her phone rang again. This time, it was Jin-won. He'd found more of her mother's jewelry inside the hidden room, along with other evidence.

Evidence that would include me in the list of kidnap victims. They'd found the embroidered name tag the bitches had cut off my school sweater. No matter how much Mom and Dad wanted to hide the fact that I'd been a victim, all of their efforts would come to naught if that name tag were made public.

"Damn," I sighed when Manta informed me quietly of what they'd found.

"Stop worrying about it," she said. "If they'd kidnapped a hundred kids, at least fifty sets of parents would probably make the same decision yours did."

"If they'd been given the chance," I said. "The others weren't so lucky."

"I may have an answer as to why you were where you were when I found you," she told me. "I'll fill you in later."

"YOU PROBABLY DON'T RECOGNIZE THIS GUY," MANTA HELD up her phone which displayed a photo. "He's the guy who was married to the kidnapped woman in Busan."

"I forgot to ask about her," I admitted.

"She was already dead when they dumped her in that room," Manta shook her head, an angry expression marring her features. "That's the reason I instructed the micro-tracker to release itself—it was clinging to the roots of her hair. I did that so we could get information on her surroundings."

"Damn," I cursed.

"Anyway, this guy has ties to Kang Dong-hyung. Who knows how many bodies he's caused to disappear in the past twenty years or so? Now that he's in custody, he's scared witless. Oh, by the way, he's the actual owner of that business, although it's registered to a fictitious company. The NIS isn't treating him gently on this, and they're hammering him to tell them what he knows about Kang Dong-hyung and his two witches."

"Why wasn't I taken to that room?" I asked.

"Well, because he has to run a semi-legitimate business out of there, or it would attract attention. Seems there was a chemical leak in the building that sent some of his workers to the hospital on the day I found you in my attic. There was a professional hazardous waste cleanup crew on-site to clear up the problem. That's why you were still alive when I found you."

"Fucking hell." I dropped onto the sofa in Manta's home office.

"It was luck. Happenstance. A miracle. Whatever you want to call it," Manta said.

"I think you were a big part of it," I wiped a hand down my face. "If you hadn't helped me, I'd be just as dead as the others."

"We won't think about that. You're here and we still have to find those ass-witted miscreants." Manta came to sit beside me. Without asking, I wrapped my arms around her and held on.

"Honey, stop worrying, okay?" She told me in English. "They have an army, we have an army. Let's see who comes out on top. It's not like Kang Dong-hyung can hide that many people forever."

"Where does our army stay?"

"Where the Monks of the White Flower have always stayed," she said. "Their monastery is built into the Hengduan Mountains of Southwest China."

"Does that mean the false monks know where they are?" This spelled disaster if it were true.

"The false monks have never had access to the actual monastery. It was locked against them years ago and nothing they can do will allow them to cross the threshold."

"Because they are false monks?"

"Bingo." Manta tapped her nose and smiled at me.

"What if they throw bombs at it?"

"Well, someday I'll take you to see the bombs they actually threw at the gates."

"They didn't explode?"

"They can't—not where they are. It's fun to see them hanging in midair like that, though."

"What part could the false monks access, then?"

"What was once the village for those who served the Monks, farther down the mountain. There's a small library there, too, which I've seen. It doesn't have a lot in it, but what little I've learned through the years I learned from reading those books and manuscripts—and sometimes reading between the lines."

"Why haven't you gone into the actual monastery?"

"It could be a mausoleum. The real Monks were destroyed somehow and there are no records of how and where it was done."

"Some sort of coup?"

"I don't have an answer to that question."

"When are you supposed to talk with the new Undersecretary?"

"Tomorrow at two, our time. We'll see what he has to say before we make up our minds about him."

"Second Monk and I will be with you," a Monk appeared in Manta's office. "I regret the intrusion, Lotus," he bowed to Manta. "But we feel that our presence is necessary for this meeting, no matter how it takes place."

"Hae Jin, this is First Monk Kija," Manta introduced us. I rose to my feet and bowed to him.

"We know you carry the Companion Stone," Kija said. "You are also under our protection."

"Uh, thank you," I stuttered.

"The monastery was empty when we found it—we know you were worried about that," Kija acknowledged. "The Companion Stone let us know," he added.

"Oh. Thank you. I was really worried that Monks had died there," Manta rose to her feet and dipped her head to Kija.

"Much of the main library is missing, however," Kija said. "We are concerned that the Monks may have been scattered in some way and were lost as time passed. This means the library may also be lost."

"Not good news," Manta sighed. "I was worried about a massacre. Instead, it could have been something more mundane, I suppose."

"Or something neither of us may suspect," Kija observed. "We cannot discount any reason at this point."

"True enough. Where do you want to be to respond to the Undersecretary's video call?"

"We invite you officially to the monastery; it will be an honor to welcome this Lotus among us. Hae Jin is also welcome."

"We'll be there," I said, bowing to Kija.

"YOU HAVE WHAT?" MANTA TURNED TO ME THE MOMENT Kija disappeared.

Tell her, the White Flower insisted.

"Apparently, I have the Companion Stone," I managed to mumble.

"What is that, exactly?"

"I ah," I fumbled for an explanation.

The Companion Stone stays with the one who loves the Lotus, the White Flower said patiently.

I can't tell her that, I hissed mentally.

Why not?

It isn't the right time.

When will be the right time?

I don't know.

"If it's that hard to explain, then don't," Manta waved off

the question and walked out of her office. She left me behind, wincing in embarrassment.

Rae-Rae

The following morning, all the news outlets were broadcasting photos of Kang Dong-hyung, Go Ha-eun and Go Aheun as the kidnappers and murderers of four teenaged victims from eighteen years before, and they hinted at some evidence found of a fifth kidnap victim.

I hadn't gone downstairs to swim yet and it was still early —I'd spent a restless, mostly sleepless night and had chosen to get out of bed at four-thirty rather than tossing and turning until five.

Perhaps Hae Jin had found a way to sleep—I hoped he had, anyway. The news was going to upset him no matter what, but it would be worse if he wasn't rested.

"Mom, they haven't released a name, stop worrying," Hae Jin spoke on his phone as he shuffled into the kitchen. "No, they haven't contacted me yet."

For now, Jin-won was holding Hae Jin's name back, and rightly so. They'd come question him soon enough, however, since they'd found irrefutable proof that the two bitches had him in their clutches when he was eleven.

The one thing that had solidified all the evidence pulled out of the hidden room was the testimony of the woman's husband, who, faced with a murder charge, was now telling everything he knew. I'd already told Jin-won to place him under heavy guard, or they'd have to deal with his murder, too.

Hae Jin hadn't slept any better than I had, which was not at all. "Do you want coffee or a nap?" I asked him when he finally convinced his mother to hang up.

"What are you having?" He nodded at the cup in front of me.

"Coffee. I have too much to do to try to sleep right now."

"Then I'll have coffee. No, don't get up, I can do this for myself."

He poured his coffee then came to sit beside me. He took a sip, then lay his head on his arms atop the kitchen island.

I rubbed his back; he was dealing with his parents and his demons at the same time. That's when Do-yoon wandered into the kitchen while on the phone.

"Auntie Sang," Do-yoon said, "I'm not in charge of the investigation. I can't tell anybody to leave Hae Jin's name out of this."

Hae Jin raised his head and blinked at me. "Just put your head back down," I told him. "You can't do anything about this, either."

He buried his head in his arms; I took the opportunity to stroke his hair. After a moment, he sighed and relaxed.

Continuing to sip my coffee, I listened as Do-yoon did his best to deflect the speeding train of Auntie Sang's imagination, which had jumped the tracks and was now running, unhindered, into uncharted territory.

"Really," Do-yoon insisted for perhaps the twelfth time, "I can't interfere in the investigation like that."

"Here," I held out my hand to Do-yoon. "Give me the phone and get yourself some coffee."

"Huh?"

"Give it." I wiggled my fingers.

Do-yoon, his eyes widening, handed the phone to me.

"Auntie Sang?" I interrupted her while she was telling Do-yoon what he should and shouldn't do about Hae Jin being the fifth victim in an eighteen-year-old criminal investigation. "This is Rae-Rae," I said when Auntie Sang's tirade stopped in mid-sentence. "I'm with Hae Jin and Do-yoon right now. They're fine. Stop worrying; things will turn out like they turn out and nothing we can do will stop that. Okay? Take care of yourself and Uncle Sang, all right? I'll see you soon. Bye."

I hung up Do-yoon's call and handed the phone back to him. He stared, mouth open in surprise. "Get some coffee. Maybe it will help," I advised. Then I pulled my phone from a pocket and dialed a familiar number at the Blue House.

BY NOON, THE NEWS OUTLETS WERE REPORTING THAT THERE was, indeed, a fifth kidnapping victim, but as that victim had managed to escape and had asked not to be identified, they were choosing to allow them to keep their identity anonymous, referring to them only as victim five in future proceedings.

I'd argued with the President and the Head of the NIS that releasing Hae Jin's information to the media and the public could paint a larger target on his back and make things ultimately more difficult for him and his family.

At least they'd listened to me and kept the information under wraps. Only a select few at the NIS had that information, so for now it would stay that way.

Auntie Sang, Hae Jin and Do-yoon were all relieved, although Hae Jin's grandfather was now insisting on meeting me. I hoped the two o'clock meeting with the new Undersecretary went well; Hae Jin, Do-yoon and I were scheduled to have dinner with their grandfather at seven.

Auntie Sang, obviously, wasn't willing to accept a simple explanation as to why Hae Jin and I knew one another, but that was a problem to solve on another day.

"Are you wearing that?" Hae Jin asked when I walked into the kitchen wearing a white silk suit—white jacket, white pants and a white silk blouse, with white shoes and pearl earrings.

"I'm wearing this," I said. "What are you wearing?"

"I was going casual," he replied.

"I see that. You look fine," I reassured him. "You don't have to talk to the Undersecretary. I do."

He was dressed in black jeans and a cream turtleneck

sweater; I'd told him it was cold in the mountains where we were going.

"I have a black jacket," he said. "I'll take it with me."

"That's fine. Grab it and we'll go."

"Don't we have to wait for Kija?"

"No."

"Uh, okay."

It took a few minutes for him to run to his bedroom, find the jacket and meet me again in the kitchen. "You ready?" I asked.

"Yes. How are we getting there?"

"Through a gate."

"A gate?"

"Like this," I held out a hand. A shining gate appeared in my kitchen. "Don't worry, this is how I questioned the former Undersecretary," I said. "Come on or we'll be late." Taking his hand, I pulled him toward the portal.

The shining gates opened and allowed us through.

CHAPTER 22

Rae-Rae

We stood outside the gates of the monastery. Carved from the rock of the mountain itself, it was both beautiful and formidable. And, as I'd told Hae Jin before, all the bombs and other incendiary devices that had been hurled at it in the past now hung suspended in midair before the massive structure.

Outside that dead zone, it was snowing.

"I hope somebody will let us in," Hae Jin dusted snow off a jacket sleeve. "It's cold out here."

The gates of the monastery began to open. I waited, prepared for anything that might be thrown in our direction. Kija stood at the forefront of a line of Monks. He bowed, then the others bowed behind him.

"Let's go," I said, pulling Hae Jin with me into the

monastery. While we covered that distance, I wondered how long it had been since the last Lotus entered this way.

"So, where is the Undersecretary?" I asked Kija as he led Hae Jin and me into a massive library. More than half the shelves inside were empty, bare of the books and manuscripts it had once contained.

"What do you mean?"

"There is no Internet connection here," I shrugged. "That means you've accepted a face-to-face between this man and me."

"Ah. I see you've known this all along."

"I have."

"I hope you will trust us this time."

"I don't trust lightly. I hope you understand that."

"There is much we don't know about you. I hope you will trust us with your history someday. For the library's sake."

"I see that much of the library is gone. I can't trust that some of my information won't be misused in the future if something like this can happen."

"The false monks were never allowed near this library, or any part of it," someone I hadn't met before walked in. He was dressed in a pale gray suit, spoke in Chinese and looked to be in his early fifties.

"Meet the new Undersecretary of Defense for the

Republic of China," Kija said. "Undersecretary Sun, this is Ong Rae-Rae, the Lotus."

"The Lotus is currently imagining the many ways you might die," Second Monk Gi informed Kija.

"Please, forgive us," Undersecretary Sun bowed low to me. "I was approached recently, both by First Monk Kija and by the Chinese Government. First Monk Kija has learned that I am the current Librarian for all the missing books. I assure you they are in a safe place and can be transported back to the monastery easily. I merely had to ensure that the Lotus Kija serves is actually the true Lotus rather than a construct, like the false monks were."

"What about the Chinese Government?" I asked.

"Ah. Well, I was an excellent strategist when I served in the military and achieved a high rank. They offered the Undersecretary's position, which I intended to decline. First Monk Kija convinced me to accept it—to keep you safe."

"You have the missing books?"

"Yes. The Librarian's position has been passed down through my family for generations, to keep it and its information safe. I am the latest in that long line."

"I think I'd like to have the tea you offered earlier," I turned to Kija.

"Of course." Two Monks left the library to bring tea.

When we had our tea and were seated around a low table, Undersecretary Sun posed a question. "What can I do to make you trust me a little more?" he asked.

"You can start by putting out wanted notices for every

member of the false monks," I said. "They were involved in the murder of Undersecretary Chin and are now in the service of a known murderer and escaped prisoner."

"Ah. You speak of Kang Dong-hyung," Undersecretary Sun nodded. "Yes, that idea has already been proposed to my superior, and, as it falls in line with a way for China to remain seemingly neutral in this, I believe it will be implemented."

"If you need help sending the information to Interpol, let me know. If we can find even one of these false monks, it may help us locate the others."

"You have one of Kang's servants imprisoned already," Undersecretary Sun pointed out.

"Kang won't do anything or go anywhere that Go Ah-eun already knows about," I said. "It's how he stayed out of prison for so long. I doubt he's willing to go back so easily, so he'll do his best to outsmart us. Besides, he has revenge on his mind because he and his murderous women have been exposed. Hae Jin will remain a target, but if Kang discovers I had anything to do with locating that hidden room, he'll bring everything he has against me."

"We will protect the Lotus, to the last Monk," Kija said.

"What about the Library?" I asked Undersecretary Sun. "Will it be restored? If so, I'd like access to read through it."

"Soon," he assured me.

"She will believe you when she sees it for herself," Second Monk Gi reported.

"You know, I'd like to keep those things to myself if you

don't mind," I snapped at him. "If I want someone to know something, I'll tell them myself."

"My apologies, Lotus." He bowed to me.

"Don't let it happen again."

"As you say, Lotus."

"I think it's time to speak with Go Ah-eun," I told Kija. "If it's convenient for you."

"It is; we anticipated this. She is still attempting to spit at us and calls us names when we bring food or water."

"I hope you've learned that her threats and insults are unimportant," I told him.

"We understood that from the beginning."

"Hae Jin?" I turned toward my companion, who'd remained mostly silent during our visit.

"I want to see her," he said, his voice steady and resolved.

"Let's go, then."

HAE JIN

Manta didn't say anything when Undersecretary Sun came with us to see Go Ah-eun. We walked down several flights of steps after leaving the library behind and traversing several long corridors.

A dungeon lay at the bottom of those steps, but it held light and warmth from somewhere, and was kept clean by the Monks.

Go Ah-eun was inside the first cell. She had a comfortable bed, a chair and a privacy screen, which no doubt held some sort of toilet for her use.

"Let me out of here, you filth," she screamed as we appeared before her cell. We stood far enough away that she couldn't reach us through the bars of her cage.

"I thought you'd be used to bars and locked doors by now," Manta spoke first.

"You bitch. We should have killed you when you were born," Go Ah-eun hissed at Manta, then spat at her. The spittle froze in midair; Manta had done that with the uncanny ability she held. Ah-eun blinked at the anomaly for several seconds, surprised, no doubt, but wishing to appear unfazed anyway.

"You remember what they say about hindsight, don't you?" I asked her.

"Ah. You came, too. I'm surprised."

"You missed your chance to kill me," I said.

"We'll rectify that."

"Not while I live," Manta snapped.

"So it was you who let him go," Ah-eun's eyes narrowed as she glared at Manta. "We don't know how it was done, but there was always the idea that you had something to do with it."

"Don't lie. Your sister thought it was my mother's ghost for the longest time."

"Ha-eun is too superstitious for her own good," Ah-eun sneered. "She always said the attic was haunted by that bitch's shade."

"Maybe it still is," Manta shrugged. "And my mother wasn't a bitch."

"If I say she's a," Ah-eun's words cut off. She grabbed her throat as if she couldn't speak—or breathe.

"Would you like to say that again—or would you prefer to breathe?" Manta asked. Ah-eun's face began to turn purple.

"Lotus?" Kija said softly.

With a wave of her hand, Manta released Ah-eun, who dropped to her knees while gasping and drawing in as much air as her lungs would hold.

"You only live because I don't believe in capital punishment," Manta glared at Ah-eun. "That doesn't mean I won't change my mind for certain cases or specific individuals. And, you've seen how easy it is for me to kill you. Now, tell us what we want to know about your sister and your puppeteer, Kang Dong-hyung. Second Monk Gi will let us know whether you're being truthful or not."

WE NOW HAD INFORMATION ON WHERE KANG DONG-hyung and his small army had stayed in Germany, but as Manta said, all that information was old news. For all we knew, they were back in Korea by this time.

Still, it gave us a place to start our search. By the time we left Go Ah-eun, she was angry and exhausted from attempting to thwart Manta's efforts to get information from her.

Second Monk Gi was a human lie detector, who could interpret the thoughts of almost anyone he was directed to decipher.

I doubted he'd ever try it with Manta again, though. Not after he'd seen the very breath freeze in Go Ah-eun's lungs.

We were back in the library afterward. Kija offered us a meal, but Undersecretary Sun declined first, saying he'd been away from his post for too long already.

"I hope you know that telling anyone about what you've seen today will not sit well with me," Manta informed him as two Monks arrived to escort him back to Beijing.

"I admit I had doubts about your authenticity," he bowed to her. "I no longer hold those doubts."

"Good for you," she said, with only the barest hint of sarcasm.

"I will contact you soon regarding the return of the library," he bowed to Kija, then.

"We will welcome the return of the missing books," Kija said, also bowing.

The Undersecretary was escorted out of the library. We waited until he was gone before speaking again.

"Our apologies for overstepping our bounds, Lotus," Kija said. "I asked Second Monk Gi to interpret your unguarded thoughts. He tells me those thoughts are now so tightly locked against him, he can hear nothing from you."

"And it will stay that way," Manta said. "How can I trust

anyone who reveals what I wish to keep hidden in front of strangers?"

"My apologies, Lotus," Second Monk Gi bowed deeply to her.

"If you hadn't redeemed yourself by reading Go Ah-eun, I'd have left you hanging upside down from the ceiling—like a bat. We're done here. Hae Jin, are you ready to go home?"

"More than ready," I replied in English.

"Awesome." Manta opened a gate and we walked through it into her penthouse.

First Monk Kija

"We have deeply offended the Lotus," Second Monk Gi sighed as we watched her disappear through a gate she'd constructed.

"We were instructed to test her," I grimaced. "Were we too heavy-handed?"

"There is something I read in her when she met Undersecretary Sun that I did not report."

"What is that?" I turned toward Gi.

"That Undersecretary Chin ordered one of the false monks under his command to crush her left foot. There was extensive damage that required several surgeries before she could walk again. She cannot run in her current condition."

"Those fools." I cursed in my first and native language, which none on this Earth could understand.

"She may never trust anyone in that position," Gi said. "Those who know what she is have only attempted to use her for their own gain—or for that of their country above all others."

"We do not have that stigma, but she won't know that, eh?"

"She is extremely intelligent. Don't make assumptions you cannot support with facts."

"This is the address in Berlin that Go Ah-eun gave us," Manta handed a slip of paper to Do-yoon. "Be careful approaching it—they may have laid traps for anyone who comes to investigate."

"Why didn't you tell us that she was captured?" Do-yoon gave both of us an accusing glance.

"Because you and the rest of the NIS won't understand where she is or how she got there," Manta said simply.

"Dare I ask?"

"Cousin, she's somewhere in Southwest China, in a mountain monastery," I clapped a hand on his shoulder. "Nobody will believe it even if they see it for themselves."

"We'll hand her over when the time is right," Manta reassured him.

"When will that be?"

"When we can capture the others," she said. "Until then, nobody they encounter will be safe."

"How was she captured?" Do-yoon demanded.

"She tried to poison Hae Jin—again," Manta grumbled. "I'm not letting that happen on my watch."

"When?"

"At the signing in Berlin," I replied. "We have the syringe in a safe place."

"But you've corrupted the chain of custody," Do-yoon complained.

"Would you rather have your cousin dead? I took the needle out of her hand myself," Manta said. "Also, if I don't go now, I won't have time to clean up and dress before going to meet your grandfather."

Manta left us standing in her kitchen to get dressed for dinner.

"She took the needle from Go Ah-eun—I watched her do it. It was less than a centimeter away from puncturing my skin when she took it, too. Be glad Manta is as quick as she is. I could have died, Cousin."

"I suspect that it isn't only Manta who's quick. Her guards must have gotten Go Ah-eun out of there with the least amount of fuss—nothing was reported to venue security."

"They're professionals," I said. I wasn't about to tell him that Manta could stop time in its tracks. It wasn't for me to say.

"GRANDPA, THIS IS ONG RAE-RAE," I INTRODUCED MANTA to my grandfather using her proper name. She'd changed into casual clothing to fit in with what Do-yoon and I were wearing.

"I was hoping to meet you one day," Grandpa took Manta's hands in both of his and patted them. "I was so proud when you won those Peace Prizes. Now I can say I've met both Koreans who've won them."

"You met President Kim," Manta smiled at Grandpa. "I never got the chance."

"And now I've met you. Come, they have our table ready."

Grandpa had chosen a small, private room in his favorite restaurant for us to have dinner. It was intimate enough that we could have a private conversation while eating. Our drink and dinner orders were taken, leaving us with a little time to talk.

"Grandpa," I reached out to touch his hand, "there are two reasons I wanted you to meet Rae-Rae."

"Other than the fact that I've wanted to meet her for several years?"

"I had no idea you wanted to meet her," I confessed.

"I kept telling your father that I did, but he just brushed me off," Grandpa complained. "And then he'd have the gall to come and tell me that Ong Rae-Rae was working on his budget or some other mundane thing. How many people are so arrogant as to ask a Peace Prize winner to correct their budgets?"

"Dad means well," I cleared my throat. Do-yoon lifted an eyebrow at me while Manta lined up her chopsticks to match the position of her fork.

"Grandfather," Manta's eyes met his, "due to unforeseen circumstances, I own thirty per cent of Sang Group. It's to my advantage to go over the budget."

"That's why he won't buy that stock back, eh?" Grandpa muttered.

"I keep trying to sell it back. He won't take it, and I don't want it in anyone else's hands."

"Because you are a shrewd businesswoman," Grandpa said. "I've been watching you since you wrestled Ong Group back from Kang Dong-hyung."

"Speaking of Kang Dong-hyung," I cleared my throat a second time. "Grandpa, he ordered my kidnapping. Rae-Rae, here, is the one who saved my life back then."

"Eh?" Grandpa turned toward Manta.

"That's her on the train with me. Look, Grandpa. She has the other half of the train ticket that I have." I pulled up the images on my phone and showed him both halves.

"Well, well," Grandpa sighed. "What are you going to tell me next that will top that?"

"I'm telling you first—Ong Rae-Rae is the one I want to marry. I haven't asked her yet, but I hope she isn't totally opposed to the idea."

"Huh?" Manta and Do-yoon yelped at the same moment.

"Grandson, I will pay for your wedding if she says yes," Grandpa chuckled. "Thank you for telling me first—I know something before your father does."

"Hae Jin," Manta whispered.

"Baby girl, please don't say no. I promise you'll never want for anything."

"Is that something you can actually say to one of the richest people on Earth?" Do-yoon asked Grandpa. Grandpa laughed.

"YOU'RE NOT GOING TO YELL AT ME?" I ASKED MANTA when we got back to the penthouse.

"Why would I yell at you?"

"Because I blurted out that I wanted to marry you."

"Well, that was unorthodox, I'll say that much."

"And?"

"And what?"

"Can you answer me?"

"I know what I want to say. I also know what I should say."

"What is it that you should say?"

"That you should have waited until the end of the season to ask. Let's face it, we don't need a yes or a no to come between us during the regular season, and certainly not during the championships. Anything good or bad between us will bring a tsunami of bad press for the team."

"True," I conceded. Lowering my head, I stared at my shoes for a moment. She was turning me down and things would happen just as she said they would. Already, my heart hurt.

"What do you want to say?" I lifted my eyes so her gaze would meet mine.

"Thank you for asking," she said. "My answer is yes."

My mouth was on hers for the first hungry kiss we'd shared since we met.

End of Book One

RAE-RAE AND HAE JIN'S STORY WILL CONTINUE IN *THE Lotus: Storm Warning (Book 2).*

Read Skyler Brooks and Lennox Winters' story in *The Seer: Betrayal.*

Read Philomena's story in *The Dragon and Mrs. Muir.*

Read even more of Phil, Rae-Rae and Skyler's story in *The Dragon Queen of Seoul* and *Wraith Zone* (coming soon).

GLOSSARY

(NAMES, PLACES AND THINGS APPEARING IN THIS BOOK)

Bak Jin-won: NIS District Supervisor, Busan.

Bhang Kwang Sun: Security guard at Ong Group Headquarters.

Binna: (Auntie Binna) Hae Jin's maternal Aunt; Do-yoon's mother.

Black Skies: Best e-sports team in South Korea.

Book of Generations: A book useful only to the Lotus; it explains how to access the records of every person, living or dead, on CG Earth 17.

CG Earth 17: Where the events of this book take place. (Control Group Earth 17)

Cha Chin-mae: Veterinarian and husband of Lee In-su.

Charles Morrison: Clothing designer and Hae Jin's best friend from college; Cheri Morrison's twin brother.

Chen Ling: See Team Manager.

Cheri Morrison: Charles Morrison's twin sister; trouble-maker who has a crush on Hae Jin.

Chief Dean Winters: An alias for a creature not born on CG Earth 17. An interloper and front man for the Devourers.

Choi Il-song: Choi Su-ho's older brother, and employee of Kang Dong-hyung (deceased).

Choi Ae-cha: Choi Su-ho's older sister, and employee of Kang Dong-hyung (deceased).

Choi Su-ho: Rae-Rae's ex-fiancée.

Chung Minjun: Backup/alternate team player for Black Skies Gaming (deceased).

Daywalker: A vampire capable of walking in daylight and able to consume food just as a human does.

Department of Confidential Security: A hidden department of the US Government which is staffed by super-natural investigators. Sometimes called the department of last resort and lost hope by its employees.

Doctor Gan: Psychiatrist for Ong Charities Hospital.

Doctor Oh: Kim Mai-an's physician and boyfriend of Shi-joon.

Gi: (Second Monk Gi) Second-in-command of the Monks of the White Flower, who protect the Lotus.

Glacier Wolves: E-sports team from Toronto, Canada.

Go Ah-eun: Younger sister of Go Ha-eun and employee of Kang Dong-hyung.

Go Ha-eun: Older sister to Go Ah-eun and employee of Kang Dong-hyung. Specializing in poisonings, she served as main housekeeper for Lee Ji-hoon and Ong Nabi for many years.

Gu Han: Team Manager/alternate player for Black Skies Gaming.

Guk: A dragon who desires the Dragon throne. With his human-turned-monster-witch wife, they plan a coup against the entirety of CG Earth 17 (see *The Dragon and Mrs. Muir*).

Hwang: Dragon royalty; formerly third in line to the Dragon Throne. Kwan's father, who carried the Lotus Stone within himself for centuries.

Im Man-sik: Former NIS agent who serves as Rae-Rae's Chief of Security.

Jiah: First Dragon King. Kwan is Second Dragon King and Philomena is Dragon Queen.

Jingfei: Guk's once-human wife and a talented black witch.

Jeong Jun-woo: Member of Black Skies Gaming team (deceased). Twin brother of Jeong Si-woo.

Jeong Si-woo: Member of Black Skies Gaming team (deceased). Twin brother of Jeong Jun-woo.

Jung Gon: Security at the building which Rae-Rae owns and where she lives.

Kang Dong-hyung: Served as CEO for Ong Group under Chairman Lee Ji-hoon, who left the running of the business to Kang. During his tenure at the company, Kang worked to take over the company with the help of the Go sisters.

Kija: (First Monk Kija) Leader of the Monks of the White Flower, the Lotus' bodyguards.

Kim Choon-hee: E-sports magazine journalist (deceased).

Kim Hu Lin: Chief Bodyguard for Ong Rae-Rae, specializing in Krav Maga and other martial arts.

Kim Mai-an: Park Shi-joon's younger, half-sister.

Kwan: Second Dragon King. See also Jiah and Philomena.

Le Chats Noir: (Black Cats) E-sports team from Paris, France.

Lee Do-yoon: Hae Jin's cousin. Works for NIS.

Lee (Sang) Hae Jin: Eldest child of Chairman Sang and heir to Sang Group, a South Korean manufacturer of small electronics and appliances. Captain of Black Skies, an e-sports team representing South Korea.

Lee In-su: Rae-Rae's younger brother (in name only). Son of Lee Ji-hoon's mistress, who made Lee Ji-hoon believe the child was his. In-su is a veterinarian, and is in business with his husband, Chin-mae.

Lee Ji-hoon: Deceased widower husband of Ong Nabi, Ong Rae-Rae's deceased mother. He was not Rae-Rae's biological father. Murdered by his mistress.

Le Cheng: (Auntie Cheng) Property Manager for Rae-Rae's building. Wife to Im Man-sik.

Lóng Hàoyǔ: An unnaturally-birthed child of Guk, a dragon, and Jingfei, an ancient, human witch. Lóng Hàoyǔ has been assigned by his parents, Guk and Jingfei, to destroy the Lotus and the Soul Witch, Philomena Muir. Both the

Lotus and the Soul Witch could destroy Guk's and Jingfei's plans of taking over the race of dragons and eventually the planet itself. He is blind and going deaf after harming the Lotus and unlike his eldest brother, is unable to fully become dragon.

Lóng Chenguang: Twin sister to Lóng Hàoyŭ. A talented witch, capable of transporting herself and others from place to place by employing her power. She assists her brothers in achieving their plans. And, like her twin brother, Lóng Hàoyŭ, she cannot turn to dragon.

Lóng Lingyun: Oldest of Guk and Jingfei's children, who not only has the talents of a powerful witch, but can achieve a full turn to dragon. He is the force behind world-wide hackings and seeks the dragon throne for himself, rather than helping his parents take the throne.

The Lotus: The bearer of Wisdom, conduit of Strength and Enlightenment and the catalyst for Spiritual Awakening.

Nam-il: (Uncle Nam-il) Hae Jin's uncle, Auntie Binna's husband, Do-yoon's father.

Nightwalker: vampire.

NIS: National Intelligence Service, South Korea.

Ong Bon-hwa: Third cousin to Rae-Rae and also her biological father.

Ong Nabi: Rae-Rae's mother.

Ong Rae-Rae: Chairman of Ong Group, Sea Eagle Security and Osprey Technology and Robotics. Also known as the Lotus.

Panthers: E-sports team from Buenos Aires, Argentina.

Park Shi-joon: Warrior-healer of Black Skies Gaming team.

Park Sung-min: Kang Dong-hyun's criminal right-hand man; In-su's biological father who is deceased.

Park Tae-hyung: Orthopedic surgeon, Hu Lin's husband and Rae-Rae's best friend since college.

PC Bang: An internet café where anyone can rent a computer for online gaming, etc. In the Korean language, bang means room.

Philomena Muir: Soul witch-turned-Dragon Queen. Her story begins in *The Dragon and Mrs. Muir.*

Pung Chung-he: President of South Korea, on CG Earth 17.

Royal Tigers: First-place e-sports team in China.

Sang Hae Jin: See Lee (Sang) Hae Jin.

Sang Chairman: Hae Jin's father and Chairman of Sang Group.

Seo Min-ho: Vice Captain of Black Skies.

Seondeok: Former Dragon Queen and King Jiah's mother.

Sung Won: Seer for the Monks of the White Flower.

Tae-yong: Dokkaebi and former military general. Currently working as personal secretary to Dragon royalty.

Team Manager: Chen Ling, former Black Skies Team Manager who has a penchant for (illegal) gambling in South Korea. Cousin to Team Owner Wu Chang.

Team Owner: Black Skies team owner Wu Chang, a

Chinese national and best friend (from college) of Zhang Bao, Rae-Rae's CEO of operations in China.

Thiwat: Rae-Rae's Thai Personal Assistant.

Undersecretary of Defense Chin: During his tenure as Undersecretary of Defense in China, has worked to either bring the Lotus under his control or destroy her (deceased).

Undersecretary of Defense Sun: Accepted the position after Undersecretary Chin's death. He and his family have taken charge of the Library from the Monastery where the Monks of the White Flower lived in the past.

Vancouver Vanguard: E-sports team from Vancouver, Canada.

Wu Chang: See Team Owner.

Yi Ha-kun: Gumiho (nine-tailed fox) and replacement member of Black Skies Gaming team.

Yun Dan-bi: Rae-Rae's bodyguard. Wife of Ma-ri, a pediatrician, and mother of their baby.

Yǔzé: A Monk of the White Flower.

Zhang Bao: CEO of Ong Group's operations in China.

Made in the USA
Middletown, DE
14 April 2023

28714424R00275